KINDRED SPIRITS

Jamie Kincaid

All rights reserved. All characters appearing in this work are fictitious. Any resemblance to real persons, living or dead is purely coincidental.

No part of this publication may be reproduced, distributed, or transmitted in any form or by any means, including photocopying, recording, or other electronic or mechanical methods, either now known or unknown, without the written permission of the publisher, except in the case of brief quotations embodied in critical reviews and certain other noncommercial uses permitted by copyright law. For permission requests, write to the publisher, "Attention: Permissions Coordinator", at the address below.

Grey Wolfe Publishing, LLC
PO Box 1088
Birmingham, Michigan 48009
www.GreyWolfePublishing.com

© 2017 Jamie Kincaid
© 2017 Cover Design by The Cover Counts
Published by Grey Wolfe Publishing, LLC
www.GreyWolfePublishing.com
All Rights Reserved

ISBN: 978-1628281125
Library of Congress Control Number: 2017933405

Kindred Spirits

Book Three of The Kismet Series

Jamie Kincaid

Dedication

    Your pen is your soul; your ink, the moments in your life. Each breath you take is a mark on this paper we call life. Each triumph, each loss, each moment in time, are your words... and the smiles, tears, and emotions made are the exclamation points. Live, love and laugh to its fullest and fill each page of your story, to make your own beautiful book of life. There is no better story than your own. Make it unique, make it intriguing, make it yours; and most importantly, make it count.

    Warmly,
    Jamie Kincaid

Acknowledgements

To my beautiful, amazing and talented children... Jacob, Joe and Julia... you make my days brighter and you make my soul smile. Each one of you inspires me to be a better person and the best mom I can be... I love you guys to the moon and back and then to the stars. There is no greater joy than being a mom, and I am blessed by your three beautiful souls. You are my heart and my heartbeat. Never doubt yourselves and never give up, no matter what. If you want it, if you dream it, you can achieve it and I'll always be there for you... cheering you on... supporting you and being your biggest fan and advocate. Thank you for your belief in me. I love you guys more than you'll ever know.

To my husband, David... Thank you so much for believing in me, for supporting me, for helping me and putting your own goals aside to help me meet mine. You never doubted my gift and that means more to me than you'll ever know. Thank you for giving me the confidence to try. Love you.

To my Sis....Time for us to celebrate dreams realized and that family is the rock and foundation; and that love is everything. Time to go Jeepin'... beep, beep...

To my Shiner... You are my shadow, my best friend and you make me laugh and smile. You never leave my side, you are always there for me... protecting me, loving me and making my life a better place. You are my forever fur baby, and I love you, Mister.

To my parents, Jim and Monsa Kincaid... You gave me the power to be who I wanted to be, to stand up for myself, and to never give up on my dreams. You believed in me first, from the little girl who used to sit beneath the stars under the oak tree and you still believe in me now, as you both watch me from Heaven above. Your girl did it. You told me I would be a writer and I am!

I feel you guys around me every moment of every day, and I see you in my children, in their laughter, their orneriness and their kindness. I miss you and I love you both, and I am so proud to be your daughter. You are the best parents a girl could ever ask for. "mnm not, dad... thunderstorms and the best talks mom on the porch swing... and calhoun nickels always. I love you guys, thank you.

And to you... life without the love of family and friends is a life not lived. I am blessed and I am humbled by the love, and support, and belief that you have given me. I have felt it from near and far.

And to Margaret... I can't begin to thank you, my friend for being my photographer and helping me. I am blessed. Thank you for helping this girl conquer the computer world, you have always been here for me. I am blessed to call you my friend; much love and here's to more dot.dot.dots!

Pray....Believe....Dream....Achieve....and always be thankful and humble.

Thank you, God, for without you, none of this would be possible. You are my rock and foundation.

Run on... Write on.

Prologue

    Liam Larson, the all-American football boy who could have had it all just for the asking, lost it all in a matter of minutes. His world ended the moment Jenny King turned away from him on Brush Creek Road and drove away. He knew their situation was dire, but he never would have guessed that what they once had was coming to such an abrupt end. Sure, he realized there were problems, but as he looked back over their past year together, he realized the sudden finality of their relationship had been coming for some time now. Jenny tried to be there for him from the beginning, but he kept pushing her away.

    He looked at the time in his truck, it was 9:11. What he tried to see as a blessing, a positive dynamic in their lives was nothing more than a grim reminder of the end. April 11th would forever go down as the day of "the accident" in the minds of those who lived in Spencer, West Virginia, but to Liam, it would go down as the day he lost his soul mate. From the first time he laid eyes on Jenny, he saw his future. He was mesmerized by her from the very beginning, and every thought was consumed by images of her. He couldn't stop thinking about her. It didn't matter that he knew nothing about the red-haired girl with the kaleidoscope hazel eyes; he was determined to learn more and finally make her his own.

Their love was uncommon only for the fact that it ran so deep. It had been born before they met; waiting for them to find each other so it could finally breathe and grow into the unconditional love that it was destined to become.

But even true love can run into obstacles, and Jenny and Liam had run into one of the biggest: Johnny Bryant. Now, only time would tell what would become of their love. Would Liam ever win Jenny's heart back or has he lost her forever? And maybe even more importantly, did Johnny finally get his way?

Chapter One
New Directions

    I'd been driving for hours aimlessly, not knowing or really caring where I was going. It didn't seem to matter; no matter what direction I headed, I traveled alone. I let my emotions control the turn of my wheel. I felt so alone and empty inside. My whole world had collapsed in only a matter of moments. I thought I would have been able to reach Liam. I thought I could break through the wall he had built up around him, but in the end, the wall was much stronger than my own will. I beseeched him to let me in so I could help him but our relationship seemed to be beyond help, and I seemed to be beyond reaching Liam. He wasn't the same boy I met over a year and a half ago. No; this was a boy who seemed to forget who he was, who loved him, and what was important in his life. His focus, for some reason, had changed and was now led by a new lease on life that entailed the fast paced life of drinking, racing and living in the limelight that he once shunned.

    My heart ached as I heard Liam's voice in my head. *"You're dead to me, Jenny,"* Those words cut straight through me as I saw the void in Liam's eyes. I couldn't believe that he could forget what we had once meant to one another. I thought about the incident that seemed to have been the precursor to our demise and realized that if I was in Liam's shoes, I might have felt the same way, eventually. He tried to sustain his anger and look past Johnny, but it had become too hard for him. Johnny's arrogant and condescending attitude left an irreparable scar on our lives, and the cut ran deep in Liam. I would have finally relented to my feelings, as well, if someone had been after Liam the way Johnny was after me. I couldn't deny that I enjoyed the affection and attention that I was receiving from both of them. Liam became my sole reason for living; my every thought, my every desire, and he was all I ever wanted or needed. But Johnny had played too much of a role in my life. Maybe the bad boy persona that I was always told to stay away from had finally gotten to me and enticed me enough that I wondered myself, what it would be like to be with such an individual. And maybe, that's why I felt myself being drawn to him even when I knew it was wrong.

    I would be lying if I concealed my feelings towards Johnny; I did love him. I was ready to admit that, but I knew it was a love that would never be given the chance to flourish. It was doomed from the beginning even with Johnny's unwavering persistence towards me. I felt so torn. I didn't want to leave Liam the way I did, but I felt as though he gave me no other choice. He pushed me away and now I was left to fend for myself, alone and scared of what the days to follow would bring all of us. I wanted so badly to turn around, I hadn't given up on us, and I wasn't giving up on Liam. I was just hurt. I knew he still needed me even though he didn't seem to think so.

    I looked at the time in my car; it read 1:11. I sighed heavily as the numbers seemed to stare back at me. I thought of that inauspicious word. Time. It seemed that was the operative term for now. We all needed some time. Grandpa Mack told me that. Even Johnny needed time; not only to move on from me but for his heart that seemed to be broken in more ways than one. I was the only one who felt differently about time, though. I didn't need any more of it. It was my enemy. When I needed it to stop, it seemed to grow in momentum, allowing my time with Liam to become too brief. I knew what I wanted, and I believed I had given Liam enough time to figure things out but my impatience was becoming my

Achilles Heel, and I had to learn to start walking instead of running. I had to go slow and give Liam the time he needed. I hoped that Johnny's time would allow him to see that too but, more importantly, I hoped that time was on his side. I knew he was dying, and I felt horrible that I had left him the way I did. But there was no other choice. My feelings for him couldn't help him; and in reality, would have only made things worse. Johnny found a weak spot in me that I didn't know existed, and I was allowing him to use that for his own benefit. Yes, this was best for us both, Johnny needed a chance to rebuild his life not only physically but mentally, and he wouldn't be able to do that if I was still there.

I kept driving until I came to an intersection in the road. I looked to my left then my right and then straight ahead. I knew each direction would lead me to a different place. The one course would lead me back home, the other to a portal that had given me sanctuary, and the final one would lead me into unchartered territory. I carefully weighed my decision. A smile came across my face, an expression that had been vacant from me for quite some time. I made up my mind and pushed on the gas.

****

"I'm going to find my way back to you, Jenny. This isn't over," Liam muttered as he drove. His cell continued to ring while he tried to ignore its stubborn persistence. He too reflected on his actions the past few months that led him to where he was now. He stared vehemently at the empty beer cans that resided inside the cab of his truck. It disgusted him to see how far he had sunk. His thoughts went to Jenny and how she tried to be there for him, but he resisted her; he was scared. He saw himself slowly turning into the monster that was his dad. He loved Jenny too much for her to bear witness to his metamorphosis. His demons were revealing themselves in more ways than one, and he knew that it was finally time to face them, or he would never see his girl again. But his lack of confidence made him wonder if he would truly be able to be the man he needed to be and do what was being asked of him. Liam was unsure and only time would tell the outcome that lay ahead for him.

The light turned green, and the incessant honking of the other cars behind him made him jump back to his reality. He had to make a decision on where to go. He had the option of going straight, turning right or turning around; he knew that each direction could lead him to his impending fate. The blaring sound of the car horns continued to pierce his ears while he contemplated his next move. He sighed heavily as he commanded his steering wheel; gunning on the gas pedal. His cell continued to ring with no regard for his feelings, so in defeat, he finally succumbed and answered it.

"Liam? Where the hell are you?" Toby yelled in a very garbled and obstinate tone.

"Why do you care, Toby? Stop trying to dictate my every move; I don't need you on my case every damn second!"

"Do you realize the race starts in less than four hours, and you haven't even checked out your bike yet? What if something's wrong with it? We're not going to have any time to fix it. There's going to be some important people here tonight, and I'll be damned if you're going to screw this up for me because of some damn puppy love you're still carrying!"

"You don't know what the hell you're talking about! You don't know me, and you don't know about my Jenny!"

"Your Jenny? Ha!" Toby's cold-hearted laughter festered at Liam like an open sore.

"Yes, my Jenny! The girl that I love and the girl that I have lost because of my own damn stupidity! I don't know if you'll ever understand what we had together because from what I see between you and Gina, your relationship is based solely on what you can get from each other, and it has nothing to do with love."

Liam's voice became eerily quiet after his rush of adrenaline. He took a much-needed breath before continuing. "Toby, I love her. I didn't forget about the damn races, but they're not half as important to me as she is, and I think I lost sight of that. I started racing because I wanted to be able to move forward with her and instead, it seems I'm moving backward, and the sad part is I don't even know how to reverse it. I should be planning my wedding right now, but instead, I'm planning my next race, a race that once I finish she won't be there waiting for me. This should have never happened this way, so just give me some damn time to figure some things out and then I'll be there."

"Where are you?"

"That's not important. Don't worry about it."

"What the hell is that supposed to mean, Liam? We've got people here already. It's not just me who is relying on you being here or the sponsors. You've got three guys here who are ready to prove to you that you're not the fastest on hell's wheels and the way you're acting right now they might be right. I thought you wanted this."

Liam paused for a moment. "I thought so too, but it was only if Jenny was going to be in my life. Nothing means a damn to me anymore. If she's not here to help me celebrate then why in the hell am I doing this? This all started because I needed to get rid of some bad shit in my life but instead, I think I've just added more to it."

Toby remained quiet while Liam spoke. He didn't want to hear this nonsense coming from his prized driver. Toby was thick-skinned and uncaring; hell, he'd drop Gina if she became a problem for him. He just didn't carry feelings like that. The only thing that did get a rise out of him was the sound of motor revving right before a race. Moments continued to pass as the silence between the two men grew. "Liam, I've had enough, I'm giving you two more hours, and if you're not here, then you might as well never come back. I'm not going to deal with this, you hear me?"

Liam hung up his phone and threw it down on the seat. He looked up only to realize he was sitting in the hospital parking lot. A heavy sigh came from his burdened body; he knew who was inside those hospital walls. All he had to do was open the door and get out, but it was much harder than he had anticipated. It was an easy task, but one he couldn't do right now. So instead, he did what he shouldn't, he just sat in his truck contemplating the inevitable. He allowed his mind to become deep in thought again until the sound of tapping on his window interrupted his thoughts. He should have been apprehensive, but he was too tired to even worry about it.

"Hello, Liam." The dulcet voice lingered in Liam's ear.

"Gertie," Liam said with no emotion.

"It's been a long time."

"Yes, it has Gertie, probably too long."

"So, how are you doing, Liam?"

He turned his head away from her. He knew she already had the answer to her question, and he really didn't want to oblige her with one, but he felt her eyes on him, penetrating into his soul, so he relented. "I'm okay."

Really?" She knew better.

"I guess you already know how I'm doing. Hell, the whole damn town knows, Gertie." He looked into her eyes and answered bluntly. "I'm a damn mess."

"I'm sorry to hear that, Liam, really I am. It's just not right that you and Johnny aren't friends anymore."

"Yeah, I guess, but there's no need for you to apologize, it's not your fault."

"Maybe not but since Johnny is my son I do feel I need to choose his side, not that I'm condoning his actions, it's just that..." Gertie looked up at the hospital. "It's just that with him being so ill, I don't care what he's done, I just want to him to be happy, and I'm sorry, Liam, but Jenny makes him happy."

"Gertie, you know she left me, don't you?"

"No, but I had a pretty good feeling that's what she had planned. She was disengaged that last time I saw her. The past few months have been horrible for all concerned but especially her. Can I ask what brings you to the hospital today, Liam?"
"I don't know. I think maybe I'm here to see an old friend." He knew she knew the reason.

"A friend?" Gertie's voice seemed amused by Liam's choice of words.

"An *old* friend," Liam said. His intent blue eyes revealing to her what he really meant. "Maybe I worded it wrong. You know as well as I do Gertie that Johnny and I haven't been friends for a while now. I don't even know how I ended up here. I was on my way out of town, and for some reason, I drove here. I don't know if I'm going to go inside. I've been here for a while, and as you can see, I'm still sitting in my truck."

"I can see that. Liam, I know how much you love Jenny, and I just think that if you could find it in yourself to repair this rift between you and Johnny it would bring her back to you. She left because she's hurting. She cares for both of you, and she can't stand how this mess is destroying what you have with her, and what you and Johnny had before she was in the picture."

"And I'm not hurting?"

"I never said that."

"You've talked to Jenny, haven't you?"

"A little. Not as much as you think and not as much as I would like. I have grown very fond of her, Liam."

"Yeah, so has your son." He knew his remark was cynical but lately, that's all he had in him. "I'm sorry. I guess that wasn't the nicest thing to say to you. But you, out of anybody, probably know why I said it."

"I do, Liam… and I'm sorry. Johnny never meant for this to get so out of hand."

"He didn't?" His cynicism was growing.

"No. He does love Jenny, but he knows she doesn't love him; at least not the way he had hoped."

"What am I supposed to do now, Gertie?"

"Do you love her?"

He looked at her as though she had been living on another planet for the past year and a half. "You know I do. I love her more than anything, more than my own life."

"Then why isn't she here, Liam?"

Liam again looked at Gertie as though she should already know the answer to her rhetorical question. "I guess it's because of me. I've been a complete ass and she finally just got fed up with me." He gave Gertie a sneering glance. "Does that make you happy to hear that I'm blaming myself for her leaving, that it's my fault, that I'm wrong, and everybody else was right?"

"Liam, no, of course, that doesn't make me happy. Whether you want to believe it or not I care for you; I wouldn't be standing here in the cold if I didn't. I would much rather be inside with my son instead of taking the time to stop and talk to you. But Liam, don't you think there is more to this than you just being an ass, as you so eloquently put it?"

"Well yeah, your son played a huge part in all of this. I caught Jenny at his apartment."

"You said you loved Jenny."

"I do, Gertie."

"Then why didn't you hear her out that night after you found her at Johnny's and why don't you believe her now, after all these months have passed? Her actions should have proven her innocence. She hasn't been with Johnny; she's been waiting for you to come back to her, and for you to forgive her."

"There's a lot more to it than just that night at your son's apartment, Gertie. Have you forgotten the accident? That was as much a part of this as anything."

"Liam, the accident was a terrible thing, it was just awful. But it was just that, an accident. It wasn't your fault, Jenny's or even Johnny's. It just happened, and it's very unfortunate that it did, but you can't keep beating yourself up over it. It could have happened to anyone."

"But it didn't, Gertie, it happened to me."

"And Jenny."

"Of course, but she wasn't the one driving, I was. I should have listened to her in the very beginning. She tried to warn me of the signs, but I didn't want to pay any attention to them. I thought that whole number eleven was just some sort of phase that didn't mean a damn thing. It's my fault, Gertie and as a result, I'm sitting here by myself without the only person who ever meant a damn to me or ever will. And from my vantage point, I see no end to this nightmare."

"Liam it wasn't the number's fault. The eleven was always just a device to be used as a guide. The accident may well have occurred whether Jenny was seeing that number or not. Sometimes our fate can't be interrupted by outside influences. Even if you had paid attention to the signs, the accident still could have happened, if not on that night, then another night. But you have to let go of the guilt, Liam, especially if you want to find Jenny again. I know the few times I've spoken with her, she was worried sick about you.

She loves you; you don't need to be a psychic to see that what the two of you have is something very special and very rare. It would be a shame for you to let it go just because you're stubborn."

Liam looked appalled at Gertie's declaration about him. "I'm not stubborn, Gertie. Does it look like I'm just being stubborn? Look at me, I haven't been the same since this shit hit the fan. I can't sleep, I'm having nightmares and they all involve your son taking Jenny away from me. Didn't she ever tell you that?"

"I know all of it. I know your nightmares are bad, and I also know she was suffering from them too. I had hoped I could have helped her or she could have at least received some help from the psychology class we were taking together. It all revolved around our dreams, but she dropped out of the class before she could learn anything."

"Wait a minute; you were taking that class too?"

"Yes, she never told you?"

"No, I never knew. But I guess she didn't want me to know."

"I'm sure it was because of me, Liam. I did try to persuade her to take the course with me, but she also seemed to have a genuine interest in it."

"I told her to stay away from you, Gertie especially because of Johnny. I didn't want her to be influenced by your family. I was scared that any amount of time spent with him or with you, for that matter, could make her realize her feelings for him were much stronger than what they were for me."

"She cares deeply for Johnny, but the love is different. Tell me, Liam these nightmares you're having, do they come every night?"

"Almost. Why do you ask?"

"You haven't gotten any resolution from them at all? Even now that you know that Johnny is out of the picture?"

"But she's still gone, Gertie. I mean, in my dream, I can see Johnny literally taking her away from me, just because it didn't happen like it did in my vision doesn't mean there isn't any credence behind it. Jenny's gone and it's because your son couldn't let go of his feelings for her. So, in my opinion, Johnny is definitely still in the picture."

"I know I can't tell you what to do Liam, but I hope you'll take what I'm about to say to heart. If you just forgive yourself, then you'll be able to forgive Johnny and Jenny as well. I do believe your nightmares will end, and you'll be able to live your life again."

"It's not that easy, Gertie. There's just so much more. It's complicated."

"Are you talking about your drinking? I think you're only using the alcohol as a crutch. Stand on your own two feet again; I know you don't need that beer as much as you think you do. You are a strong man, and that's who Jenny fell in love with. He's still inside of you, just let go of your anger, and you'll see what I'm talking about." Gertie placed her porcelain fingers over Liam's hand that was still clutching his steering wheel.

"Why are you doing this for me? There's no reason for you to want to help me."

"Because I still see that little boy that used to play pee-wee football with my son. I still see a young man who adores his grandpa and found true love without even looking for it. I see the man you are becoming who holds the ones he loves close to his heart and has morals that he believes in. I see a man who knows right from wrong and that at the end of the day realizes the power of forgiveness is much more powerful than he's willing to admit. This interruption in your life doesn't have to change you. You still have Jenny even though she's not here right now. You can find her again, Liam. Just look inside of you, and you'll see those demons will disappear as soon as they realize you're not holding onto them anymore. You're much stronger than you're giving yourself credit. Remember, you're the one in control, not them."

"You know when this all started with the nightmares, Jenny wanted me to see you. She told me she believed in you and thought you could help me, but I said no. I still don't think I need your advice, Gertie, but I'm glad we've had this chance to talk."

"Have you made up your mind? Are you going to see Johnny now?"

Liam stared despondently at the hospital window. "No, I don't think so. I can't, Gertie... not yet."

"I know he would like to see you, Liam, whether you believe me or not."

Liam looked down at his lap as he played with the turquoise beads on the leather bracelet that Jenny had given him. "How is he, Gertie? I mean really? Is he going to make it out of this?" Gertie's sullen look was all the answer Liam needed. "Gertie?" Liam begged with a more pressing voice.

She sighed heavily. "He needs a new heart, Liam. His is failing him, and there's nothing we can do about it. The doctors are out of options."

"Do you have a heart?"

"No, not yet. I hope we can find one, but he has a rare blood type. It's going to be difficult. But I'm not giving up, and neither is Johnny. We're going to make it out of this, and he's going to be able to live the life he deserves." Gertie paused for a moment. "You should go and see him, Liam. I think it would do the both of you a world of good."

"You're probably right... I just don't think I can step inside there right now. It's hard for me; too much has happened between us. How much time does he have?"

"I don't know. They have him stabilized for now, and he's going to be able to come home in a few days. They just want to run a few more tests before they release him. Liam, I understand your reasons for how you feel, but you need to remember the times you and Johnny had together before Jenny. You guys used to be inseparable when you were little, and you turned into brothers as the years passed. Even though you were enemies on the field, you were always friends off of it. Both of you need to remember that before it's too late. You're already here; all you have to do is get out of your truck and walk a few steps inside. He's on the second floor, room 209."

"I can't, Gertie... I'm sorry."

"I see. Well, at least I tried. So, where are you off too then?"

"I'm supposed to be in Glenville. I have a race tonight."

"You're still racing, Liam?"

"Yes. There's a guy who's been looking out for me. I thought it would help me prove to myself and maybe some doubters that I was still man enough. You know, since the accident."

"And has it helped? Did you receive the respect you were seeking?" Liam didn't answer. "That's what I thought. Liam, no one has ever doubted you but yourself. Trust me when I tell you the answers you're looking for aren't going to be found in racing or your new friends; they're going to be found right here, inside of you."

"Gertie?"

"Yes?"

"Can I ask you something?"

"Of course, anything."

"Do you know what is in store for Jenny and me? I mean, will I ever see her again? Is she gone forever? I don't think I could go on living if I thought that was the case. My goal has always been to get her back and for us to be the way it used to be. Maybe not the way it used to be, but better. I love her, Gertie. I love her so much. I should have never let her go. I feel like such a fool."

"You know people come to me and ask me a plethora of questions. They want to know if they'll be rich, if they'll have a baby or if they'll find the love of their life. I don't always have the answers they're looking for. Sometimes it's because I can't always see it and other times I think it's best if they don't know. I can sense their vulnerability and weakness and can tell if they're ready to handle what my visions show me. I try to use my gift wisely. Sure, I know for some it's just pure entertainment, and I understand that, and I do enjoy that part of it too; but it's still not easy when you know something that that one person doesn't and you're not quite sure if they're truly ready to hear the answer. I will be honest with you, Liam. I don't know. Maybe it's because my son is sick and my energy is concentrated on him but you and Jenny are also close to me, and I can tell that the path you're seeking is not going to be an easy one. This is a test, possibly for all three of you; and right now there are no clear answers. But I do know that if you want her back, you have to let go of your past, and that includes the conflict between you and Johnny. I do know she loves you, Liam, but sometimes that's not enough. So, if you want to find out if you'll see her again, I can't answer that for you, only you can. I don't think you'll ever lose her. Right now you both just need to find each other again. Everybody believes in you, even Johnny, and it's about time you did too." Gertie looked up at the hospital window again. "Well, I better go inside. I'm sure Johnny is wondering where I am. Can I tell him I saw you?"

"I don't think so. It might not be such a good idea. I need to go too... bye, Gertie."

"Goodbye, Liam. Liam?"

"Yes?"

"Please be careful."

Liam didn't answer her, only nodding as he drove off. The race was in less than two hours, and he had to redirect his focus, even though he knew what Gertie told him was right, in his mind, he still had something to prove.

Chapter Two

Superstar

The road that led away from the hospital and into the belly of Spencer was long and winding as it snaked its way down the hill. Liam drove it slowly even though he knew he was pressed for time. Glenville was a good hour away, and at the rate, he was progressing, he would just make it in time for the race, something that was sure to piss Toby off even more than he already was. But once in town, Liam still felt something pulling him away from the road that would take him to the race. At the light, he looked to his left. He couldn't help but feel a sense of nostalgia as memories of times past began flooding his mind once more.

The light turned green and once again he was rudely made aware of that fact by the incessant honking from behind him. He looked at the road in front of him; a little over an hour away was a race that was waiting for him but to the left of him was a place that was calling to him for a long overdue visit. The car honked again reminding Liam to get a move on. He took one more glance in front of him before turning his steering wheel to the left and driving down Jenny's street. He drove cautiously, taking in the view that led to her house. It had been a very long time since he occupied space in her driveway. He used to do it countless times when they were in school, just to be near her. He looked up to the darkened window that was draped in its blue curtains. He imagined her figure standing there as she blew him a kiss goodnight and wrapped her hands around her body to let him know that her hug was for him. He felt so alone as he sat there. He was hoping against hope, as he blinked his eyes in a futile attempt to change the hands of time and make everything right again, to reverse the tragedy that was unfolding right in front of him, but as he sat in his seat, the magic that he was seeking ignored his pleas. How he wished he could just blink his eyes and make everything right again, to make things the way they used to be and the way they should be.

    He closed his eyes and whispered something under his breath that was only audible to him as he lowered his head. It's becoming too much for him to be here, he thought it would help, but as his knuckles grew a greyish white, gripping the steering wheel, he was beginning to wish he hadn't made the turn down her street at all. But he was here, and even though the absence of Jenny made his misery grow, he needed to walk in the footsteps of his past before leaving once and for all.

    He got out and perused his surroundings. The street looked completely deserted and desolate as he peered at the vacant buildings that once occupied life within them and as he made his way up the steps that led to Jenny's porch he was startled by the movement of a pale white curtain on the second floor of Mr. King's apartments. He wondered if Mildred was being her usual nosy self. "There's nothing much to see," Liam said in a whisper. He turned from the apartment building and stood staring blankly at Jenny's front door. A myriad of memories engulfed him as he re-lived a happier time. He seemed to have become frozen in time as the recollections again reaffirmed that those happy times were over. His thoughts were interrupted by his dismal reality as he heard his cell ring incessantly as it sat in the car seat. He took his time walking back to his truck and reluctantly answered it.

"Yeah," he answered with a disinterested attitude.

"Are you coming or not?" Toby's voice was ruthless.

"I told you I would be there."

"Well, you better be on your way. Everyone's asking for you and they're all expecting a race with *you* in it," Toby said.

Liam turned off his phone while Toby's belligerent voice kept babbling. He didn't need any more reminders of where he should be; right now he was where he needed to be.

"She's not here." The male voice surprised Liam from behind. He thought he was alone.

"Excuse me?" Liam said turning to meet the stranger's voice.

"You're Liam Larson aren'tcha?"

"Yes, I am."

"I'm Billy. I'm managing the apartments for Mr. and Mrs. King. You're Jenny's boyfriend, right?"

Liam looked down. "Yeah." He said, not wanting to think otherwise.

"Well, she's not here. Hasn't been for a while."

"You mean she was here?" Liam's voice was filled with anticipated optimism.

"Yeah, but she's not now."

"Did she tell you where she was going?" Liam asked as if his life depended on Billy's answer.

"No, I never actually saw her, but I figured out who you were by your truck and thought you might be looking for her. I must say Liam, it's a pleasure to meetcha. I'm a big fan of racing, and I've heard a lot of great things about you. I would also like to say how sorry I was about your accident last year, I'm glad it didn't stop you from racing. I heard you do a lot of motorcycle racing in Glenville, is that right?" Billy asked, while his chew trickled from his mouth.

"Yeah, I do some," Liam said despondently. Right now the mere mention of racing made Liam sick to his stomach, another grim reminder of how his life seemed to be playing out.

"Some? Well hell, I heard from folks around here that you're hell on wheels. I'd love to see ya race, even though I know they're not normally advertised." Billy poked Liam in his side with a mischievous snicker. Liam was annoyed. The races were kept a secret if only so the police wouldn't find out. Billy knew that, but that still didn't stop half the State from having them, or for that matter, coming to them. It was always a race, whether the participants were racing against each other or from the cops—either way, the danger was there, and that was part of the draw.

"Well you should, I'm actually racing tonight."

"You're kidding? Well, that's a darn shame, I can't tonight. I gotta fix Miss Mildred's hot water tank. She's been complaining for weeks, and Mr. King will have my hide if I don't get it fixed soon. Mr. King's been a friend of mine for many a year, and I owe him a lot for giving me this job; I can't let him down or Miss Mildred, for that matter. But I'll keep my eyes and ears open for the next one." Billy seemed oblivious to Liam's unhappy nature or to the fact that Liam could have cared less about talking to him. Once the subject was off of Jenny, he stopped listening to Billy altogether. The moment became quiet and very awkward between them as Billy waited eagerly for Liam to engage in his conversation but Liam didn't oblige. "Well, did you need something? I mean if you need to go inside their house I can let you in. I'm sure they won't mind, especially since you're Jenny's boyfriend."

Liam again lowered his head on hearing those last two words slip from Billy's mouth. *His thoughts were more that he is Jenny's fiance' instead of her boyfriend, didn't Billy know about them...their history? The entire town of Spencer seemed too.* But at this point, he was willing to hear anything that associated him with her in a positive way.

"Thanks, but I have my own key." Liam turned to let himself inside, hoping that Billy was wrong, and he would find Jenny inside waiting for him. He inhaled. The house still smelled of Mrs. King's baking. "Jenny?!" Liam exclaimed hesitantly walking further inside. He heard nothing but his own voice. "Jenny?!" Once more he called out her name only to be continually disappointed by the silence of the house. He made his way into the living room and slumped himself onto the oversized sofa. He looked at the clock on the mantle; Toby would be expecting him soon. He knew he should be leaving but instead, he put his feet up and made himself even more comfortable. "What have I done?" he whispered. He scanned the room and the adjacent hallway. I can feel her presence. Her smell lingered around me. I stood up, taking one last look before leaving. I realized it was useless being here, there was no healing, or for that matter, even closure. I walked out, shutting the wooden door carefully behind me. I never looked back, and within the hour, I was at Toby's.

****

"It's about damn time! I thought I was going to have to come after you myself! How damn long does it take you to say goodbye?" Toby asked scolding Liam.

"Back off, Toby, you don't need to go there. I'm here just like I told you I would be. So save me the grief of your lecture by not breathing down my neck and let me get ready."

"Get ready? You should've been here last night to be ready; right now I'm just expecting you to be at the startin' line and to finish... first!" Toby demanded as if there should be no other ending to the impending race.

There must have been a hundred people to watch Liam race. His reputation had preceded him, and most of the people in attendance wanted to see if he lived up to his name. Liam angrily passed Toby and went to the garage to check on his bike, only to be met by Gina, who felt that it was her duty to help him out.

"What are you doing?" Liam blasted at her.

"Helping you since you don't seem to care enough to help yourself."

"What the hell is that supposed to mean?"

"It means that if you don't give a damn about making sure your bike is in tip-top racing condition, then I'd better. Toby and I have too much riding on you to risk you not being fully prepared. You should have been here the entire weekend prepping for this race, you knew it was coming!"

"I had something to take care of."

"You mean your sweet little Jenny? Why do you care so much about her anyway? I thought after what you saw of her and her other boyfriend you were through with her. What's your hang-up with her anyway, why can't you get over her? You should be glad she's out of the picture, she didn't seem to care about you anyway!"

Liam had never in his life hit a girl or even wanted to, for that matter, but listening to the garbage that was spilling out of Gina's crimson traced mouth made him what to shut her up with his fist. It was all he could do not to follow through with his wicked thoughts as she stood there babbling on to him.

"You better be careful, Gina."

"Or what, Liam?" Gina was egging him on, and in the state of mind he was in it wasn't going to take much to push him over the edge. But instead, he took a deep breath and stepped backward, *it isn't going to do me any good to take out my frustrations on her, she isn't even worth it.* Or nothing, Gina. Just leave me alone. I am here to race, and I am here to win, so don't worry about the bets you and Toby have made on me, they'll all come through when I cross the finish line. I haven't let you down yet." Gina gave Liam a condescending smirk as she began to leave. Liam grabbed her arm and pulled her back in. "And for the record, Johnny isn't her boyfriend, never has been and never will be, you got that." His voice was cool and even toned but Gina got Liam's message, it was loud and clear even if he wasn't.

"Sure, whatever you say, Liam, just next time there's a race, and you're the star attraction, be sure not to keep us waiting so long. We let you have your time yesterday, you belong to us tonight. Don't forget that. Toby isn't always the carefree, fun-loving guy you've come to know and enjoy, he's got a nasty side to him, and I'd hate for you to see it just because you want to go kiss and make-up with your girl." Gina gave Liam an arrogant smirk as she walked off, the sound of her gum smacking between her crimson lips echoed in the stale air as Liam kicked his bike in frustration.

"Fifteen minutes," Toby reminded Liam entering the garage. Liam didn't respond.

"Did you hear me?"

"Yeah, I heard you. I'll be there, don't worry."

"I don't mean to put any added pressure on you, but there's talk outside that some big shot by the name of Aaron Dent is here to watch you race.

"So."

"So? Hell, Liam, if he likes you, it'll be easy street for us."

"For us? I thought he was here to see me."

"Of course, he's here to see you, but he wouldn't even be here if it wasn't for me. I'm the reason there's a huge crowd out there, and I'm the reason you're making money, and I'm the reason why there's a big name sponsor outside too. He's the real deal. You'd better not screw this up for us."

"But are you forgetting that it's me who's winning the races. It doesn't mean a damn thing if I'm not coming in first, Toby."

"You can say whatever you want, Liam. Go ahead and use that cocky attitude to your advantage, I like it. Like I said, tonight's not the night for you to screw up. It's when you're all riled up like this that you win, much better than when you're thinking about that girl."

Liam's pulse began to race as he listened to Toby. "Keep her out of this, Toby, it's the last time I'm telling ya, I've already told Gina to leave her alone, and now I'm telling you. I don't want to hear you guys talk about her again. You got it? Do you even realize what has happened to me? Do you even give a damn? I don't need any grief from you or Gina or from anybody regarding her. I love her no matter what happened, and I'll be damned if you or anyone else will talk bad about her. She was the best thing in my life, and she's the reason that I'm racing. I'm going to get her back, and I'm going to do it the only way I know how. I'll win tonight, you can count on it, but it won't be for your benefit or anybody else's, it'll be for Jenny and me."

"Whatever you say, Liam. I really don't care what pushes you past the finish line as long as you pass it in first place. Like I keep sayin', I like it when you're like this, you got fire in your piss or something, it makes you want to win, and that's what I need from you. I'll see ya out there. Don't be late."

Liam pushed his bike out of the garage to the cheers of his name echoing in the air. "Liam! Liam! Liam!" In years past, there were times he would have accepted the attention he was receiving with a gracious and humble smile. He would have embraced the chants that were being thrust upon him, but that was when he was happy when he gave a damn, and when Jenny was by his side. He pulled up to the starting line and gave a nod in the direction of his opponent, he knew the guy, his name was Bobby Frasier, a fellow football player from Ripley. Bobby acknowledged the nod and returned it. Both of the men mounted their bikes.

Their engines revved as they waited for Gina to shoot the gun. She was the polar opposite of Julia Shipman who always came dressed in her monochromatic white ensembles and perfectly coiffed hair. Gina was dressed in full black attire, her leather pants painted on her as she positioned herself a few feet in front of Liam and Bobby. Her black-ink hair fell irregularly down her back, and the front was tucked neatly behind her heavily pierced ears. Her hand was raised high above her with the starting pistol carefully nestled within it; the only visible signs of color were her crimson nails that always seem to match her lips.

Liam took one more glance to his left; Bobby was securing his helmet while waiting for Gina's cue. Liam's crystal-blue eyes went to the crowd; he scanned the numerous strangers who seemed to want to be his best friend. All of them cheering wildly as they waited for Gina's sign. Out of the energized crowd, Liam noticed one individual who didn't seem to be joining in the climatic fanfare. He stood passively with his arms crossed. He looked like your average run of the mill guy, a little older, Liam concluded, possibly in his late twenties or early thirties. His jeans were torn at the knee but the brown leather jacket he wore told Liam that he had money. Nothing else was a giveaway except for the baseball cap that rested on the man's dirty blonde hair. It was a brown cap with white lettering that said Dent Enterprises. This was the man, *the* Aaron Dent. Just as Liam's eyes met his, Gina's gun went off.

The race covered an open stretch of terrain that Toby made just for tonight. There were six hills and four kiss-your-ass turns that would bring the contender back to the beginning of the race and the finish line. This was going to be Liam's first race on his newly restored motorcycle, and he was wondering how well the bike was going to handle the course. It was only April, and the winter had been harsh in more ways than one for Liam. The previous races had been handled inside Toby's huge indoor garage.

Bobby was the first to pass Gina; her hair flowed into a horizontal pattern as the wind picked it up from the aftermath of his bike. Liam gunned on his gas but the bike stalled, he gunned it again only to have the bike spit out another sputter. Liam kicked the gas pedal with an igniting fury that possessed him. This time, his bike came to life and charged past Gina like a bat out of hell. In seconds, he was on Bobby's ass and within a few more, Liam passed him. The first turn was a few hundred feet in front of them, and as they approached it, Bobby inched his way back into Liam's space. In a moment of rushed adrenaline, Liam's natural instinct took over, and he knew what he had to do. His Fatboy took the approaching kiss-your-ass turn with ease bypassing Bobby for the final time.

Huge smiles arose on Toby and Gina's faces as they saw Aaron Dent break into a rare but pleasing smile that seemed to be as wide as his wallet. The race covered a little less than two miles and by the time Liam made the last turn; Aaron Dent was shaking hands with Toby. The crowd went into a frenzied hysteria when Liam got off his bike. Bobby followed close behind his former teammate and congratulated Liam before leaving. Liam was civil and accepted Bobby's well-wishes but showed him no emotion. There was enough from everyone else to take care of that. Liam hardly had a chance to get his helmet off before Toby was smacking him on the back for a job well done.

"I knew you had it in ya! Thanks for scaring the livin' hell out of me in the beginning, though. Did you plan on having your bike stall like that? It was pure genius if you did, just pure genius." Toby exclaimed as Liam continued to show no emotion. Gina too, was beside herself hugging Liam tightly. Their previous encounter seemed nothing more than a mere memory for her as she showered him with affection. And still, Liam remained strangely quiet. "I want you to meet somebody, Liam." Toby moved to the side as the man with the torn blue jeans, and beautifully supple leather jacket came into view. "Liam, this is Aaron Dent. Aaron, this is Liam Larson... your next superstar."

Chapter Three
Aaron Dent

Liam sighed heavily, he was not in the mood for the conversation that he was about to have with Aaron. This was not his idea, this was all Toby's doing and Liam let Toby know his feelings with a huge frown. His thoughts were still with Jenny as he imagined her running towards him after he won the race. *"You did it baby, I love you!"* She would have exclaimed, smothering him with her sweet scent. He could feel her velvet skin touching his, enticing his senses and her auburn hair tickling his face, igniting the passion that had never died inside of him. His eyes were still closed with those thoughts when Toby's gruff and demanding voice reminded him it was just another dream.

"Ahem, Liam this is Aaron Dent."

"Hi, Liam. That was an amazing race you just won."

Toby gave him a critical look. The same look that a parent gives a child when they are being reprimanded for not acknowledging the person who is speaking to them. "Ahem." Toby voiced again.

Liam looked coldly towards Toby. "Thank you. It really wasn't anything."

"Really?" Aaron asked amused. "I beg to differ. You handled yourself extremely well on that bike, and that was a damn good time. I haven't seen anybody race that fast in a long time. You seem to be born for this," Aaron said showcasing his million-dollar smile again.

"Well, I don't know if I was born to do it, but I do enjoy racing. I've been doing it for years but only on a bike for a couple of months."

"You're kidding. What did you race before?" Aaron was intrigued by Liam's unpretentious behavior.

"My truck." Liam directed his glanced towards his black beast that seemed to be waiting patiently for his return.

Aaron's grin only seemed to widen as Toby and Gina both hugged each other. In their eyes, this was a done deal. There were dollar signs dancing in their eyes while they watched Aaron talk to Liam. It didn't even matter to them that Liam seemed out of sorts, as long as Aaron promised a future that was filled with guaranteed cash advancements, they were happy.

"I would like to talk to you, if that's alright, not here of course, but some place where we can sit down and get to know each other a little better."

Liam looked at Toby knowing that if he said anything but yes, Toby was going to be madder than hell at him. "Sure, that would be great." He answered in a drone but still appeasing voice.

"I'm going to be in town for a couple of days, why don't we get together tomorrow night? Toby said there's a place called *The Dock*, I could meet you there at eight o'clock."

"Eight o'clock then, Mr. Dent."

"Call me Aaron. All my friends do, and I think you and I are going to be the best of friends." Aaron extended his hand to Liam's as he tentatively accepted it. "Until tomorrow then. See ya, Toby, goodbye, Gina." He tipped his cap before leaving on his custom Harley Softtail.

"This is just the beginning for us, Liam. Do you know what it means for *the* Aaron Dent to even want to give us the time of day? He's known throughout Ohio for only sponsoring the best. He must see something special in you to make a trip all the way down here to our little old Glenville."

Liam could have cared less. He was sick of seeing the unbridled enthusiasm that everyone seemed to be pushing on him. He had come here and done what was asked and expected of him. All he wanted to do now was go back home. He pushed his bike onto the bed of his truck and prepared to leave.

"Where are you going now?" Toby was confused by Liam's strange behavior.

"Home."

"Home? Why the hell for? You can't go home now. You just won, and *the* Aaron Dent is interested in you. We've got to celebrate."

"You can do that for me, there's nothing I want to celebrate, Toby. I did what I came here to do, and now I want to go home. Give me my share of the winnings, and I'll be back tomorrow, but I have no intention of spending the night here with you guys. This is the last place I want to be."

Toby didn't push it, this time he indulged him and handed Liam a clump of hundred dollar bills. Liam shoved them in his pocket and drove away, allowing his faithful F-150 to take him back home.

Later on that evening, Grandpa Mack walked into Liam's room placing a piping hot cup of black coffee on his nightstand. Liam's heavy snoring informed him that he finally had succumbed to the much-needed sleep he had been hoping for his grandson. The night was hard on him. Grandpa heard Liam screaming for Jenny earlier in the evening. He didn't want to wake him now, even though there were a thousand questions he needed to ask. He was a patient man, and he could wait a little longer if that's what was needed.

A few hours later Grandpa Mack was given his opportunity. He was greeted by Liam, who brought the untouched cup of caffeine back into the kitchen. Liam sat down next to his elder while he lowered his head on his arms, letting it rest on the table. He was tired… mentally and physically. Grandpa Mack gently placed his rugged hand on Liam's head and rubbed it softly, the way he used to when he was a little boy.

"You okay, son?"

"No." Liam raised his head to meet his grandpa's concerned face. They're identical eyes transfixed on each another. "I've lost her for good, haven't I? I seem to lose everything that I love."

"I wouldn't say forever, Liam. She just couldn't stay here anymore and watch you self-destruct. She loves you, not Johnny. I know that, and you know that. I've had some long talks with her these past few months and her love for you has always been there. But you can't keep going down this road you're on if you want her back. That's what pushed her away in the first place.

"Grandpa?"

"Yes, Liam?"

"I know nothing happened that night at Johnny's."

"You do? Then why didn't you believe her?"

"I don't know. I really don't have an answer, I guess I was just caught up in my drinking, and I let that do the believing for me. I knew all along she would never hurt me like that but..." Liam's head went to the table again as his voice trailed off.

"Liam you've got to listen to me. You've got to let go of this, you've got to let go of Johnny. He's been able to, and now you need to do the same. He can't even bother himself with this stuff anymore, not in his condition. And more importantly, you've got to stop drinking before it destroys you."

"It already has, Grandpa. It's too late."

"It's never too late. You don't need the beer just like you don't need to race. Is that where you were last night?"

"Yeah. I won."

"Does that even matter, Liam? Why did you even start again? Does it have to do with that Toby character I keep hearing about? Is he the reason?"

"I guess, partially. I mean, he didn't force me into it, it was still my idea. He just helped nudge me in that direction a little bit. Grandpa, he's got a guy who wants to sponsor me. He's a pretty important person in the racing circuit, and he wants me. If I can get him to sponsor me, I can race on a much larger scale. I could really make something of myself. I'm supposed to meet him tonight in Glenville."

"No matter how big the scale is, Liam, it's still street racing, and it's still illegal. All it takes is one bust from the cops, and this so-called career you're pursuing is over. Anyway, what about the shop? Are you ready to throw that away? I thought this shop was important to you? You can't be racing all of the time and still run a business here in Spencer. It doesn't work that way. And why do you want to make something of yourself, Liam? You could have had all that attention in football? It was yours for the taking. Why racing and why now?"

"I don't know, Grandpa. I guess I'm thinking of my future without Jenny in it. I saw us being together forever, that's why I bought into Joe's shop. But that doesn't matter anymore. There's nothing to keep me here. It was only important with her in my life."

"What about Joe and Parker? Are you willing to leave them for your new friends? Liam, this just doesn't seem like you, it's not your character. You know, son, I heard that you asked Joe to buy his share of the shop back from you. I think you're acting too hastily, that's the wrong thing to do." Liam didn't reply. "Listen, you don't have to do this. Your home is here, and the people who care for you are here too. From what I've gathered, this Toby character only cares for you as long as you're making him money. He doesn't want anything to do with you unless it's got a dollar bill tacked onto it." Grandpa hesitated before continuing. "You're still having your nightmares, aren't you? Don't lie to me, Liam, I've heard them."

"They're not as bad, Grandpa."

"They're not, are they? Is that why I was up half the night tonight listening to you scream out Jenny's name?" Liam lowered his head again. "You know what you've got to do, son. Once you realize that, your nightmares will disappear, and you'll find your way back to her. I just know it. Why don't you go to the shop today before heading back to Glenville? Parker's been asking about you. He said the last time he saw you, you guys got into a heated argument."

"I've already been told what I should do to make things right. I know I should just let go of my demons, I guess we'll just have to wait and see about that. And as far as Parker is concerned, we did have a pretty nasty argument, but it was my fault, not his."

"To be honest, Liam I kinda thought so. Why don't you go see him? I think it would do you good to be at the shop, from what I hear, you haven't been there for a while."

Liam knew his grandpa was right. If he stayed at the house, he would only become more depressed. The whole house reminded him of Jenny, and he could hardly stand it. "I guess, Grandpa." Liam stood up and began to walk away but stopped before exiting the kitchen. He turned around, "I love you, old man. Don't ever forget that, no matter what happens."

Grandpa just looked at him wondering what the real meaning was behind his statement but knew that in asking he might not like what he heard, or he might not be told the truth, so he just let it go. "I love you too, son."

The clock read 11:00 when Liam pulled in. Parker's lime green truck was parked in its usual spot. He carefully got out and walked inside as Avenged Sevenfold's *Nightmare* played in the background. *How fitting.* He found Parker underneath the body of a beautiful gunmetal '68 SS Camaro with red racing stripes down its hood.

"Hey."

Parker appeared from underneath. "Hello, asshole," he said with full meaning.

"I guess I deserve that."

"What are you doing here?" Parker's words were cool as they rolled off his tongue.

"I wanted to talk to you."

"What about? I don't think we have anything to say to each other. I think we said enough the last time I saw you."

"I guess I deserve that too. I came here to apologize. I'm sorry for what happened between us. I know you were only trying to help me, I just didn't want to hear what you had to say."

"Is that all?" Parker asked.

"What do you mean?"

"I mean is that all? What's going on with you, Liam? You know I was only trying to get through to you and to help you see what I think you're missing, not to mention that I think your drinking is out of control. You can't hide that from me, remember who you're talking too; I've known you a lot longer than those assholes you've been keeping company with lately. I know your past, Liam."

"It's not that easy to explain, Parker."

"Come on, Liam. Tell me the truth. I know you're not your dad, was this all about Jenny and the accident?"

"I guess, and Johnny, of course. I was carrying, and still am carrying, so much pain, Parker. I drank to forget the pain. Not so much the physical pain but the emotional pain. You know, ever since my parents died I have put my all my energy into being the best damn football player I could ever be. I was invincible, and I loved it. But I didn't know what love really meant until Jenny entered my life. She made me realize what was important; now nothing seems important." Parker wasn't amused by Liam's little pity party he was throwing for himself.

"I don't know, Liam. I don't know what to say to you anymore. You say nothing seems important to you, but you sure seem to think racing is important when in reality Jenny should have been your priority. You lost sight of her, and your friends, and this shop. Are you ever coming back here?" Parker gave Liam a curious look. "Do you want to tell me why you sold back your share of the shop to Joe?"

"You wouldn't understand."

"Try me."

Liam let out a heavy sigh. "I guess, Parker, I just felt with me being gone so much I wasn't doing anybody any favors by holding onto it. I couldn't be here to help the way I should, and it wasn't fair to you or Joe."

"And?"

"And what?" Liam asked, wondering what Parker still meant.

"And Jenny."

Liam sighed again. "Yeah, and Jenny. This was our future, and now that there's no future with her, I didn't see the need to keep it anymore."

"You know Joe never accepted your offer, he never signed off on the papers you left him. He wants you to come back whenever you're ready. All you have to do is say the word, and he'll tear up the papers, and for what it's worth, I feel the same. I didn't come on board until you asked me, this was your dream first."

"Well, that's nice of both of you, but I don't see that happening anytime soon. Like I said, this was for Jenny and me; besides, I told you, I don't have the time anymore. I never wanted to be an owner in name only, I wanted to work here and build this place up. But that's in your hands now, you and Joe can do it, you're just as talented as I ever was; hell, maybe more so. This is how it should be. Listen, Parker, I didn't come here to talk about the shop. I came here to apologize. I hoped that this would be easy."

"Why should it be easy for you? You haven't made it easy for Jenny and me or anybody else, for that matter. So why should I make this easy on you? You deserve this. You've had it coming for some time now if you want my honest opinion." Parker wiped the grease from his brow with a cloth that was just as dirty as he was.

"I guess I deserve that too. I'm sorry, man… really I am."

"For what's it's worth, Liam, your apology doesn't mean shit to me. You should be standing in front of Jenny telling her this, not me."

"I can't."

"Why?"

"She's left town, Parker."

For a second, Parker felt some empathy for his friend. "Sorry, I didn't know."

"Yeah. I really screwed up this time."

"Well, I can definitely agree with you, you've been an asshole for a while now, and it doesn't surprise me that she finally had enough of your shit. But in your defense, I know how she feels about you, and you don't know for sure that she's gone for good. She might just need a break, some time away."

"Well, it doesn't look very good. I don't even know where she is."

"Maybe she's with her parents. They're in Myrtle Beach, right?"

"Yeah, but they moved there when all this crap was going on between us, I don't even have a phone number for them."

"Have you tried calling her?"

"A thousand times, Parker. It just goes to her voice mail."

"Look, Liam, this has been hard for her, really hard. I watched her fall apart every time I saw her. You never gave her a chance. She wasn't cheating on you with Johnny. I mean, she had plenty of opportunities to do so, Johnny wanted her you know that, hell everybody knew that, he didn't exactly keep it a secret. But still, even with his persistence, she didn't allow herself to go there. She told me what happened, and you have nothing on her. If anything, it's still Johnny. But that's not important anymore," Parker said, as he thought about Johnny in the hospital. "She didn't know what to do or what to think after that mess at his apartment. I know you've been going through your own hell; but man, Liam, you totally shut her out, and she just couldn't stand it anymore. She wanted to help you but what else was she supposed to do when you totally alienated her; and then to top it off, you weren't there for her. You've made this all about you when you forgot she was hurting too. You became a different person…to all of us."

"What if she decides we're through for good?"

"I don't know man, like I said, it wouldn't surprise me. I can't sugar-coat this for you. I guess you're going to have to cross that bridge when you come to it. But I do know she still loves you, Liam. It was always just you."

"I know that now. I just hope I get the chance to let her know that again."

Both of them stood side-by-side, neither one of them knowing what to do or what to say next.

"So… you feel like doing some work?"

"I guess, I don't know. I can't stay long, though, I've got to go to Glenville tonight to meet somebody."

"Who?"

"You don't know him. His name is Aaron Dent, he's from Ohio. I think he wants to sponsor me."

"Sponsor you? You mean for racing?"

"Yeah."

"You're not serious, Liam, are you?"

"Maybe, I haven't made up my mind yet. I need to at least hear him out, see what he has to say to me."

"I see," Parker said indifferently.

"I know this isn't what you want to hear, Parker but I'm still dealing with a butt-load of crap. I still have nightmares, and now they seem to have come true. Jenny's gone, and I'm not even asleep. I started racing to see if I could find myself again and possibly even redeem myself to everybody but in the process, I let Toby take control, and I lost Jenny. You've known me most of my life, and you know once I start something I have to finish it."

"Just like that damn race, do you still feel the need to finish it?" Parker asked.

"Maybe I do, to me, the race is still on. I know how Jenny feels about Johnny, but it still kills me to know how he feels about her."

"You know he's back in the hospital don't you, Liam?"

"Yeah, I went to see him yesterday, but I just couldn't bring myself to go inside." Liam paused as he reflected on his thoughts. "Listen, Parker, why don't you go with me tonight to meet this guy. You've always been my partner in crime; I'd like you to be there."

"I don't know, man, I've got a lot of work to do here, and Joe is out of town buying supplies for the shop, and since you haven't been around, we've been behind the eight ball for a while. Besides, just because we're talking doesn't mean things are cool between us or that I approve of your new lifestyle. You know how I feel about all this. I don't think you need to be racing, and I especially don't think you need to be racing with Toby Raines always looking over your shoulder. I've heard a lot of bad stuff about him. He's only in it to make money off of you, I don't understand why you don't see that."

"You don't know him like I do, Parker. He's not that bad. Yeah, I'll admit he's a hothead, but he's had my back from the beginning. I've been racing really well these past few months, and he's always been there for me. Things could change for me if Aaron wants anything to do with me. That's why I need to see him. I could make some real money. Hell, it could give me the chance to prove myself the right way. This wouldn't be happening for me if it wasn't for Toby. Come on," Liam pleaded. "We haven't spent any time together in a long time. You've always been there for me, please don't turn your back on me now, I need a friend in my corner, especially now. You, out of everybody, know what I'm going through. I haven't forgotten what Kelli meant to you, I'm feeling the same stuff over Jenny. Just come with me and hear him out. That's all I'm asking." Liam entreated Parker.

Parker hesitated. For once in what seemed like a long time, he looked into the eyes of the man before him and saw the friend he used to know. "Yeah, I guess. But if I don't like what I hear, Liam, I'm going to tell you. I'm all for having a good time, you know that, but I think your future is here and not on some damn motorcycle. Don't forget what you're really fighting for. If you want Jenny back, you better think hard about what you're about to do with your life."

Liam didn't answer but just gave his old friend a hug.

****

The Dock was busy, as usual. There were at least five girls at the bar trying to persuade the bartender to put their bra on the chandelier. You could tell that he was enjoying the attention that the college beauties were giving him. Liam and Parker meandered their way through the bar until they found Aaron Dent at a back table with what looked to be his entourage. Aaron instantly rose from his seated position at Liam's approach.

"I was wondering if you were going to show," Aaron said extending his tattooed arm to him. Liam graciously accepted his gesture.

"Sorry I'm late but I'm here now, and I brought a good friend of mine with me. Aaron this is Parker, Parker this is Aaron Dent."

"Glad to meet you, man." Aaron extended his same inked arm to Parker.

Parker wasn't as willing as Liam was in reciprocating the gesture. He instead kept his hands in his pocket and gave Aaron a slight nod. Aaron realized by Parker's cold demeanor that he wasn't going to be as easy to win over as others had been. "Well, take a seat, both of you. Can I get you guys something to drink, would you guys like a beer?"

Parker's eyes bore into Liam's. "Nah, thanks, we're fine." "Where's Toby? I thought he would be here for this little meeting?"

"He's on his way, he called right before you guys arrived saying he was running late. But we don't need to wait for him; it's you that I want to talk to."

"Well, like I said, I'm here and all ears."

"I was blown away by your racing, Liam. You seem to have been given a gift from God. I haven't seen skills like that on a bike since I used to ride," Aaron said in an arrogant tone.

"You raced?"

"Yeah, back in the day but I had to give it up. I had a bad crash that almost cost me my life about ten years ago."

"What happened?" It was the first time Parker showed any interest in what Aaron had to say.

"I was rounding a turn, and my tire blew. I went right into a retaining wall, head first. I was in a coma for almost three months, when I finally did wake up; I had three steel rods in my leg. I suffered a nasty concussion and had my spleen removed. The doctors said I must have had an angel looking over me; I should have died at the scene. This was actually my third accident; the doctors said one more time would probably be my last. That's all I needed to hear, I had to make a decision. I knew I couldn't give racing up totally; I love it too much. So I decided to turn my addiction into a business. Once I was out of the hospital and on my feet again, I began spreading the word that I was looking into sponsoring some races. I took my savings and began building my business… word spread like wildfire, and by the end of my first year, Dent Enterprises was born."

"Wow. That's impressive," Liam said while Parker remained apathetic.

"Yeah, I've done well for myself over the years. And, I've been watching you for a long time, Liam. Your name isn't quite new to me."

Liam seemed confused. "Me? What do you mean? I thought last night was the first time you had seen me race?"

"It was. But I've known about you for a couple of years now." Liam's confusion grew. "Don't look so baffled, Liam. You've been racing for a while haven't you?"

"Yeah."

"I've got my own spotters who travel the tri-state area looking for new talent. We found you a couple of years ago when one of my boys raced against you. He came back and told me how you seemed to have had the race figured out before the flag went down. How you came from behind just in the nick of time to win the race as though it had all been perfectly choreographed beforehand. It was then that I began watching you. Last night was no accident on my part."

"But you acted surprised when I told you that I had raced my truck."

"Yeah, it was just to make small talk. I didn't want you to become disinterested, so I needed to keep the conversation going so I could have you agree to meet me tonight." Aaron waited for Liam to speak. "You are still interested in what I have to offer, aren't you?" Liam didn't say anything. "Please tell me this isn't a waste of my time. I see something in you, Liam, and if you give it half a chance, you could be ten times what you are now by this time next year. All I'm asking is your trust." Liam's eyes bore into Aaron's as he heard the last word. Trust. That's what Jenny wanted, and he realized they didn't have it. He wondered how could he give a complete stranger his trust when he couldn't even give it to her. With some hesitation, Liam extended his hand. Parker immediately pulled it back to his surprise of everyone at the table. "What?" Liam asked Parker more than a little annoyed.

"I don't mean to pry, but you did bring me along because you wanted a trusted friend by your side, didn't you?" Liam waited for what Parker had to say. "Well, I don't think you should be shaking hands on a deal quite so soon. I don't mean to be this way, Mr. Dent..."

"Call me Aaron, all my friends do."

"Thank you, Mr. Dent," Parker said, "but right now I don't really know you, and I wouldn't consider us friends... at least not yet." Aaron gave Parker the same stare that Liam was giving him. "I just think you should mull this idea over a little while, maybe sleep on it before you shake hands with him. It wouldn't hurt you to talk to your grandpa about this. This seems like a pretty big deal you're about to embark upon, I'm just sayin' as a friend, that before you agree to anything, you should think and I mean really think about what you want." The last few words seemed to have a double meaning for Parker. Liam began to speak only to be interrupted by a voice behind him.

"I don't think he needs to think about anything except how much money and fame Aaron Dent is going to bring us." The gruff voice was undeniable, only Toby spoke with such a brash and harsh tone to his normal everyday voice. He extended his right hand to Aaron while using his left hand to intentionally brush against Parker as he patted Liam on the back. "I'm sorry I'm late, Aaron. I had a few things I needed to tend to back at the shop. You know, it won't run itself," he finished with a hearty laugh.

"No problem, I completely understand," Aaron said. "As a matter of fact, it looks like you came at the right time, we were just finishing up, and I think your boy here was about to become part of the Dent Enterprise family."

"Wonderful. That's exactly what I want to hear." Toby gave Liam another hearty pat on his back, this time almost knocking him into the table. "Well, Liam...what are you waitin' for? Shake the man's hand. He's about to change our lives forever." Liam stared at Toby, then at Parker, and then Aaron. His eyes went back and forth in a feverish, triangular pattern as the room began to spin before him. He felt pressured and knew that if he didn't make this deal now that his name would be mud in the racing circuit; but then again, a voice was telling him that he was about to make the biggest mistake of his life. It was Jenny's voice and as Liam's hand reached out one more time to grab Aaron's; her voice began to fade away. It became muffled by the boisterous laughter of Toby and the exuberant cheering at the table as Liam's palm rested securely into

Aaron's. The deal was done. It was as if the devil himself had made it. Parker just sat back in his chair shaking his head in disbelief as Liam was thrust into the center of all the chaotically enthused revelry.

Chapter Four
Aaron's Heartbeat

  Liam drove slowly on Ripley Road as he made his way out of Spencer. This road which held the name of the malevolent spirit himself, amused Liam as it seemed to be so rigid to Liam's feelings or for the fact that this inanimate entity had taken his soul and spit it out without regard to him or Jenny. Liam felt trapped. He kept thinking back to his night at *The Dock* when he literally gave his life away by shaking hands with Aaron Dent. He squeezed his palm, trying to squeeze the remnants of Aaron's touch from him. His hand felt dirty. Liam could envision Parker's face giving him a worrisome yet evil eye as his longtime friend followed him from behind.

  Parker knew the mistake he was making but was unable to help his friend, unable to help him turn back the hands of time and unable to help him realize that time was running out.

  Liam sighed heavily as he gazed upon the empty seat to the right of him… Jenny's seat. He could still smell the scent of her as if she were sitting next to him. Her essence was embedded in every fiber that was a part of Liam. He came to an intersection; he braked slowly before coming to a complete halt. His life for the past two years seemed to be a series of intersections; he was always deciding which way to go, what turn to take and what would be waiting for him once he made the turn. His decisions were always hanging in the balance, waiting for the answer that seemed to be vacant from him, and the last decision he made, the one with Aaron, seemed to have sealed his fate. He sighed. But no matter what he had done, all the mistakes and drama that had occurred, he knew that Jenny should still be here with him. It was killing him that she wasn't and he knew with each passing day that she was gone, only meant that her return to him would become even bleaker until eventually, she would be nothing more than just a memory of his sordid and pathetic past.

A car honked from behind then. He was in a trance at the intersection, unable to move forward without thinking of his past mistakes. It was déjà vu about Spencer. He realized that seemed to happen a lot. He couldn't keep his mind in the present when all he could do was think about the mess that had been created from April 11th. The annoying driver not only blared his horn this time but also yelled a few obscenities to make sure he was getting his point across. Liam got the disgruntled driver's message and heeded to it, but not until rolling down his window and thanking the driver for the courtesy by giving him a very poignant and effective hand gesture as the driver passed him. He didn't care anymore about anything, and on that moving note, he entered the ramp onto 77 North that would take him to Dover, Ohio.

In only a couple of hours, he would be signing his contract with Aaron Dent, not with a handshake this time, but in writing, and in Liam's mind, not with ink, but in blood. The highway seemed as cold and dark as Liam felt. He was positive that this new stretch of asphalt had seen as much heartache as Liam and Jenny had on Ripley Road. He drove in a daze up the strip of blackened artery that would lead him to his new life. His foot never letting up on the gas as he hastily made his way, he could hear his bike in the back of the F-150, strapped in for the ride, as it rattled back and forth from the bumps and potholes that decorated 77. All sorts of vehicles tried to pass Liam, only to fail in their attempt as Liam pushed harder on the gas. He was still racing, if only against himself.

Although he didn't want to be a part of Aaron, or Toby for that matter, he didn't have anything to look forward to anymore. So, even though he wanted to go back in time, a time where Jenny was with him, he was ready to move forward in time if it meant that time would bring her back to him. So, in order to do that, he drove like a maniac letting the interstate take him to his new fate, at least, for the time being. And before he could have a change of heart, Liam was exiting 77 and entering a new stretch of road that led him to his master: Aaron Dent.

Aaron Dent and Parker were waiting for Liam as he pulled into the massive lot that was a part of the Dent Enterprises. Liam was impressed by what was in front of him. There were not only one or even two steel-framed buildings that graced the property but eleven, even here in Ohio, that menacing number seemed to follow him. All of them were branded with the words, *Dent Enterprises* written in heavy black lettering to stand out against the red exteriors. The buildings were massive in size, covering what Liam thought to be at least two to three football fields in length in total. On the right of him, Liam could hear the familiar sound of engines rumbling as he noticed a motorcycle race on a track that seemed to be as large as Spencer. There were people everywhere, all wearing something that said *Dent Enterprises* on it and the most repulsive of them all, was none other than Toby Raines. His huge frame that held a girth that could never be concealed as it poked out from beneath an already filthy *Dent Enterprises*, t-shirt, made its way to Liam at an alarmingly fast pace.

"There's my boy!" Toby exclaimed, giving Liam a bear hug and a bit of chew as it trickled from Toby's mouth and onto Liam's arm. "Where the hell have ya been? We've been waitin' for ya." Liam continued looking at Aaron as he made his way towards the three of them.

"I'm glad to see you, Liam," Aaron said as he interrupted Toby's hug and gave Liam his own signs of affection with an even bigger embrace. Liam didn't reciprocate but allowed Aaron to showcase his enthusiasm. "Did you have any problems finding my place?" Aaron asked.

"No, not at all," Liam replied. "It was an easy ride up 77, just like you said. I could have done it blindfolded." Aaron and Toby both let out a laugh, knowing that Liam's little remark held more credence than he probably meant... pretty much anything Liam did when it concerned driving, he could do blindfolded. He was just that good. Parker on the other hand, remained quiet.

"Of course you could," Toby remarked. "Aaron and I ain't fools, we know a superstar when we see him." Toby winked at Aaron as Aaron looked on. Liam didn't like to be the center of attention, especially when it was being forced upon him by the hands of Toby... and now Aaron. He had a bad feeling ever since their meeting at *The Dock* when he could have sworn he had heard Jenny's voice pleading with him not to become Aaron's latest puppet. He tried to dismiss the gnawing feeling in his gut, but he knew that it was his conscience trying to remind him what everybody else had been telling him.

"You have a remarkable place, Aaron," Liam said as he gazed at the Dent Enterprises, property.

Aaron followed Liam's gaze, "Thank you. This is my heart, and now you are going to be a part of this and make my heart beat even louder and faster Liam," he continued as he put his hand on Liam's shoulder. He gave Liam an uneasy stare. Aaron's grip on his shoulder was tight and made Liam feel that Aaron was securing his claws into him.

"What do you mean?" Liam had to ask, all the while, Parker continued to remain quiet as he took in the atmosphere that the Dent property was providing.

Aaron gave out a wicked and hearty laugh, "Nothing, Liam, no need to become defensive. I just see in you the chance to be something much bigger than what you are now, just like Dent Enterprises. It started out as a small track in some back woods, now it's this," Aaron said as he waved his arm to showcase his property. "I gave it my nurturing touch, and in time, my baby has turned into this spectacular place that has never let me down." Aaron became pensive as he continued, "And, you, Liam Larson, are my new blood, and will pump new life into Dent Enterprises making my heart beat even stronger. I intend on nurturing you with the same care I have for my company and turn you into the star I know you are. And with that, I know you won't let me down either." Aaron's last remark seemed more of a threat than his intended flattery.

"I won't let you down, Aaron. That's a promise."

"Good, boy. That's all I needed to hear." Aaron's smile looked like it came from the devil himself. "So, why don't we get down to business? The papers are ready for you to sign."

Liam followed Aaron and Toby into one of the buildings to the far left of them as Parker unpacked his truck. Upon entering, Liam saw a woman sitting behind a small desk; her total attire could have been a billboard for Dent Enterprises. "Hello, Mr. Dent," she said in a sultry voice.

"Hi, Roxy, this is Liam, the boy I was telling you about. I need the contract papers I had you do for him yesterday." Without saying a word, Roxy rose from her seated position, showing off her assets that were tightly concealed in a Dent Enterprises low-cut t-shirt. She walked passed Liam brushing his side but not without first giving him a very seductive and alluring smile. Opening a drawer behind Liam, she pulled out a manila envelope that contained Liam's new future in it.

"Here you go, Mr. Dent."

Aaron took the envelope without another word to her and then motioned for Liam to follow him. They walked past Roxy's desk with Toby close behind and entered a room; Roxy remained focused on Liam, her charismatic emerald eyes sizing him up as the door closed behind him.

Aaron's office was quite different from the room that Roxy occupied. Where hers was minimalistic in nature... a small desk with a computer on it, some cabinets and one window that allowed her to look at the massive buildings around her for her view, Aaron's was much larger and opulent. In the center was an enormous mahogany desk with antique replicas of tiny race cars from years gone by strewn across it, an ornately decorated leather chair sat behind the desk, with gold beveled tacks outlining its frame. The walls were painted in a deep red with white and green racing stripes centering it and they were covered with signed posters of famous race car drivers. Unlike Roxy's office, Aaron's had not one, but four large six-paneled lead-glass windows that overlooked the backdrop of Ohio. Liam was impressed, but what impressed him even more, or perhaps scared the living hell out of him, were the stack of papers Aaron was still holding. In them, he saw his future, a future that did not hold the happiness that Aaron had been promising him; instead, he saw more misery and loneliness. He wondered if he should high-tail it out of Aaron's elaborate office before another word was spoken. All he could hear was Jenny imploring him to not make the biggest mistake of his life.

Aaron perused the mass of papers in a very quick and composed manner, his half-moon specs resting comfortably on the tip of his nose. "Well, Liam looks like everything is in order." He gave Liam another huge money-making smile as he handed the papers to Liam along with a gold pen. "All you have to do is sign at the 'X', and we're off to the races... literally," he said, letting out a very boisterous laugh as Toby joined in.

Liam didn't partake in the obstinate hilarity, he, instead remained quiet as he took the papers and began rifling through them.

"Is something wrong, Liam?" Aaron asked as he wondered why Liam felt the need to review the paperwork. "Everything is in order, just like we discussed at *"The Dock,"* you won't find anything missing or different." Aaron was pressing Liam to him to sign.

Toby seemed agitated too. "Liam, what the hell, just sign your damn name on the dotted line."

Liam gave both of them a very disconcerting look and with a heavy sigh; he took the gold pen that contained the poison that would seal his fate and signed his life away. Liam could hear Jenny's voice, but it was much more distant this time and slowly faded away as Aaron and Toby's exuberant clapping took over. Liam smiled indifferently to both of them, knowing there was no turning back the hands of time now.

"I'm going to put these in my vault. And then, why don't you get settled in, Liam. The last building to your right is made up of a bunch of rooms for my drivers. Your room is the first to the left as soon as you enter the building. You can put your stuff away and then you can meet me at track eleven - I chose that one just for you - and we'll start testing your bike on one of the courses. I think you'll like what you'll see.

"Thank you, Mr. Dent."

"Remember, call me, Aaron, Mr. Dent is my father."

"Of course... Aaron. And thank you. I'm looking forward to this new venture." Liam was lying. Something he was getting used to doing when it came to Aaron and Toby. He turned to leave only to find Aaron's assistant, Roxy waiting for him as he exited. He just gave her a half-smile as he passed her, ignoring her efforts to let him know she was interested in him, he could not have cared less. And once she realized her attempts were in vain, she gave out a loud and disgruntled huff, one for Liam to hear, only making Liam laugh at the sound of it. No one could reach him, not even her, and the only person who could, didn't seem to want anything to do with Liam anymore.

The next twenty-four hours consisted of Liam testing his bike on the numerous courses that encompassed Dent Enterprises. He felt like a kid in a candy store as he rode them. And for all the misery he was feeling, Liam seemed to come alive when he was riding. He decided to not to think about his past for the time being and begin to embrace his new life, and by the end of his first week at the Dent compound, he had won all five of his heats, leaving Aaron's best in Liam's dust. Aaron and Toby were beside themselves as their minds began counting the money they were going to make off of Liam.

Aaron met up with Liam in his private quarters, hoping to entice his new protégé, not only with the meal in front of him but with a new, much more lucrative offer. Liam sat down, ignoring the spread in front of him. Aaron had noticed that Liam only seemed to be alive and excited when he was racing, at all other times, the boy seemed to be uninspired. "Liam, I hope you are enjoying your stay at Dent Enterprises."

"I am, Aaron. It's amazing."

"Thank you. I must say, I am even more impressed with what I'm seeing from you; your driving skills surpass anybody I have come across. You have my entire staff in awe of your talent." Aaron said as Roxy walked in at that very moment. She gave Liam the same sultry glance she had days earlier and Liam gave her the same as he did days earlier: his ignorance. He wasn't interested in her. She handed Aaron a beer but not before clipping the top off for him and pouring the pale ale into a frosted mug.

"Would you care for one?" she asked Liam, still smiling. She leaned closer to him with the ale in her hands, allowing the beverage to spill on her skin-tight white dress.

"No, no thank you, I'm fine," She stood silent, allowing Liam to soak her in. Her efforts still went unheeded. Aaron motioned her to set the beer down and with a flick of his wrist, told her it was time for her to leave. He took a large gulp from the frosted mug and turned his attention back to Liam.

"I have a race for you, Liam. It's in a few days, this Saturday to be exact. I do a lot of business down south, and I have a client who would like to take you on. He's well-known in the Carolinas and Tennessee area. His name is Eli Nazareth, and he's never lost a race. I think it's time that the two of you face each other and see who the better man is.

Liam remained quiet for a few minutes. He felt insulted by Aaron's remark, as though he was questioning his talent. "I'll take him on, Aaron. I'll do it right now if you want, he won't beat me, as a matter of fact, you can bet your compound here that the closest he'll even come to me is his face in my tail pipes as he swallows my dust."

A malevolent snicker escaped from Aaron's lips as he took another sip of his beer. "That's exactly why you're on my team, Liam, and Eli isn't. I don't expect anything less from you. Eli will be here tomorrow morning, which gives him a couple of days to get used to the courses.

"I'm ready for him now, Aaron. Bring him on." Liam stood up.

"Aren't you going to eat?" Aaron asked as he waved his hand across the mass amount of food that was laid upon them

"Nah, not hungry. I'll see you in the morning, Aaron." Liam turned from Aaron and walked back to his room. He should have been excited about this race, this is why he signed with Aaron. He wanted to take on the best, to take on those whose reputation seemed as great as his, and to prove to all of them, that there was only one who held the honor of being the best, and that was him. But instead, Liam was despondent, and out of sorts, he felt alone, even with Parker by his side. He realized that his hope to get rid of his demons was nothing more than a façade and that perhaps his demons were more of his reality than he thought. He sighed heavily. He plopped himself down on the grey comforter and took his wallet from his back pocket. He rummaged through the few $50's and a couple $100's until he found the most valuable item in the piece of worn cowhide: Jenny's picture. He stared at it intensely, rubbing his hand across her face... gazing at her as if she was right in front of him. "I miss you, babe. I miss you so much," and with that, he put her picture back in his wallet and took a beer from the fridge and used the rest of the night to drink his sorrows away.

****

The next morning, Liam found Parker and Aaron talking to a guy whom he concluded to be *the* Eli Nazareth. Liam sized up his new nemesis, his stature was tall, easily meeting Liam's height, and his hair was bright red and hung poker straight down the side of Eli's face. Liam could tell by the bulging muscles that protruded from Eli's cut-off black leather biker jacket that besides his love for racing, he seemed to have a love for pumping iron as well. Liam guessed he should be intimidated by this gift from the south, but to the contrary, Eli's presence did nothing more to Liam but ignite a rage inside of him that was bursting to be released, and Liam was more than ready to release the rage... and he would, in two days, allowing this Eli character to see that the real nemesis in this race was Liam.

"There you are," Toby said between spits of chew. "We've been waiting on you."

Liam looked past Toby. "I'm here, Aaron. Hey Parker," Liam acknowledged.

Parker pulled his friend to the side before giving Aaron the chance to speak. "Are you sure about this?" Parker asked with genuine concern for the first time since arriving at Dent Enterprises.

"What do you mean? Eli is no threat. Trust me, friend, after Saturday, this Eli character will be dreading the day he ever crossed my path."

"You can say whatever you want, Liam. But I've seen him ride. He's good, real good. And his bike is built for speed. It's not that I don't have faith in you, but Aaron told Eli that you guys would be racing on Reaper's Bluff." Reaper's Bluff was Aaron's most dangerous course, a three-mile stretch of road with six hairpin turns, two water hazards and a forty-five-degree hill that would put their bikes in flight before they crossed the finish line. It's no coincidence that it's named Reaper's Bluff, three of Aaron's best are now on disability, with one in a wheelchair because they didn't respect the course… its goal was not only to compromise the driver but to come for his soul, just as its name suggested.

"I'm not afraid of the Bluff, or of Eli, give me some faith, man, remember who you are talking to, I'm going to win, and Eli is going to go back where he belongs, especially after I'm through with him."

Parker wasn't as convinced but decided not to argue the point anymore. "Okay, whatever, Liam, but don't say I didn't warn you." Parker stepped back for a second putting his hand to his nose, "Man, have you been drinking, Liam? You reek! You better sober up before Saturday or your promises on making mincemeat out of Eli will all be said in vain."

"I'm fine, Parker, nothing I can't handle." Parker's remark annoyed the hell out of Liam. He didn't need his friend's two cents of advice. He could handle his drinking just like he was able to handle his racing.

"Finally," Aaron said as Liam approached them. "Your little pow-wow with your friend over?" Liam didn't answer. "Well, anyway... Liam this is Eli Nazareth, Eli this is my new star, Liam Larson."

Eli reached out his hand to showcase a full sleeve tattoo, "Glad to finally meet the legend. Your name and reputation for driving have made it all the way down to my neck of the woods, I'm looking forward to our race on Saturday." He then grinned, allowing Liam as well as Toby and Parker to see his gold-capped tooth smack dab in the middle of his mouth.

"It's nice to meet you, too, Eli. Aaron has told me a little bit about you. I'm looking forward to seeing what you bring on Saturday. I'm sure neither one of us will disappoint the crowd." Liam said still staring at Eli's gold tooth.

"Of course you won't," Aaron added. Aaron also noticed the smell of alcohol coming from Liam's breath. "Eli, why don't you clean up and get something to eat. We'll catch up later."

"That sounds great, Aaron. I'll see you guys later... and I'll see you, Liam in a couple of days. I hope you're ready." Eli let out a subdued but still sinister snicker before getting on his bike.

"Come with me, Liam," Aaron insisted.

Liam followed. "What's up, Aaron?"

"You smell, Liam. You've been drinking. I don't care what the hell you do in your off time, but when you're on the clock, I expect you to be on time, and not drunk. You're not only carrying your reputation, but you're carrying mine, and I will not let it be tainted because you can't handle your liquor. Do we understand each other?"

"I'm not drunk." But Aaron and Liam both knew better.

"I don't give second warnings, Liam or second chances. You've got two days to get ready for this race against Eli, and I expect you to come ready to show Eli and everyone else that I haven't made a mistake in sponsoring you."

Liam looked at Aaron. "I am the best. You already know that, and on Saturday, every one of your other little puppets will know that too... including Eli Nazareth."

"Then let the games begin," Aaron declared, giving Liam a satisfying grin to Liam's decree.

Chapter Five
Eli Nazareth

Liam awoke Saturday morning to the banging of his bedroom door. "Liam! Get up! It's eleven o'clock, your race is in less than an hour!" Parker yelled as if his own life depended on it.

Liam groaned heavily. His night had been weary with little sleep, and the the sleep he did catch was interrupted continuously with images of Jenny imploring him to leave Aaron Dent and return to her. He sat on the edge of his bed, running his fingers through his greasy hair, "I'm up, I'm up," Liam grumbled unlocking his door.

"What the hell, Liam, you should have been at the track hours ago! Aaron's already madder than a hornet's nest." Parker threw Liam a pair of jeans that were wadded up on the floor as well as a dirty white t-shirt, "Here put these on. I'll wait for you outside, we need to do a check on your bike, and then you have to get your ass to Reaper's Bluff."

Liam wasn't as eager as Parker seemed to be, but he knew that it didn't matter, no one seemed to care about what he was going through anymore, and he was tired of hearing that he was throwing himself his own little pity party, so instead of thinking about Jenny and the dream he just had about her, he got himself up out of bed, got dressed, threw some cold water on his head and put on his game face. It was time.

Liam and Parker were greeted by Aaron and about thirty other of Aaron's other minions. The day was bright, but you wouldn't have known it by the look on Aaron's face. "Is this what I should expect from my prized driver?" Aaron said callously.

Liam remained stoic. "I'm here, Aaron. Let's get this race on."

In the distance, Liam could hear the sound of a very loud engine as it careened its way through Reaper's Bluff… it was Eli. "As you can see, Eli is preparing himself for the race. I hope his efforts don't surpass yours, Liam," Aaron added in a sarcastic tone. He seemed to doubt his new star since he arrived. Liam's behavior seemed genuine on the surface, but Aaron could sense that his mind was never where it should be, and that was here, at Dent Enterprises.

"As I told you the other night, you have no worries when it comes to me and my racing ability. You signed me on because you liked what you saw, I have no intention of letting you down now… or myself, that's not how I operate. I can win this race with my eyes closed." Liam's tone was smooth and confident.

"Good, that's what I want to hear," Aaron said coolly.

At that very moment, Eli drove up next to them. "Hello, Liam, looks like a great day for a race."

"Yes, it does, Eli." Liam extended his hand to Eli's, "May the best man win."

Eli looked at Liam's hand, studied it for a moment, wondering if his opponent was being sincere and then with the same gesture, extended his, "may the best man win," and then gave the crowd his best gold-tooth smile.

"You guys have about thirty minutes before the race. I suggest you use it wisely," the meaning of Aaron's remark seemed to be for Liam much more so than Eli.

"Sure thing, Aaron," Eli said.

"I'll be waiting at the finish line," Aaron said looking directly at Liam.

"I'll see you at the start, Eli," Liam said as he began to walk away with Parker.

"Liam, could I have a moment with you?"

Liam looked perplexed, "We don't have much time, Eli before the start of the race, what is it?" Liam said as the two of them left Parker standing by himself.

"We didn't really get the chance to talk the other night, and I was hoping we could this morning before the race, no matter who wins, I'm leaving for Nashville as soon as the race is finished, I've got some races down there I'm in, and I need to scope the area before I race them."

"Sounds like you're pretty busy, why take the time to come here and race me then, if your schedule isn't allowing it? It's not like I'm anybody special." Liam added.

"On the contrary, like I told you the first day we met, I've heard about you, Liam for some time now, if Aaron hadn't called me, you would have seen me anyway. I've wanted to race you since your days back in Spencer, and I wasn't going to miss this opportunity when I heard from Aaron."

"I see… well looks like you'll get your chance today, Eli." The two men just stood there, letting the awkward silence take over. "Is that it, Eli?" Liam continued.

"I guess, and to let you know that even though your reputation precedes you, I think you might have your work cut out for you today. I'm the best, Liam, not just in my parts but up and down the Eastern coast. Eli Nazareth doesn't mess around and this little race today that your boss is putting on, might be for show for him and for you too, but I never get on my bike unless I plan on leaving somebody in my dust, and today, that somebody will be you." He smiled again, something Eli seemed to like to do, if anything, to show off his gold tooth. They were close to each other and Liam could smell the stench of his breath as well as see that his face was littered with scars, remnants he was positive of, from races past. He cupped his fists while his muscles bulged from his arms, he was wearing the same cut-off leather jacket and worn jeans. Eli's cocky confidence was bold as it was obnoxious. "Most people when they hear they are racing against me, walk away, and if they don't, they're usually carried away," he added with his wicked grin.

"Well, I'm not most people, Eli and if anyone is carried away, it will be you. You might talk a big talk, but that's only because you haven't raced against me, that'll change, I promise ya, after today."

Eli continued with his grin adding with it, his sinister laugh. "I'll see you at the starting line, Liam. Nice talkin' to ya." And with that, Eli walked away.

"What was that about?" Parker asked as Liam approached him.

"Nothing. Nothing at all." Liam was fuming, and all he wanted to do now was show Eli Nazareth the way home... on a stretcher.

****

Liam drove his bike to the starting line. There were easily a couple hundred people that had come to watch this race. Liam was amused. He thought this was just going to be something between Eli and himself, but then he looked to his right and saw his boss and realized that when Aaron Dent was involved, even a lap around the track would be considered an opportunity for Aaron to make some money. And from the kiosks selling Dent Enterprise t-shirts, hats, and other paraphernalia, he knew he was right. Aaron turned his eyes towards Liam and gave him his toothy smile with a nod and a thumbs-up; he then took his seat along with the couple hundred other spectators.

Liam nodded in return while adjusting his helmet and turned to see that Eli had pulled up beside him. Neither one of them spoke a word to the other, both realizing that enough words had already been spoken earlier that morning. There was no Julia Shipman dressed in white or even a Gina dressed in black to drop the flag; instead, over the noise of the crowd, Liam heard only one voice, an announcer as he began his countdown. It was race time. At that very instance, the crowd rose to their feet, as their voices reverberated from the Ohio hillsides, some carried banners with Liam's name on it while others showed their loyalty to Eli.

"Ten, nine, eight, seven, six, five, four, three, two... one."

Eli was the first to punch his accelerator, keeping his promise to Liam, at least for the moment, that he would eat Eli's dust. But the moment was fleeting for Eli, because within seconds of leaving the gate, Liam was upon Eli's back, and by the time they had approached the first turn of Reaper's Bluff, Liam had passed Eli, this time letting Eli eat Liam's dust.

Aaron stood amongst the crowd, binoculars and walkie-talkie in hand to keep tabs on Liam's position. He remained calm amongst the revelry of the spectators. Liam and Eli were both out of sight and except for a few of Aaron's employees who were tactfully positioned throughout Reaper's Bluff's, the two racers were alone. Liam was a good twenty yards ahead of Eli when he felt his bike begin to fishtail. He looked in his rearview mirror to see

Eli on his ass, punching his back tire with his bike, his gold grin sparkling in the wind. Eli was playing dirty. Liam kicked his bike into overdrive allowing him to pop a wheelie before entering the next turn. He didn't see Eli anywhere, and as he approached the water hazard, he became airborne only to find that somehow Eli had caught up with him and had taken the lead by the time both of them had landed.

He gave Liam a defiant "thumbs-up" with his middle finger as he passed him and disappeared in the final turn before the last water hazard. Aaron kicked his chair in a fit of rage as he listened to his spotters giving him the play-by-play of the race. There was only less than a mile left before the finish line. He could hear Jenny's voice, *"come on, baby, you've got this, don't give up now. I'm right here with you,"* her tender voice was all he needed to hear and gave him the strength he needed to turn this race around and make it his own. He gunned his gas pedal so hard that the heel of his boot came off, he accelerated in speed and within seconds he was on Eli's tail. A few moments more and they were both neck-and-neck, and as they entered the ramp and became airborne, Liam passed Eli landing at least ten feet in front of his racing nemesis. He gunned his gas again, this time reciprocating Eli's earlier gesture, but instead of one "thumb-up," Liam let go of his handlebars and with full glory, gave Eli both of his middle fingers straight up in the air, laughing as hard as he could as he disappeared from Eli's sight.

Aaron was pacing back and forth, his baseball cap turned backwards as he waited patiently to see who would round the corner. Parker too, was anxious, waiting to see if his friend would not only round the corner first, but make it out without crashing. Moments seemed like hours, the enthusiastic crowd who had been showing their support with thunderous commotion was all but still as they too, waited to see which driver would appear first.

The silence was deafening, and then as the hills picked up the sound of a bike's engine, the crowd rose to their feet again and began to clap at a fevered pitch as they saw Liam come down the homestretch. Aaron was turned to Parker and shook his hand as they both walked down to greet Liam at the finish line. Liam could see him, and as he began to relax knowing that he was seconds from crossing, he felt his bike beneath him as it began to shake and fishtail one more time, it was Eli, still sportin' that gold-tooth grin as he shadowed Liam only yards from the finish line.

"Oh no you don't," Liam whispered. Eli was next to him, both of them were prematurely claiming victory, Eli pushed his bike into Liam's, causing Liam to swerve even more, he was mad, not for Eli's vindictive actions but for allowing Eli to even get this close to him. Liam looked at the finish line, he saw Aaron and Parker and about a hundred other people he didn't know. But then he saw her, he saw Jenny, she was standing there, her beautiful presence amongst the sea of unknowns, clapping and jumping up and down wildly as she cheered him on to victory. That's all he needed, he looked at Eli one last time and charged down on the gas, as he pushed his bike into Eli's causing his nemesis to spin out of control and slam into a guard rail. Liam never looked back and crossed the finish line finally, to the applause of the crowd.

The crowd surrounded him as he dismounted his bike. "Now that's what superstars do," Aaron said pleasingly as he hugged Liam for the very first time. "And that's why you're on my team."

"Thanks, Aaron. I told you, you didn't have anything to worry about."

"That was a great race, Liam, I'll never doubt you again." Aaron patted Liam on his back as Toby and Parker looked on.

"I knew you would do it, Liam," Toby added as if it was because of him Liam won.

Parker stood by his friend and just shook his hand. "Nice job, friend." Liam smiled at him, letting Parker know that having him there with him, meant the world.

"Thanks, buddy."

The celebration continued only to be interrupted by Eli Nazareth who had made his way to them. Liam stared at Eli. Eli stared at Liam. "Nice race, Liam."

"Thanks, Eli. I think we left the crowd satisfied; it was a good match-up. I'm glad we had the chance to race each other." Liam said genuinely.

Eli gave out a snicker, he then grinned, and Liam noticed something different about Eli. The prominent piece of gold that graced his mouth was missing. "I'm sure you are, Liam, there's never been anybody been able to say they have beaten Eli Nazareth... that is until today... that's some karma there for ya, if you ask me... I'd be careful with it. Karma always has a way of coming back to bite you in the ass." Eli turned to thank Aaron and then left Dent Enterprises and his ego behind. Reaper's Bluff had not claimed any souls that day, but it did claim one Eli Nazareth's ego... and one gold tooth.

Liam felt validated that day for the very first time since April 11th. He didn't exactly know what Eli meant by his comment about karma, but he didn't care; he felt that finally, after a year of bad karma, his was finally making a turn for the better. He was ready for his new-found fame and glory and whatever else Aaron Dent had in store for him. Yet in the back of his mind, he could still hear Jenny's voice inside of him, it had never left, his heart still went back to her and to his hometown of Spencer.

He knew he would always be wrestling with it, still wondering if he had made the mistake that Jenny's voice had warned him about or if he was finally beating his demons and winning the race once and for all.

But as he joined in the celebration with his new friends, he could only hope that their paths would cross again… and as time went on, and Aaron's clutches dug deeper into Liam's soul, Liam's fate seemed sealed and his past… became nothing more than a memory.

Chapter Six
Six Months Later

    It had been almost six months since I had been home, or 173 days, 12 hours, 29 minutes and 11 seconds, if I was keeping count. I left on a lonely night after one of the worst nights of my entire life. As I made my way back home through the winding roads and the kaleidoscope skyline that the autumn season brought to the mountain state, I felt the usual but distant tug in my stomach return. The knot that had formed from so many turbulent times in my past had never gone away, it was just nestled deep enough in the pit of my belly that it only made itself known when necessary... and right now, it deemed itself necessary.

    I tightened my grip on the wheel as I approached the long stretch of black top that had become one of my biggest adversaries. I slowly braked, my apprehension grew exponentially as I made my way to the top of the crest; *Devil's Bulge* was before me. My heart pounded looking at the black asphalt ribbon that had changed my life forever. This had become my nemesis, an inanimate object that launched itself into my life, turning it into a living hell. The road seemed innocent enough as it conveniently welcomed me with its ominous tease but I knew better, there was nothing innocent at all about this menacing road.

"Well, well if it isn't the return of the beautiful Miss. Jenny King, it's been a long time, my friend. Why don't you come closer so we can get reacquainted again, I've missed you..." It seemed to be mocking me as the knot in my stomach grew larger with every breath that I tried to inhale. "*Are you still scared? Why?*" A single, sinister laugh echoed in the air. "*What are you waiting for? Come on, Jenny, I'm not going to bite, that's not my style. We've been through too much for you to be afraid of me now. We have a history together or have you forgotten in your estranged absence? Besides isn't that why you came back... to see me, to see if your fears have been conquered? I know it can't be to see Liam. You're over him... right? Good riddance to the loser, if I may be so bold.*"

I could feel the tears stinging my cheeks while they made their way down my face. I buried my head into my hands to avoid the sounds that I thought I was hearing, I knew it was all in my head but the voice that continued its mockery of me seemed so real and painful. I thought I could handle this but I was wrong. *Hasn't enough time passed for me? Shouldn't I be able to come back and not be haunted by these same memories? Where is my strength, my resiliency?*

I felt so weak sitting there and so very, very alone. I did what I was told to, Grandpa Mack, Parker, my family, and even Gertie had convinced me that I needed some time, some time to let the wounds heal and time to think about what to do. But it hadn't worked; if anything the only thing time had done was make me realize how fragile I really was. And more importantly, how much I missed Liam. My love for him had not diminished but had grown stronger with each second I had been away from him. That's why I had come back, I needed resolution from him. I needed to know if we still had a chance or if it was once and for all, over. I couldn't stay here; this road that meant everything and nothing to me, all at the same time was killing me slowly. I felt myself wasting away the longer I stayed idle, so I lifted my foot from the brake and pushed down hard on the accelerator. My car seemed to take the road effortlessly, gliding over the black pavement leaving its mark securely on it.

Familiar landmarks passed quickly before me, memories from my past stinging my senses and then, before I had time to breathe again, *Devil's Bulge* made itself known to me once more. The ominous voice that had chastised me earlier returned to continue its rant, taunting me as I drove through the hairpin turn, but not once did I flinch or break down. My only focus was to keep a steady foot on the gas and brace my steering wheel with a vengeance as it took me away from the ugliness that made up the menacing curve. I wasn't about to let my will be continually weakened by an object that wasn't even alive. I was determined, and as I exited *Devil's Bulge* I felt a calming come over me. The inanimate voice that haunted my mind quickly faded as did the sight of the turn in my rearview mirror. Its sinister laughter muffled by my own. A sense of accomplishment overtook me and I moved onward towards my home.

The house carried an austere and somber feeling to it. I walked closer looking at the new cracks in the concrete steps and overgrown weeds that resided in the yard. A multitude of cobwebs had made residence in every corner of the porch and a settling of dust had occupied the wicker table and porch swing. It was a dismal sight, this house that at one time produced so much life and activity in it seemed destined to be nothing more than a depressed and broken-down shack that rested only on its memories.

I walked to the door; the creaking of splintered boards beneath me announced my arrival. The lead panels of glass that bordered the vast, wooden door entreated me to enter its domain. I carefully but intuitively put the key into the hole watching it effortlessly unlock for me. I walked in and my heart was home, even though the interior of the house looked older than usual with flecks of paint falling from the ceiling and the addition of new cracks that had spider-webbed itself onto the walls, I didn't care, I was home... finally.

The air was stale and gave off a peculiar smell that stung my throat once inhaled. The austere feeling that I received on the outside continued on the inside of the house as well. The living room furniture was covered in white sheets and as I touched them a cloud of dust rose into the air stinging my senses even more. I moved on, continuing my walk until I found myself standing at the base of the stairs. The huge stained glass window that occupied the second floor landing seemed more brilliant than ever as the sun rays beamed through the multi-colored panes sending a sense of warmth into the cold and dreary house. I took the steps one-by-one until I had reached my bedroom. I felt nervous for some reason but still, I yearned to be in my own space and be surrounded by my belongings. I clutched one of the few teddy bears that still sat tolerantly on my bed, and I fell on it as I had a thousand times in my past, contemplating what my future held. I closed my eyes and welcomed my dark and trustworthy friend.

My body was truly enjoying the sleep I was permitting it and was nowhere near happy to withdrawal from the lingering slumber it obviously needed; but the persistent ringing of my cell begged me to answer it. I reluctantly fought with my sub-conscious to finally wake up. I rubbed my eyes vigorously glaring at the number that was so rude in interrupting me. I recognized it and the anxiousness that befell me made me instantly hold my stomach tightly. I hadn't seen this number grace the screen of my cell in a long time. The ringing continued until the vibration began to make my hand go numb.

"Hello," I said with an eager but still guarded tone.

"Jenny?" The voice was unusually curious.

"Kendra."

"Oh my God, Jenny, I can't believe it's you. I thought I had seen a ghost when you drove through town. I saw you at the red light and I couldn't believe my eyes. I didn't think I would ever see you again."

"Well I didn't think I would ever be back, Kendra."

"Are you okay? How have you been? Are your parents alright? Are you alright? Why did you come back?" The questions flowed from Kendra's mouth with a choreographed fluidity to them.

"Yes, Kendra, everybody is fine… considering, I mean my dad's health still isn't great but he is doing much better since he and mom moved away. And I guess I came back because I was homesick, this is still my home and I've missed it.

"How have you been, Kendra, are you enjoying motherhood? How's the baby?" I too, seemed to have an ample amount of questions.

"Allie is great. She's almost three months old. Can you believe it? I'm the mother of a three month old little girl! She's gorgeous, Jenny. I can't wait to introduce you to her."

"I want to meet her. And I'm sure she's beautiful if she looks anything like you."

"Well, I am a little bias but she is perfect. I can't believe she's mine." There was a long period of awkward silence once we both realized the initial greetings were over. We had been the best of friends for as long as we both could remember; able to finish each other's thoughts and sentences without hesitation but at this moment, neither one of us knew what to say to the other. In the six months I had been gone we had become acquainted strangers. "So…" Kendra finally interjected, "what really brings you back home?"

"I don't know, Kendra… I guess it was just time."

"Were you with your parents the entire time?"

"Most of it, but being around my dad made me even more depressed. I know that sounds really awful to say, I thought being with them would help but it didn't. Don't get me wrong, it was great to be with them, it was time together that we needed but after a few months I couldn't stand it anymore. It's still hard for them to carry on a conversation with me without bringing up Liam's name. I couldn't handle it. I went away to try and forget him but instead my parents kept reminding me of him, so I left and spent the past couple of months in California with my sister."

"Wow, Jenny, I don't know what to say. I knew this time wouldn't be easy for you. I'm so sorry. Are you doing better now?" Kendra was cautious with her question.

"It's alright, Kendra, you don't have to worry about what you ask me. I'm not going to break, I'm doing fine. I'm not going to lie to you; it was very difficult coming back here. I thought I was ready until I hit Ripley Road."

"You didn't come in that way did you, Jenny?"

"I did. I guess I wanted to see how it felt. It was hard but I needed to do it and I'm glad I did." The next few minutes were spent with Kendra talking a mile a minute as her nerves began to show. She was my second sister, a trusted confidante that in the past, I could always rely upon but the months that had come between us had changed us both. I could feel her anxious energy while she tried to act like nothing had changed. But we both knew better. We weren't the same two, giggly teenagers who used to talk for hours on end while our favorite songs played in the background. No, now we had turned into two young adults who had been dealt a new hand in life. And after what seemed like hours of endless monotony over nothing, Kendra finally asked what had been bearing on her soul since I first answered the phone.

"Jenny, don't you have something to ask me?"

"What do you mean?"

"You know, aren't you going to ask me about Liam?"

I sighed heavily. All along, those were my intentions but after the few minutes we had shared with one another, and Kendra not volunteering any information on her own, I thought maybe I wouldn't want to know. Maybe Kendra was intentionally avoiding the subject. "Kendra, I'm confused. He's been out of my life for six months now and in reality maybe even longer. The entire time I've been gone he's been my one singular thought, even when I was with Ashley. I want to know everything about him but I'm afraid to know anything at all. It's weird but I feel somewhat jealous."

"Jealous? Why in the world do you feel jealous, Jenny?"

"I don't know. I guess because it seems he's been able to move on with his life. We haven't spoken since that night at Brush Creek Road, I was so much a part of his life and to find out that he's been able to carry on his without me… well, it's hard for me to swallow. I don't know if I want to know how he's been but then again, I don't think I will be able to stand it if I don't know, if that makes any sense."

"Awww, Jenny, it's okay, really. And it does make sense. I will tell you everything I know. I've always been here, I've missed you terribly and I know you've been hurting."

"Thanks, Kendra, I needed to hear that. I thought coming home would be different but I've felt so alone since my arrival. I don't know if I made the right decision. I'm seriously thinking I should just leave and, this time mean it when I say never look back."

"Don't, Jenny. You belong here just as much as anyone, this is your home. Listen, why don't I come over and bring Allie with me. We could order a pizza from Lougini's. It would be just like old times."

"That would be great. I haven't had a Lougini's pizza in like forever."

"Then it's a date. We'll be over in a little bit."

Kendra showed up exactly when she said she would with a large Lougini's pizza in one hand and Allie in the other. I didn't realize how much I had missed my old friend until we embraced. I needed to see a familiar person from my past that was just as happy to see me as I was them. We spent the first part of our evening just talking and catching up, and I had the privilege of holding little Allie, who was, on all accounts, a perfect angel. Her full name, Alison Jenny Bishop was after her great grandmother on her mother's side and the middle name was after me. I was beside myself and felt so honored that Kendra named her little girl partially for me.

Even though I was hesitant in knowing anything that had happened while I was gone, Kendra knew full well that once she arrived and we became comfortable with each other I would want her to spill the beans on everything… and that's exactly what she did.

Apparently, after my departure, Liam didn't waste any time in moving on with his life. His racing had become his mistress and according to Kendra, he embraced her 24/7. I was sad to hear though that Toby and Gina were still very much a part of Liam's livelihood but happy to hear that Parker had re-entered it by becoming his manager. I felt at least a little at ease knowing Parker would be by his side. He would try to keep Liam on the straight and narrow, if that was even possible anymore. But the biggest surprise was hearing about Aaron Dent.

This so-called "redeemer" seemed to have saved the day for Liam, as rumor had it. He had signed a lucrative deal with Dent Enterprises that allowed him to continue racing in the underground circuit without the threat of police. On the surface, Dent

Enterprises was a well-known auto body company that worked closely with the regional police departments in southern Ohio. This made it easy for the racing to continue. Aaron helped the police and the police, in return, turned their heads for his races. Most of them took place in Ohio and apparently, Liam had become a phenomenon on two wheels there, racing almost nightly and making himself, as well as Dent Enterprises and Toby Raines, more money than they knew what to do with.

My heart sank hearing this. It killed me a hundred times over every time I thought of him racing. This wasn't the same boy I had met two years ago who shunned away from the notoriety that football had given him. He hated the mere thought of a reporter zoning in on him for an interview or the frenzy of so-called friends who flocked to his side. Liam never enjoyed the public eye or having any amount of attention put on him. I guess he really had changed because the boy I fell in love with would have walked away from what this boy was now doing with his life.

I wondered where Grandpa Mack stood with Liam's new lifestyle. Surely to goodness, he would have tried to talk some sense into him but then again, this past year Liam seemed hell bent in proving how strong he was without the support of loved ones. I had hoped our time apart would have changed him but it obviously hadn't. But still, even learning all this, I still needed to know if Liam thought about me, if he asked about me or even cared anymore; but the words eluded me. I was too scared to ask because I was too scared to hear the answer. Kendra sensed this and knew I needed to hear the truth.

"Kendra, do you know if Liam has ever asked about me?"

"Jenny, I don't know much. I have only spoken to Parker occasionally, and when we have talked the only thing he has told me is that Liam hasn't been the same since you left."

"Is he still drinking?"

"I'm not sure, Jenny. I never asked Parker and he never offered the information. I don't want to tell you he hasn't and give you false hope either; I think that's something you're going to have to find out on your own."

"Do you ever see him?"

"Sometimes, when he's in town, which isn't much. But the few times I have seen him I can tell you, that he doesn't look well. He's let himself go. I ran into him at Lougini's about a month ago and it took me a second to realize who he was, and when I did say hello to him, it was as if he didn't even know me. Grant it, last time he saw me I probably wasn't carrying a little baby in my arms but still, it took me saying my name to him a couple of times before he said hello. It was like I was a stranger."

"That's all? Are you sure Parker hasn't said anything to you?"

"I really don't talk to him, Jenny. But I do know wherever Liam is, so is Parker. I can tell you that Liam's given back his share of the shop to Joe."

"What? How do you know this?"

"It's a small town, word spreads, Jenny especially when it involves you guys."

"I don't understand, Kendra. Why?"

"Liam didn't want to keep it; the shop reminded him of you. He bought into it when he thought the two of you had a future together and after last spring he realized that wasn't going to happen." I lowered my head into the sofa pillow. "I'm sorry, Jenny. I don't think Liam really believes that you guys can't work it out."

"Really, Kendra? Then why did he give back his share of the shop to Joe?"

"Maybe he's confused, Jenny. It would make sense. He hasn't been the same since..." Kendra stumbled over her last few words.

"What, since the accident?"

"Yes, Jenny, since the accident."

"Jenny?"

"Yeah?"

"There's something else you haven't asked me."

"What's that?"

"Johnny."

"Oh," I said placidly. I hadn't forgotten about Johnny. If Liam was my one singular thought since I had been gone, Johnny would have been my second. The few seconds I spared myself of Liam I allowed myself to think of Johnny. The last time I saw him, he lay feebly in a hospital bed. I could still see the misery in his face when I left him. I lay awake on so many nights wondering if he was still or alive or if he had passed away because of a broken heart.

"I don't know if I should allow myself to know how he is, Kendra. It's enough knowing what's happened to Liam."

"Well, I know you better than that and I'm going to tell you. He's hanging in there, Jenny, much better than anyone expected."

"Do you mean he's better?"

"Well, he's not cured, if that's what you're asking but he did make a remarkable recovery in the hospital last spring. He surprised everybody, including the doctors. They said he shouldn't even be here but it was like he found some sort of inner strength or something."

"Did he find a match for a heart?"

"No. He's taking meds to keep everything working but it's still only a matter of time, Jenny. He won't be able to live a life with the heart he has now."

I remained quiet. As a matter of fact, after that conversation the rest of the evening became very uncomfortable for us. We tried to continue our talk but each sentence we ended led to prolonged periods of silence. The only thing that kept us going was Allie's necessitating cries for her mom. We found that after a few hours of much needed bonding and a new found awkwardness between us, our evening had finally come to an end. Kendra was ready to walk out my front door when she abruptly stopped. "What?" I asked perplexed.

"I can't leave yet. I think there's something you should know, Jenny."

"What is it, Kendra?"

"I haven't told you everything about Liam."

"There's more?"

"There's a race coming up and Liam is going to be in it."

I really didn't see the significance of Kendra's remark, he apparently had been racing all summer, the importance of this race seemed strange to me. "So, Kendra. He's been racing for a while now, why should this one matter anymore than the others?"

"It's just that it's going to be a pretty important race." I still didn't understand what Kendra was getting at. "Jenny, he's going to be racing here in Spencer. It's the first time he's raced back here since April 11th. I just thought you would want to know about it." My heart sank. "I didn't know if I should tell you but I couldn't leave tonight with a clear conscious without telling you. I thought you would want to know, Jenny."

"Thanks, Kendra. I'm glad you told me but if he's changed like you said he has, it's not going to make a difference if I know or not. It's not like I can change his mind anymore, it seems he has forgotten about me. I'm nothing more than another notch in his belt and a faded memory of his past."

"Well the race is in three weeks..." Kendra hesitated.

"Where, Kendra?"

"It's going to take place on Ripley Road."

"Ripley Road! No!"

"Yeah, Jenny, that's why I thought you should know. Parker told me. It was apparently Toby and Aaron's idea. Toby told Aaron about the accident and all the drama surrounding it. Aaron loved the story and thought it would be great to recreate the night. Everyone associates Liam with racing now and almost everyone knows about the accident. They thought it would be a good draw to re-enact the race, but on motorcycles this time. They even tried to get Johnny to race against him but he won't do it, or maybe he can't do it."

"But why would Liam agree to this, Kendra? I mean, it's one thing for him to choose this crazy career but why would he want to relive that night again? Did I mean nothing to him? If anything, you think out of respect for me he wouldn't do it. It's like a slap in my face. I thought...."

"Jenny, I don't think he wants to do the race. From what I've heard, he's being forced too. Aaron pretty much runs the show and if Aaron says jump, Liam jumps. There's a lot riding on Liam, a lot of people have invested not only their time but their money in him. I think Liam's hands are tied in this. He's got to do the race no matter what."

"Oh my God, Kendra, this is crazy! Can't anyone stop it? I mean, it's not like he signed his life away, why can't he just say no? Does Grandpa know about this?"

"I'm sure he does, but he never sees Liam anymore. It's like Toby and Aaron have some sort of hold on him. I thought having Parker with Liam would balance things out, but they seem to just shuffle Parker around and half the time he doesn't even know what's going on until it's too late."

Allie was screaming at the top of her lungs by this time and wrestling for her mother's attention. "I'm sorry, Jenny but I better go. She must be hungry or something."

"It's okay, I totally understand. It was good to see you, Kendra. Thanks for coming over and for the talk. It's been too long."

"I agree. And Jenny, it's going to be okay, I just know it. Maybe enough time has passed; maybe Liam will be more receptive to you now. Just because you haven't heard from him doesn't mean he doesn't care. I know he loves you. That's one thing Parker did tell me. I should have mentioned it to you earlier but this whole night's been weird for me. I just didn't know what you wanted to hear."

"Like I said, Kendra, you can tell me anything. I've grown a pretty thick skin since I met Liam. I can take almost anything."

"I can see that. Well, I better go," as Allie continued her crying fit.

"She's beautiful, Kendra. You did well."

Kendra hugged me one more time before leaving, as I watched her leave, I saw the shadow of a truck turn the corner. I could have sworn that it was a black Ford F-150.

Chapter Seven
Relief

I looked at my calendar; a cool breeze informed me of the approaching weather. It was the 11th of October, two years to the date of my first encounter with Liam Larson. I circled the date and gently laid the pen on the table. I advanced to the window and inhaled the fragrant wind. The town was busy preparing for the forthcoming festival. The entire town had bedecked itself in its usual brown and gold ribbon and every store in town had adorned their doors with the autumn regalia. I wasn't joining in on the festivities this year. There was no need for it. It wouldn't be the same without my family and Liam. I would go about my normal routine as of late which included becoming a recluse in my own home.

It had been eleven days since my arrival back to town. In that time, the only people that I was certain knew I was back were Kendra and Billy. I had been unable to reach out to anybody else or maybe my will just wasn't allowing it. I had become a chicken; afraid of the rejection I knew I would receive from the one person I needed more than ever to welcome me home. I had dialed Liam's number numerous times only to hang up before the first ring. I even called Grandpa Mack only to hang up when his soft but raspy voice answered. But I knew I couldn't continue this isolated lifestyle for much longer. So, for the first time since I had been home I went into town.

    I drove down the streets that had been so much of my childhood, taking back streets and alleys recalling a time in my life that wasn't so complicated. My car steered itself through the rural neighborhoods. I felt good as I went about my way… until I found myself sitting in the parking lot of the high school. It was here where I let my emotions get the best of me. I went to this school for four years but it only took the last year to leave the biggest impact. I missed him, and what hurt the most was I didn't think Liam missed me at all. I wondered what he was doing right now, if it was him who I saw the night that Kendra was leaving my house and if it was, why didn't he come see me? I wondered about everything but mostly about what he was doing at this exact moment while I sat alone thinking of him. I closed my eyes.

****

    Liam rounded the last turn and plowed down the finish line. He didn't wait for anybody to help him; he took his bike into the garage and prepared to hoist it onto his truck.

    "What are you doing?" Parker asked.

    "I'm leaving."

    "You know, Liam, I'm not the enemy here. You can talk to me. I've been your friend a lot longer than these guys. I know who you are and this act or whatever that you've been putting on lately isn't very convincing, especially to me."

    "I don't know what you're talking about, Parker."

    "You don't? Huh. Okay. I can keep playing along; I have been for the past six months. But don't act like you're fooling me. I know what's going on with you, Liam and the sooner you admit it the better off we'll all be."

Liam strapped his bike into the bed of his F-150 and proceeded to leave. "Look, Parker, I'm just doing my job, what they want from me and what they expect from me. I don't need you or anyone else telling me how messed up things are in my life, I tell myself that enough."

"Fine, but let me remind you this race Aaron and Toby are expecting you to be in is wrong. You can't do it. It's the worst thing you could possibly do, especially to Jenny." There was a long pause between them as Parker waited for Liam to speak, but he didn't. "Fine then," Parker continued. "I've said my piece. I'm here because I want to be, Liam, because I'm your friend and I believe you need somebody who really cares for you in your corner." And still, Liam remained silent. "Dammit, Liam! You know I've never agreed with this and I'm not going to let you prepare for this asinine race without trying to talk some sense into you!"

"I understand, Parker. But what the hell do you want me to do? I signed a contract with Aaron, if he wants me to race, I have too!"

"Nobody bent your arm in signing that contract, I was there, remember? And from what I've learned contracts are made to be broken!" Liam just sighed heavily. Parker knew he wasn't getting anywhere with his friend. "Liam, did you hear whose back in town? Do you really think she would approve of what you're about to do?" With those last few words, Liam stomped on his gas pedal and left Parker in a pile of dust.

"What the hell was that all about?" Toby asked coming up from behind Parker.

Parker couldn't stand the thought of Toby Raines and to be next to him made him ill to his stomach. It was all he could do not to say how he really felt about him but he kept his mouth shut for his friend. It had become harder than hell for Parker to stand in the background while Toby and Aaron treated Liam like their damn puppet. "It was nothing, nothing at all, Toby. Just a couple of friends talking." Parker walked away while leaving Toby standing alone, scratching himself.

Liam's truck came to a screeching halt at the doorstep of his home. It was dusk and Grandpa Mack was in the field bringing Sugar Dumplin' into the barn. He waved to acknowledge Liam and in return Liam gave a slight nod in his grandpa's direction making his way inside. This was how it had been since Jenny had left. Liam was rarely home anymore, and when he was, he spent his time in his bedroom, secluding himself from the one man who had always been there for him. He plopped on his bed while looking at the picture by his bedside of he and Jenny. He wondered what she was doing at this very moment and if she ever thought about him.

****

Jenny thought she was dreaming. She thought she heard her name but the sound of tapping glass overshadowed it. She had fallen asleep while sitting in the parking lot. "Jenny, Jenny." The voice anxiously called. She rolled her eyes trying to wake herself up. "Jenny," The voice said once again. She looked to her left in disbelief; she thought she was still dreaming.

"Johnny." Instead of rolling down her window, she opened her door and jumped into his arms holding him tightly.

"Whoa!" Johnny was taken totally off guard by Jenny's fervent greeting towards him.

"I'm so glad to see you, Johnny. I've missed you."

"I can tell." He reciprocated in her very affectionate hug. "What are you doing here in the school parking lot by yourself in the dark, and for that matter, what are you doing back in town?"

Jenny didn't want to let go of him. She just wanted to hold him. She needed to be held and if it meant being the instigator then she was more than willing to do it. He felt good against her body and she just wanted to relish in the moment.

Johnny knew not to let go of her. "Jenny, are you alright?" He could tell that there was more behind her bear hug than just an old friend being glad to see him.

"Yeah, Johhny, I'm fine. Now that you're here." She let go of the tight hold she had on him. "I'm just really glad to see a familiar face."

Johnny went back to his original question. "What are you doing home?"

"I got homesick, Johnny. I missed being here."

"So…." he continued. "Are you…." Jenny knew where he was going with his interrogation.

"No. I'm not back with Liam. As a matter of fact, besides you, the only person I've seen is Kendra. I've been home for almost two weeks and I haven't seen or even talked to Liam. I don't think he knows I'm home."

"Well, believe me it's going to be a shock to his system once he finds out. I thought I had seen a ghost when I drove by."

"That's what Kendra said to me too. You would have thought I died or something." Jenny said with a soft chuckle. Johnny looked much better than the last time she had seen him. "How are you, Johnny?"

"I'm doing well, Jenny, considering my circumstances."

"What does "well" mean?"

"It means for the time being, my heart is in good shape. I'm still on the donor list for a new heart but until that happens mine is treating me fine." The look of concern must have said it all. "Don't worry, Jenny. I wouldn't lie to you, like I could if I wanted too. I've come to learn that I can't seem to hide my feelings towards you anyway," Johnny said, somewhat laughing at his own remark. "Really, I'm doing fine. I promise."

"Johnny, I'm sorry the way I left things. I didn't mean to do it that way; I just couldn't stick around here anymore, not with everything that had happened. I didn't feel like I belonged and I needed some space. It was horrible for me to leave the way I did when you were so sick."

"No apologies are necessary, Jenny. You were going through a really rough time in your life and believe me; if I was able, I probably would have left too."

"So, I heard that you're back at home with your mom, is that right?"

"I am. I don't think she's going to let me out of her sight for the next hundred years," Johnny said with the same laugh. "Once I got out of the hospital, she didn't want me to return to Glenville. I've been home ever since."

"So you're not going to school?"

"Not this year, at least. By the time I was released from the hospital I had missed registration. I'm helping mom at her shop for now. I'm supposed to take it easy, so mom has me doing menial jobs. Honestly, she could do them herself but I know she's just trying to keep me busy so I don't think about stuff." Johnny lowered his head as he spoke.

"What kind of stuff, Johnny?"

"You know, Jenny." She did know. He meant her. He was still in love with her.

"Johnny," she said softly.

"It's okay, Jenny. You don't have to feel weird around me, I'm not going to try and corner you anymore. Those days are over. That is, unless you want me to." The same nervous laughter continued to spill from his mouth. There was a long pause afterwards though. "So, are you going to try and see Liam?"

"I don't know, Johnny. Kendra filled me in on some of the stuff he was doing. You know, while I was gone we never communicated; not even once. I haven't talked to him since the night I left Brush Creek. I don't know if he even wants to see me anymore. I'm scared to find out. I've been hurt enough, I don't think I can take any more rejection from him and that's exactly what I think I'm going to get."

"So you haven't tried to call him?"

"Well, sort of."

"What's that supposed to mean?"

"I've called him a few times but I hang up before it even starts ringing. Like I said, I'm scared, Johnny."

Johnny pulled me to him allowing me to bury my head into his chest. I could feel his heartbeat pulse against my temple in a rhythmic, almost melodic manner. "You're trembling, Jenny and you're ice cold."

"I'm okay, Johnny, just my usual mess." I looked him square in the eyes. "Do you think things will ever be normal again... for any of us?"

"I don't know. I would like to hope so but I don't think so. I would like to think that all this stuff we've been through has been instruments to help guide us as we grow older. It had to be happening for some damn reason. I guess time will only tell." Johnny pulled back from me. "You still love him, don't you?"

I couldn't deny the fact that I had developed feelings for Johnny that were more than I had ever thought they could be but they still paled in comparison to what I felt for Liam. "I do, Johnny. I love him more than anything; maybe even more than when I left. Isn't that crazy? I mean, the guy pretty much dumped me for fame and fortune and I still can't stop thinking about him."

"It's not crazy; Jenny and he didn't dump you for fame and fortune. He just got caught up in some crazy shit while he was trying to figure himself out. Don't forget that I've been friends with him for a long time. This stuff he's involved in isn't Liam and I think in time he's going to realize that too."

"But how much time does he need, Johnny?"

"I don't know. I can't answer that. I will tell you that through the grapevine, I've heard that he isn't drinking as much."

"Really? How do you know this for sure?"

"Jake told me. He's been to some of the races Liam has been in for Dent Enterprises. I guess he's unstoppable, Jenny. One night Jake ran into Parker at a race outside Dover, Ohio, they started talking bullshit and Liam's name came up. Parker told him that he hadn't seen Liam take a drink in over a month. That was about two months ago. I don't know how true it really is but I don't know why Parker would make something like that up."

Relief swept over Jenny as she heard this. It gave her hope that maybe; just maybe, Liam was returning to his old self and with that, maybe remembering what they once had together.

"But he's still racing, Johnny. Kendra told me that he gave up his share of the shop to Joe."

"I heard that, too."

"Johnny?"

"What?"

"I know about the race on Ripley Road."

"You do?"

"Yes I do. Is he really going through with it?"

"I think so. They asked me to race him but I said hell no. If anything, it was out of respect for you, besides I don't want to race Liam anymore, or anybody for that matter. Those days are over for me."

"I wish they were over for Liam. I just can't believe the boy I fell in love with who didn't give a damn about all the notoriety would stoop so low as to recreate that awful night. We almost died, Johnny. I don't get it."

"Nobody gets it but you can't give up hope, Jenny. The Liam we know is still inside of him and I know Parker's been giving him an earful about doing the race. I can guarantee he's not going to be able to go through with it with a clear conscious. He knows who really cares about him."

"I'm not giving up on him, Johnny but how can I help him when he doesn't even want me around?"

"Do you know that for sure, Jenny? You said you haven't spoken with him, how can you say that until you hear it come from him?" I knew what Johnny meant but I was still a chicken.

"You, out of anybody, know Liam's heart." Johnny's comments were true and my guilty conscious was agreeing with him. But right now it was easier for me to be a chicken shit than to be brave.

"I'm sorry, but I need to go, Jenny. I really don't want to. I can't tell you how good it's been talking to you. I've missed you but duty calls. Mom is expecting me. I was actually on my way to pick up some supplies for her when I saw your car. I'm sure she's wondering where I am but then again, being who she is, she probably already knows," Johnny said with the same laughter he had been providing since our encounter began.

"Tell her hello for me."

"I will. You should come see her. It would make her day to see you again."

"Maybe I will, Johnny."

"Jenny, I'm here for you. You don't have to go through this alone."

"I know, and I appreciate it. I just have to take this slow. It's been a little overwhelming for me since I've been back. I'm just trying to absorb everything and take it one day at a time."

Johnny embraced me with the same force I had given him earlier. His body felt so good against mine. I felt alive for the first time since I had arrived home. We were still holding each other when the sound of a vehicle rounded the corner. I knew the sound of the engine and as Johnny and I pulled away from our embrace, the black Ford F-150 accelerated in speed as it passed us.

Chapter Eight
Grandpa's Regard

Liam threw the sacks of feed into the barn in a careless manner with no regard to where they would fall. He then took the broom and swept Sugar Dumplin's stall without even paying any attention to her. He was in his own little world, just going through the motions of his routine. He left the barn leaving the remnants of his half-ass job behind him. He stomped through the kitchen and past Grandpa Mack without even a hello in his direction.

Grandpa had had enough of Liam's pity party, that's all he ever saw from him. "Liam, I want to talk to you."

"I don't feel like talkin', Grandpa."

Grandpa wasn't going to take no for an answer. "Well, I do. What's going on with you? Did you get the feed for Sugar Dumplin?"

"Yeah, it's in the barn." Liam was spiteful in his answer. He stormed up the steps taking them two at a time as he let his brute strength slam the door shut. The deafening sound reverberated all the way from the second story to the kitchen windows on the first floor, making the blue floral china shake in their case.

Grandpa walked calmly up the stairs, trying to keep his anger to a minimum, reminding himself that this wasn't his grandson's normal behavior. He knocked repeatedly until Liam finally asked him to come in.

Liam's room looked like a tornado had gone through it. There were clothes strewn haphazardly on the floor, drawers opened, the sheets from his bed had been pulled from the mattress and food paraphernalia was everywhere Grandpa's eyes could see. He just breathed. "Son? Can we talk?" Grandpa was trying to be polite whereas Liam wasn't. Liam sat in his chair and stared out the window and into the meadow behind the barn. Grandpa walked over the mess that now decorated Liam's once clean room and tenderly placed his rugged hand on his grandson's shoulders. Liam didn't even flinch by his grandpa's touching act. "Do you want to tell me what's bothering you?" Liam's attention remained stoic. Sugar Dumplin' was sauntering her way to the field, her tail flipping back and forth while she swatted the horseflies that were pestering her hind quarters. Liam seemed mesmerized by the horse's actions. "Liam?" Grandpa asked again.

"Nothing's bothering me; I've just had a long day, that's all." Grandpa knew better.

"I see, well you've been working on this farm since you were six years old. I know what hard work is for you, but cleaning the stalls and putting away a few bags of horse feed shouldn't wear you out."

"I also had to test my bike today, Grandpa. I was doing that most of the day before I ran your errands. There's a race in a few weeks, and I've been trying to prepare for it."

"Do you mean the one on Ripley Road?"

"Yes, you know about it?"

"Yeah, I do."

Liam almost felt ashamed. He lowered his head and looked away from his elder.

"Are you really going to go through with it, Liam?" Liam only answered with a heavy sigh. "Liam, I'm talking to you dammit, now answer me, boy." Grandpa was becoming frustrated by Liam's ongoing childish behavior.

"Yes. Aaron's overseeing it." Grandpa took a long breath in disappointment as Liam explained. "I have too, Grandpa, you don't understand, I've signed a contract with him. I have to do this race. It's money not only for me but for Aaron and a lot of other people too."

"You don't have to do anything you don't want to do. I've raised you to be an independent person who can stand on his own two feet. You were born with a mind of your own, and I expect you to use it," Grandpa said adamantly. "Ever since you've become involved with Toby and Aaron Dent your whole demeanor has changed. You're never home anymore, and when you are, you walk around half the time with this blank look on your face that I can't understand... and to top things off, you just sit in your room. I know what this is about. Go after her, Liam!"

"I can't, Grandpa."

"Why?"

"I saw her today."

"That's great! So, she's back in town. Did you talk to her?" Grandpa asked with genuine excitement for the first time since their conversation began.

"No, she was busy."

"Busy? Doing what?"

Liam recalled seeing her and Johnny as they hugged each other. "It's nothing, Grandpa. I'd rather not talk about it if you don't mind."

"You better do me one better than that, Liam! What was she doing and why didn't you talk to her?"

"Because, Grandpa, Johnny Bryant's arms were wrapped around her! I didn't think I should interfere!" Liam was acting like a spoiled child crossing his arms and remaining steadfast in his seat while kicking his foot on the wall in front of him.

"Are you sure it's what you think? If I know that girl like I think I do, I know she still loves you and she wouldn't do anything intentionally to hurt you. A love like that doesn't just die off overnight. She probably feels all alone right now. I'm sure she's wondering where you are, why you haven't been by to see her. But hell, the last time she did see you, you gave her the impression that you didn't want her around. To be quite honest, Liam this is all your fault, what did you think she would do? Come running back into your arms?

For the first time since Grandpa Mack had entered Liam's room Liam stood to face him. "What's that supposed to mean?"

"Don't forget that you pushed her away. She was always waiting for you; it was you who caused this." Grandpa's words cut through Liam like a hot knife through cold butter. He didn't want to admit Grandpa was right. But he was and so was Parker. Everybody seemed to see it but him. Instead of turning to her, like he should have in the beginning when his nightmares took control, he turned to a bottle of beer which in turn led to Toby and Gina and eventually Aaron Dent. The domino effect had been crippling. Now in his state of mind, it was too late.

"If you don't like what you are seeing, Liam then you should do something about it. I'm not condoning Johnny's behavior, but he's doing exactly what any man would do in his position. He's taking advantage of an opportune situation. Jenny's a beautiful girl and you know he's had his eyes on her from day one. Hell, he doesn't even have to do it behind your back anymore; you've given him a free ticket to jump right in your place. If you don't want Johnny around your woman, then do something about it. And I don't mean a goddamn race! I don't like it! I'm tired of you acting like the world owes you a favor, it don't! All this nonsense with your drinking and you acting like there's nothing for you here anymore is nothing more than a bunch of goddamn cockamamie bullshit! Forget about the accident, your nightmares, the drinking, Johnny, and everything else you've been using as a crutch this past year, and look at what's in front of you. She's back, and you better take advantage of it before she leaves and never comes back. If I was Jenny, I wouldn't give you the time of day but I'm not, and that's why I know there's a good chance if you did see her she would take you back in a heartbeat. All she needs to hear is that you want her. Don't think she's going to make the first move either, it's not hers to make, it's always been yours. She came to you last spring, and you left her brokenhearted: if you want her back then go after her, Liam." Liam had never heard his grandpa talk to him with such a demanding tone. Instead of trying to hear Grandpa Mack out, Liam excused himself from his own room. "So, that's it?" Grandpa was completely baffled.

Liam turned his head back before leaving. "Yeah, I guess that is it. Sorry, Grandpa but that's all I've got." He walked away leaving the sound of his fading footsteps in grandpa's ears. Moments later, Grandpa heard the sound of Liam's truck as it sped away, leaving a cloud of dust behind it. He sat down in the chair that Liam had just occupied and wondered if he had made a mistake speaking so bluntly to him. His grandson was in a place he couldn't reach and the only person who could, might not want to help him anymore.

"Jenny, do you want me to follow you back to your house?" Johnny asked.

She was still in shock from seeing Liam pass her without even a nod in her direction. Did he really hate her that much? She was wondering. Had the past six months of their separation been confirmation of how Liam really felt, was he really able to let go of her that easily? She thought she meant more to him, the way she felt now she was no more than what Shanna had been to him. Her heart dropped, not that it could drop any further than it already did. It had already taken residence in the bottom of her stomach since that fateful night at Brush Creek Road.

"No, that's okay, Johnny. It was just seeing him. I guess I wasn't as ready as I thought I would be, but I'm fine. You don't need to baby me, I'm a big girl." She forced a sullen smile.

"A big girl with a broken heart," Johnny said as he brought her to him. She didn't want to have this bond with Johnny. She had fought too long to keep him at a distance, to keep him at arm's length but, in the end, he still never gave up on her and right now, his arms were the only thing keeping her together. He was always there, no questions asked or even needed. She hugged him tightly as a few of her tears found their way to his chest. His beating heart reminding her that he was still here and still very much alive.

Chapter Nine
Chasing Shadows

You can't turn back the hands of time. This is one statement that I have learned over the years to be very true. No matter how hard I wished for the clock to turn back before that fateful April night, it would never happen. The events that unfolded since then seemed to be writing my new life as well as Liam's.

I had been in town for almost a month, and in that time I had seen Billy numerous times, Kendra twice, Johnny on a few occasions, and Liam only once, or so I thought. It was just the passing of his truck that I saw and although there were dozens of black trucks in the Spencer area, there was only one that held the presence that Liam's did. It was his that I was certain I had seen. I hadn't come back to Spencer to chase shadows, but then again, I didn't think I would have to.

I checked my cell; there were no pending messages to hear. So I did what I had been doing for the past three and a half weeks. I went to my room. It was a beautiful, bright, sunny afternoon in Spencer, the autumn weather had been generous with its mild temperatures but in my state of mind, the only thing it meant to me was that it was another glorious day without Liam. I didn't like having these feelings. I left six months ago with a focus. I was strong and ready to move on while Liam took his time deciding what to do next. I was convinced he would have returned to me by now and maybe that's what the problem was. He hadn't. My intuition was wrong and maybe our relationship had been wrong too. My judgment was clouded by what I hoped would be between us. That's why I sunk into a depression that I promised myself I wouldn't allow again. I'd been there too many times before. But it was just so easy. I became accustomed to the darkness my sleep provided. It was my refuge that always seemed to welcome me with open arms when reality wouldn't. It wanted me to be there and begged for my presence, unlike Liam who didn't seem to care if I was in his life or not. For being so distraught so much of the time, I found that sleep came easily to me; I allowed it to lull me into its dark abyss where I lay in its comfort, protected by its mystery. Time continued to tick on by, and as it did, I questioned where my loyalty should lie. Liam seemed to be over me, whereas Johnny still needed me and wanted me. I begged for an answer as thoughts of Johnny instead of Liam filled my head.

****

"Johnny?" Gertie called for her son from the basement of *The Spiritual Ship*.

"Yeah, Mom?" he answered back.

"I need help lifting these boxes, are you busy?"

Johnny, in fact, had not been busy since being released from the hospital over five months earlier. His time had been spent either sitting on the sofa as he watched countless reruns on TV or with his best friend, Jake Pittman while they cruised their small town; the same thing that they had been doing since they learned to drive. Dr. Thompson gave him strict orders that his life, for the time being, would be filled with calm, non-chaotic behavior. No stress or drama whatsoever. *Ha*! If only he knew how much stress and drama Johnny had been enduring. But Gertie did know, and she was making sure that he followed these orders to a "T." It wasn't until two months ago that he was allowed to lift anything over the weight of a toaster. She welcomed the reprieve that had come with Jenny's absence and Liam's new-found life. Johnny had been going stir crazy and only came to his senses when he found Jenny sitting alone in the high school parking lot. She had given him a renewed strength and purpose that he had been missing. "No, Mom, not busy at all, I'll be right there," Johnny said as he took the steps two at a time.

"You seem to be in good spirits today. Anything you want to tell me?" she asked in her beautiful, melodic voice.

He was discreet. "No. I can't think of anything in particular." But in fact, he had Jenny on his mind. She had never left his mind, and in the three and half weeks since her return, for the first time, he thought time was on his side.

"Really?" Gertie asked skeptically enthused. Johnny knew that it was next to impossible to keep anything from her. He loved his mom but at times wished she didn't have the gift she carried; it made it next to impossible for him to get away with anything. Sometimes she knew more about him than he did. But he was determined not to let his news of Jenny's return slip by her. Gertie loved her too and the interrogation he would receive for not informing her would be almost too much for him to take.

"Really, mom." But his secret was not to be kept, for at that exact moment, as both Johnny and his mom reached the top of the basement stairs, they heard the harmonious sound of the *Ship's* entry chimes ringing in their ears.

"Jenny!" Gertie exclaimed rushing to Jenny's side.

"Hello, Gertie!" Jenny's voice shared Gertie's excitement. The two women hugged for a long time while Johnny looked on. "I wasn't sure if I should stop by. Is it a good time?" Jenny seemed a little apprehensive.

"Whatever do you mean, child? You are always welcome here, always." Gertie validated her comment by embracing Jenny even harder this time. "How have you been? When did you get back and why haven't I known about your return? Did you know she was home, Johnny?" Her questions rambled out of her almost faster than she could ask them. Jenny could hardly contain herself from the laughter that was emanating from her.

"It's really good to see you, Gertie. I've missed you." She paused for a moment. "I hope you don't mind me showing up, it's just that since I've been home, I haven't really been anywhere or seen anybody and…." Gertie didn't allow her to finish.

"Hon, like I said, you are always welcome here. Please, sit down." Gertie led Jenny to the familiar velvet-cloaked chairs that she remembered from her very first visit. Johnny followed suit and sat down between them. If Jenny could hardly contain her smile for feeling welcomed, then Johnny could hardly contain his for having Jenny so close to him again. Gertie sensed that she could have walked away and never be missed. Neither Jenny nor Johnny stopped staring at each other since they sat down. It was a very satisfying site for her to behold. For the next hour, the three of them talked incessantly while Jenny informed Gertie of what her life had been like since her departure last spring. The entire time, Johnny remained absorbed by Jenny and only after their prolonged conversation did Gertie give her son the indication that it was time for him to leave so she could have some girl time with Jenny. Johnny left the room but not until he hugged the girl that kept his heart beating.

"So, hon why don't you tell me what's going on? Gertie always could read Jenny. She sighed heavily. The happiness that befell her only moments earlier was quickly replaced with her tears.

"Gertie, I don't know where to begin or even what to say. I don't think anything has or will change."

"Have you talked to Liam?"

"No. I can't explain it, Gertie, I left Spencer feeling empowered and confident, but on returning, I lost those feelings. I thought I would hear from Liam. I thought we could talk like two mature adults and figure out what went wrong, but it hasn't happened. I needed to come home, I've been so homesick. Even being with my parents wasn't the same. All they talked about was the hope of Liam and me getting back together; and after a few months of not hearing from him, I couldn't stand hearing his name anymore. They've been so sad lately, and I know it's because of my dad's declining health. I couldn't pretend to be happy around them, that's what they needed, and I couldn't provide it. I was so sure that Liam would contact me and when he didn't, I just couldn't bring myself to call him. Don't get me wrong, I dialed his number a thousand times, but I always hung up. It seems like since he hasn't reached out to me, then he doesn't want to hear from me. I'm scared that it's really over between us, Gertie."

"Jenny, I knew this time was going to be hard for you, and I'm so sorry that it seems even more difficult than you expected. I don't think I can give you the answers that you want to hear. And I know it's not making it easier to have my son fawn all over you. His demeanor lately has been so upbeat; I should have realized it was because of you," Gertie said with a sly smile.

Jenny smiled back looking in the direction that she had seen Johnny leave. "I love your son."

"I know that. But not like you love Liam, right?" Gertie said with certainty.

Jenny always felt somewhat ashamed for not carrying the same feelings for Johnny, especially now, when he was there for her and giving her the support that Liam wasn't.

Would it help to tell you that I've tried to feel the love for him that he feels for me?"

"No, because you would be lying... to me, to Johnny, and most importantly, to yourself."

"What am I going to do then, Gertie? I don't want to leave again. I feel like I have nowhere to go. I'm just wandering aimlessly from day to day hoping Liam will show up and whisk me away. I keep waiting for my knight in shining armor to rescue me. Liam is supposed to be him." My voice wavered as I spoke.

"Listen, I can't stand to see you in this much pain. What would you think about coming here to work for me a few days a week? I could use the help, and it would get you out of the house and away from brooding over Liam."

"Gertie, I'm not like you. I can't give readings or tell people what their number is or what it even means."

Gertie let out a soft, melodic chuckle. "I don't mean that. I'm in the process of changing things up in the store. Johnny has been great in bringing up boxes or moving heavy things for me but he really doesn't have an eye for decorating, and I've been too busy lately to put the time into it that my shop deserves. That's where you would come in. You can help me with that." There was a long pause between them. "Please, Jenny." Gertie implored.

Jenny was trying to rationalize the ramifications if Liam ever found out but then again, she realized it probably didn't seem to matter. "Yes. I guess I will. If you're sure you want me."

"Of course, I do, I wouldn't have asked you if I didn't want you. Great, then it's settled, you can begin tomorrow."

"Thank you, Gertie. I think this is going to be just what I needed. I need to keep my mind busy instead of worrying about the race that will be coming up on Ripley Road."

"Are you serious, Jenny?"

"Dead serious. You didn't know about it?"

"No, dear. I didn't, but then again, Liam hasn't been my priority."

"Well, he is."

Gertie's vibrant skin was instantly drained from all the blood it carried. "Jenny, you can't let him drive in that race." Her hands were on Jenny's squeezing them with an icy grip. Gertie knew something, Jenny could tell.

"Why? What's wrong, Gertie, what do you know?" Jenny began trembling uncontrollably.

"You have to stop him, Jenny; you have to stop him from participating. I don't have a good feeling about it." Gertie's voice was disconcertingly different. There was almost a shrill tone to it as she spoke. Her face became gaunt and sallow, and her eyes seemed sunken into her face to portray a forthcoming trepidation that wasn't there before.

"Gertie, what's wrong? You're scaring me. Is Liam going to get hurt if he races?"

"I don't know Jenny, but I do know that there is a black cloud lingering over this race."

"What am I supposed to do?"

"Go to him, Jenny. Talk to him. You're still the only person who can reach him."

"What about Grandpa Mack?"

"It's got to be you; don't you understand that, Jenny? This racing stemmed from you and it's still only you who can talk him out of it."

"But he didn't listen to me last time. Why should he now? I'm not going to be able to help, Gertie. He's going to turn me away like he did last time. I won't be able to handle it if I lose him again like that."

"Would you rather lose him for real, Jenny? If he's in this race something horrible is going to happen. I know you don't want to live with that knowledge, knowing you could have prevented it." Gertie's voice was trembling as she spoke, the shrill still there. This wasn't her intention, but at the same time, she needed to get her point across. "Listen, Jenny. I just don't feel good about this. When you told me where the race was to take place, I got this awful feeling in the pit of my stomach. I have made a career out of listening to my gut instincts, and I can't begin to start ignoring them now, especially when they concern people I care about. Tell me, when is the race supposed to take place?"

"A week from now," Johnny said as he came from the back room.

"Were you listening, Johnny?" his mom asked, alarmed.

"Not your entire conversation. Just the last part."

"Are you sure about the date?"

"Pretty sure. It's pretty much the talk of the town. Mom?"

"Yes, dear."

"Liam was supposed to race me."

"What?!"

"I was approached about a month ago by Aaron Dent. That's the guy sponsoring Liam. He learned from Toby about the original race and how people still talked about it. He wanted to re-enact the event since we never finished it."

"Johnny?"

"Don't worry, Mom, I told them no."

"But Liam is still going to race? If you're not his opponent, then who is he racing against?"

"I don't know. The last I heard, they hadn't found anyone crazy enough to do it. Everybody around here feels it's messing with karma to race Liam, especially on that road. I think they're trying to find someone from outside our area."

"So there's still a chance the race might not happen, right?" Jenny asked, hopefully.

Johnny wanted to indulge her optimism but couldn't. "I guess, Jenny, but don't count on it. Aaron has plenty of people who work for him, if they don't find a willing participant, he'll just have one of his regulars race Liam. I know he's not going to let this race go. It's already making him money, and there's still over a week before the race."

"What's that supposed to mean?" Gertie and Jenny both asked at the same time.

"Just that if Aaron Dent is involved, then there's money in it. That's how he makes his real money; not through the auto shop, that's just a cover-up so Aaron can concentrate on the racing. And that's why Liam signed on with him, for every race Liam wins; Aaron gets a huge cut of the winnings."

My head dropped in disappointment. "See what I mean, Gertie. Liam doesn't need me in his life anymore. He's replaced me."

"Jenny, it's going to be okay," Gertie said as she escorted Jenny to the door. "I'll make sure of that. Now go home and get some rest, if you can. I want to see you here bright and early tomorrow morning." Gertie embraced her as she gave Jenny a forced but heartfelt smile.

"Alright and thanks, Gertie. I really meant it when I said I had missed you."

"What do you mean bright and early tomorrow morning?" Johnny asked after Jenny left.

"She's going to be working for me here at the store." Johnny's smile widened from ear to ear. "You can wipe that smile off your face. I didn't do this for your benefit. I did this for her, she needs this, she's suffering. It'll do her good to keep busy."

"And you think having her work for Liam's worst enemy's mom will help the cause? Mom, this is insane, you're just going to make things worse. If Liam finds out where Jenny is spending her time, he'll flip out, not that he hasn't already," Johnny said the last part under his breath.

"That's exactly my plan, son."

"What are you doing, Mom?"

"Nothing, just trust me. I need to find out where Liam stands. Jenny doesn't think he wants her anymore, if that's the case, then he won't care at all that she's spending her time here."

"But, Mom, this can't be good for Jenny. Don't you think she's already suffered enough? She wants Liam back; this little scheme of yours is only going to backfire on Jenny and who's going to be there to pick up the pieces for her when Liam refuses her again?" Gertie just gave Johnny an endearing smile. Johnny immediately knew what his mom was up too. "Oh, Mom, really? I thought you liked Jenny?"

"I do. She means the world to me, and that's exactly why I'm doing this. She needs to know how Liam really feels about her and if he's not willing to make the first move, then I'll make it for him.

"But it's none of your business."

"The minute Jenny walked into my shop almost two years ago and the minute I saw how you felt about her, it became my business. You have to know, Johnny, you deserve that. Time is not on your side anymore."

"You don't know that, Mom. I'm feeling stronger every day."

"I know that but don't you want to know where you stand? If Liam rejects Jenny one more time, I guarantee you that she will turn to you; and this time, she won't discard her feelings. She has them for you; they've just been covered up by Liam's. This way we can all move on."

"Mom, I don't won't Jenny's affections unless they're genuine. I don't want to be the rebound guy. I want her to want me on her own terms."

"They will be on her terms. She's confused right now, she needs to know that Liam doesn't love her anymore, once she gets that validation, her feelings for you will come to fruition and grow stronger, and she will turn to you for the comfort she's been missing from Liam and realize that it's always been you. I'm just taking the bull by the horns and eliminating the problem."

Gertie gave Johnny a kiss on his cheek. "Trust me, son, I know what I'm doing. If anyone deserves this, it's you; you've been waiting in the wings long enough."

Chapter Ten
The Bucket List

"Great," Liam's sarcasm was more than evident as he watched Toby and Gina drive up in Toby's prized Mustang. Liam knew why they were here, the upcoming race was a few days away, and they were making sure their investment wasn't getting cold feet. It was what Toby did when he had a stake in you.

"Hello, Liam." Gina's annoying voice made Liam want to puke at the sight of her. He let out a chuckle as he imagined doing exactly that, vomit spewing from his mouth as it landed perfectly all over her skin tight jeans. It would almost be worth the wrath he would receive from her as he continued to snicker under his breath.

"What are you laughing at?" Gina blurted at him.

"Nothing, Gina, nothing at all."

"Are you ready?" Toby added.

"I guess," Liam said chewing on a piece of grass. He didn't offer Toby or Gina any more insight. Ever since he had signed on with Aaron Dent he had a gut instinct that he had done the wrong thing, but the deed was done; in his mind, and everyone else's, he had signed away his soul to the devil, it was irrevocable. So, instead of making idle conversation that wouldn't mean a damn thing to any of them, he decided to remain quiet, letting Toby take the lead.

"Did you hear if Aaron found someone to replace Johnny?" Toby asked.

"He did. It's someone from Ripley."

"How appropriate," Gina said. "The race is taking place on Ripley Road, and you're going to be racing someone from Ripley." She was laughing and looking at Toby to see if he got the joke she just made. Neither Toby nor Liam got her humor.

"I don't want you to forget about what happened to you on that road, Liam."

"What do you mean, Toby?"

"I mean, I want you to dig deep into yourself and bring out those feelings you have been hiding since that night when you raced Johnny and had the wreck. I want you to feel the raw emotion of seeing your girlfriend lying next to you all bloodied and mangled. It's those inflamed feelings that are going to give you the edge and win us the race."

"Don't worry; I haven't let you guys down yet, have I? And for the record, Toby, she's my fiancée."

"Not anymore," Gina said with her same stupid laugh.

"Watch your mouth." Liam was in her face. She just turned her head and looked the other way, her vicious laughter dwindling while Liam continued his staunch stare on her. It was perfect timing though because Grandpa Mack came from inside the house. He sauntered to Liam's side with an uneasy gait and waited for Liam to introduce him to his new friends.

"Hello, Liam."

"Hi, Grandpa. Grandpa, this is Toby and Gina, my friends from Glenville."

"It's so nice to meet you," Gina said as she extended her scarlet-nailed hand to Grandpa.

"It's nice to meet you too," he said politely without reciprocating her gesture.

"I've always wanted to meet the man behind Liam." Toby had walked right up to Grandpa Mack and put his face right into his. Grandpa wasn't impressed by Toby's boldness or by the smell of his breath. He backed away to put more space between the two of them. There was complete silence as the four of them stood waiting for the other to speak. Grandpa had already decided that he didn't like Liam's new friends and after their introductions, he didn't see the need to say anything else to them. So instead of shooting the breeze over stupid shit, he turned his attention to his grandson.

"Liam, can I have a word with you in private."

"Sure, Grandpa." He looked at Toby and Gina to let them know that it was time for them to leave.

"It was so nice to meet you, sir. Bye, Liam." Gina gave Liam her best syrupy smile.

"Yes, it was very nice to meet you. I'll talk to you later, Liam," Toby said as the two of them got into his black and yellow Mustang and drove away.

Liam followed Grandpa inside and sat down at the kitchen table. "What did you want to talk to me about, Grandpa?"

"Liam, did you know that I saw Jenny the other day?"

"Where?"

"I don't think you're going to like it."

"Where, Grandpa? Tell me."

"You know the past couple of weeks I've been going to Kanawha County to take Sugar Dumplin' to see the vet for her leg."

"So? What does that have to do with Jenny?"

"Well, you know Johnny's mom owns that shop on the bypass. I have to pass it on my way to the vet's. About a week ago I thought I noticed Jenny's car in the parking lot. I didn't think much of it except it was there the next day and the day after that. I've taken Sugar Dumplin' to the vet about five times in the past two weeks, son and each time Jenny's car has been there." Liam was silent. "I just thought you should know. I know I would want to know."

Liam didn't know what to say. His feelings for Jenny had never been stronger, and the ironic thing was, it had been six months since he had last seen her. "What am I supposed to do, Grandpa? I mean, it seems as though she has decided who she wants to be with."

"Do you really believe that, Liam?"

"What else am I supposed to believe?"

"Did you call her like I told you to do?"

Liam lowered his head. "No."

"Why? I know she's probably been waiting to hear from you. I told you it was you who had to make the next move. She already felt like she didn't belong here, I guarantee you that Johnny took advantage of your absence, and that's exactly why she's been at their shop so much. Don't you want her back, Liam?"

"You know I do, Grandpa! But it's not that easy anymore. I'm not the same person she met. I've changed."

"Have your feelings for her changed?"

"No. I love her more than anything, and that's why I haven't contacted her. She didn't want to be with me if I was going to continue my racing and that's exactly what I'm doing. I told you, I'm under contract with Aaron. I would just hurt her more if I were to ask her back. She's better off with Johnny, anyway. He's not going to hurt her, at least not like I did."

"My God, Liam do you hear yourself? You're still talkin' up the same cockamamie bullshit from before. I give up. I totally give up," Grandpa said as he flung his arms in the air. "If you want to believe that crap then go right ahead, but I'm not supporting you in it. I just hope one day you can open those damn eyes of yours and see what you let go. Right now you're just handing Jenny over to Johnny on a silver platter, why did you go through all the drama last year if this is what you had planned on doing in the first place?"

Liam didn't answer his grandpa. Instead, he pushed his chair back from the kitchen table with such force that when he stood up, the chair fell to its side, knocking a second one over, as well. Liam quickly went to the back door only to stop himself in the entrance. He paused as his hands grasped the frame of the door and his knuckles turned a bone white. He tried to hold in his anger, but that's all he had been doing lately, so he allowed himself the privilege of releasing it by slamming his right fist into the kitchen wall leaving a huge hole. Grandpa just looked on as Liam let loose. He waited for Liam to say something, anything to help him understand why he wasn't trying to get Jenny back. After what seemed like an eternity of silence between the two men, Liam turned to face his mentor, his face finally showing the pain he had been enduring since Jenny left. His crystal-blue eyes filled with tears.

"You know Grandpa; as soon as I heard that she was in town, my heart jumped into my throat. I was so happy to know she was back, that she was close to me. I felt like this was our second chance. I felt alive but then I realized what tore us apart, and all those happy feelings were gone again. She doesn't want me like this, and I don't know if I can change, Grandpa."

"You're wrong, Liam, she does want you, and you can change. I've seen it in you already. When's the last time you had a drink in your hand, son?" Liam just shook his head back and forth; it had been at least a month if not longer since alcohol had touched his lips. "Exactly," Grandpa said. "You haven't been drinking, just like I thought. That's a change, and you know it. And this racing, I've already told you that there's nothing written in stone, you don't have to keep doing this. I know for a fact that Joe would have you back in a heartbeat at the shop. If you want, I'll go talk to that Aaron Dent myself and get you out of this so-called contract you're under."

"No, I can fight my own battles, Grandpa."

"Then why don't you? Stand up to the man. You act like he's got you horse-whipped."

"You don't understand, this race is a done deal. I have to do it."

"Why? What point are you still trying to prove?"

"Don't you get it, Grandpa? I still need to prove to myself that I'm worthy. I lost myself after the accident, and I'm not going to be good to anyone, especially Jenny if I can't get the old me back again. It doesn't matter what you had to say or the fact that Jenny was there for me. I still felt like a loser; and then to add insult to injury, there's Johnny. I know Jenny loves me, but I can't get past the fact that Johnny loves her as much as I do and she seems okay with that. I know I let you guys down, but I let myself down the most. Everything just seemed to spiral out of control and then that night when I found her at Johnny's apartment, it just seemed like that was the final straw. Maybe I was looking for an out, and that was my opportunity." By this time, Liam had walked back into the kitchen, picked up the fallen chair, and sat down as the anger that was controlling him finally subsided. "I know Jenny didn't do anything at his apartment, but at the time, I was just too drunk to care: all I cared about was the racing, the rush it gave me. I felt bigger than life, and I know that's no excuse, but I was craving that attention. I thought that would complete me and then I could come back and be the man that Jenny first fell in love with but that hasn't been the case. I don't feel any better about myself, and that's why I haven't contacted her. I don't blame her for not trying to reach out to me; I wouldn't either if I was her. Grandpa, I've picked up my phone a thousand times only to put it back down again. I'm afraid."

"Afraid, Liam? What of?"

"Afraid that once Jenny sees me again, she'll realize that she made the right decision when she left me at Brush Creek Road. I keep thinking that our time apart has proven to her that she doesn't need me in her life." There was a long pause before Liam spoke again. He fiddled with his fingers on the table, collecting his thoughts before carrying on. "Grandpa, I know Jenny's been at Gertie's shop."

"You do," Grandpa asked surprised.

"Yes. Parker told me. She's working there, I guess."

"Oh," Grandpa said.

"You see, she's made her decision. It's Johnny."

"You don't know that for sure, son."

"Yes, I do. Why else would she be there? It's not like she needs the money. I know it's to be close to him and maybe it's because of his condition. No matter how she ever felt about me, I know she carried a small torch for him, too."

"That small torch she carried Liam, was of gratitude for what Johnny did for her at the accident. You need to stop foolin' yourself. Everybody knows how she felt and everybody knows how she felt about you. You're just too damn blind to see it for yourself. And as far as her making up her mind, you're probably right. But it's not Johnny, it's still you. I just know it. I will say it again; she's leaning on Johnny because you haven't tried to reach out to her. It's up to you, son, and only you. She's always been there for you; it was you who wasn't there for her. Maybe that's not what you want to hear, but it's the truth. If you want Johnny to win at this game, then you're doing a pretty good job of helping him. Grandpa put his rugged hands over his grandson's in an act of genuine love and concern. "Listen, Liam, I know this isn't what you had planned when you first met Jenny. Nobody said it was going to be easy. The best things in life don't come easy and trust me, she's the best. Don't let your past keep you from having a future with the woman of your dreams." There was another pause, this time from Grandpa. "Liam, how are your nightmares? Are you still having them?"

"Sometimes. But they've changed."

"What do you mean? Are they getting better?"

"I don't know about that. It's just that they were always about Johnny taking Jenny away from me and now when I do have one, they're just about me. It's still the same scene of the accident, but Jenny is nowhere to be found. It's like she's really gone. I guess it's not a dream anymore, Grandpa... she is gone, at least from me."

Grandpa had heard enough. He said his piece to his grandson and now felt as if it was up to him if he wanted her back. "Liam, I've known you for your entire nineteen years of life; and in those nineteen years, we have laughed together, cried together and worked together. I have loved you unconditionally and worried about you without ceasing, but there is one thing I haven't done until tonight."

Liam looked at his grandpa with an apprehensive curiosity. "What's that?"

Grandpa raised himself up from his seated position and removed his rugged hands from Liam's... "I've never been disappointed in you until now." With those final words, Grandpa walked out of the kitchen leaving Liam to be alone.

****

Jenny took the duster and began doing what she had been doing since her first day at *The Spiritual Ship* over three weeks ago; she cleaned and reorganized the front room for the hundredth time. "Here, let me help you with that," Johnny said as he came up from behind her.

"Thanks, but I've got it." Both of them were facing each other with only a few inches separating their bodies from touching. Johnny had grabbed her hand in a small attempt to grab the duster, but Jenny knew his intentions were otherwise. "Johnny?"

"Yeah, Jenny?" his voice was tender as he spoke to her.

"What am I doing?"

"Huh?" Johnny seemed confused by her question.

"Your mom doesn't need me here. The entire time I've been here, the only thing I've accomplished is going through five cans of furniture polish and rearranging the same pictures from their original spot to their new spot. Your mom didn't need my help, did she?"

Johnny just sighed as his futile attempt to hold Jenny's hand went unnoticed by her. "Mom just worries about you. She didn't want you to be all alone in that big house of yours."

"Johnny, I'm okay."

"Are you, Jenny?"

"Yes. Why are you guys so worried about me? I'm fine."

"Because you're still in love with Liam," Johnny said.

Jenny gave him a somber stare. "Listen, it doesn't matter what my feelings are for him anymore. He's been out of my life for months now, and I'm none the worse."

"Are you sure?"

"Why do you keep saying that, Johnny?" Jenny threw her dust cloth to the ground.

"Because of the love you two shared. Don't you wonder why he hasn't tried to come to see you or at least call? I know for a fact that he knows you're back in town."

"Why? Because he saw us at the school parking lot?"

"Well that's not what I meant, but yeah, he saw us then. But also, because Jake talked to Parker a while back and your name came up. I'm sure if Parker knows you're in town so does Liam." Jenny walked away from Johnny's endearing stare. "Well?" Johnny persisted.

"I don't know, Johnny. Maybe it's just as hard for him as it is for me. I haven't exactly been clamoring for his attention either."

"But you miss it... right?"

"Johnny, you already know these answers. I am still head over heels in love with a boy who doesn't want anything to do with me. I am madly in love with *the* Liam Larson; the one boy who swept me off my feet over two years ago and today doesn't even care where my feet land. I'm sorry if this isn't what you want to hear, but I can't just turn my feelings for Liam off overnight."

"Overnight, Jenny? You guys haven't been together for over six months now. I would think that would be enough time for you to mend your broken heart."

"And what about yours?"

"My heart is doing fine."

"It is? Then why can't you get over me? You've been given the same amount of time to mend your heart." Johnny continued to give Jenny an uneasy stare but before he could answer he began to sway back and forth. "Johnny? Are you okay?" She ran to his side. Johnny was holding his chest with one hand while he tried to steady himself with the other. He clung to the velvet chair while trying not to fall over it.

"Yeah, I think so. I'm sorry, Jenny, I just got really dizzy there for a moment. Just give me a minute, I'll be fine."

"Are you sure? Should I get your mom?"

"No, please don't do that." he implored. "She'll just make more out of this than there needs to be. Really, I'm okay; like I said, it was just a dizzy spell, that's all. Just give me a moment to catch my breath."

Jenny held onto Johnny's clammy hand allowing him to become comfortable in the velvet chair. Within moments, his normal color vanished, and his once-tanned face had turned to a sickly grey. His chocolate eyes were now dull and revealed the true nature of Johnny's health. He was still sick and from what Jenny could see, very sick. It was something Jenny had somewhat forgotten since she'd been back. Their time together had been unusually normal, and his demeanor reminded her of the way he used to behave before she knew about his condition. "I think I should get your mom." She handed him a glass of water. Johnny took it appreciatively drinking it voraciously.

"No, Jenny. I don't need her." His response, this time, was a little more assertive than the tenderness he had portrayed earlier. "Please, I don't want to be coddled, and that's exactly what Mom will do. I know when I'm fine, and I'm fine, just a little dizzy, that's all."

Jenny didn't believe him. "If you say so." She relented to his bidding.

"I'm sorry, Jenny. I don't mean to upset you; it's just that ever since Mom found out I need a heart transplant she walks around me on eggshells. I can't go to the bathroom without her checking in on me. I know you meant well and of course, it meant even more because it was coming from you. I'm just tired of feeling like I'm living in a bubble. I've had this condition for most of my life now, and Mom still feels the need to baby me."

"That's what moms do. And if you don't mind me saying, I can understand why she feels that way, Johnny. It's not like you're getting over a cold. It's a little bit more serious than that. You just startled me when you grabbed your chest. I haven't seen you react that way since I've known you. It just really scared me." Jenny gave Johnny an engaging stare. "Johnny, I'm sorry for what I said earlier. The timing sucks. I never would take advantage of your condition, I'm really sorry."

"It's okay; I kind of egged you on. And please, I get enough of it from Mom; you don't need to treat me like I'm dying."

"But..." she said.

"I know, I guess I am dying," he said laughing. "But please, don't remind me of it." The two of them both started laughing this time.

"You know, it's been a while since I've laughed," Jenny said.

"You have an amazing laugh; you should always find a reason to be happy."

"That's easier said than done these days."

"Jenny, for what it's worth, I'm sorry too. I didn't mean to bring up Liam. I know it's still none of my business; it's just that my feelings for you are sometimes really hard to hide, no matter how much time has passed between us, I don't think I'm ever going to stop worrying about you." Johnny contemplated on whether he should ask his next question but decided *what the hell*. Jenny?"

"Yes."

"Would you like to go get something to eat or even go for a cup of coffee?"

She knew he meant well, and he was genuine with his affections, but she still knew that Johnny would take it for more than what it really was. He saw this as an opportunity, and she just saw it as having a bite to eat with a good friend.

"Johnny... I, I don't..."

"I understand, I didn't think you would say yes."

"No, it's not that. I would love too, I just don't know if I should. I mean... it would be different if..."

"If I wasn't in love with you... if it was Liam asking you?" he asked, making eye contact with her.

"Johnny, please try to understand. This whole town knows our history. Everyone knows that Liam and I are together..." she paused... "well... were together," she said sadly. "But he's moved on and..."

"And you can have a sandwich with me." He stood up without the aid of her help. "Listen, I know what everybody thinks, and I know that people will talk, but they are already talking. Do you really care what anyone thinks?"

"I care what Liam thinks and that's who I'm afraid will find out."

"I'm not trying to cause more problems or add fuel to the fire; I just thought that it would be nice to get something to eat. You do still eat don't you?" Johnny's innocent flirtation was humoring Jenny.

"Yes, I still eat."

"Then, what's the problem? Hey, you can look at it as the boss taking his employee out for employee appreciation day."

"You're my boss? I thought that title belonged to your mom?"

"Well I'm the boss' son, that's pretty close to the same thing, and I know she would want me to make sure her employees are well taken care of. *The Spiritual Ship* does have a reputation to uphold. We can't have our customers thinking we don't take care about our employees, now can we?" He was pleading to Jenny with his brown eyes for her to give in. "Please. We don't even have to go anywhere here in Spencer; if you're worried about someone seeing us together. I know this great little spot in Walton. It's not much to look at on the outside, but they are world-famous for their cheeseburgers."

"World-famous? Really, in Walton?" she asked rhetorically, realizing she didn't see any harm in having a cheeseburger with Johnny. It isn't like he was taking her back to his place to try and have his way with her, they are just going to have a bite to eat and then part ways. He will go back to his house, and she will go back to hers, it is just two friends sharing some time together; but then again, if it was so innocent why was she having such a hard time convincing herself of that. But on the other hand, she didn't have anything better to do, and she was hungry. She had convinced herself. "Okay."

"What?" He couldn't believe what his ears heard; he thought there would be a lot more coaxing required. He bent his body downward to watch her mouth move. "Did my ears deceive me or did Jenny King just say 'yes' to me?" The coy grin he gave her earlier was now an ear-to-ear smile.

"Yes, I just said 'yes' to your invitation to grab something to eat, but there's nothing to this, just like you said; think of this as two colleagues having dinner together, this is not a date, Johnny Bryant."

"Yes, I'm good with that. However, you want to perceive it is alright with me."

****

Jenny felt extremely at ease driving with Johnny to Walton. It was less than a half an hour away, but for some reason, she wished the drive was farther, she was enjoying his company. She relaxed in her seat and perused Johnny's Bronco. This was only the second time she had been in it. It looked pretty much the same but cleaner than the last time and the scent of pine was evident. She watched Johnny driving; he had his left hand securely on the wheel while his right hand rested comfortably on the seat. It seemed unusually lonely, and Jenny knew that it was Johnny's way of inviting her to put her hand on top of his. But she didn't accept the invitation; instead, she kept her hands nestled securely on her lap, where they belonged. She scooted her body closer to her door without having the handle jab her in her side. It reminded her of the first time she had been in Liam's truck and how she did the exact same thing. He didn't care, he knew that they would be together and her trying to prove otherwise only made Liam try harder for her affections... and it had worked. She had fallen for him. She sighed heavily engaging in those memories of Liam, she didn't even realize that they were now sitting in the parking lot and Johnny was standing there holding the door open for her.

"Jenny, are you coming in or should I order our food to go?" he asked jokingly.

"I'm sorry, Johnny, of course, I'm coming in. I didn't even realize we were here, I must have really been enjoying the ride."

"You seem to be in another world, you didn't say one word on our drive here. Are you alright?"

"Yeah, just tired, that's all."

"Well, I hope you're hungry; like I said, this place is known for the best cheeseburgers you will ever eat in your entire life."

Jenny looked up at the sign that hung on the dilapidated building where Johnny had parked. Although he warned her that it was just a hole-in-the-wall, she was still taken aback by the actual condition of the building. The wooden structure looked like it was a hundred years old and the green paint that covered its exterior was faded and chipping in numerous places. The rusted, red tin roof leaned to the right, making Jenny think of the illustrations from children's books. But of course, the most intriguing sign was the huge neon kicking bull that resided on the one side of the roof. It was appropriately named, *The Greasy, Buckin' Steer.* "Wow," was all Jenny could say as she tried to find a more appropriate word to describe the interesting eatery but couldn't. "I see you don't spare any expense for your employees." She couldn't help but burst out laughing.

"You just wait; you'll be begging for me to bring you back. One bite of their amazing cheeseburgers and you'll think you have died and gone to cheeseburger heaven."

This was all he ever dreamed of, just having her to himself without the feeling that they were sneaking around. He couldn't have been happier if he tried.

Jenny's senses were instantly enticed when she walked in by the overpowering smell of grease as it wafted through the air. Usually, she didn't care for the smell of grease, but she was hungry, and this place smelled wonderful. The entire restaurant was bulging at the seams with hungry customers, all of them indulging in the enormous cheeseburgers that Johnny had informed her about. "I can't believe I've never heard of this place, it's obviously very popular." There wasn't a seat to be found, but Johnny took her by the hand and led her to the back. "Where are you going, shouldn't we wait to be seated?"

"We already have a table."

"We do?"

Johnny continued to lead Jenny to the back of the room. He nodded off and on to people he passed as they returned the greeting. It was becoming very apparent to her that he was a frequent customer of the establishment. At the very back of the room next to an old Jukebox that played 45's was a vacant table that seemed to be waiting for their arrival. He pulled out one of the old wooden chairs that were covered in a faded red and white checkered seat cover and motioned for Jenny to sit down.

"How did you know there would be an empty table waiting for us?" Jenny asked, very interested.

"I used to come here a lot when I lived here; my dad went to school with the owner. I bet ninety percent of my meals during high school came from this place. This is the place to be, especially after home football games and this is the table I would sit at with my friends. When you agreed to come here with me, I called the owner, Louie, and he told me my table would be waiting for me."

Jenny perused her surroundings as an aging waitress dressed in western gear and faded red cowboy boots showed up with two glasses of water in mason jars.

"Well hello there, stranger." The waitress seemed excited to see Johnny. She hugged him tightly allowing her protruding chest to press against his body. "It's so good to see you, deary. It's been a long time."

"Hello, Loretta, it's good to see you too. Loretta, this is Jenny."

"It's nice to meet you, darlin'. My, my aren't you a pretty thang," She gave Johnny a deliberate elbow to his shoulder and a wink of her approval.

"Thank you," Jenny said modestly.

"Jenny works for Mom at her shop in Spencer," Johnny informed Loretta.

"Oh, how is your mom? I heard about your parents' divorce. I'm so sorry, Johnny. They're both such nice folks, I can't believe they're not together anymore."

"It's okay, and they're doing fine, getting a divorce was probably the best thing that ever happened to them. They get along better now than when they were married."

"I'm glad to hear that, but I'm still sorry, though, I hate to hear when good folk have to part ways. Well, I'm just ramblin' now, enough of this small talk, I'm sure you guys are hungry, will it be the usual Johnny?"

"Yes, and we'll take a couple of root beers too," Johnny added as if he knew that's exactly what Jenny would want too. "Is that good for you, Jenny?"

She didn't want to say otherwise; both Loretta and Johnny were looking at her for her approval. "Yes, that sounds great."

Loretta left Johnny and Jenny to be by themselves, and as Jenny took a drink of her water, she noticed that Johnny conveniently scooted closer to her. "So, what do you think?" he asked as he motioned to *The Greasy Buckin' Steer's* ambiance.

"It's nice. It definitely has character. I can't believe I've never heard of it though, but then again, I can't remember the last time I've been in Walton."

"Didn't your dad do a lot of business here?" Johnny asked.

"Yes but it was mostly deliveries, and he usually had one of his employees do those for him."

They continued to make small talk for the next few minutes when Loretta finally showed up with two of the largest cheeseburgers that Jenny had ever seen. "Well, here you go, kids," Loretta said with her southern draw, placing the two mounds of meat on their table. "Dig in. I hope you're hungry."

"Are you kidding?" Jenny peered over her cheeseburger to Johnny.

"Yeah, they're not exactly small in size, but I promise you, that you'll be begging to come back before your stomach has a chance to think about it."

"That is, if I can finish this one."

During the next hour, Johnny and Jenny engaged in small talk while they tried to consume the ginormous burgers. Johnny finished his easily while Jenny's looked like she had barely begun. They were enjoying each other's company, but still, Jenny couldn't help but periodically look around to see if anyone recognized her. It was on her mind constantly and even though Johnny was acting just like a friend, (except for him continually scooting his chair closer to hers) she still felt very awkward.

"What's wrong?" Johnny asked after noticing Jenny looking over her shoulder one too many times.

"Nothing, I'm just full. I don't think I could eat another bite even I wanted to." She said giggling while the *Steer's* special sauce dripped from her chin. Johnny couldn't help but smile. "What?" she asked as she took one final bite.

"I love your laugh. It's one of the most beautiful sounds I've ever heard." Jenny turned to face the jukebox to avoid eye contact. Johnny reached out to her face as she grabbed his hand to stop him. "I'm sorry, but you've got sauce on your face." He leaned in to wipe it off only to find himself practically nose to nose with her. Both of them became deadlocked in each other's stares. He carefully brought her face even closer to his, he wanted to kiss her. He wanted her so badly at this moment that he could hardly stand it; but still, he controlled his desires for her and instead just wiped her face gently with his thumb. She sat there frozen. She knew what he wanted but didn't dare move just in case he thought she was obliging his feelings. She couldn't give him the wrong impression even though her heart was telling her something different. She was lonely, it had been a long time since she felt the touch of a man against her, but she couldn't go there, she just couldn't do it.

"Jenny," Johnny whispered. She didn't answer him; he didn't give her a chance. Johnny's lips were on hers in that very moment, his soft lips surrounding hers, locking them into place. He needed her, and the contented groan that he conveyed made it clear. She tried to stop him, but her will went unheeded; and as he placed his free hand behind her neck and pulled her closer to him, she finally gave in to him. It felt like it was just the two of them while the crowd surrounding them seemed to disappear. He held her close, his hand continually squeezing the nape of her neck while his other hand found its spot between her thighs. He squeezed them making a warm sensation flow through her deprived body. He wasn't letting go, no matter how hard Jenny wanted him too. His lips were on her, but Liam's face was all she could see. She was confused. The kiss lingered while the *Steer's* patrons went about their business; and just when Jenny thought it would never end, his lips parted from hers with the gentlest of efforts. He pulled himself back from her but never took his eyes or his hands from hers. She could still taste him.

"Johnny."

"Please, Jenny, please don't tell me what I already know you're about to say. Please, just let me have this moment." The noise that surrounded them seemed to be muted, their stares, still on each other. Jenny was positive that Loretta had come over to ask if they wanted anything else but she couldn't tell, everything and everybody seemed a blur to her. The only person in focus was the one person that should have been a blur. Jenny became distracted as Loretta's cowboy boots clicked behind her. She was taking someone's order, mingling with the customers and then suddenly the muted silence was broken, and Jenny came back to reality. It startled her, she watched the patrons come to life with their conversations and laughter.

"Jenny," Johnny cooed. She turned her head away from the restaurant and back to Johnny as she heard him call her name. She remembered what happened between them and realized what could happen.

"I think we should go, Johnny."

He rose from the chair, perplexed, and helped her to her feet. "Whatever you want." He knew her emotions were raw, and he cared enough about her that he didn't want to push any more than he already had. He could hold it within him just like always. He took a twenty dollar bill from his pocket and laid it on top of his plate. He then proceeded to take Jenny's hand and guide her through the sea of patrons who were all preoccupied with their own lives, oblivious to the kiss that had happened between them.

"Ya'll come back real soon," Loretta yelled to Johnny and Jenny as they exited the *The Greasy Buckin' Steer*.

The two of them sat in his Bronco in shock, the heat defrosting the windows, still keeping quiet, watching the icy moisture melt away and slide down the windshield. The silence between them was deafening. Finally, after what seemed like hours of awkwardness, Johnny realized Jenny wasn't going to address what had just happened inside. "Jenny, please don't be mad at me. I didn't plan on kissing you. It... it just happened," he said almost apologetically. She looked down at her hands, her fingers methodically twirling around themselves. "Jenny? Come on; please don't give me the silent treatment. I promise, kissing you in there was not my intention. I... I can't explain it, it just happened. You have to realize by now that I can't always control myself when I'm around you, no matter how hard I try." He placed his right hand on top of her left thigh. Jenny scooted as close to her door as she could and crossed her left leg over her right, making Johnny's hand drop to the seat.

"I'm not mad at you, Johnny, I'm angry at myself for allowing it to happen. I can't do that. I'm sure you noticed that I didn't try to stop you. I should have, but I didn't. I'm not even going to blame you, I blame myself." Jenny turned to face Johnny. "Ever since my return, I've felt so alone. Don't get me wrong, I've seen you and Gertie, and even Kendra, but still I go home to an empty house and an empty heart. I miss him, Johnny. I miss Liam more than I can ever explain. I know you don't want to hear that, but it's the truth, and I guess when you kissed me you caught me at my most vulnerable. I..."

"What, Jenny?"

"When you kissed me, Johnny, I imagined it was Liam kissing me, and I think that's why I didn't stop you. It felt good, and I'm sorry, I know you don't want to hear that, but I can't lie to you or to myself. I miss his lips on mine."

"Oh, I see," Johnny said with disappointment. "I guess it doesn't surprise me but it still doesn't change how it felt to me, and it never will." Johnny scooted himself over to her, surprising Jenny as she pressed herself into the Bronco's door even more. The handle was wedged in her spine as Johnny pushed himself against her. He looked ardently at her. "The hell with it," he said taking his hands and bringing her lips to his once again. He thrust his tongue deep into her mouth, their spit culminated into each other. She didn't even have time to breathe. He was kissing her with all the tenacity that seemed to keep him going. She tried to stop but the more she struggled with him, the deeper they seemed to connect. *Didn't he hear what I just said*?

He pulled her body to his and not once did he let go of her. His strong, masculine scent overpowered her as he had his way with her. The only thing she could do was allow him to finish; and when he did, after what seemed like an eternity of swapping spit, did he allow Jenny to speak. "There. Now tell me you were thinking of Liam." Jenny tried to say something, but Johnny had taken her breath away. He scooted back to his side of the truck and without even the slightest look in her direction, he drove back to his place instead of the shop.

She remained quiet, keeping her focus on the passing scenery. She didn't want to look at him, it just reminded her that this night went totally wrong... *just a bite to eat, that's all, ha!* He pulled up to his house and helped her out of the Bronco. Her heart was pounding as she allowed him to take her upstairs to his room, neither one of them said a word to the other. She knew where this was going and still, she followed him. Johnny's room was large but quite minimalistic in décor. The only furniture occupying the huge room was a king size bed and a dresser. There wasn't even a desk or chair. The walls were grey with a green border and vacant of any pictures or posters. She sat meekly on the bed while he took his shirt off. His physique was remarkable, and she couldn't help but compare it to Liam's. And still, in her mind, Johnny paled in comparison.

He knelt in front of her and kissed her body, hovering his lips over her thighs, making his way up. She didn't move. Johnny continued, moving his free hand up her thigh to the top of her waist. He pressed gently on her stomach, making her fall backward and lay prone on his bed. He crawled on top of her, holding her arms down with his hands, making her a prisoner of his desire.

She knew this was wrong, but she felt torn. She knew this is what Johnny had always wanted, and in her mind, she thought if she allowed this to happen then she could justify it, and he would be satisfied. He could have this time and fall back on the memory when the world stopped, and their desire joined them together, if only for a moment. *He is dying; maybe this would be the only time he would ever get.* She tried to put herself in his place, the feeling that time was not on his side, and the only thing he ever wanted was what he couldn't have. *Doesn't he deserve this?* She knew his heart was fragile, and there was no guarantee or promise of what tomorrow would bring for him. But still, the little voice inside her head kept telling her that this was wrong. *It won't be enough for him.* Johnny would want more and the more she gave, the more he would take; more than she was willing or even able to give. *He will become greedy with his needs.* The little voice kept reminding her of Liam as images of him besieged her mind. Johnny was now undoing the buttons on her blouse. He was methodical in his movements, letting her know just how much he adored her. She got lost in the moment, her body ached for more, but no matter, it still wasn't Liam's touch she was feeling, she had to stop Johnny before it was too late or better yet, she had to stop herself from allowing it to continue.

"No." Jenny's voice was strong, but when the word came out, it was only a hush above a whisper. "No, Johnny. We can't do this, stop!" Her eyes pleaded with his as he slowly stopped his quest. Her heart was beating hard as she tried to regain her composure. She felt awful, not for what almost happened but because she didn't allow it to happen. She re-buttoned her shirt and pulled herself off of the bed and stood up. She turned to look at Johnny as he lay on the green and grey covers in defeat. He sighed heavily. "I'm sorry. I'm so sorry." She turned away and ran to the door only to have Johnny get up and stop her.

"Don't go, Jenny."

She looked at him with bewildered eyes. "You can't mean that, Johnny?"

"I don't want to be alone, not now. I promise I won't try anymore. I mean it; please just stay the night with me. I don't want to be alone."

"Why?"

Johnny pulled the hair that fell over his eyes to the side, walked back to his bed and sat down. "I'm always alone, Jenny. I just want to fall asleep with you next to me. I never thought I would have this much time with you, and I don't mean because of what happened between you and Liam, but because I shouldn't even be here. I should have died months ago. I've cheated death so many times in my life that I don't think it's going to let me get away with it again. Maybe I am taking advantage of your situation, but I have to take what I can get when I can get it. I know I should have never brought you here or even kissed you, trust me, those weren't my intentions in the beginning; I really did just want to get something to eat with you. But when you're on borrowed time you kind of don't think of the consequences, you just react to your needs and I need you. I didn't have anything to lose by kissing you or trying to make love to you." Johnny paused for a moment as he chuckled quietly to himself.

"What?" Jenny asked curiously.

"It's nothing; it's just something my mom told me."

"What is it?" she persisted.

"It's just that, well, you know Mom being who she is has always believed that everyone should make out a bucket list and fulfill it. She said that people take for granted what's in front of them or the time they have because they always think they have tomorrow. Maybe she believes this because she knows stuff that she doesn't always say. Well, since the age of eleven, I've never had that luxury. I've been on borrowed time for over half of my life now, and I just realized that in order for me to fulfill everything on my bucket list, I have to start and stop with you."

"I don't understand, Johnny."

"You, Jenny, you're my bucket list. You are my everything that I want to experience before I die; before my heart finally gives in and releases me from this hell I live on Earth. I would easily accept my fate and die tomorrow knowing that tonight I had this time with you. And I don't mean that kind of time, although making love to you would be the ultimate bucket list wish come true for me. I mean having you here for one night, next to me, while we sleep together would fulfill my every wish, my every dream, Jenny."

"Johnny, you've got so much to give. I know you're going to make it, and you're going to realize that there is someone out there who will fulfill you and give you back what you're willing to give to them. Why do you want me knowing I can't give that to you? Don't you want someone to give you the love that you have to give? I don't love you, Johnny, no matter how special you are to me, it's not there, and if I never get back with Liam, I still wouldn't be able to give you my all. My all will always belong to Liam. I couldn't do that to you; believe it or not, I do care enough about you to be this honest with you. I care enough about you that I don't want to see you hurt anymore. Please…" Jenny said as she went to him and placed her hand on his beating heart. "Please, Johnny, give up on me."

He placed his hand over hers. "I can't. It's not in me to give up and I won't, even with my last dying breath. It's just not my nature." He brought her hand up to his mouth as he lightly kissed it. "I don't have much time, Jenny. It's the truth, and I'm not saying this so you will feel sorry for me. I'm scared, and I've never told anyone that, not even my mom. I want her to be strong, and she can only be that way if she doesn't see the fear in my eyes. I want to remain positive around her, so I keep my fear to myself, but I am scared, Jenny and I'm tired of being alone. They can't find a heart for me, and I know my time will run out before they do. My blood type is too rare, I understand my reality. I can live with the fact that you will never love me, I've lived with that knowledge from the very beginning but please Jenny, just stay with me, just this one time, just for tonight. Even if you do it because you feel sorry for me, I'm fine with that, I don't care what the reason is, just as long as you can find one. I just don't want you to leave. I just want to remember how it feels to be with someone that I want to be with and not because they're a convenience." Johnny pulled an object out of his jean pocket. It was the silver pocket watch his mom had given him in the hospital last spring. "My mom is such the optimist. She knows the truth but is afraid to admit it. The way she thinks makes her a believer in a lot of the nonsense. She really does think that this watch will give me the time that she couldn't." He put the watch back in his pocket and looked away from Jenny.

"It's a beautiful gesture, Johnny and I think the watch represents hope. If we don't have hope then what do we have? I know your mom's not giving up on you and neither am I. You are going to live, and you are going to have a fulfilled life, but it's going to be a life with someone else. What happened to Charlene?"

"You know she never meant anything to me, I want to feel you against me tonight. Please, Jenny, I'm willing to beg for this opportunity, I'll get down on my hands and knees if that's what it takes; just don't go, not this time." Johnny held her hand tightly within his.

Her chest heaved as she watched him implore with his brown eyes to agree to his request. She didn't have the heart to say no to him. *The reality was that I was lonely too, and I also missed the feel of a body against mine. If it couldn't be Liam's, then maybe, I thought it would be alright at least for one night, if it was Johnny's. I will, Johnny, I will."*

He smiled at her and hugged her tightly. "Thank you."

Chapter Eleven
The Kiss

Jenny remained with Johnny that night and stayed until the wee hours of the next morning. She slipped out quietly while he was still sleeping leaving him a note:

Johnny,
I believe in you, please believe in yourself.
As long as there is hope, there will always be
the promise of a bright tomorrow.
With love,
Jenny

He saw it next to his bedside table neatly secured by his pocket watch. He found himself feeling profoundly alone reading it, but he didn't care, the night before had been magical for him; it was exactly what he needed. She had stayed with him and that time would always be something that Liam would never be able to take away from him. It was something that the two of them shared, and he would forever be grateful.

****

It was almost two weeks later before Johnny saw Jenny again. She didn't show up for work at *The Spiritual Ship,* and she wasn't answering her phone. Johnny had, for lack of better words, become an incessant worry wart. He wondered if their night together had backfired and instead of bringing them closer together, it had pushed them apart; and that if she wasn't going to make her whereabouts known to him, then he would find her. His thoughts were having a field day with him as he wondered if Jenny had found her way back into Liam's arms. Was their last encounter so big as to drive even a bigger wedge between them? He tried to shake it off knowing that at least for the time being; Liam's time was being spent preparing for the upcoming race on November 11th. He was fairly positive that Jenny wasn't with him even though in his heart, he knew that's where she wanted to be. But he still needed to make sure she was all right, so he went to the first place that came to his mind.

It was a familiar sight as he pulled up to Jenny's driveway and saw her sitting on her porch swing, swaying back and forth. It reminded him of the last time he saw her sitting there when he came to visit her, almost two years ago, after her horrific accident. He had signed her cast that day, writing that she would always hold a place in his heart; little did he know at the time, how much truth that statement would hold.

"Hello, stranger. So this is what I should expect? You spend one night with me and then I don't hear from you," Johnny said with some humor.

"Hi, Johnny." The brightness in her eyes was gone when she answered him, but her tone was still sweet.

There was a long pause while he waited for an explanation to her sudden absence but Jenny volunteered nothing.

"So... where have you been?" he finally asked.

"Here." Jenny was being very elusive.

"You know, my mom's been very worried about you. You haven't been back to work since our night together. Why not?"

"I'm sorry; I didn't mean to do that, it's just that I felt like I needed to be alone for a while. After that night, I needed some time to myself. I didn't think your mom would really miss me. She never really needed my help anyway, you know that. She was being the sweet person she is because she's worried about me. I knew from day one why she hired me."

"What about me?"

"What do you mean, what about you?"

"Don't you think I missed you? Can you really spend that kind of time with someone and then just leave them like that? Besides, I thought we knew each other a little better. You could have waited until I woke up."

"I left you a note, Johnny."

"I know," he said as he pushed his hand into his jean pocket, she could hear the sound of crumpling paper as he grasped it.

"Johnny, I am so happy that we shared that time together, it meant the world to me to be there for you, but when I left, I just felt this horrible feeling inside of me, like I had cheated on Liam: and in retrospect, perhaps I did."

"But you didn't, Jenny," Johnny said adamantly.

"Maybe not in your eyes but for Liam it probably would look different. Like I said, I'm glad I was there for you. I know the hell you are enduring, and it kills me that I can't do more for you. I don't want you to be scared and to be honest, I think you are one of the bravest guys I've ever met but I came home that night feeling ashamed, and I did a lot of soul-searching because of it. I appreciate your kindness and your mom's generosity more than you'll ever know but what happened between us can never happen again, and I believe that if I keep working at your mom's store, you might hope it will. I will become a daily reminder to all of us that I'm not going to stay. It won't be permanent, and I know that's what you're hoping for. I can't go back.

"Didn't you feel something between us that night, Jenny?"

"Yes, I did, but you caught me when I was at my most vulnerable. I miss being held too. I miss the spark that happens when I'm touched, the energy I feel when I'm kissed. But I also realized that it wasn't so much what I missed but who I missed... I miss Liam. I love him, Johnny and I always will."

Johnny sighed. "I know, Jenny. I know you do. I'm sorry; I should have never used my condition to persuade you. It was wrong of me. I know you love Liam; I've always known that... that's been part of the game for me. I'm a true competitor and when I want something, or should I say, someone, like I want you, I don't give up; but that night I realized just how much you do love Liam."

"What do you mean?"

Johnny's chest heaved heavily as he sat down next to Jenny on the swing. "I couldn't believe that I had you to myself that night. The last thing I wanted to do, Jenny was sleep. I just wanted to make sure that I wasn't dreaming and that you were really lying next to me in my bed. I don't think I could have slept even if I wanted too. It felt so good to feel your warmth against me, to have your smell linger when you moved. I just wanted to breathe you in. You, on the other hand, fell fast asleep, and it was then when you told me how much you loved Liam. You had probably been asleep almost an hour when you started calling his name. I just listened to you calling out to him. It was so pure, I knew then, more than any other time since I've known you, that you really do love him. I now know it's not and never has been me. I guess I hoped that all my persistence over the last couple of years might have left some sort of sympathetic love dent in you but it hasn't."

"I'm sorry, Johnny. I didn't know I did that."

"How could you know? There's no need to apologize. I guess I'm the one who should be apologizing but I just can't. Even though I know where your heart lies, I'll still cherish the night we had together for the rest of my life, however long that may be. It meant more to me than you will ever know.

"It meant a lot to me too, Johnny. You mean a lot to me. The past couple of years have been nothing but a roller coaster for all of us, and even through the turbulent times, you have always thought of me with no regard to yourself. I can never repay you for that."

"But you have, Jenny, the night we spent together was all I've ever dreamed about. I meant it when I said I could die today and be happy with my life. I know I will never have what you and Liam have together, maybe I don't even want it... but I do have what I need, and that's thanks to you. I do love you, Jenny King, whether you want to hear it or not."

Jenny smiled at him. "I hope you understand why I can't come back to help your mom."

"Yeah, I do, and I'm sure she does too. I will admit it was nice seeing your face every day, but I get it." Johnny stood up. "I think I should go, I just wanted to make sure you were okay... you are okay, aren't you, Jenny?"

"As good as I can be."

Johnny realized that after he left Jenny this time, things would be different forever for them. He left reluctantly. No matter how much he tried to convince himself that it was over, he still didn't want to believe it. He didn't want to leave her.

Jenny was relieved as she saw Johnny's Bronco disappear around the corner. She walked into her kitchen and grabbed a bottle of water from her fridge. She wanted to talk to Liam, that's all she wanted anymore, she missed the sound of his voice, the clicking of his boots when he walked into a room, and his crooked but still beautiful smile when he saw her. There was just one thing she had to do to capture those moments again, and that was to go to him. She was tired of waiting for Liam to come to her. She made it as far as the car when her nerves began to wane. She sat in her seat thinking about Johnny's visit while she tried to find the will to pull out of her driveway. She'd almost found the courage when her cell started ringing. "Now what?" she said displeased by its intrusion on her privacy. "Hello?"

"Jenny?"

"Parker."

"It's been a long time," he said with some anxiety.

"Yes, too long, Parker." Jenny paused. She wondered why she was hearing from him now. "So, what do I owe the pleasure, Parker?"

"I just wanted to see how you were doing. You've been missed."

"I have, Parker? By whom?"

"By lots of people, Jenny. Me, Kendra, Grandpa Mack and…"

"Liam?" Jenny interjected. There was silence on Parker's end of the phone. "Just as I thought. Parker, my heart has already been broken enough, and I have pretty much concluded after my return that he's gotten over me. I really didn't need this phone call from you to confirm it."

"But, Jenny, you're wrong. Liam does miss you."

"Really? Does he know I'm in town?"

"Yes, he does."

"Then why hasn't he tried to reach out to me or come by to see me?"

"It's not that easy for him, Jenny. He thinks since he hasn't given up the racing then you don't want anything to do with him."

"Parker, the racing wasn't the issue. It was the drinking and him shutting me out. Instead of confiding in me and letting me be there for him, he decided Toby and Gina could have that honor. He hurt me, Parker. I never stopped believing in him. It was Liam who gave up on us... Parker?"

"Yeah, Jenny?"

"Is he still drinking?"

"I don't think so, I won't promise you anything, but I haven't seen him take a drink in a couple of months."

"What about his nightmares?"

"I couldn't answer that."

"What about Grandpa? Is he doing alright?"

"He's fine. He misses you too. It hasn't been the same since you left town."

"I miss him too. But I can't call him just like I can't call Liam. It doesn't feel right for some reason."

"I guess I can understand, but that's one of the reasons why I'm calling you."

"What do you mean?"

"I'm sure you've heard about the race on Ripley Road tomorrow night?"

"Yeah, I know about it. Why?"

"I just thought you should know that this wasn't Liam's idea. He doesn't want to do the race, but he's being forced too."

"By whom? Toby?"

"Well, Toby is partially behind it, but it's Aaron Dent. Liam signed a contract with him after you left town and he's bound by it to do any race Aaron sets up for him. Aaron heard through the grapevine about your accident, and he thought it would be great publicity for Liam to re-enact the race on his motorcycle. Not to mention that it's going to be on the eleventh. Aaron wants it to be as much like the first race as possible, that's why it's tomorrow night. He'd have you there if he could. Aaron already tried to get Johnny to race Liam."

"So Parker, Liam is racing because he has too not because he wants too?"

"Yes."

"I still don't understand why you're telling me this, though. It's not like I can do anything about it."

"I don't believe that, Jenny. I think that if you were to talk to Liam, you could talk him out of it. I don't think he should do it, not just because of the accident but because Aaron is a snake, and I don't trust him. Besides, I don't think Liam is in the right frame of mind to be out there doing some of the crazy shit Aaron expects from him. And to make matters worse, Liam's not listening to anybody. He's in his own little world, and nobody can seem to reach him, not even Grandpa Mack and believe me, he's been trying. I know this might be difficult for you to hear, but I'm asking you to remember who you fell in love with, and as Liam's best friend, to consider my request. That race is going to be dangerous, and I'm afraid for him. I just thought maybe he would listen to you."

"I don't know, Parker. It's not that easy, too much time has passed between us."

"Please, Jenny. I know he wouldn't do it if you told him not too. I just know it. Please, will you at least think about it?"

She didn't want to tell Parker she had already made up her mind to see him that she was sitting in her car trying to find the courage to turn on her ignition. Okay, I'll try."

"Thank you, Jenny. I knew you wouldn't let me down."

"No promises, Parker. I still don't believe I can make a difference. We're not the same two people anymore. I can only try, and that's all I will promise."

"That's enough for me, Jenny."

"Bye, Parker."

"Bye, Jenny." The phone clicked as Jenny heard a tap on her window.

"Is there anything you need Miss Jenny?" It was Billy.

"Huh?" She rolled down her window to acknowledge him. "I'm sorry, Billy, I didn't see you standing there."

"That's okay, Miss Jenny, I was just wondering if somethin'

was wrong? You've been sittin' in your car for a while. Is there somethin' wrong with it? I can check it out if you want me to," he said kindly.

"Oh, no, Billy, thank you, nothing's wrong with my car. I was just getting ready to leave."

"Are you sure? I don't want you to get out on the road, and your car break down on ya."

"No, really, everything is fine. I guess I was just daydreaming."

"It's a nice day for it. Well. I'll let you go. Are you on your way to see your boyfriend?"

Jenny was taken aback by Billy's comment. "Ummm..." was the only thing she could produce from her mouth. She didn't know what to say to him; apparently, he didn't know that they weren't a couple anymore.

"Well if you are, tell him I wish I could see him race. I'd give anything to be there tomorrow night, but I'll be working on the plumbing in Mildred's apartment. It's going to take me most of the weekend to get those pipes fixed. But you tell Liam I'll be rootin' for him. It's going to be one helluva race... if ya don't mind me saying so. That boyfriend of yours was born with a gift. He's going places, you mark my words and one day I'll be seeing his face on some sort of racing magazine with you next to him. That'll sure be the day."

Jenny just stared at him while he spoke about Liam as if he was some sort of racing god. "I gotta go, Billy," She had become very uncomfortable listening to Billy's excited rant over Liam.

"Okay, Miss Jenny. Have a good evenin' and don't forget to tell Liam to kick some ass for his ole' buddy, Billy," Billy's belly was bouncing up and down while he laughed; the brown spit that culminated in his mouth from his chew was now resting neatly on his chin. He tipped his hat while Jenny backed out of her driveway.

"Okay, that was totally weird." She grasped her steering wheel tightly for support as she made her way to Liam's house. Her stomach was in knots as she took the turn-off and drove down the crooked dirt road that would end at Liam's house. It had been a long time since she frequented this place she used to call home. The winding trail that was usually covered with tree branches and bushes was now bare and unadorned, as it gave way to a clear path before her. She came to a stop when the house came into view. It was as if it was waiting for her return. She was in awe of it. It was just as beautiful as she remembered it. Everything was still in place, the old barn to the right, the two oak trees that resided on either side of the house and the broken steps that led to the front door. Even Blue was in his usual spot, fast asleep by the front door. But still, the house seemed to hold an ominous presence to it. As she sat there in her car, she contemplated on whether she made a mistake in coming here. She should have called first, but her intuition was to do this in person, and not over the phone. She wanted to see Liam whether he wanted to see her or not.

"You can do this, Jenny, be brave. It will be okay. Just put the foot on the gas pedal and go, you're already here anyway; just pull up to the house." She didn't move. "I can't, I just can't." She bent her head down and started crying into her hands. She was too emotional to move on. She wanted to be here so much but was more afraid that Liam would tell her to leave. She just couldn't handle the rejection. But then again, she thought about what brought her here. She had to do this, if not for her sake but Liam's and Grandpa's too. She had to find out why Liam had agreed to race.

So with the last bit of courage she had left in her, she finished her drive. She stopped at the front steps and stepped out of her car slowly. Blue awoke instantly and ran to her side; he wagged his tail fiercely trying to get Jenny's attention. *I could tell he was glad I was her.* He thought to himself.   She pet him kindly while Blue showered her with his affection. She inhaled sharply. "Okay, let's do this. Just take one step after the next, Jenny, and you'll be at the front door. Don't turn into a coward now," she said, still trying to give herself more encouragement. She stepped carefully over the broken boards that led to the porch and the front door. It was the longest and loudest eleven steps she had ever taken. With another deep breath and a quick prayer, she knocked on the door. She messed with her hair while waiting patiently for Liam or Grandpa to answer it. She knocked again, this time with more force so the sound would resonate louder throughout the house; still, nobody came to answer the door. She looked around; she realized that she hadn't noticed Liam's or Grandpa's trucks parked anywhere on the premises. She sat down feeling relieved and let down simultaneously.

      She didn't understand why seeing Liam would scare her so much, but it did. He used to be the only person she could ever rely on and now they had become strangers. Blue lay next to her feet just like he used to, almost consoling her the way only a dog could. He was still completely oblivious, though, and in his mind, all was right with the world. *If only she could believe that too.* It was an hour later when she finally decided to give up and go home. *Obviously, no one is here.* She gave Blue an affectionate pet and got up. She made it about three steps when she heard the sound that used to make her heart jump into her throat... Liam's truck was nearing. She didn't know what to do. Her first thought was to run and hide, but she was sure he would see her. So instead, she stood frozen as the black F-150 pulled up next to her. If it hadn't been for the erratic beating her heart was making, she was positive that it would have come to a complete stop.

      She held her breath as Liam locked eyes with her. He seemed to be just as shell-shocked to see her as she was him. He didn't move. She knew she should say something, anything, to break the silence between them but all she could think about was how good he looked. His hair was shorter, but his dirty blonde locks still fell beautifully around his masculine face; his eyes were still crystal blue, and she found herself already getting lost in them. He wore a grey flannel shirt that had the sleeves cut off showing the rippling muscles in his tanned arms. He was breathtaking, and Jenny was finding herself becoming weak in the knees at the sight of him. She tried to remain in the present instead of daydreaming about him. Finally, she spoke.

"Hello." It wasn't much, but it was better than she expected. She was worried that when her mouth opened nothing but air would come out. After almost a year without seeing the only man she ever loved the only thing she could say was a two syllable greeting. *How generic.* Liam turned off his ignition and scooted over to the other side of the truck. He opened the door and got out, he was slow in his movements and Jenny wondered if it was from the shock of seeing her or the disappointment. She still didn't know where she stood with him. They were now standing only a few inches from each other, their bodies only a movement away from touching each other and as the wind swept between them, Jenny found herself becoming drunk with his scent. Her heart was beating out of control, waiting for him to say something back to her. She was scared, excited, relieved, and anxious all at the same time... wondering what was going through his head. So much time had passed between them that she didn't know what to expect from him anymore. Aside from her weak acknowledgment to him, the two of them hadn't spoken a word to each for over six months. He continued to stand there, not breaking eye contact.

"I guess you're kind of surprised to see me at your doorstep," she said laughing in a stupid and nervous way. His blue eyes never left hers, but she found herself shifting her eyes back and forth. She was becoming increasingly uncomfortable with his conspicuous silence. Her hope that he might be happy to see her was diminishing, gradually being replaced with the disappointment she thought she would feel. It was becoming apparent to her that she wasn't welcome, just as she had feared. "Well, I guess I should go..."

"Go? After you just got here?" he said. She was so startled by his voice that she lost her train of thought. He seemed larger than life to her as he stood in front of her and she was finding it difficult to put two words together.

"It's just that..." Jenny paused again, knowing she was making excuses. She breathed in deeply, allowing Liam's scent to encompass her. "Liam, it's just that after all this time, I thought you would react differently to seeing me here. I mean, I know things are different between us but aren't you glad I'm here? It has been a while."

Liam stood there as he also breathed in Jenny's scent. *If she only knew how much he had missed her, if she only knew what it meant to him to see her standing here when he drove up and if she only knew just how happy he was she was here but it wasn't that easy for him to tell her.* He was still carrying the torment of his past, and he still felt as if he had let her down. In his eyes, he hadn't proven himself to her yet. "I am glad to see you, Jenny; it's just that I didn't expect to see you when I pulled in."

"Is that a good thing or not?" She didn't know if she wanted his answer.

"It is but..."

"But it still doesn't change how things are between us? Is that right, Liam?"

He didn't answer her. *Why couldn't I just let go of everything and be happy for the opportunity I have been handed right now?"* Instead, all he could think about was that he had a race in less than twenty-four hours. He realized that Jenny's visit was a little too coincidental. "Jenny, why are you here?"

"It used to be that I didn't need a reason to see you, Liam."

"Well things change, don't they?" He thought about seeing Jenny at the high school parking lot with Johnny.

"I guess. Listen, Liam, I've missed you, and I've been home for over a month now, and I suppose I was tired of waiting for you to show up. I thought you would have at least called me."

"You've missed me?"

"Yes, why do you question that?"

"I don't know, maybe it's because of what I've seen and what I've heard."

"And what would that be?" She was hoping he would have lost that arrogant tone, but it seemed to be in full force today.

"How could you miss me, Jenny when you seem to be spending all your time with Johnny? I saw you at the school parking lot, and I know you've been at his mom's shop almost every day. If you've missed me that much, you sure have a hell of a way of showing it. It looks like you're doing fine. I didn't see the need to see you; I would have been just intruding on your friendship with the one and only Johnny Bryant." The sarcasm was quite evident to Jenny. Liam was still angry.

"I'm not seeing Johnny. What you think you saw and what the truth is are two totally different things. There was nothing going on in the parking lot if you must know, he was just trying to console me because I was upset about you. I didn't think I would come back to this. I never heard from you while I was gone and it about killed me, Liam. I thought for sure you would have come after me. All I've ever wanted to do was be there for you. I told you that at Brush Creek. I meant it then, and I still mean it, why don't you believe me?" She could feel the tears welling up in her eyes; this is what she didn't want to happen, to expose her fragile state, to become a blubbering idiot in front of him. She needed to stay strong.

"Jenny, really? You still don't get it? I can't stand the sight of Johnny. He has been a thorn in my side since he moved to Spencer. He went after you with full intent knowing we were together, and you allowed it. I can't and won't compete with him anymore. I told you that it was either him or me. So when I saw you with Johnny and heard where you were spending your time, I realized you had made your decision. That's why I never contacted you. And as far as that goes, you have a phone too, you could have called me."

"I'm here now, aren't I? I've been scared to death to see you because of how we left things last spring. What was I supposed to think when you never tried to come after me? I love you. I don't love Johnny. I've been so lonely since we broke up. Johnny's mom offered me a job just so I would get out of the house, that's the only reason I've been there, I've been working for her. She was worried about me, that's all there was to it."

"How convenient for Johnny."

"He's been a friend to me since I've been back, Liam nothing more."

"Maybe I should just be friends with Shanna too. Would you like that? Can't you see how that looks? The whole damn town thinks you are with Johnny, how could you do that to me, Jenny? You want to work things out, but you go to Johnny? Come on, Jenny how am I supposed to take that?"

The tension between them was mounting, and Jenny realized that they weren't getting anywhere. She felt sick to her stomach. This definitely wasn't going how she had hoped. She threw her hands up in the air and turned to walk away from Liam. This had been a huge mistake.

"Where are you going?" he asked following her.

"I'm leaving. It's obvious you don't want me here. I came here with good intentions and the hope we might be able to talk like two civilized adults, but I guess that's not possible." Liam grabbed her arm. It was the first time he had touched her in over six months, and the electricity that went through her body almost made her fall over. She gasped as he held onto her. It felt so good to feel his skin on hers that she didn't want him to ever let go, even if he was upset with her.

"Stop, Jenny, listen I don't know what's going on between us, but I'm trying to figure it out. I don't like this tension between us either. I have missed you too, but I still need to get rid of my ghosts that are hanging around. I'm getting there, but it's taking time."

"Is that why you're racing tomorrow night, Liam?"

"I thought that's why you came here. How did you know?"

"I have my ways, and it's really not important how I found out. You shouldn't do this race, it's not worth it. Why would you be willing to risk everything just to race on that road again?"

"Because, I need to finish the race. It doesn't matter that I won't be racing against Johnny; I just need to do this for me, it's personal."

"Personal? What was I? Wasn't I personal enough for you? Correct me if I'm wrong, but I do believe we became very intimate when we were together, and it wasn't just the sex! We shared something between us, Liam, that I know nobody else would ever understand. Don't you see, after everything I'm still here for you? That should count for something. I feel like we've been through hell and back, I don't know anybody else who would still be standing here after what we've endured. That must mean something," Jenny said as her voice softened. "And for what it's worth, I don't believe you. I think you're being forced to do it for the publicity because Aaron Dent is making you, and maybe even Toby and Gina. You were always a leader, when did you start following other people around? That's not you. Where's your integrity, your heart? Why would you sell yourself out for fame and fortune? You never wanted that. Did I do that? Did I change you? Because you certainly weren't this way when I first met you."

"I know it sounds crazy, but I've got to do this. It was never my intention to ever race Ripley Road again, but when Aaron explained it to me, it kind of made me think that I could put this behind me if I did do it, it made sense. That's why I'm racing on that road again, not for the glory or the money. I've never cared about that stuff, you know that."

"You sure seem to have painted a different picture to everyone else, especially since you met Aaron. It definitely seems like the money and notoriety have something to do with why you gave up your life for racing. It's no secret the name you've made for yourself. I always knew you were good, but I never thought you would use your talent in such a superficial way. I thought the shop was your dream. I guess I was wrong, I guess maybe I never knew you; but then again, how could I when you wouldn't let me see the real Liam Larson."

"That's not fair, Jenny. I tried to let you in, but there wasn't room for you and Johnny."

"You won't get over that will you?"

"How can I when the first time I see you, you're with him. You say you didn't know me, but maybe I didn't know you either. I have always loved you, and I never would have allowed anyone to come between us. I was willing to fight for you, even die for you. You knew how I felt; all you had to do was tell Johnny no."

"Are you serious, Liam? That's all I've ever said to him. You pushed me towards him when you shut me out! I feel like I have been alone ever since the accident. I came back for you. Thank God Johnny was here for me because you certainly weren't. It took everything in me to come out here today. You shouldn't be racing, and you shouldn't be hanging out with Aaron Dent. It's wrong, something bad might happen. I am right here, Liam. Please stay me with so we can talk this out, don't do this race. I'm begging you."

Liam just stood there as his hand dropped from Jenny's arm. He had been holding it the entire time. "I'm sorry, Jenny but I have to."

Jenny sighed heavily. "Are you still drinking... what about your nightmares, are you still having them?"

"My nightmares are fine, I'm handling them. And as for the drinking, don't worry that's under control too."

"I see. Well, I'm glad to hear it." The way they were talking to each other hurt Jenny beyond words. It was if they were just casual acquaintances instead of the soul mates she thought they were. "I'm going to go now, Liam, because if I don't I'm going to start crying and that's the last thing I want to do in front of you. I feel like that's all I ever did and I'm not doing that anymore. I may not be able to change your mind about tomorrow night, but I hope I've given you something to think about. You've got plenty of people here who love you. Think about your grandpa, he doesn't need to worry about you, and I know he is worried. Try to remember what we had and could still have, please Liam, it's not too late."

Liam stared at her. It was taking everything in him not to whisk her away and let her know how much she meant to him. He wanted to tell her how sorry he was for putting her through all the pain and that he loved her with everything he was or could ever be, but something inside of him just wouldn't let him do it.

"Okay, well I guess I've said my piece." She started to walk away when she stopped dead in her tracks with a revelation. She turned quickly around to find Liam still standing in the same spot, his blue eyes bearing into her. She ran to him and threw her arms around his muscular neck and placed her deprived lips on his. She held on tightly and kissed him hard. She made sure he was aware of what he'd been missing since she'd been gone. She kept her one hand securely around his neck while she let her free hand explore the bottom part of his torso. They both groaned in unison. Liam was trying to breathe, but she wouldn't allow it. She wanted him to inhale only her.

It felt good to him as their mouths molded into each other. He tasted her sweetness as her tongue thrust deep into his mouth. The kiss seemed to last forever, and when she finally released her hold on him, she looked deeply into his eyes.

"Remember, Liam, this isn't over between us, this is who we are; we were made for each other. If you still need time, then I'll give it to you. I'll wait forever for you if I have to. I love you."

Liam slowly took a step backward, he didn't speak or better yet couldn't, instead he watched Jenny get in her car and drive away.

"Wait," he said, but it was too late, she was gone.

Chapter Twelve
The Race

The next twenty-four hours after seeing Jenny dragged for Liam. He kept reliving her visit and her leaving again, it seemed that's all he saw any more, the back of her car as it drove away.

****

"It's time, Liam." Aaron walked into the trailer ignoring Liam's odd demeanor. "You need to get your bike to the starting gate. Five minutes to show time." Aaron was eager with anticipation as he rubbed his hands together. There were hundreds of people outside to watch this infamous race, and he had at least ten times that in bets. If Liam won the race, like he knew Liam could, Aaron would be a much richer man by night's end. He had a lot riding on this race and on Liam.

Parker stood next to his long-time friend giving him a judgmental look. *I wondered if Jenny had been able to talk to him, if so, her talk must have not worked since Liam was here and ready to race. But then again, I hadn't told Parker that I had seen her or what had happened.* He was still trying to digest it himself. Neither one of them said a word to the other. They were just going through the motions until it was time for Liam to arrive at the starting line.

Liam already knew how Parker felt about this race, so it didn't really matter if they exchanged words or not. It wouldn't matter one way or the other, he hadn't changed his mind. He gave Parker a nod to let him know he was ready and then left him where he stood, pushing his bike to the starting gate. His opponent was already there, revving his engine while waiting for Liam to line up next to him. The intended intimidation didn't work, if anything it only pissed Liam off. There was no way in hell he was going to let this guy think he could mess with him just by showing off what kind of power his bike possessed. Liam ignored the attitude of his opponent and concentrated on his own stuff. He was checking his brakes when he heard Jenny's words resonate in his head. *Don't do this, Liam. Please."* Her words begged him to stop, but instead of heeding her plea, he just shook his head until she disappeared from his mind.

He looked to his right where he found his fearless opponent waiting. He didn't recognize him, but then again, it was hard to tell who he was behind the green and white helmet. The guy gave Liam an ominous stare as if to say that tonight belonged to him. He didn't seem intimidated by Liam's presence or the reputation that preceded him. Liam could usually stare down his opponents but not tonight. He, in fact, realized that he was probably more scared of the race than the guy who challenged him. *This wasn't going to be like the countless races I had been in before. No, this one was different, this is where it all happened, this road and the race that took place on it almost two years ago was the beginning of the end of what I thought would be my destiny. This is where I had lost her. I knew that winning wasn't the key but finishing the race was.* Ripley Road wasn't going to hold the title of beating Liam Larson any longer; he was more determined than ever to win.

The two challengers stared blankly at each other for minutes, watching each other's every move. But finally, Liam took the lead by breaking the stare on the green and white helmet and turning his attention to Julia Shipman, who had just arrived. She was dressed in her all-white attire and holding her infamous white flag high above her. Liam waited impatiently for the cloth to drop from her hands. It seemed to take forever, and as time stood still, Liam found himself searching the crowd that occupied the two sides of Ripley Road. Everything seemed the same on this fateful night, just as it did on April 11th. It had even begun to rain. The chaotic behavior of the crowd, the churning feeling in the pit of his stomach as he comprehended the magnitude of the event, and finally, the obvious adrenaline rush right before the flag dropped. That had never changed. He couldn't deny the feeling. The only thing that changed was that Jenny was absent. He didn't ask her to watch, not that she would have; but he hadn't even thought about it when he saw her. He was so taken aback with her presence that it never entered his mind. But then again, their conversation hadn't gone too well; so it made sense that she wouldn't be here. But as always, he looked for her angelic face in the sea of fans hoping against hope that she would be there. He hoped that maybe she would find a reason inside herself to come on her own... just because.

He was lost inside his own thoughts when Julia began her countdown. The flag dropped, slowly descending from Julia's fingertips until it eventually hit the black pavement. Liam didn't waste any time coming back to reality as he zoomed past the guy who wore the green and white helmet and began to make this race his own.

The race had been designed for them to drive down Ripley Road and into Devil's Bulge. They would then proceed onto a stretch of grassy road with three massive dirt mounds and two obstacles that were forty-five degrees in their turns only to see a water hazard that they would have to jump over before crossing the finishing line. He was aware of the danger but mentally prepared for this challenge. He was well ahead from the very beginning, leaving the green and white helmet several hundred yards behind him. Liam made it through Devil's Bulge without flinching. Everyone was impressed, especially Parker, whose eyes never left Liam. But little did he or anybody else know that as Liam so superbly rode the race that he was constantly praying for Jenny's guidance. He was a mess inside and only when he concentrated on her face did he find the will to continue. That was the one secret he didn't reveal to anyone. It was her spirit that gave him his strength to continually win.

Liam was alone as he made it up the homestretch; the green and white helmet was nowhere to be seen. He met the challenges that were given to him and saw victory was imminent. But as he headed for the finish line, he glanced to his left and thought he saw the one person who he hoped he would see. His eyes searched for Jenny, her beautiful auburn hair and hazel eyes gracing her face while she waited for his victorious return. But she was nowhere to be seen in the frenzied sea of fans, his mind was playing tricks on him, as it usually did. His will weakened and he remembered the last words she said before leaving him. He mumbled something under his breath. It was then he realized he was riding the berm of the road.

His bike began to fishtail. He tried to regain control, but the circumstances had become dire. His bike had a mind of its own, and as it hit a patch of loose rocks, the bike popped its front wheel and then flipped on him, sending Liam flying through the air. He hit his head hard on the pavement with a crashing thud, causing his helmet to crack in half. He lay there on the cold ground, his face embedded in the black asphalt. Ripley Road had claimed victory once again. He was dazed and tried to focus on the images that were besieging him. His mouth tasted of metal as red liquid began to puddle in it. He saw footsteps running towards him but what he noticed more was the finish line; it was still in front of him. Once again, he had failed to cross it.

Parker ran to his side, "It's going to be ok, Liam, I'm here. Just lay still, don't close your eyes, help is on its way!" Parker repeated those words hoping to reassure his best friend as watched the blood pour from Liam's head.

Liam tried to obey his words and remain conscious but the darkness was calling him, and he didn't have the will to refuse it. His eyes were stinging from the blood that trickled into them from the massive wound on his head. His blurred vision frightened Liam; he was scared and frantically searched for Jenny. He thought he heard her sweet voice, as her soft touch caressed his battered body. *"I'm here, baby, don't be afraid, I'm not going to leave you."* It was then that he knew he was in bad shape. He knew she wasn't there, this was all part of his marred mind, toying with his soul before he lapsed into the subconscious. Liam yelled for Parker.

"I'm right here, buddy." Parker was trying to remain strong and hold Liam down, but the sight of his friend's contorted body was making him lose his own will.

With all the strength left in him, Liam lifted his bloodied hand to Parker. His mouth was moving, but Parker couldn't understand what his best friend was trying to tell him. He leaned closer to him; Liam painfully whispered only one word to his friend before giving in to his injuries.

"Jenny."

Chapter Thirteen
Losing Control

Jenny awoke in a panic. She was finding it difficult to breathe, it was as if someone had laid a ton of bricks on her chest and was pressing down with all their might. She was confused but even worse, she was scared, her gut instinct told her that something was wrong... seriously wrong. She sat up to find her bed in a rumpled and sweaty mess, the sheets were pulled from their corners and her blue and yellow comforter was thrown to the floor in a jumbled state. The weird and frightened feeling kept gnawing at her like a horrible toothache, and as much as she tried to shake it, it just wouldn't leave her alone. She was drenched in a sticky sweat, and as she pulled back her wet hair from her drenched face, she became aware of what time it was. She gasped in horror. The clock read 2:11 in the morning. *That damn, stupid, idiotic, crazy and bizarre number. Dammit, why?* She hadn't had any occurrences in months and now as she sat in her rumpled mess of a bed; the mirror digit of itself in all its menacing glory decided to remind her that it was still very much alive and kicking. It didn't bring her the comfort she sought; instead, it was nothing more than a grim reminder of how her life had fallen apart. There was nothing good about it, no promise or hope that she had so naively convinced herself that it held. It was a carrier of disease and despair, ripping souls apart and leaving heartache in its path. It infuriated her to no end that she believed in it with the wonder of a child instead of the maturity of a scorned and bitter woman. She had a knot in her stomach the size of Texas, and as the seconds ticked away, the knot grew larger.

She tried to take a breath only to have the ton of bricks press harder on her chest. Her anxiety was growing as the gnawing feeling kept its vigil over her. She couldn't go back to sleep, that would be senseless; so she got out of bed and went to the bathroom where she splashed cold water on her face until the clamminess that lingered was replaced with the water's icy chill. Her hands were trembling so much that she had to hold on tightly to the basin just to keep them from not moving. Her thoughts went to Liam, this strange behavior she was experiencing, she was positive was because of him. *It has to be, there is no other explanation for it.* She had seen him in her dream. She knew something had happened, and she was sure it was the race.

She quickly ran back to her room and picked up her cell, there were no missed calls or messages. Her disappointment was obvious. She sat on her bed and squeezed her pillow. Something was wrong, and it wasn't just because she was all alone in her house, she just knew something bad had happened. Something had happened to Liam. "Liam, please what is it, baby?" she whispered. "Please dear God, what is wrong? What is going on?" And as if He knew she needed an answer, she heard a knock at her front door. She raced down the stairs taking them two at a time, knowing that it had to be Grandpa Mack or even Parker, but instead she found none other than Johnny standing on her stoop.

"What are you doing here, Johnny? It's the middle of the night, and I'm really not in the mood to talk."

"Jenny, it's Liam." Johnny didn't care what she had just said, he let himself in any way.

"It's the race, isn't it, Johnny?"

Johnny nodded yes. "I'm sorry, Jenny, but it's not good news."

"Oh my God! I knew it! Were you there? Are you sure it's Liam?"

"Yes, I'm sure, and no, I wasn't there but Jake was, and he called me immediately after it happened. It sounds pretty serious, Jenny. I rushed over as soon as Jake called."

"Johnny, I want to see him. How bad is he?"

"I don't know, but I do know he had to be airlifted from the scene."

Jenny's mouth opened as she covered it with both her hands, this was almost too much for her to take. Her knees gave way while her body gave in; Johnny was beside her immediately as she fell to the floor. "Johnny, I can't lose him, I just can't." She was going into shock, her bewildered and frightened eyes imploring Johnny to tell her this was all just a bad dream, but he couldn't do that.

"I know. That's why I'm here. I'm going to take you to him, Jenny."

"But what if they won't let me see him, or even worse... what if Liam doesn't want to see me. I'm scared. I hate this feeling." Jenny was crying so hard that she was almost inconsolable, her body dry-heaving from the outpour of her emotions. But Johnny remained her constant rock; he was there to help her. Even though he knew where her heart belonged, his still belonged to Jenny. He was going to be there for her even if it meant helping her get to Liam. He loved her that much, enough to take Jenny to the love of her life. He had lived without reciprocating feelings from her from the beginning and would forever. It was all he knew. The one thing Johnny couldn't stand was seeing her in pain, and right now she was in a lot of it, maybe not physically but emotionally, she was hurting.

"We'll make sure you see him. They're not going to turn you away, and I'm guessing that as soon as Liam sees your face, he's going to beg you to stay."

Johnny gave Jenny time to get dressed. She was a pro at it, and within minutes was already bolting back down the stairs ready to go. "I'm ready."

"Then let's go," Johnny insisted.

****

The scene at the hospital came right from a war zone. There was chaos and confusion from every angle of the hospital, and the staff seemed to be trying to do twenty different things all at the same time. Half of Spencer had shown up to keep vigil over Liam. Johnny and Jenny were finding it next to impossible to get anyone's attention. "You go take a seat. Let me find out where Liam is." Jenny took Johnny's cue and found a chair near the adjacent wall. She was in the worst frame of mind, and the nervous energy that consumed the hospital made her feel like she was going to lose it at any moment. Jenny checked her cell a million more times only to find there were no messages for her. She still couldn't understand why Johnny was the only one who seemed to think enough of her to tell her about Liam.

Aromas from the hospital drifted around her recalling her previous hospital visits. She wanted to gag. Her legs were anxious, and the only relief she felt was when she stood up and paced the hall. Her nails were bitten to the quick and stung as blood trickled from the open sores, but she didn't care, she knew this was nothing compared to what Liam was enduring. Down the long, stark hallway were an infinite number of closed doors, she knew Liam had to be in one of them. Her imagination ran wild as she envisioned his bloodied body being pumped with unknown liquids in an attempt to save his life. She was so engrossed in the image that she didn't even realize Johnny was back by her side.

"Jenny?"

"What, Johnny? What did you find out? Is Liam okay?" she asked as her pinky finger remained in her mouth.

"He's in intensive care. The nurse said that they almost lost him in the emergency room. He's listed in critical condition. She won't tell me any more because I'm not family."

"Well, I am. I'm his fiancée!" she screamed at the top of her lungs. "She'll have to tell me!" Jenny was crazed with emotion, her tears were replaced with a pure adrenaline that came from deep inside her. Ever since she woke up with that horrible, gnawing feeling, she knew something bad had happened. It was that second sense that validated to her why she and Liam were soul mates. It didn't matter that they were at a crossroads in their relationship; her heart knew they were still connected, their souls were still one, bonded together forever. Jenny stormed past Johnny almost knocking him to the floor as she headed to the nurse's station.

"Stop, Jenny. She's not going to tell you anything. She already saw you come in with me. Don't you think I told her who you were? It doesn't matter. Unless your name is Grandpa Mack, she's not going to tell you any more than what she told me." Jenny couldn't believe it. *Why was Johnny telling me this? It did matter.* But nobody saw that anymore. The last thoughts this town had of she and Liam was that she left him standing at Brush Creek Road. The only thing that mattered to the nurse with the tight-cinched bun that seemed to restrict her rational thinking or even her soft spot for true love was that Jenny wasn't considered family.

"What am I going to do, Johnny? I've got to know what's going on. I have to know before I go crazy."

Jenny was being irrational, and Johnny was trying his best to be there for her, but it was hurting him to see how much she loved Liam when Liam didn't seem to give a damn anymore. Johnny did give a damn about Jenny, and he didn't care what he had told her before. He wanted Jenny for himself. But he realized that this wasn't the time or place for him to start feeling jealousy over someone who wasn't even his.

"Jenny, you just need to go upstairs and make them let you see Liam. I promise if you do, you'll run into Grandpa Mack. I can't help you anymore; I've done all I can for you." Johnny's words were sincere but still carried a hint of defeat and Jenny saw that. She knew how hard it was for him to see her break down over Liam.

"Johnny, thank you but more importantly, thanks for being here for me. I needed you whether you believe that or not. I couldn't have done this without having your undying support."

"You're welcome. Now go." Johnny pushed her away as he pointed her towards the elevator at the end of the long corridor. His heart was breaking on a regular basis lately, and tonight it was almost broken beyond repair. He put on his best face and threw her a kiss; she smiled weakly before turning away. The elevator doors seemed monstrous in size, and as the bell rang and their stainless frames opened to welcome her inside, she felt like she was shrinking with each step she took. *I stood feebly inside the steel crate that carried me to the next floor, shrinking with each second that passed, positive that by the time the doors opened, I would be completely invisible. But this could work in my favor, if nobody could see me, then I could avoid the impending sorrow that I knew awaited me.* But the disillusionment was nothing more than wishful thinking. She was just as real as anybody else in the hospital, and she received that confirmation as soon as she stepped out and saw Grandpa Mack. She knew Grandpa never held any ill-will towards her but as she stood before him and the silence steadily grew, she thought that just maybe he had found enough of a reason to resent her for leaving and not staying to fight for Liam's love and their future.

"Jenny, I'm so glad you're here." His masculine voice began to break. Her theory seemed to be wrong.

"Grandpa, I've missed you so much." She wanted their embrace to last forever; she missed the feeling of being wanted. "How is he?" She was almost too afraid to know.

"It's bad, Jenny, real bad," Grandpa said in a very solemn tone. "They don't know if he's going to make it." Jenny thought she could feel some resentment in Grandpa's voice, but discarded it to him feeling worried over Liam.

"Oh my God, Grandpa. No, this can't be!" Jenny broke down and fell into his embrace. "He... he can't die, not like this, not before we can make things right. He can't do this to me, Grandpa. He can't leave me. Not yet. We're supposed to grow old together. Please tell me this is a nightmare, tell me he's going to be okay, please." She stuttered her words between wails of desperation.

"There, there, Jenny. I'm so sorry that you have to go through this. You two have had enough pain to last two lifetimes. No one deserves this. I wish I could tell you things were going to be better but I can't, not this time. He's broken up pretty badly." Grandpa pulled himself away from her and looked her straight in her eyes. "Do you want to see him?"

"I... I do, but I'm afraid. What if he doesn't want to see me? I don't think I would be able to take it. Besides, the nurse downstairs said only family, I'm not..."

"You're family, Jenny, always have been and always will be. Everybody knows that, even Dr. Garrett. He told me earlier that if you were to show up that you should see him. Jenny, Liam would never turn you away. But I should tell you that he probably won't even know you're here. He's been in a coma since they brought him in." Grandpa stood back. "Now go on, Parker's in there with him right now. You can send him out so you can be alone with Liam."

Jenny looked at him questionably, still wondering if she should go but Grandpa remained adamant and reassured her with those same blue eyes that he shared with his grandson. Those eyes told her that this was the right thing to do. "Okay." The word came out in a feeble whisper.

The intensive care unit was set up with eight rooms in it, four on the left and four on the right with the nurse's station positioned in the middle. Liam was in the second room on the left, room 227. *It added up to eleven. I wanted that number to just disappear altogether and stop reminding me of its power over me. Of course, it would add up to eleven; any other number would mean it would be somebody else.* Jenny exhaled sharply and then with one foot in front of the other, she entered Liam's room. Her footsteps were heavy and slow, she approached his bed, the sound of the beeping monitors kept a perfect cadence with her walk.

"Jenny." Parker came quickly to her side. His heartfelt hug made her feel so much better. He let go of her in time for his eyes to tell her what his mouth couldn't. It was just as Grandpa had said; Liam was in a bad way.

Jenny turned her attention to Liam's broken body. She was in shock. If she didn't already know who he was, she wouldn't have been able to recognize him. His head was completely covered in bandages, and his left arm was broken and hanging from an elevated pulley. His right leg was broken, but the cast was soft and covered in a blood-soaked bandage beginning from his hip and ending at his toes which were scraped and bloodied. What she could see of his face was distorted, and the left cheek seemed to have been shaved raw from hitting the pavement. "What happened?" she asked as if the sight of him wasn't enough of an answer.

"He lost control, Jenny, right before the finish line. It was like April 11th all over again." Jenny looked at Parker in disbelief. He didn't know what to say to her, so instead, he hugged her again before leaving the room, knowing the best thing for her right now was to be alone with Liam.

Liam's bruised eyes were swollen, almost completely hiding the blue that Jenny begged to see. She took a seat next to him and placed her hand over his. There was an unusual tremble in her movement, a nervousness that she wasn't expecting as she faced him. She prayed to God that he would feel her touch through the bandages that concealed his skin and respond but he didn't; his hand remained still. "Liam," she whispered. "It's me, Jenny. Baby, I'm right here. Can you hear me? I love you. I love you so much; I'm so sorry for everything, please don't leave me. You have to get better, you just have to come out of this, please, baby I need you." She begged softly as her eyes never deterred from him. She longed to hear his sweet voice just one more time but the only voice she heard was her own, and it was overshadowed by the incessant beeping of the machines. "Please, baby just open your eyes one time for me, I know you can hear me. I know you're in there. Please wake up." And still, Jenny spoke in vain. The nurse came in several times, but she ignored the nurse's mandate to leave and it became adamantly clear to the staff that she was not leaving unless it was on her terms.

Jenny remained by Liam's side for the next few hours, watching him continuously. She kept her time by telling him stories of the way they used to be and watching to see if there was any movement from him. Her hope was that even though he was unconscious and seemingly unaware of his surroundings, he would recognize her voice, and hear the stories and remember the good times they shared... and possibly could share again. She had one of the nurses bring in a radio so she could play his favorite George Strait songs; and even then, Liam was unresponsive. She fell asleep with her head resting next to his arm. She woke up when she felt the warm touch of a hand on her shoulder.

"Jenny, we have to go. They're not going to let us stay with him."

"I can't leave him, Grandpa."

Grandpa's firm touch remained on her shoulder and reminded her that he wasn't leaving without her. She stood up and leaned closer to Liam's face and whispered softly in his ear before kissing his bandaged head. Almost everywhere she tried; she touched some foreign material that was compromising her ability to actually touch him. She didn't want to touch the bandages or the tubes that were enabling him to live, but she had no other choice. *At least I was here with him and not just imagining his presence the way I had for the past few months.* Grandpa guided her outside and down a corridor that led to a subdued room that allowed the families of critically ill patients to get something to eat or drink or to just take a rest from the nightmare they were experiencing.

"Would you like some coffee?" Grandpa was pouring some for himself.

"No, thank you," Jenny said politely.

Grandpa sat down next to her. She wanted to ask him a million questions but didn't know where to begin, and at this point, she was almost too exhausted to try. But he knew that she needed to talk and was waiting patiently for her to begin. It only took a few minutes before the questions began to pour from her.

"Grandpa, why didn't you call me? I had to hear about this from Johnny."

"Jenny, I'm sorry. I wanted to; believe me, as soon as Parker called me my first thoughts were of you. But to be honest, I didn't know where we stood anymore, hon. It's been a long time since our last talk."

"But I would have thought you would have wanted me here. I needed it to come from you, not Johnny."

"Well, I know and I'm sorry, but that was the other reason. It's no secret that you've been spending a lot of your time with Johnny. It's made Liam think that it's really over between you two. I figured that Johnny would tell you, word around town is you two have been seeing each other. I just didn't think it was my place to call you, anymore."

Jenny was mortified with what she just heard. "Are you kidding? There is nothing going on between Johnny and me. I told Liam when I saw him."

"So the rumors aren't true? I've heard a lot of talk lately that you're at his mother's shop more than you are at your own house. Is that not true?"

"It's not because I'm dating Johnny. His mom offered me a job, that's why I've been there. Listen, it was really hard for me to return home, Grandpa. I didn't hear from Liam after I left town. I love you guys more than anything, but even after my return, I never heard from Liam. I was a complete mess, and Johnny and Gertie knew that. They were worried about me. I wasn't doing anything but staying at my house and sleeping. Gertie offered me a job to keep me busy, to get me out of the house and keep me from becoming even more depressed than I already was. That's all. There's nothing romantic going on between us. I promise, Grandpa."

"Does Johnny think that too?" Grandpa asked with sincere skepticism.

"I know what you're thinking. I know Johnny still cares for me but Grandpa, there's still nothing there for me. He's just turned into a friend and as of late, one of my only friends."

"Jenny, try to see it from my perspective and Liam's, it's like you've taken sides. No matter how sincere and innocent you might think Johnny's gestures are towards you now, there's still a vehement history among the three of you. Liam still can't forgive Johnny. You say you're wondering why you haven't heard from Liam but do you really expect him to call if you're patronizing with the enemy? I must admit it threw me for a loop when I found out where you've been spending your time. It just doesn't seem like you. You had to realize that Liam would find out and that this would hurt him. Why would you do that to him? If you want my opinion, I think you're enjoying this. You like this attention, you liked it before, and you like it now, maybe it's because you're feeling sorry for Johnny and his condition or maybe it's something else, but whatever it is, I think you like it."

"That's not true! I love Liam; he's the only one I care about. But it's Liam who doesn't seem to care about my feelings! He's the one that's changed! I didn't make him race; Toby, Gina, and that guy Aaron Dent did! You don't think that hurts me? And that's exactly why we're here right now, because of his racing and his new friends!"

"I guess there are still a lot of unresolved issues, and I'm really sorry about that, Jenny. I never would have guessed that you and Liam would be so distant from each other. It's just not right, but then again, nothing has made sense lately. I don't want to rehash old wounds, but I think you need to make a choice. Liam thinks you already have and if he makes it out of this, there's a lot you two need to work out. That is if you want to work it out."

"Of course I do Grandpa; I love him."

"I do not doubt your love for him, but you're definitely sending him, and everybody else in this town mixed messages. I know Liam, and I know he hasn't tried to see you because of Johnny. He's been trying his best to clean up his act. It just about killed him that night you left him and mentally, I think he was already gone. But as time went by he knew he had to make a change and one of those changes has been his drinking. He hasn't had a drink for over two months now and as far as the racing is concerned, last night was supposed to be his last race. He left me a note telling me that it was going to end after tonight. He didn't care if he won or not; it didn't matter to him anymore. I don't know if he really meant it, I want to believe he did, but it looks like the choice was made for him when he crashed.

"Jenny, if he comes out of this I don't think he would be able to ride even if he wanted too, he got messed up pretty bad, and the doctor said he will be lucky if he comes out of this walking. He crushed his pelvic bone and both hips, I'm just praying for a miracle for my boy, and I think you should too. I can't tell you what to do. Hell, I don't even know what you want. I'm sorry if I sound offending to you, but my concern lies with my grandson, and not you or your relationship with him. I can't begin to tell you how happy I was to hear of your return, but it's been overshadowed a few times since then; the first time being when you didn't reach out to me. I've told you I would always be here for you, and I meant that; all you had to do was call me, dear and I would have been there for you in a heartbeat. The second and probably the most upsetting to me was when you went to Johnny and his mother for the support you should have been asking for from Liam and me. If you love someone as much as you and Liam say, then you keep fighting, and you don't give up. You don't let your differences get in the way of what's right and what's real. It seems both of you dropped the ball, but I also thought for sure you would have been able to fight a little harder. It seems you gave up when you came back to Spencer, I just hope your choice hasn't sealed your fate. And for what it's worth, I have defended you to Liam on more than one occasion but honestly, girl, I did it with false pretenses from what I've been seeing and hearing."

"But, Grandpa..."

Grandpa held up his hand to interrupt Jenny from finishing. "Jenny, like I said, I'm not here to chastise you, but I've needed to get this off my chest for a while now. Even though this isn't the place or the time, I feel it still needed to be said. You asked me why I never called you about Liam's accident; well I think I've explained my reasoning. I'm glad you're here, and I believe Liam knows you're here too. You were always the one who could reach him, and I hope that still rings true. You once said it was Liam who pulled you out of the darkness when you were slipping away, maybe you can do the same for my boy now. But no matter what, I'm sticking by him, Jenny. I love you, dear, like you were one of my own, but I can't pardon your actions lately. You need to make up your mind. I think you came back thinking the fight was over, but it looks like it's only just begun. I saw Johnny bring you here, and that was a mighty bold act on his and your part. You can't have your cake and eat it too; it just doesn't work that way. My boy's hurt and not just physically. His wounds run deep and some things can't be fixed with a band-aid. I know you're hurting too but the minute you decided to take up your time with the Bryant's was the minute you made your decision. Jenny, you have a passionate heart, and I know you are partially trying to be a friend to someone whose heart isn't healthy but Liam's heart is broken too, and you should have been thinking of his a little more than Johnny's." Grandpa rose from the vinyl sofa and threw away his cold cup of coffee. He didn't even say goodbye to Jenny as he left the room.

Chapter Fourteen
Liam's New Reality

The rain beat steadily on their skin, but it didn't matter, neither one of them were aware of it. They were both too wrapped up in each other's embrace to take notice of the world around them. She lay softly on the ground, her moist legs wrapped around his lower torso. She could hear the beating of his heart take cadence with the beating of the rain. It sent a chill up her spine knowing that it beat for her. He was trying to be gentle with her, but his insatiable passion was overpowering his will to slow the moment down. He wanted her, and more importantly, he needed her. It had been too long for him, and he had missed her too much. He missed her voice, her laughter, her smell, her touch and he missed the feeling when he found himself deeply inside her, loving her the only way he knew how. It pleased him more than anything to see the satisfaction on her face while he continued to move inside her with the ease of a composed dance. All he ever wanted was to make her happy.

She, of course, felt the same for him. She wanted to please him at all times, to satisfy his needs and give him what he desired from her. She exhaled, and became dizzy from his efforts. Nothing felt better than the charge she received when they made love. A feeling that pulsated inside her making her go crazy when he touched her. It was a charge that escalated, a fire that burned deep inside of her that grew when their bodies became one. Then, and only then, did her senses allow her to climax and deliver the pleasures that only he could release from her.

"I love you," he whispered in her ear. His hot breath tickled her making a giggling gasp escape from her lips as the three words rhythmically fell into her ear. He was hovering over her, their bodies kissing each other as they moved together, a dance they had performed a hundred times before but each time was more powerful and poetic than the last. His sweat trickled from him, falling with the rain; the star-lit night illuminated the droplets making them glisten upon her skin like tiny crystals. There were no inhibitions between them. Their love-making was animalistic and yet still sweet and pure mimicking the characteristics of virgins meeting for the very first time.

"I love you too," she whispered back in between staggered and contented breaths. Her pulse was racing as his fingers delicately clutched her body, he moved faster within her, the motions stronger with each thrust, causing them both to peak in unison with each heightened act. As many times as they had made love, she had never grown tired of this. She groaned in complete satisfaction. He could stay here forever. Their eyes locked into each other. She had become greedy when it came to him and grasped him even tighter. Her body was covered in his sweat, and yet it was still parched as it grew thirstier for his touch. "Deeper," she begged. He willingly obliged her sweet command.

He suddenly stopped, causing her to almost go into a euphoric shock, her eyes piercing his, wondering why. He was teasing her. "Do you want me?" He knew the answer but yearned to hear it fall from her perfect lips. He moved one hand down her body until it stopped between her thighs, she trembled with the anticipation, arching her body closer to help him meet his goal.

"Yes." It was only a one syllable word, but it held the power to move mountains for these two lovers who could not get enough of each other.

"I've missed you. I don't ever want us to be apart again," he said.

"Me neither." Her hands found their way to the nape of his neck. His long locks of dirty-blonde hair became tangled in her fingers. The harder he pushed the harder she pulled, his groans telling her that he was happy; but more than that, he was telling her that when he was with her, he was home, where he belonged. Their sensuous acts intensified while they rolled effortlessly on the ground. The wet blades of grass stuck to them, and only after each of them had pleased the other many times over, did they finally give in to their exhausted efforts and fall to each other's side. And even then, though their bodies had separated from being one, they still did not relinquish their touch from each other. Their hands forever entwined.

"I'm never letting you go."

She knew this. "I know. I don't want you to." Her words were serene.

"Can you forgive me?" he asked apologetically.

"Only if you forgive me," she added.

He rolled her on top of him, her auburn hair falling down and kissing his rugged face. "I hated the time we were apart. I don't want us ever to be separated again."

"I was never away from you; I was always in your heart and in your dreams, just like you were for me. That's what kept me going, my love," she said in a beautiful, dulcet tone. "The time we were apart was wasted time, but it made us realize what was important in life. We held too much negative energy towards each other, life is too short for that. I would rather die a thousand deaths than to live a life without you in it."

He brought her even closer to him, holding her porcelain face only inches from his as she sat on top of him, "we'll live together, and we'll die together, that is my promise to you." He brought his lips to hers, molding them once more into hers. She reciprocated as she begged with her body for him to satisfy her needs once more.

"Please," she whispered while she guided his free hand to her area of desire. He fluently took her heed and once again obliged her.

"Is this what you want?"

"Please," she begged again, forcing him inside her where he belonged. "This is exactly what I want." Her voice was exasperated as she sighed in pleasure.

"Your wish is my command, my love. I am only here to please you; my only reason for existence is to fulfill your needs and to make you forever happy," he said.

"As am I, my love. I love you, today, tomorrow and for always." The smile that appeared on his face from hearing those words fall from her sweet mouth only broadened with each breath he took.

"You are my life, my love and my only reason for being, without you I am dead, a body without a soul, you are my essence and the reason why my heart beats." He closed his eyes with those words, the rain continued to fall on them. He thought about his life and how it led to this moment... and he was happy. It didn't matter the mountains he had to move, the valleys he had to tread or the crosses he had to bear, what did matter was that he was with her for now and for always.

Chapter Fifteen
Reality Interrupted

It had been fifty days since the accident. In that time, Jenny had been by Liam's side for forty-nine of them. On day fifty, Liam had begun to show signs of life. Everyone seemed to breathe again, to relax and have hope that the worst was behind him. He had been nothing more than a corpse for the first forty-nine, allowing a machine to breathe for him, sending a false sense of hope to those who cared about him. Nobody wanted to believe that he might not bounce back from this; he was *the* Liam Larson, indestructible and resilient in every sense of those words. But hope was fading those first forty-nine days, and it looked as if the grim reaper was about to pay him a visit. But on day fifty, a Sunday as it turned out, the first day of the New Year, Liam seemed to have his own intentions about breathing life into his stagnant and broken body, and with that, he left the reaper at the doorstep, at least for the time being.

It was gradual, but the first sign of life was the movement of his right forefinger, nothing much in the grand scheme of things but to those concerned, the effort of that small appendage still wrapped in gauze from being broken in two places was monumental. The second, and most assuredly more important was the brief opening of his eyes. It was, of course, a struggle for him not just to open them but to keep them open. They had been soundly closed for forty-nine days... forty-nine days visualizing another world. Perhaps a world he preferred to the one he was now beginning to live in again. And still, the day wasn't over. In his world of darkness, he saw nothing but shadows and forms that made no sense to him, he felt lost and of course, longed to see the one person that had been absent from his side but never from his mind. Jenny was there for him. She had been with him; not just literally, as she remained faithfully by his bedside, but she had been with him in those dark and obscure places between life and death.

The nurse removed the ventilator, and Liam gasped for air like a newborn baby. In that fleeting but instrumental moment, he gave everyone reassurance that he was finally back. All eyes were on him. He looked at his surroundings, puzzled by what he saw. His last memory was not of the accident that he had endured but of Serenity Hill. It was the most sensual and real memory of he and Jenny being together. He could still see them, the vision as clear and vibrant as if it had just happened. *But didn't it?* Even though his body was riddled with a multitude of bandages and tubes, internally he still felt that same carnal charge that he only received when he made love to Jenny, an ache that only Jenny's touch could take away. He knew he didn't just dream it, he felt her, and it couldn't have been just a façade, a reality that didn't exist. They were happy, the way they used to be. His eyes that had suffered the lesser of the evils still had been tarnished with the ill effects of the accident. They were hazed, turning their blue clarity into a grey cloud. *I was confused, not only by my surroundings but by the vision that I thought I was seeing. She looked like the girl I once knew but that time seemed like a lifetime ago for me.* He blinked his lackluster eyes incessantly, trying to make the image in front of him clearer. *Was it Jenny?"*

Liam," she whispered. "It's me, babe." She tried to wipe away the excessive amount of tears that kept falling. She wanted the first time Liam saw her to be as he always remembered her, not this way, with her face red and swollen. Dr. Garrett was checking his vitals while Parker remained close to his friend at the foot of his bed. Everyone carried a weak but still optimistic smile; they had been waiting for this moment since November eleventh.

Liam wanted to speak, he had so much he needed to say; Dr. Garrett put his hand gently on his shoulder. "Liam, you've been in an accident, you've had a tube down your throat for a long time, don't try to speak right now." Liam gave him a very confused and perplexed stare. He looked at his grandpa for answers. He didn't understand what was going on. Grandpa looked back at him, trying to give his grandson the support he needed to see from him.

"I love you, son."

Liam tried to tell him the same, but the pain in his throat was too strong to allow it to come out.

"I think we should let Liam get some rest," Dr. Garrett said. Liam's eyes got wide, he didn't want them to leave, especially Jenny. He tried to make some sort of movement to let them know that he wanted them to stay, his eyes went to Jenny. She tried to give him a comforting look. He tried to speak, but it was in vain. She held tightly to his hand. "What, Liam?" She leaned closer to him, his voice barely audible. "I'm trying to understand you but I just can't. It's all right; you don't have to say anything right now, just rest. You can tell me later." But Liam shook his head. He motioned with his one finger for her to come closer. "I'm here, Liam." He again motioned for her to come even closer. She did as he asked and when she leaned in, she couldn't believe what she heard, *it has to be a mistake* she thought, *I have to be hearing him wrong,* she looked at him once more as he whispered the words again to her.

"Go away," Liam said in an exasperated exhale.

Jenny's head bolted back while her heart sank further than it ever had before. *This can't be...Liam didn't want me. I just couldn't believe it. Nothing mattered anymore or ever would. It was over and obviously it had been for Liam for some time now if that was the first thing he wanted to say upon his awakening.* She ran out of the hospital room knocking the chair she had occupied for the past forty-nine days to the floor. Everyone she passed became a blur to her, pushing them aside, as she ran almost blindly into them. She didn't care; she wanted to get out of that hospital as fast as she could. Parker and Grandpa both ran after her, but they were no match for her newfound strength and speed. She heard them cry out her name, but she ignored their desperate pleas, and not until she had reached the outside did she finally collapse into her grief. She had never felt so alone or heartbroken than at this very moment. Not even Brush Creek Road could compare to the misery she was experiencing now. *He didn't want me, he told me to go away.* She felt abandoned, unloved and unwanted. She thought there would be hope, but all hope had been diminished within those fleeting seconds when Liam opened his mouth. She lay limp in the gravel, praying for some sort of insight that would help her make sense of the tragedy that was unfolding around her. She was in a fetal position when Grandpa Mack found her.

"Jenny." He picked her up. She didn't want his pity or his help and tried to fight him off, trying to wrestle her body free from his grip as he carried her to his truck. He didn't know why but he knew she was hurting and with each comforting word he gave her she threw another hard jab into his chest. He let her. He didn't stop the frenzied madness; he knew she needed to release the anguish that had been pent up inside of her. He gently sat her in the cab of his truck, her arms still flailing while he covered her with a wool blanket.

"Now, now, hon, what happened back there?" he asked in a consoling tone. He had no idea what Liam had said to her. She couldn't speak; all that came out of her were stuttered breaths and whimpering sobs. Grandpa knew something horrible had to have happened to make her lash out like this but for the life of him, he couldn't understand what it could be. His boy finally woke up, this should be a time of celebration, not more heartache and sorrow. "Jenny, please, what happened with Liam to make you this upset?

What did he say to you?" Jenny nodded her head up and down. "What?" he asked sympathetically. She shook her head this time back and forth. She didn't want to say it out loud. "What, Jenny? What did he tell you?"

Jenny looked at Grandpa Mack, her eyes revealing the pain she was feeling. "He told me to go away, Grandpa. He doesn't want me anymore, and it seems you don't want me either. I should have never come home; it's been the worst thing ever for me."

"Jenny, you are wanted. I still love you, hon I'm just disappointed in how things have been. You can't expect me to be happy. The two people who mean the most to me have been acting ridiculous, and that's the God's honest truth. I've never seen two people more in love than you and Liam and instead of trying to work it out together, both of you would rather do it alone. It doesn't work that way. You're both so damn stubborn. I don't understand why you went to Johnny. I'm being honest about how I feel."

"I never went to them! I told you! I waited for Liam, but when he didn't call me I couldn't bring myself to come to you or him! I was afraid that he didn't want me and I guess I had reason to be scared. He just told me to go away! Grandpa, I never…oh why am I even bothering? I've already tried to explain this to you and Liam, but it hasn't mattered."

Grandpa tried to bring her to him, but she fought him off again. She wasn't feeling the love from him anymore. Right now she felt completely unloved; more than she ever had in her entire life. She wanted her dad to hold her and to tell her that everything was going to be okay. She wanted his arms wrapped securely around her trembling body. The last place she wanted to be was with Grandpa. She didn't want to listen to his words of advice; all she could think of was Liam telling her to go away. Those two words screamed inside of her as they ripped her heart out. She knew she couldn't stay here any longer; she bolted from Grandpa's truck and ran into the night. Grandpa was yelling for her to stop but the attempt was in vain, she never looked back.

****

After that night, Jenny wasn't seen by anyone. And to make matters worse, Liam slipped back into his coma. The momentary consciousness he had was brief and unexpected, he was already out of it by the time Grandpa Mack returned to his room. Dr. Garrett had no explanation for it and gave no answers to when or if he would ever wake up again. Grandpa Mack was beside himself with worry not only for Liam but about how he treated Jenny. He tried numerous times to call her and even enlisted the help of Kendra and Parker to try and reach out to her, but Jenny was not to be found. It was if she just disappeared off the face of the planet.

****

The month of January was hell for all those who were worried about Liam. Aaron Dent had been a regular visitor to the hospital, but as far as Toby and Gina, they had given up on Liam almost from the beginning. Toby saw his business opportunity with Liam die the night of November 11th. Once the prognosis seemed doomed, Toby cut his ties with both Liam and Aaron.

Grandpa hoped that by February, there would be some positive change in Liam's condition, but to his dismay, there hadn't been. The hospital halls that used to be packed with concerned well-wishers had all but disappeared; they too had realized what seemed to be the inevitable and moved on with their own lives.

Dr. Garrett considered what his next option for Liam should be. His vitals were stable, and his body was healing but still, he was puzzled about why Liam had not emerged from his unconscious state. By all accounts, he should be awake. All indications led the medical staff to believe this, but it was as if he was being held prisoner by unseen forces that were beyond the doctor's expertise.

It had been eighty-three days since the accident and thirty-two days since the last time anyone had seen Jenny. Nothing made sense to anyone anymore, and for the most part, most of the people concerned were letting fate decide if Jenny and Liam would ever be together again.

Even Johnny had begun to move on, too. His heart took a turn for the worse and now his focus was on himself. He was at the hospital almost on a daily basis. He didn't have the energy to think about Jenny and why she left again. Of course, he did think about her, but it was just memories now and not of the hope of what could be. His efforts were spent trying to live in the present and not live in the past. Although his heart would always belong to her, he couldn't live in that fantasy world any longer. It was obvious to him that no amount of effort on his part would ever change her feelings for Liam.

Even Gertie realized that her efforts were futile. Her little attempt to keep Jenny near Johnny had backfired. *I wondered if I was losing my touch, my edge, my intuition muddled. But my thoughts were of my son, he was dying, and that took precedence over everything else in my life.* She knew Jenny's fate had been sealed; it had been for some time. She knew what waited for Jenny and Liam, but she didn't want to tell her for fear it would scare her. She knew, as she always knew that these two lovers who had been torn apart almost from the beginning would learn about their destiny in their own time without the help of her gift.

Grandpa Mack and Parker continued to be regulars at the hospital. Occasionally, a friend from the past like Joe and even Kendra would come by. Aaron Dent though, had come to the conclusion that at this point, if Liam did wake up, he may never be the same. The future he'd planned for his new superstar seemed to be over. He made the decision, like so many others before him, that it was time for him to move on.

****

Dr. Garrett walked into the room where he found Liam's grandpa sitting solemnly in a faded vinyl chair next to the window. It had been Grandpa's spot since Liam had taken residence there. He was staring intently outside while the rain beat steadily on the window pane. He seemed mesmerized as it pelted down at a horizontal angle making beautiful patterns form on the glass. He was in his own little world. He knew this talk with Dr. Garrett was coming, and now, with it only moments away, Grandpa Mack sipped his coffee frequently, though he wasn't thirsty, but realizing he needed something in his hands to keep them from shaking. Dr. Garrett pulled up a chair next to Grandpa. Together, they took in a deep breath.

"Mack."

"Doc."

The doctor looked down at the floor. He had been friends with Mack Larson for most of his life, and he knew Liam since the day he was born. He had given this talk a hundred times before to grieving families, but this impending conversation seemed to be the hardest of all, taking a toll on the doctor. His personal feelings were overriding his professional judgment and the words he spoke had to be tactful but still respectful. "Mack, I have looked at Liam's charts more times than I can count, and I just don't understand why he's not waking up. By all accounts, he should have woken up weeks ago. His vitals are stable, and his wounds are healing; even his pelvic bone is almost healed. I was hoping that at this point, Liam would be in physical therapy but he's not, and there's just no explanation for it. Mack, you are a friend of mine, and I have taken a personal and vested interest in Liam's case, so, what I am about to say, doesn't come easy. But I believe that what I'm about to tell you I would do if it was a member of my own family, and with that, I hope you know that this is coming from my heart and I have exhausted all other avenues. This is all I have left to offer you. I'm sorry, Mack."

"So, what are you trying to tell me, Doc?"

"I think we need to think about our next step."

"And what would that be?"

"We've done all we can. There's a facility near Charleston that specializes in cases like Liam's. He would receive outstanding care there and when and if he wakes up..."

"If he wakes up? You don't think he's going to wake up, Doc?" Dr. Garrett just looked away hoping he wouldn't have to answer the obvious. "Well, Doc?" Grandpa insisted.

"I don't know, Mack. Like I said, he should be awake right now talking to us, but he's not, and I don't know why. It's beyond my medical training. I've consulted with doctors all across the country, and there's nothing new they can tell me. He hit his head hard in that accident, and the brain is a complex and mysterious organ, it will heal in its own good ole' time, not mine or yours."

"Dammit, Doc, stop talking to me like you're the damn grim reaper or somethin'! Liam is a strong boy, and there's nothing that's going to keep him down. He is going to wake up! He's going to make it through this, and he's going to do it without the help of some old folks rest home that you want to put him in! You're his doctor, and I expect you to live up to the oath you made when you went to school! I need you to help my grandson, Doc, not someone else." Grandpa stood up and pointed his finger directly into Dr. Garrett's face. "You can't weasel your way out of this. Liam is going to get better, and he's going to do it with the help of you, do you understand me?"

"But, Mack..."

"There's no ifs, ands, or buts about it, I won't hear of it."

Dr. Garrett knew not to press the issue anymore; he stood up and put his hand on Grandpa's shoulders. "Okay, Mack. I just wanted to let you know about your options, but if you don't want to hear them, then I won't waste any more of your time or mine. I will help Liam." Dr. Garrett thought he could see a tear trickle down the old man's face. In the fifty plus years he had known the man, he had seen him cry on only two other occasions; when he lost his daughter and then when he lost his wife. He was known to keep his emotions to himself unless it concerned his family. He hugged Grandpa as Grandpa reciprocated it with a stronger one.

"Thank you, Doc. I know you can help him, I have faith in you. I know my boy will wake up, I just know it."

Chapter Sixteen
Day Eighty-Three

    It was almost nine o'clock when Grandpa raised himself from his seated position. He scooted the worn blue chair that he had occupied over the last eighty-three days back to its original position. He was tired; Dr. Garrett's conversation from earlier in the day had been weighing heavily on his mind. He looked down at his grandson who seemed to be sound asleep instead of in the stupor that didn't want to release him. Liam's body was resting comfortably under the three blankets that were protecting him. Grandpa had hope that it was only a matter of time. *I wished to God that he could just say my name and my boy would hear my voice and open his eyes. If only it could be that easy.*   "Good night son, I love you, I'll see you bright and early tomorrow morning." He talked to him like Liam could actually hear what he was saying. He bent down and kissed Liam on the forehead, squeezing his hand tightly but still with a gentle touch. He was about to let go when he thought he felt something, a movement of some sort but as he stared intently at his grandson's hand, there was nothing. Grandpa rationalized he was more tired than he realized and quickly dismissed his arbitrary thought. Again, he went to let go of Liam's hand only to feel the same pressure. He turned to look again, knowing for certain that he didn't imagine this a second time. He watched carefully at Liam's hand, and as if in slow motion, he saw his prayers being answered right before him. Liam ever so slightly squeezed on his grandpa's pinky. "Oh my God, Liam. Can you hear me?"

"Grandpa." His voice was weak, and the word barely escaped from Liam's mouth.

"Liam! I'm right here. I'm right here, son." Grandpa could hardly contain his emotions.

Liam slowly opened his eyes, one at a time and turned them to the male voice he heard. "Grandpa?"

"Yes, son, it's me, I'm right here."

"Grandpa." The voice was raspy, and Grandpa could tell that it still hurt for Liam to talk.

"Don't try to say too much."

"Where am I?"

"You're in the hospital. Don't you remember?"

"No."

"Do you remember the accident, son?" Grandpa tried to jolt Liam's memory.

"No. What accident, Grandpa?"

Before Grandpa went into detail about the accident, he called for Dr. Garrett. The look on Dr. Garrett's eyes and the nurses who followed, were of sheer shock and disbelief as they examined Liam. In the far corner, Grandpa could not help but release his emotions as he thanked God for saving his boy.

"How is he, Doc?" Grandpa asked with a reserved excitement.

"It's a miracle, Mack, I just can't believe it, and I have no explanation for it, but this was an act of God. He's going to be fine. Your boy has beaten the odds once again." Dr. Garrett was smiling from ear-to-ear. "You knew. You knew all along this day was coming, and it's finally here." Dr. Garrett gave Grandpa a hug and walked out the door, the two nurses, who were just as excited and in shock followed suit carrying the same smiles.

Grandpa went to his grandson and held his hand tightly in his. The two men, stared at each other with the same blue eyes conveying more than any words could express. But Grandpa knew that Liam had questions, and so he spent the next hour explaining to Liam what had happened to him and why he had been in the hospital for the last three months. But for all the questions that Liam should have asked, he only produced one for his Grandpa: "Where's Jenny?"

Grandpa Mack didn't answer him immediately. He didn't know what to say. He didn't know where she was. He called her parents and had looked high and low for her to no avail. Nobody had seen her, and that was the mystery. "I don't know, Liam." He could see the disappointment in Liam's eyes.

"What do you mean? I saw her; I remember seeing her sitting next to my bed. You can't tell me I dreamed that?"

"No, you didn't. Jenny was here, Liam. She had been here from the very beginning but do you remember talking to her that one time you woke up?"

"I thought it was part of my dream, I told her not to go away. I was so happy to see her. I couldn't believe she was here, after everything that had happened between us I couldn't believe she was next to me. Everything felt so right, like it used to be. Grandpa, I did talk to her right before the race, and we still left things unresolved."

"You told her not to leave?" Grandpa seemed confused.

"Yes. Why, Grandpa?"

"Because, Liam, I don't think that's what she heard. She ran out of here that night in a hysterical fit. I couldn't imagine what you had said to her, but I think I understand now."

"What do you mean?" Liam's voice was cracking from the strain he was putting on it.

"Well, when I finally got her to talk to me she told me that you told her to go away. It just about killed her, Liam."

"No, Grandpa, I was so happy to see her. Can you bring her back to me? I have to let her know that's not what she heard."

"I wish I could, son, but I can't."

"Why?"

"I don't know where she is. I told you. I really don't have any idea where she went, nobody does. Everybody's been looking for her. I even called her parents, but they haven't seen her since she left last Fall. I don't even know where to look anymore, Liam. I'm sorry, I'm truly, truly sorry."

The sincerity in Grandpa's voice told Liam that he was telling the truth. Liam turned his head away. He was being dealt a lot since awakening, and he really didn't want to think about anything anymore. He closed his eyes, this time on his own accord. He recalled the dream where he was with Jenny again. The way it was supposed to be for them. He wanted to will himself back to that place again. When he was dreaming, he was happy, and that's exactly how he wanted to feel again. He wanted her scent surrounding him, and he wanted to feel her skin against his once more.

****

The next month was met with a barrage of emotions for Liam and his grandpa. Not only was Dr. Garrett and the rest of the medical staff fairly convinced that Liam's awakening was nothing short of a miracle but Liam himself was making great strides in getting better. With the help of his therapist and his trusty cane, he was learning to walk again. The first weeks found him wanting to give up and give in, but by the third week of February, Liam had found a new confidence to continue to improve. He was determined to walk out of the hospital on his own two feet without the help of the staff or a wheelchair. He had a mission and to accomplish that mission, he had to be able to walk on his own. So he continued with a fervent perseverance. He was inundated with visitors, all of them happy to see the once all-American boy spring back to life; even Coach Green and his wife paid him a visit. Liam even received a phone call from Jenny's parents. It almost killed him to talk to them. They were sincere and spoke of how happy they were to hear the news of his recovery but how sad they were about not hearing from Jenny.

That mystery was what kept Liam going. *I was determined to find her. She came back to me and once again, I let her slip through my fingers, I'm never going to let that happen again. I am ready to let my demons go once and for all. Whatever the future holds, I want to meet it with her by my side. I have to find her, that's all there is to it.*

By month's end, Liam was walking almost as well as before. The limp that lingered from the April 11th accident was now enhanced with a stronger stagger in his gait, but it was something Liam had become accustomed to.

"You are doing amazing," Grandpa said as he watched his son during his therapy session.

"I'm trying."

The nurse walked in to hand Liam his pain medication. "I don't want it," he said pushing the pills away.

"It's doctor's orders," the nurse said with insistence.

"No, thank you." Liam was becoming annoyed with her persistence. He tried to tell her again, this time in a more civil tone. "Really, I don't want them, but thank you."

She left in a huff leaving the medication with Grandpa. "You know, son, she's only trying to do her job. There's no need to get upset with her. You need to take your medicine."

"No, I don't. I'd rather feel the pain."

Grandpa knew when to quit trying. "Well, it looks like you're doing fine but if I were you, I would still take the medicine, instead of trying to be so bull-headed." Liam didn't respond, he just kept concentrating on his exercises. "Well, I think I'm going back to the farm and finish some work. You're not the only one with a bum leg. I need to take Sugar Dumplin' back to the vet. Her back leg is bothering her again."

"Is she okay?" Liam asked. Liam had always seen Sugar Dumplin' as Jenny's horse. The horse had taken to Jenny from the very beginning, and that was the only reason why Grandpa kept her. That horse loved Jenny, and she hadn't been the same since she left. There was no way Grandpa or Liam were getting rid of her.

"Yeah, she just needs some tendin' too, that's all. I'll be back later, son." Grandpa hugged Liam harder than usual. He knew how close he was to losing him, and he wasn't going to take for granted the opportunity he was given to have him back.

Liam continued his exercises for the next hour on his own, when he was done, he walked down the long corridor that led back to his room. On his way, he heard a familiar voice. When he turned the corner, he saw none other than Johnny Bryant talking to Dr.

Thompson. Johnny glanced in his direction as Liam passed him.

"Liam, wait up!" Johnny yelled. Liam didn't want to stop. "Liam, wait up!" Johnny yelled again. Liam had turned the corner by this time and disappeared down the hallway. Johnny didn't see him anywhere.

The next day, Liam had his therapy session at the same time and upon leaving he again passed Johnny. Liam rushed past him hoping Johnny wouldn't see him, but he did, and again, Johnny tried to catch up with him. Liam had become good at this new cat and mouse game they were playing and once more avoided a confrontation with his nemesis. By day three, Johnny had taken the upper hand and waited in the wings for Liam to finish his therapy session. By the time Liam made it to his room, Johnny was already there. Liam sat in the chair that faced the window and made himself comfortable. He was unaware that Johnny was only a few feet away, waiting patiently for him in the darkened corner. He walked slowly to his side. The cadence of Johnny's footsteps made Liam turn quickly towards the sound.

"So, this is what you are rushing back to when you leave therapy?" Johnny's voice said from behind Liam. "Hello, Liam." Johnny pulled up a chair and sat down next to him.

"What are you doing here?" Liam's cynicism was quite apparent to Johnny, but that's what he had come to expect from his one-time friend.

"Well, I thought it was time we had a talk."

"I don't have anything to say to you, Johnny."

"Oh, I would beg to differ. I think we have a lot to talk about."

Liam scooted his chair closer to the window and farther away from Johnny. He tried to cross his legs only to have an immediate pain shoot through his thigh. He carefully put his leg back down, grimacing from it.

"How are you doing?" Johnny asked.

"I'm fine."

"Look, Liam, my intentions were never to see you again. I think we both know how we feel about each other, and I'm fine with that, but when I saw you, I figured what the hell. I'm really sorry about your accident, and for what it's worth, I'm glad you're getting better. From what I heard, it was touch-and-go for you for a while."

"Like I said, I'm fine, couldn't be doing better," Liam said with even more cynicism and a touch of arrogance.

Johnny overlooked his behavior. "I need to talk to you about Jenny."

Liam gave Johnny a dirty look. "I'm sure you do, I bet she's always on your mind."

"Maybe, she is, but that's not why I'm here."

"I've talked to her, Liam, not recently of course, since nobody can seem to find her but a lot before your accident."

"I guess you did, especially since she was at your mom's shop so much. You guys must have gotten really close."

"Okay, that's fair, still a cheap shot, but fair. I deserve that. I've been able to talk to her a lot, but it's only because she didn't have anyone else to talk to. She would have much rather been talking to you, but you didn't seem to have the balls to call her up."

"You bastard, how dare you say that to me! It's none of your damn business if and when I talk to her! What are you doing here anyway? Just leave me the hell alone!"

"I'm not leaving until we talk this out. This conversation is long overdue, and I'm staying until we talk or fight it out. Your choice, Liam but either way, we're going to get some things settled between us." Liam gave him a glaring look. He turned his chair one hundred eighty degrees away from Johnny. "My God, Liam are you going to be so childish with me that you can't even face me? What happened to us? We used to be good friends, really good. Are you willing to throw that away without at least trying to fix this? Don't you think it's been long enough? What went so wrong?"

"You know damn well what went wrong, Johnny. If you would have just kept to yourself instead of trying to take the only thing that ever meant a goddamn thing to me, then we wouldn't be enemies right now. It's your fault that Jenny and I aren't together. You need to own up to that."

"Are you really going to place all the blame on me? I'll admit that I shouldn't have gone after her but God, Liam, you have to blame yourself for at least a part of this mess. I didn't drive you to drink or to hook up with Toby and Gina. And I certainly didn't make you sign your life away for some stupid adulation and attention. And then you're given a second chance when she comes back, and you decide it's better to be Aaron Dent's latest puppet. That was you and all you, and that's why Jenny left again. The racing is what took Jenny's place, and you totally lost sight of her. You were so hell-bent on proving your self-worth that you lost sight of her. She was always there for you and she always loved you. No matter how hard I tried to convince her otherwise; and believe me, I've tried, she still didn't give a damn about anybody but you. It's always been you. She came back because of you. She loves you, Liam and she's been waiting for you to come for her."

"If that's the case then, why in the hell was she spending all her time with you?"

"She was lonely, and she felt like there was no hope. My mom felt sorry for her, and she offered Jenny a job to keep her busy. That's all there was to it. She was spending every waking hour alone in that house, and if you weren't so wrapped up in your new life, you would have seen that. Hell, Liam, I was just trying to be a friend to her. She came back here for you. And you know, if you weren't going to be there, I was. I was willing to give her that shoulder to lean on."

"I'm sure that's not all you were willing to give her."

"You know you're one damn lucky man, and you don't even know it. You had everything right there for you and you didn't even see it because of all your bullshit. You're goddamn right I was willing to give her what I had to offer, she already knew that I loved her, but she didn't love me, can't you get that through your thick skull. You're making this about you and me when it isn't. Liam, I don't have the time to waste on this. I want her to be happy, and that's why I'm here. She needs you, and I know you need her." Liam remained quiet. "Listen, I don't know what else you have to prove or what this is about anymore. But if it's about the demons in your past or the drinking or the racing or something else that I don't even know about, you just need to go to her and let her help you. That's all she ever wanted… to be there for you. Stop shutting her out before it's too late." Johnny didn't know that Liam had already started letting go of those demons, that he did want her back, and he was ready to find her no matter what.

"Before it's too late?"

"Yes, before it's too late. The last time I talked to her, I got the impression that she wasn't planning on staying in Spencer much longer. It just about killed her to find out about your accident. It was bad enough when she learned you were racing on the eleventh and on Ripley Road, but then you had to go and get hurt again. Did you know I was the one who brought her here to see you? Isn't that proof enough to you that I'm willing to give up the fight?"

Liam looked away from Johnny. "Liam, this little disappearing act of hers may have been her last one. It might already be too late. I told you she didn't feel wanted here anymore." Johnny waited for Liam to say anything that would make him think that he had ignited some sort of spark inside of him to make him realize just how dire the situation really was. "Liam, do you want Jenny back?"

"Of course I do. You know she came to me before the race and told me everything you're telling me now. I wanted to tell her okay, but at the time, it wasn't that easy for me. I still felt ashamed. I thought she would be better off without me, and to be honest, when I heard she was seen at your mom's shop, I thought maybe the decision had been made. I love her, Johnny, more than my own life but I'm not the same guy, and I'm not the guy that everyone looked up to in high school. To be brutally honest with you, I still can't get over what you did for her. You will always be known as the hero, and I will always be known as the boy who almost killed her. Do you know how that makes me feel? I promised her I would always be there for her, to protect her and take care of her and I couldn't do it. I feel like I failed her in so many ways. It's an awful feeling. I feel like the race still isn't over, and it won't be until I cross the finish line. That's why I did the race, and that's why I wanted it to be against you. But I couldn't do it and maybe I never will. It's just not in the cards for me; it's just another failure I can add to my long list."

"So, that's it?"

"Listen, I don't need you to tell me how to run my life. Did you forget that you're part of the reason why my life is ruined? I don't need you in it anymore. Understand?" Liam stood up causing his leg to almost buckle beneath him. "Either you go, or I go but, either way, one of us is leaving this room. This isn't over between us no matter what you say. I'm really sorry, man, about your heart and it sucks but our friendship is dead." Liam hesitated, "You know, I tried to see you last summer. You were here in the hospital, and I actually made it all the way to the parking lot, but I just couldn't bring myself to come in. Your mom found me sitting in my truck, and she did her best to convince me to come in. I couldn't then and I still don't care to see you now. I'm sorry man, but you need to stay out of my life; and for what it's worth, I'd appreciate it if you would stay out of Jenny's life too. I don't care if you're just trying to be a friend or not. You can't fool me, Johnny; I'm sure even this little stunt of showing up now is for her benefit, to show her that you're above the bullshit that's going on between us."

"Whatever, Liam. Don't bother about leaving, you stay, and I'll go. I came, and I tried. You go ahead and think what you want. But just one more word of advice from someone you used to call a friend. Jenny may love you with everything she's made of, but if you're not willing to show her how much you love her, you're going to lose her, and if you're not careful you may have already; and this time, it will be forever. I heard the finality in her voice, she's ready to end this, she's tired of the drama. You can't expect her to keep waiting for you to solve your problems, life's way too short for that, take that from someone who knows. Remember, actions speak louder than words." Johnny began to walk away but turned once more to face Liam. "I just have one more question to ask you?"

"What is it?" Liam asked despondently. "Has it been worth it?"

"Huh? What the hell do you mean?"

"Your racing, this whole thing with Aaron Dent, has it been worth it? Was it worth losing everything to make a name for yourself?" Liam didn't answer. "I didn't think so." With that, Johnny walked out of Liam's room and Liam hoped Johnny walked out of his life forever and hopefully, out of Liam's life forever.

Chapter Seventeen
Finding His Religion

Liam sat on the floral sofa in his living room and watched Grandpa tending to Sugar Dumplin' in the field. She was still favoring her one leg, and Grandpa was helping the Tennessee Walker back to her stall. The horse missed Jenny. Liam knew exactly how the horse felt. He sat still and unwrapped the soft cast from his leg. Dr. Garrett had given him orders to wear it for the next month, but as usual, Liam wasn't one to follow protocol. He didn't see the need for it when he was able to get along just fine without it. To him, the brace was just a bunch of nonsense that he felt Dr. Garrett needed to enforce. Of course, without the cast, his leg bothered him more but Liam was happy to experience the pain, it reminded him of what happened, and he didn't want to forget. He looked up to see Grandpa give a wave. Apparently, someone had come to pay them a visit. Within a few minutes, Grandpa walked in with Aaron Dent.

"Look who I found outside, Liam."

Liam rose slowly from his seated position to greet him. "Hello, Aaron." Liam extended him his hand.

"It's good to see you, Liam. I must say you look 111% percent better than the last time I saw you. I hate to admit it, but I really didn't think I would ever be talking to you again."

"Well, I think most people would agree with you. I guess someone was looking out for me."

"You can say that again. I'm glad to see you on your feet."

"Aaron, I need to get back to work but can I offer you something to drink before I go?" Grandpa asked cordially.

"No, but thank you. I really can't stay long; I just wanted to talk to Liam before I head back to Ohio." Grandpa shook Aaron's hand graciously but gave Liam a troubled look before exiting the room. Liam and Aaron both sat down.

"So, to what do I owe this visit?" Liam asked. "I must be honest, Aaron, I didn't think I would hear from you again. I know Toby has written me off and from what Grandpa gathered, I thought you had too."

"I know Liam, and I'm sorry, but you've got to understand that I don't make money unless my drivers are healthy; and well, like I said before, I didn't think I would see you anymore. You were in really bad shape there for a while, I know even the doctors were ready to write you off. I just figured that I should give your Grandpa some peace and just leave. I know he has always felt that I've taken you away from him. Hell, I'm sure he blames me for the accident. But I'm not here to hash up the past, I'm here on business. I won't beat around the bush, Liam; when I heard that you were out of the hospital, I was ecstatic. You have been my best driver since I took you on last year, and I don't want to let you go. There's a bunch of races coming up in the next month throughout the tri-state area, and I think it would be great practice for you and help prepare you for what I'm really here for."

"And what would that be?" Liam asked warily.

"Ever since you told me about the race between you and Johnny Bryant, I haven't been able to get it out of my mind. You know my hope was that he would have raced you last November, and since it didn't happen, I think it's time we try again. Correct me if I'm wrong but the two year anniversary is just over a month away, I think it is fate that you had the accident in November. I think you were meant to do this particular race on the actual date."

"What?" Liam blurted out. "Aaron, there's no way in hell. I do not want to do that race on that road ever again. It's over. I'm coming to grips with that and learning to live with the fact that maybe some races aren't meant to be won or even finished. That race has caused me so much heartache, and ever since I got out of the hospital, I've been making peace with my past so I can move on with my future. I lost myself and even more importantly, my girl, over it, and my only intentions now are to find her and win her heart back. I'm not going to chance losing her again just so you can make a couple of bucks off of me. There's just no way in hell I'll do it. Let me save you the trouble of trying to convince me, my answer is no!"

"Liam, I don't have to convince you. I own you right now," Aaron said malevolently, "or have you forgotten? You signed a contract with me, and you have to abide by it. Maybe you didn't read the fine print or don't remember it, but I didn't come here to ask you, I came here to tell you. You need to get back on your bike and start practicing."

"My bike was totaled, Aaron."

"I have other bikes you can ride. Your grandpa told me that aside from being stiff and sore and your bum leg, you're pretty much back to your old self. I'll give you a few more days to rest up, but I want you at Toby's training facility by next Monday, no excuses, Liam. I've already spoken with Toby, and he's agreed to help out again, he's expecting you. That gives us three weeks to get you back on the racing circuit and almost a month to get ready.

This will happen, and I want it to be against Johnny." Liam looked at Aaron mortified; he couldn't believe what he was hearing. "Don't worry about Johnny, it's going to happen. That race is all I've heard about since I signed you on. It's like some kind of an urban legend around here. It's going to be a huge money maker for me, and I have people interested in watching you as far away as Georgia. If they like you, then the sky's the limit, not just for you but for me too. And furthermore, don't worry about the bike, you'll be racing your truck; I want this race to be identical to the first one, authentic all the way down to the last detail. That's why it has to be against Johnny. I've already contacted Joe, and he's agreed to help too."

"But Johnny can't race, he's sick."

"Yeah, I heard, he's got a bad heart or something, but I also know that he's not dead yet, and he's not an invalid. Look, everyone knows your history with him and Jenny, I'm sure he would like to get this resolved just as much as anybody, plus money talks." Liam had never heard Aaron speak with such callousness, it was as if he either raced or he died trying but, either way, he wasn't letting him get out of it. "And furthermore, don't try and get all high and mighty on me and think since you got hurt you won't be able to do this one. You will Liam, and I expect you to win. I'm not willing to accept sponsoring a second place finisher, especially with your background." Aaron stood up and adjusted his worn out baseball cap, he perused his surroundings for the first time since he had come in; he nodded his head in approval to what he saw. "You've got a real nice place here." He then proceeded to walk over to the fireplace and look at the numerous pictures that graced the mantel. He picked up the one that was of Liam and Jenny. "My, my, if she's not a vision, Liam. I'd go crazy too if she was out of my life. I can see why you're so in love with her; she'd keep my head spinning too." He held the picture and faced Liam. "Do it for her, Liam, win this one for your girl."

Aaron was always a polite gentleman to whomever he met. It was only after you got to really know him that you found out what a complete jackass he was and how he had no regard for anyone except himself. That's why he had been so successful. Liam watched Aaron exit his house and shake Grandpa's hand before leaving their premises. Grandpa knew what kind of snake Aaron was and wished to God Almighty that he had interceded before Liam had signed his life away to the Devil himself. Liam knew he couldn't get out of this, his mind starting clicking when he realized what he had to do. He picked up his phone and began dialing.

"Hey, I need to talk to you, can we meet somewhere? It's really important. Great, I'll see you there."

Liam left his house with a heavy heart. *I knew I couldn't get out of this race and furthermore, I began to realize that my chances of ever seeing Jenny again were becoming slim to none. There was no way in hell she would approve of this race. I looked over at the empty seat next to me, I missed her so much. I grabbed the bandana that was hers. I kept it in the truck so for these times when she wasn't' with me; I could still take it and smell her sweet scent. I should have listened to her when she came to see me before the race.* He pulled into the high school parking lot and waited patiently, within minutes, he saw the white Bronco turn the corner and come to a stop next to his. Johnny gave a nod to Liam, and both of them got out of their vehicles.

"Hello, Johnny."

"Hello, Liam," Johnny responded back. "So, Liam I must say I was pretty shocked when you called me. What's this about?"

Liam was chewing on a piece of straw. "Why don't we take a walk?"

They walked in silence up the hill that led to the football bleachers. "I haven't been here in a long time," Johnny said.

"Me neither," Liam added sitting down. The field was empty on this cold, March evening. It felt weird for Liam to look at the field. He kept imagining his high school days when his world seemed so simple. He also remembered seeing Jenny as she lay on the turf after the team had almost trampled her and how beautiful she looked as he lent her his hand to help her up.

"Liam, is everything okay? I mean why did you want to meet with me?"

"Tell me something, Johnny are you a religious man?"

"Huh?" Johnny asked confused.

"I mean, do you believe in fate, destiny, that things happen for a reason?"

"I don't know, I guess I do. I almost have to with my mom. She believes in all that kind of shit. Why do you want to know?"

"Well, I never did believe in religion. I guess I kind of lost my faith after my parents died and then my grandmother. I didn't understand why God took them away from me, and I carried a lot of resentment against Him for that. I was six at the time, and I have to tell you, that's a lot for a little boy of that age to endure. And then as I got older, I tried to find my faith but I still couldn't. Grandpa did his best with me, you know he did what any Elder does for their children, he took me to church every Sunday, I went to church camp; hell, I was even in the church plays and sang in the choir. But I was only going through the motions; you know, none of it meant a damn to me. I did it because I was trying to make my grandpa happy. He was so worried about me; he didn't know what to do for me. It didn't even matter that he was grieving too; hell, he lost his only daughter and his wife, but he put all his focus on me. I was, and still am, his only concern. He knew I was suffering, and he thought by taking me to church and trying to teach me that there is still good in the world that it would eventually sink in and I would feel better. But I still had no faith. I just couldn't believe in something that was so willing to take my everything away and rip my world in two. It just seemed hypocritical for me to believe in that stuff. It wasn't until Grandpa got me involved in pee-wee football that it started to make sense to me. I loved it so much. It took my mind off of my reality and allowed me to hit people without getting into trouble," Liam said with a slight chuckle. Johnny remained quiet letting Liam continue without interruption. "I felt alive for the first time since my parents' death. And Grandpa saw a big change in me. I started talking and laughing and looking forward to the next day. I couldn't wait to get back out there and play more ball, it was all I thought about."

"I remember, Liam. We used to play a lot of pee-wee ball together as kids. That's how we first met."

"Yeah, I know. You were this scrawny little kid from Walton. I didn't even know where Walton was but man, I thought the best football players came from there, you were that good. I used to think that Walton must be some sort of place where the football gods lived. I guess that's why we hit it off so well when we were young, we both loved the game."

"Well, you were pretty good yourself, Liam and if I remember my history correct, you turned out to be one of the best damn football players this entire State has ever seen. I had nothing on you. You know all people have to do is say football and your name pops up, it's pretty much synonymous with the game."

"Well, maybe a few years ago but not anymore." Liam touched his bum leg. "I've never told anyone this, Johnny, but you're the reason why I worked so hard to be so good."

"What?"

"Yes, it's true. I was so afraid that I could never compare with your skills, that's why I worked out so diligently, I had to be better than you even back then." Liam sighed heavily. "And I guess I'm still trying to be better than you."

"Liam that's all water under the bridge."

"Is it? We used to be the best of friends and now we're known as enemies, and we're still competing, maybe not for the game anymore but for something that's a whole hell of a lot more important. And that's why I asked you if you were a religious man. Like I said, once football came into my life I thought I found my religion, I found something to live for or at least, I thought I did, until August 11th."

"What happened on August 11th?"

"That's when I first saw Jenny and to be honest when I fell in love with her."

"Oh." Johnny finally realized where this conversation was going.

"I fell head over heels in love with her, and I didn't even know her. Isn't that one of the craziest things you've ever heard? It was insane. I didn't know what had taken over me, all I could think about was her, and that's all that ever mattered, even then, before we met, I knew we would be together, it was like some sort of damn epiphany for me. Hell, we had been going to school since kindergarten, but I never noticed her until that day. I thought I was going to throw up when I saw her," Liam said with that same slight chuckle.

"And then I thought I would never be able to talk to her. I didn't think anyone that beautiful would want anything to do with someone like me. But I was willing to find out, to take that risk. I had to know for sure, I could hardly concentrate on anything, especially football, so I had to find out before the coach kicked me off the team." Liam chuckled again at his own expense. "So finally, after a couple of months of pure misery and some pushing from

Parker and Tony, I got my nerve up. It was hard in the beginning; she didn't want anything to do with me. But I persevered, and I never gave up, I just knew we were meant to be together and finally, we were. It was the best damn feeling ever. I didn't know what my life had been missing until she entered it. She filled that void that had been missing since I was a little kid and it was only after we were together that I began to have real faith again. I didn't hate God anymore. I remember thinking that maybe he was just waiting to show me what I needed in my life. I knew from the very beginning that I would marry her. I can't explain it except that it was fate or if you were to ask Jenny, Kismet. We were so happy, and everything seemed so perfect. I finally began to believe that I was allowed to feel something more in life than the anger and sadness I usually felt."

"But you seemed to be having a pretty good life in high school. I remember us having some great times," Johnny said.

"Yeah, I guess, but none of that meant anything to me. It was just shallow feelings that covered up a lot of pain. I learned at a very early age how to mask my true feelings. I had to grow up fast. Like I said, it was only after Jenny came into my life that I realized what true happiness felt like. And it wasn't just her beauty that mesmerized me, it was her inner beauty that shined through. She was silly and funny, and she was carefree, and she loved life; and at the same time, she had these quirks that helped define who she was. Even her number eleven, I swear I thought she was crazy when she first brought up that damn number to me but when I saw how much it bothered her, well, it bothered me too. I didn't care about anything but her and making her happy, that was my goal in life, and I loved it because when she was happy then so was I; and nothing could compare to the smile that she wore or how she laughed. But then…."

"Then I moved to Spencer." Johnny finished for Liam.

Liam looked Johnny squarely in the eyes. "I have gone over what happened between us, and I have to say, Johnny, I would have never guessed that I would one day not call you my friend. We never held any animosity between us, even when we were in football but what you did to me," Liam paused again as he tried to collect his thoughts. "Well, it was probably the cruelest thing a friend could do to another friend." Johnny looked away. "I'm not going to go there right now like you said, that's water under the bridge, and I've been trying really hard to let that water wash away. I don't know if I'll ever fully be over what you've done but I can at least finally say that I understand why you fell in love with Jenny, it's the same reasons I did. I'm not saying that I'm okay with it, I just get it now. I get why you came to see me in the hospital. I know she loves me, and I know you're ready to give her up. Like I said, Johnny, I never claimed to be a religious man, but when Jenny entered my life, I found my faith and I'll be damned if I will lose it again."

"What are you getting at and what's this got to do with me, Liam?"

"Tell me, have you gotten any phone calls from Aaron Dent recently?"

"No. Should I?"

"Yes and soon."

"I don't understand this, Liam, why would Aaron be interested in talking to me?

We don't have anything to say to each other."

"Well, let me just say that Aaron doesn't take well to being told no."

"Does this have to do with the race?"

"Yes, but not the one in November, this one has to do with one coming up."

"What do you mean? Does this include you too?"

"Aaron will be calling you asking you to race against me on April 11th."

"No way man, do you mean to tell me that once isn't enough for that son of a bitch? Let me guess, it's going to be on Ripley Road again?"

"Yeah, he still wants to create the whole scene from two years ago."

"First of all, I'm not into racing bikes, Liam, you know that and even more important, I wouldn't do it if the guy paid me a million dollars. There's no way in hell that I'll say yes to this, I'm sorry man, I can't do it, and you shouldn't do it either."

"I have no choice," Liam said sullenly.

"Yes you do, just tell him no. How hard can that be?"

"It can be really hard when you've signed a contract with him. I guess I should have read the fine print better, but at the time, I didn't really care. I can't get out of it, Johnny, he owns me. And we aren't racing bikes, Aaron wants me to race my truck, and he wants you to race your Bronco."

"What the hell, Liam, are you serious? Why? Why is he so hell-bent in recreating that damn race? What's in it for him?"

"What do you think? Money, and lots of it. He said that it's become some sort of urban legend around here and there are people as far away as Georgia who are willing to come in for it. All he cares about is his next dollar. He knows we didn't finish the race and so he's hell-bent on making sure we do. I didn't get it done in

November, so he sees this as his opportunity to do it right; and what better way than against you and in our trucks."

"What about Jenny? You know she will be livid once she finds out."

"If she even finds out."

"Did you try calling her?"

"Yeah, on my way here but it just went to her voicemail. I thought about just going to her house, but I don't know."

"I told you, Liam, all you had to do was go to her; she's ready to take you back, but I don't think she's at her house, I've checked, and the house looks empty. Tell me, does Aaron want Jenny in the race?"

"I don't think so. He only mentioned her name when he saw a picture of us together. He said something about doing the race for her, so I think if he wanted her to be a part of it, he would have said so. But I would never agree to that." Liam looked at Johnny for his answer. "So, even though you said no, would you be willing to reconsider, maybe mull it over for a few days?"

Johnny sighed. "Liam…"

Liam wouldn't allow Johnny to finish his thought. "There's another reason why I think you should consider doing this race, Johnny."

Johnny seemed intrigued. "Another reason? What would that be? Are we going to come out of this friends? Or I know, maybe I will get a new heart out of the deal? Does Aaron have one back at his headquarters?" Johnny asked with a note of sarcasm.

"Listen, Johnny, can you just hear me out before you make up your mind? I think after what I have to say to you, you might want to reconsider."

"And what if I don't like what I hear? I really can't imagine you have anything that would make me want to say yes to this, Liam. Hell, I don't think you should be doing it in the first place, but then again, I can't control what you do just like you can't control what I do."

Liam began to explain in lengthy detail his reasons. They talked for hours and by the time the sun went down the former friends had shaken hands on a done deal. Johnny was reluctant in the beginning, but once he heard what Liam had to say, he couldn't say no. They had a lot of work to do before the race, both of them knew what they had to do to prepare for it and for the first time, they were going to do it together, and for the right reasons.

Chapter Eighteen
The Promise

      Jenny looked at the calendar and counted. "One, two, three…" until she reached her number. "Nine, ten and… eleven." She sighed in despair. Eleven more days until April 11th, how she dreaded this number and how she dreaded the date that she knew she would have to endure for the rest of her life. This time would never come easy for her. She started doubting herself recalling the night all over again. *If only I would have, even the accident I thought might have been avoided if I hadn't been so hell-bent on being by Liam's side that night. He was always looking at me, keeping his focus on the race but at the very same time keeping his eyes on me. Maybe if he hadn't been so worried about me; he could have remained steadfast on the race and possibly seen the deer.* But all this was hindsight now, her fate and Liam's, seemed to have been sealed as soon as he hit the deer and there was nothing she could do to change that. There appeared to be no turning back the hands of time. She chuckled thinking of how everyone felt that time was all they would ever need. Time would heal the wounds, time would give them space and time was supposed to be on their side. She had been given plenty of it, and nothing seemed to get better. If anything, time had only solidified that she and Liam were over. *Our love had become nothing more than a fleeting high school romance that had finally run its course. But in my heart, I knew that wasn't true. The love we shared was uncommon and unusual and real. I sighed. My life felt empty without Liam. There was nothing to look forward to.* The life he promised her had slipped through their hands in an instant. They should be married now, but instead, they were living their lives apart; and she was taunted by the 'what-ifs' and 'maybes' that seemed to besiege her on a daily basis. She touched the calendar one more time that held the number eleven in its grasp. It too seemed to be a prisoner to this ominous digit.

"So, are you ready?" Kendra asked coming from behind Jenny.

"Yeah, I guess." Jenny perused her bedroom one more time before leaving. This time, for sure, she knew she would never fill its space again. There was no turning back, she tried, and she failed, mission not accomplished. She knew about the race being planned for April 11th, and it pained her to know that not just Liam but that Johnny too, had finally agreed to be part of the debauchery that Aaron Dent had created. Kendra picked up one of Jenny's bags following her down the stairs. "Wait." Jenny stopped when she reached the front door.

"What is it, Jenny?" Kendra asked.

"I forgot something, I'll be right back." Jenny dashed up the stairs and rushed into her room where she opened her closet and fervently began rifling through the scant amount of clothes that still hung sadly before her. "Where is it?" she asked herself while the clothes fell from their hangers. Jenny searched in vain until finally, she exhaled; the one article of clothing she had been desperately searching for came into view: Liam's letterman's jacket. She reached deep into its pockets and clutched the item tightly in her grip. It was the letter Liam had left her at Serenity Hill. Even though its contents had never given her much hope, it was all she had to hang onto, and she couldn't leave without it. It was a part of Liam, and she needed every part of him that she could still get. She held it close to her heart before carefully putting it into her purse.

"There," she said with a huge sigh of relief.

Kendra was now waiting in her car. Jenny walked down the steps slowly and looked back only once. In that moment, she saw her entire life pass before her eyes. Before her, stood a little girl holding on to her daddy's pinky. A few years later stood a young teenager laughing with her mom as they returned home from one of their numerous shopping adventures and then, finally, before her stood a young woman being escorted down the steps with Liam by her side. She held onto that image the longest.

"Jenny, we should go, mom can only watch Allie for a few hours."

"Right, sorry Kendra, just daydreaming, I'm ready." Jenny hopped in the car, and they began to drive away. She noticed Billy walk across the road, he waved goodbye to her. His huge girth protruding from the suspenders that tried to keep it contained.

"Are you okay?" Kendra asked sympathetically.

"No, but I guess I will be... in time."

Kendra knew that right now all Jenny needed was some time to think. She didn't try to overwhelm her with questions or try to convince her best friend that she was making the biggest mistake of her life by leaving again; no, instead, she remained quiet, allowing her friend the space she needed while she drove Jenny to her destination. They were making their way through town when Kendra noticed a familiar vehicle behind her. She drove slowly; Jenny seemed oblivious to her surroundings until Kendra finally pulled into a gas station.

"What are you doing?"

"I'm thirsty, can I get you something?"

"No, I'm fine, but please hurry, I just want to get out of here." Jenny sat patiently listening to music while she waited for Kendra's return.

"Hello, Jenny."

She looked up. "Johnny, what are you doing here? I don't have time for another talk." She looked back to find Kendra sitting on a bench. Kendra just shrugged her shoulders, and Jenny rolled her eyes in disapproval. This had been a setup.

Why?" Was all he asked.

"Because, I just don't." Jenny didn't want to explain why she was leaving. It was nobody's business, especially Johnny's.

"Okay, I see," he said somewhat aloof. "I can play along if that's what you want, but I just think you should know that what you're about to do is wrong."

"How do you know what I am about to do?"

Johnny looked over at Kendra, who was now pretending to mess with her phone. "I have my ways."

"Oh, I should have known." Jenny followed Johnny's eyes. "Listen, Johnny, you have been more than a great friend to me, especially since I came back. But things just aren't working out like I had hoped. I know I'm leaving without explaining myself, but I feel it's best if I do it this way."

"Really? Can you at least tell me where you've been? No one has seen you since you left the hospital that night. Don't you think we deserve to know why?"

"We? Who are you talking about? You and your mom? Liam? I'm not wanted here by Liam, he told me himself that night in the hospital. And as for not telling you or your mom anything, I don't have to. I knew you guys would try and stop me. I can't stay here any longer, Johnny it hurts too much. I tried, and Liam doesn't want me, he's made his decision and it's time for me to accept that. And as far as you're concerned, I will always care for you but I can't give you the love you need. I never could. You've got enough problems without adding me to it. It was a mistake for me to ever come back here." Johnny looked at her with a peculiar glare. "What?" Jenny asked somewhat sarcastically.

"A mistake? You think it's been a mistake for you to return? You don't get it do you, Jenny?"

"Get what? What are you trying to tell me?"

"Liam does want you. He never wanted you to leave. He has been a complete mess since he realized that you had been at the hospital. It wasn't a mistake; it was the best thing you ever did. It showed Liam that you didn't give up on him, that you still love him as much as he loves you."

"Johnny, I heard him tell me point blank to leave."

"No, Jenny, he was telling you *not* to leave. He wanted you to stay with him."

"I don't believe you. Besides if that's the truth why hasn't he tried to reach me?"

"He has!" Johnny blurted out. "But you disappeared into thin air like some sort of damn ghost. No one has been able to find you. Where the hell have you been, Jenny?"

She didn't want to tell Johnny that she had been spending her time at Serenity Hill, that Kendra had solemnly sworn that she wouldn't tell a soul where she was or that it was Kendra who was keeping her informed on what was going on. Kendra had been trying to convince Jenny from the onset that Liam and Johnny were both looking for her but she didn't want to believe it. She looked at Johnny realizing he wasn't going to be satisfied until he received an answer from her.

"I've been at Serenity Hill, Johnny, if you must know."

"What?"

"I couldn't stay here, I didn't want to be found, but I still needed to be close to Liam." Johnny couldn't believe that Liam had never even thought about going there to look for her, he had searched everywhere but hadn't once thought about going to the most obvious of places. "And where is this behavior coming from, Johnny?"

"What behavior?"

"This. All of a sudden you're defending Liam, you're on his side now? Shouldn't you be glad? I thought this was as much your power game as it was his. Why aren't you here for me? I don't see Liam anywhere, so you've got the perfect opportunity to try and have your way with me again. What's changed?" Jenny asked, more pissed off the longer she thought about it.

Johnny still had all those feelings for her; he would always carry that torch. His heart was pounding out of his chest with the love he felt for her, but he had made a promise to Liam, and it was a promise he wasn't going to break. He ignored Jenny's question and turned the conversation back on her.

"Do you know what's about to happen, Jenny?"

"What?"

"I'm sure you're aware of the race coming up, aren't you?"

Jenny got out of the car and stood next to Johnny. She looked over at Kendra, who seemed to be intent on reading the contents of her pop can. "Yes, I know about it but what am I supposed to do? I'm definitely not putting on my rally cap to cheer you guys on to victory. And why, Johnny?"

"What do you mean, Jenny?"

"Why did you agree to race Liam? You still haven't answered me. Why this time? You had the chance last November, what changed your mind now?" Johnny didn't say anything; he instead just turned and looked the other way. "Anyway, what about your heart? You're in no condition to do this race, what if something happens to you?"

"Do you really think it matters anymore? Whether I die today, tomorrow, a year from now or on the eleventh, it won't really be a big deal, aside from my parents, no one is going to miss good ole' Johnny Bryant. I've lived a pretty good life, short but good, I have no complaints or fears, and no regrets. Everybody who has ever meant a damn to me already knows how I feel about them, I've made my peace, and I'm ready whenever that time may be."

Jenny was in disbelief. "You seem sure of your fate."

"I've known for a while that my time on this earth would not be long, the fact that I'm coming to the end of it isn't any surprise to me."

"You seem ready."

"As ready as anyone can be who's facing their demise. It's not like I have a choice in the matter, there isn't a heart out there for me; and mine, well you know better than anybody, it isn't going to fix itself. It's broken... in more ways than one."

"How am I supposed to take that comment, Johnny?"

"Any way you like, my dear. I'm ready to race, and I'm prepared for the outcome. This race is going to produce a winner, whether it's Liam or me but you can count on there being a victory for somebody. It's been two years of hell for everybody concerned and it's time one of us closes the gates to that inferno."

"You know, when I heard about the race, I really couldn't believe it. I mean, once was enough and then it happened again, and I thought, wow, this is some sort of never-ending nightmare. And now, to hear you talk like this makes me wonder whose side you're really on."

"I'm on nobody's side; I'm just doing what I think I should. I've thought about it, and I'm ready. That's all there is to it," Johnny said surreptitiously. "You, on the other hand, you should not be so worried about me and my heart but about Liam and his. You think mine's in bad shape, Liam's is probably ten times worse. He needs you, Jenny and he's having a hard time living without you. I know he's been hard-headed, and I've probably contributed a lot to that behavior, but this is different, you need to be there for him. He needs to know when he crosses that finish line you'll be there waiting for him."

"I still don't understand why suddenly you're pushing me towards him."

"Don't you want to be with him?"

"Of course I do, Johnny, but what happened to make you realize that? I've been trying for two years to convince you, why now? You were part of the reason why I left Spencer, why Liam and I aren't together. What am I supposed to think right now?"

"Just that I'm trying to do what's right, that's all, Jenny. My feelings for you haven't changed; I've just been made aware of the bigger picture."

"Huh?" Confusion swept over her face.

"Never mind. The race is going to happen; it would be nice if Liam knew you were going to be there for him after it was over."

"What am I supposed to do, stand next to Julia Shipman and wave the flag as you two begin another death match against each other? I just can't do that. It's not like this is any other race, this is the race that destroyed everything, both of you are crazy for doing it. It doesn't matter if I'm there, it never has and it never will."

"That's where you're wrong. It does matter. That's what I've been trying to get through to you. This race is all about you and getting you back. Are you going to stand in front of me and tell me that you're willing to leave Liam behind once and for all because you're tired of trying? What happened to your backbone? I thought you would never give up on him, isn't that what you always told me, that he was your soul mate, the two of you were some sort of Kindred Spirit, that it was Kismet? I'm telling you, if you leave right now, it will be the worst thing you will ever do."

"The worst thing? I came back for Liam. I came back because I couldn't stand to be away from him. I have bared my soul to him and look where it got me!"

Johnny seemed more frustrated with each word Jenny spoke. "Am I speaking to a wall here? Why won't you believe me, Jenny? What do I have to gain from this? For once in my life, I am trying to do the right thing, and I'll be damned if you'll be too stubborn to believe me. I have never lied to you, the feelings I feel for you have come from my heart and you know that. I'm standing here telling you that you need to go to Liam; I'm telling you this because it's the truth and it's important. God! Both of you need your heads checked because you're both crazy! He doesn't think you want him, and you don't think he wants you. You know what? You both deserve each other!" Johnny tried to settle himself down and remain calm. "Listen, I can't keep you from leaving, I've done my part but if you have made up your mind, at least before you leave, talk to Liam."

"Why are you racing, Johnny?"

"Because I made Liam a promise, it's between us; I've already told you that."

"And you said I'm crazy. That's the stupidest thing I've heard come out of your mouth yet. You've never done anything you haven't wanted to, Johnny. You and Liam hate each other, why would you even make him a promise?"

"I can't tell you, plain and simple, so please stop asking, you're not going to get it out of me. All I want is for you to talk to him before you leave."

"I've already tried to talk to him and looked what happened; he raced and ended up in the hospital."

"Jenny, please!" Johnny pleaded. "This needs to happen!" The urgency in Johnny's voice was very apparent as patrons of the gas station looked in his direction.

Jenny was dumbfounded. She exhaled in disgust. She didn't have a clue what this was all about. "Kendra is taking me to pick up my car at Serenity Hill. I'll be there. If you're telling me the truth Johnny, then I'll believe it when Liam shows up. He can come to me this time."

"He'll be there, Jenny, just don't leave."

"I still don't understand your change of heart, Johnny."

"You know that you will forever hold a place in my heart. I believe that's why I'm still alive, you've kept my heart alive, you've kept it beating, but this race is bigger than all of us now, I have my own reasons for being in it, and that's all you really need to know."

"Okay, fine, keep it a secret from me. I don't care to know why you're acting like such an asshole to me!"

"No, I'm just not obliging you with an answer."

"Oh, I see. You force me to talk, but when the shoe is on the other foot, you clam up."

"I just don't think it's necessary to go into it, that's all. Let's just say I have found a new reason to race Liam and maybe it doesn't involve you."

"And this reason, Liam knows about it?"

"Yes, he was a big part of it. And if you're so determined in understanding my reasons for doing the race, you can ask him. Maybe he'll tell you and maybe he won't, that will be up to him. But I've said my piece, I've got to go, I have a lot to do before April 11th." Johnny gave Jenny an endearing and thoughtful smile, his anger and frustration subsiding. "Jenny?"

"Yeah?" she sat back in her seat.

"I do love you, a lot more than you think." He put his two fingers to his lips as he kissed them and then placed them gently on hers. "A lot more than you'll ever know, maybe you'll realize how much after all this shit is over." Jenny just sat there as he got into his Bronco and drove away. She felt angry, confused and in some weird way, betrayed.

"Ready?" Kendra had returned. Jenny just gave her a look. "I had to, Jenny. You needed to talk to him before you left."

"Whatever but no more surprises, alright? Please let's just get out of here."

Chapter Nineteen
The End of A Chapter

"Are you going to be alright? I can stay if you like, mom said she was taking Allie to the park, so I don't need to get back as soon as I thought I did."

"I'll be fine, Kendra and besides, after seeing Johnny, I am actually looking forward to having a little bit of alone time. You go; I know how much you miss being with Allie."

"Are you sure?"

"Very sure but thanks for being here for me, I don't know what I would do without you; and I don't mean just today but for all the times you've had my back."

The two friends embraced. "I will always be here for you." She looked Jenny squarely in the eyes. "This is going to work out; you do know that, don't you? I've never seen two guys more in love with one girl in my entire life. I know you might not believe this, but you're very lucky to have their love. Whatever happens, Jenny, just remember that."

Jenny didn't seem as convinced; her belief in the fairytale was waning. "It's just weird, Kendra, I was ready to let go but after

Johnny's visit, I'm right back where I started, still hopelessly in love with Liam and still very much alone."

"Ready to let go of what?"

"I had made peace with the fact that maybe we weren't supposed to be together, but now I feel torn again. It's not that I wanted Johnny to stop caring for me, but if you could have only heard him, he was so adamant about his feelings. He really seemed like he was over me and that's never been the case. There was just so much finality to his words, it actually scared me."

"Correct me if I'm wrong, Jenny but isn't that what you always wanted?"

"Of course it is, it's just that for almost as long as Liam has been in my life so has Johnny. I was used to him."

"Listen to me, I'll be the first to admit that I don't hold the answers when it comes to love, look at me, I'm a single mom. I know your feelings for Johnny run deep but I also know you're love for Liam runs much, much deeper and that's where the difference lies. I can still see it when you speak his name, it's in your voice, in your eyes and the way you carry yourself. If you doubt your love for Liam, you shouldn't."

"I want Liam to be head over heels for me like he was before. We didn't have a history, and now we do, I'm just worried that our history won't allow us to love each other with that same raw emotion that we first enjoyed. Everybody has been trying to tell me that he wants me back but that's just it, it's everybody but Liam telling me. How do I know it's true? It hasn't been easy to love him, yeah maybe in the beginning but the beginning of our relationship was so fleeting. I'm scared to love Liam the way I want to, I can't be hurt anymore, I'll just die, Kendra."

"Have faith, Jenny; please just have a little more faith." Kendra looked at her watch. "I guess I should go. I love you. Call me if you need me."

"I will and thanks, I love you too." Jenny hugged her.

Jenny made herself comfortable in the gazebo as she watched the sun set. It was the kind of evening that Jenny loved, a picture-perfect evening with the setting sun radiating shades of purple and orange across the sky. The cool breeze reminded her that there were still many days left before warm weather would finally settle in. She looked lovingly at the gazebo. Nature had been kind to the structure, the paint still glistened and the starry night sky still sparkled with life. It was here that she felt closest to Liam. She looked towards the beaten path that would bring Liam here; the deafening silence reminded her that he was nowhere near. *I breathed in the night air; my nerves were getting the best of me as I awaited his arrival. It was so unlike me to feel this way about seeing him. Sure, my body always became anxious when I knew of his imminent arrival but this nervous tension was originating from a different place inside me, a place that was still unsure if there was a future for us.* It was with that thought that she heard the hum of the F-150 make its way towards her.

She stood up; her heart came to a stop when the truck stopped. She could see Liam's rugged frame sitting behind the wheel, her stomach felt strange... those same butterflies that used to visit her on a regular basis early in their relationship had revived themselves once more. She wasn't ready for this; her bravery was being swallowed up by the evil, cowardly monster that had been harboring inside of her. She hadn't even spoken to him and yet she was already on the brink of passing out. Only Liam had this effect on her, no one else. She waited patiently for him to move, he just sat there watching her watch him. Maybe she was supposed to go to him, maybe he was waiting for her, confusion swept over her and while she tried to figure out what to do Liam stepped out of his truck. His frame looked strong and stout as he stood beside his trusty beast. It was amazing to her that he could be standing there so full of life when only months earlier he was so close to death. He began to walk towards her; he seemed nervous which made Jenny feel oddly better. She studied him closely; his walk was different. He produced a much more evident limp, obviously a result of his latest injuries. He was now only inches from her, and as he stood there, so close that she could feel his breath pass her, she saw the boy that she had fallen in love with. His blue eyes were full of color, they had her mesmerized and danced with the same emotion she remembered. His scent was stimulating, and she inhaled it deeply while still trying to keep her balance. Her mind began to make her doubt her own self-worth for the first time since she had known him. *How could anyone who looks like Liam want anything to do with someone like me?* She still didn't understand it, but as always, when she doubted herself, he renewed her confidence just by speaking.

"Hello." His voice was tender. She didn't return the greeting, perhaps because she was lost in his eyes, but it didn't matter, he went for her hand anyway, and when he finally touched it, they both gasped.

"Hi." Her voice was weak but still carried the same tenderness.

He inhaled deeply. He didn't waste any time. "Jenny, can we talk?"

"Yes, definitely."

He led her to the gazebo. She walked slowly with him, understanding that a slow walk was about as fast as he could go. Once there, he noticed numerous articles that were haphazardly strewn about the floor.

"So this is where you have been?"

"Yes. I've been here since I left you."

"Why, Jenny?"

She just looked at him. "I had to, Liam. I didn't know where else to go."

"You could have gone back to the house."

"No, I couldn't. I left the hospital that night thinking you never wanted to see me again and then to add insult to injury, Grandpa made me feel worse. I couldn't stay where I didn't feel wanted."

"First of all, Grandpa feels horrible about how he acted towards you. He didn't mean it, Jenny, he loves you. He wanted to apologize, but nobody could find you. It's killed him that he hasn't been able to apologize to you, he would never hurt you like that, I hope you know that. Secondly, and definitely most importantly, I never told you to go away. I wanted you to stay, I was telling you to *never* go away. I'm sorry you didn't hear that."

"I know that now, Liam."

Liam looked around him. "You know, it never crossed my mind to come here. I don't know why; it's the one place I should have come first. It makes sense you would be here, it's where I would have come too... Jenny?"

"Yeah, Liam?"

"I remember you being at the hospital. I could feel your touch on my skin, and I remember waking up seeing you beside me. I thought it was a dream at first because I had been dreaming about you... about us. I've missed you so much, and I'm so sorry for this past year, I should have never let you leave that night at Brush Creek Road. It was selfish of me." She didn't know what to say. She had so many questions and nowhere, to begin with them. "What?" he asked, watching her reaction to him.

"I'm just confused, Liam, I don't know what to think anymore."

"You're confused about me, about us? Have your feelings changed for me since we've been apart?"

"No, I love you, Liam, but you're here because Johnny told you to come see me. It doesn't make sense to me that the one guy you have detested, the one guy who seems to be behind all of our misery, has now turned into one of your biggest supporters. I saw him earlier, and his mannerisms towards me were completely different than they have ever been. It was as if he had thrown in the towel."

"And that upsets you?" Liam asked disputably.

"No, I'm not upset, I'm just curious as to why it happened or better yet, why it didn't happen. He was trying to convince me why I should be with you. It was so strange. What happened to you guys?"

Liam exhaled sharply as he sat down on the stoop of the gazebo. He brought Jenny with him, never once letting go of her hand. "Would you believe me if I told you that Johnny and I have made a truce with each other?"

"A truce? No, I don't believe that, you said that before, and it turned out to be a lie, why should you mean it now?"

"Because I've changed and I know what's important. A few weeks ago I had a long talk with him and after it was all said and done, we had come to an agreement. I'm not saying we're the best of friends, but we're not sworn enemies either."

"I still don't understand, Liam. If you guys are on better terms then why are you doing this race? If the fighting is over then, there's no need to prove anything."

"I wish it was that easy. It's more complicated than that, Jenny. I have to race. I'm still under contract with Aaron, and I can't get out of it, at least not yet. It's turned into this crazy media frenzy, and it's going to generate a lot of business for him which means a lot of money. I have to do it. Besides, if I don't, Aaron will just make me do another race and another until he gets what he wants and what he wants is for Johnny and me to finish the race from April 11th."

"Why can't you just tell Aaron to go to hell? Just walk away from him, you still have your share of the business with Joe, you don't need to work for Aaron."

"I promise you, Jenny, that after this race, I will be done; there will be no more racing for me."

"So... you're not going to tell me about Johnny?"

"Does it matter, Jenny? I came here to see you not talk about Johnny." Jenny implored Liam with her eyes. "You're not going to give up on this, are you?"

"No, I'm not. I deserve to know."

"Fair enough, but I have to start from the beginning, or it won't make any sense. A couple of days after I awoke from the coma, I was talking to Grandpa. He was trying to fill me in on everything... including you," he said looking at Jenny with indulgent eyes. "Anyway, he thought it was time I knew some of our family history. I thought I knew everything there was to know about my background but boy, was I wrong."

"What did he tell you, Liam?"

"I think you already know, Jenny. He told me about the race."

"You're not talking about the one we were in, are you?"

"No, I'm talking about the one Grandpa was in. He told me everything and how it changed his life. He didn't leave out one part, including the part when he started drinking or how Grandma saved him. I didn't realize how much we were alike. It made me realize that if he can live through that then so can I. Jenny… my grandpa had Grandma, and I have you."

"I'm glad he told you, Liam, you deserved to know. But how is Johnny a part of it?"

"Do you remember Grandpa telling you about the boy who died in the race, his name was Lee West?"

"Yes. He was Grandpa's best friend."

"Yes, he was. He was also Johnny's great uncle."

"What?!"

"It was on Johnny's mom's side, her dad's brother."

"You mean Lee West was Gertie's uncle?"

"Yep. That's why Johnny is willing to do this race. He sees this race as his opportunity for redemption for his great uncle and for his mom."

"Wait a minute… is this what you told Johnny?"

"Yes, I figured if I was going to have a clean start then I needed to be upfront about everything, including telling him what I knew."

"So, he's doing the race because of what happened years ago? It has nothing to do with you or me? It's just his way of trying to finish something that his uncle couldn't?"

"Well, not in the beginning. I confronted him about the race because Aaron wanted me too but after Grandpa talked to me, I didn't think it would hurt to let him know about it either. Besides, I thought it might help in his decision."

"It didn't matter to you that he's not healthy enough to do the race? You know any kind of stress could literally kill Johnny, don't you?"

"I know his health isn't good but Aaron expects this race to go down, and he expects me to win it. I didn't necessarily twist his arm. Johnny's a grown man and if he really didn't want to do the race he wouldn't. Remember, he wasn't willing last November; he just has a reason to do it now. We both have something to gain from it."

"Like what?"

"I know it's probably not what you want to hear, but I can finally end this chapter of my life. I still need to finish the race; it will never be over until I can do that, Jenny. And as for Johnny, he gains redemption for his family."

"Who would have guessed our paths would cross so much with each other. Who knew that your grandpa's best friend would also be the great uncle to your worst enemy? The connection between you two is just crazy!"

"I know," Liam said. "It's pretty insane."

"Liam, after everything you've just told me, I still don't have a good vibe about this race. Can you be honest with me about something else?"

"Always, Jenny. I promise, and I do mean that." Crossing his heart with his hands.

"Are you setting Johnny up?"

"Hell no! This race will be fair, but like always, I don't plan on losing. I will cross that finish line and then we can leave all this bad shit behind us once and for all, I promise. I'm ready to move on, and I'm ready for us to be together, forever, without anything holding us back." Liam paused for a moment before continuing. "Jenny, there's something else you should know about me."

"What?"

"I've stopped drinking. I don't want it, and I don't need it. I'm over my demons, and there are no more nightmares either. All I want to do is to start my life over… with you. I love you; it's never ended for me." His words were strong as they fell from him along with his tears. "I will do anything to prove to you that I have changed, just please don't leave me again, please," he begged her.

"Liam, I do want to believe you, this is all I ever wanted was from you, to just be honest with me and allow me in. I want to be there for you, in the good times and the bad. I want us to be there for each other."

He carefully brought Jenny's face to his putting his lips on hers. He hesitated, cautious as he wondered if Jenny wanted this as much as he did, but his instinct entreated him to continue. The touch of his lips against hers sent a scintillating feeling throughout her that made her body react immediately to him. This was exactly what she wanted. Their lips molded into each other. The nervous energy that they were sharing only moments earlier had been replaced with an animal magnetism that neither one of them could ignore. He closed in on her, if that was even possible, causing her to bend backward as he showed her just how much he had missed her. He took in her breath with each gasp she made, replacing it with his own. She felt alive for the first time in a very long time. She didn't want him to stop, he continued to kiss her face with small but endearing caresses that ignited her inner senses. "I love you," he whispered.

Her tears were flowing freely now as he held her close to him. Her head nestled deep into his rugged chest. It had been such a long time since she heard the soft beating of his heart against her ear. She missed the sound of it.

He pulled her face to meet his. "Jenny, please forgive me for everything, I want to come home, and I want to come home to you. Please take me back."

She turned herself to him; positioning herself on his lap as she wrapped her legs securely around his torso. She didn't say a word but kissed him emphatically as she held his hair tightly in her grip. It was all the answer he needed from her. He responded to her by gently laying her back down; making sure her body was tightly in his hold. His authority over her excited her, and she was more than willing to indulge him.

"I've missed you, Jenny. I've missed your smell, your touch, your voice and I've missed being inside of you."

She looked at Liam with adoration as she arched her body to meet his. She wanted him too. He wanted to take it slow, and he was trying, but his heart and head both needed him to go faster. He couldn't help it. He needed to be closer to her; he needed their bodies to become one. The anticipation of feeling himself inside her grew, and his urge was more powerful than his restraint. He became rushed in his quest with her and quickly stopped in fear that she would be upset with his actions, but on the contrary, she demanded him to continue by returning his favor and placing his hand between her moist thighs. It was just like his dream. They undressed each other in swift, choreographed movements, she unzipping his jeans while he unbuttoned her blouse. His breath became labored as her blouse fell from her shoulders. She directed his face to hers and implored him to touch her; he lovingly obeyed her wish and kissed her breasts with the lightest of touches. He rose up and looked deep into her eyes waiting for her consent to let him in. With a nod of her head and one guided movement from her they became one. The love they made was euphoric and sensual, raw in its rarest form but still sweet and tender as only Jenny and Liam could make it. When it was over, their desperate efforts had been triumphant, and both of them gave in as they collapsed in each other's embrace, totally in love and finally fulfilled.

They lay in each other's arms for hours, neither one of them wanting to relent to the morning sun that beckoned for them to arise. They were still exhausted from their enraptured efforts, but they rose with a voracious appetite for what their lives had in store for them.

"I am never going to take you for granted again, Jenny."

"I never thought you did, Liam. We both made mistakes, and I'm just glad it's almost over."

"Almost?" Liam asked.

"Yes, you still have to race, so after that, I can officially say it will be over... for both of us. It's been a two-year nightmare that I'm ready to wake up from."

"You're not going to be there when I race, are you?"

"I can't, I still can't do that. You know that, don't you? I mean, you know that I can't be there? I will always be here for you, and I will be there for you when you race, it just won't be me in person. I will definitely be there in spirit."

"I know. I had to ask. Will you wait for me here? This is our place, and this is where I want to find you when it's over."

"Of course. This is our place and that will never change."

"Will you do me at least one favor?" he asked.

"I will if I can."

"Will you please come home with me, you can come back here for the race but you should have never left, and it hasn't been the same without you. Ask Grandpa, even Blue and Sugar Dumplin' haven't been the same. Then, once the race is over, we will start building our lives here at Serenity Hill. Besides, Grandpa would love to see you again."

"I will if you're sure."

"Never doubt that it's your home too, but if you don't want to stay there then I'll go where you go, my home is where you are, Jenny, no matter where that is."

Liam helped Jenny pack up her things and put them in his truck. He opened his side of the door, and just like the gentleman she always remembered him to be, he helped her in. It was like old times, he had her as close to him as he could without actually having her sit on top of him, and his right hand as always was snuggled deep between her legs. She put her head on his shoulder and sighed affectionately. Life was finally looking good.

Chapter Twenty
The Dance

Jenny sat quietly at the kitchen table while Liam poured her a cup of coffee. She fidgeted with her hands. Her eyes kept going to the door waiting for it to open.

Liam tried to calm her down. "Would you stop worrying, it's alright."

"Where is he?"

"He'll be here soon."

"What if he's still mad at me?"

"I told you he isn't, and I'm not lying to you." Liam squeezed her fidgety hands to try and reassure her.

She took a sip of her coffee only to miss her mouth, the hot liquid running down her chin, as she heard the kitchen door swing open. She turned quickly as she heard the uneven gait of Liam's grandpa make his way to them. He stood tall at the entrance offering a powerful presence before them. Her heart leapt into her throat, she waited for him to tell her to get the hell out of his house... but he didn't. He took a few steps into the kitchen and stood next to her. She looked politely at him, waiting for him to say something; anything to break down the wall she felt that had built up between them. He bent down and with both arms embraced her with the biggest bear hug she had ever received from him, crumbling the wall to the ground.

"Welcome home, hon, it's so good to have you back where you belong."

She exhaled while Liam erupted into a boisterous laugh. "Thank you, Grandpa; it's good to be home."

The three of them sat down, Grandpa Mack taking the chair next to Jenny. "Sweetheart, I am so sorry for my actions towards you at the hospital. I hope you can forgive this old man for being such a dumbass. I don't know why I spoke to you in such a harsh manner, I'm truly sorry, Jenny."

"It's okay, Grandpa."

"No, it isn't, and there was no excuse for my behavior. I love you like you were own flesh and blood, and that's the God's honest truth. I'm just so happy to see you here with Liam; the sight of you two back together again gives this old feller something to smile about again. It's been long overdue, and I'm just so happy that you guys have found a reason to be together."

Jenny and Liam exchanged glances at each other.

"So tell me, what's your plan now Liam?"

"I still have to do the race, Grandpa but after that, I'm finished, and Jenny and I can start concentrating on what's important… us."

"That damn race, I swear it's going to be the death of all of us. I wish I never would have told you about what happened to me. It was a long time ago. I was just a young kid and felt it was the best thing to do at the time; it was foolish."

"It's alright, Grandpa, I would be doing the race whether you told me or not and I have a feeling so would Johnny. He wants to put this behind us as much as anybody."

"So, Jenny, Johnny's finally given in and given up on you. All I can say is it's about damn time."

"Grandpa!" Jenny exclaimed.

"I know, I know. The boy has a sick heart, and that's a terrible, terrible thing. I don't wish any more ill will on him but that still didn't give him the right to pursue you like he did and that's all I'm saying on the matter. In my opinion, it's ancient history. I'm done with it. Well, I'm gonna give you two lovebirds some time alone, I just wanted to welcome you back and apologize to you, hon. I will see you soon, sweetheart." Grandpa leaned down and kissed Jenny on her forehead.

"What's gotten into him?" Jenny asked Liam after Grandpa had left the kitchen.

"He's just really happy for us. I told you there was nothing to worry about. He hated how the last two years treated us. It's almost been as hard for him as it was for us, Jenny." Liam leaned in and kissed her. He couldn't seem to get enough of feeling her lips against his. "Are you going to be alright while I'm at the shop?"

"Yes. The shop?" Jenny asked as she pulled back from him. "Have you started working there again?" She was hoping.

"No, not necessarily. Joe and Parker are helping me get ready for the race."

"It's just like old times; they helped you back then, too."

"But this time, it's different; after I win the race, we're finally moving on with our lives, no more interruptions or diversions, remember my promise to you."

"Ahhh, yes you did promise me that."

"Yes, I did." he said, his lips brushing over hers.

"I'm holding you to that, Liam." Her tone was more serious this time.

"You can hold anything you like of mine, Jenny, just as long as you never leave me again. Promise?"

"That's a promise I intend on keeping."

Liam couldn't contain his feelings; he brought her to him and held her close to him while he carried her upstairs to their room. The magic continued between them.

"I won't be late," Liam said to her hours later.

"I'll be waiting right here." She wore a vexing but contented smile on her face.

Liam left that morning feeling better than he had in a very long time. He had a new spring in his step, and his uneven gait was hardly noticeable. He looked forward to what the day would bring him knowing that at the end of it, Jenny would be there for him. Nothing could ruin it.

"Hello, Liam." Toby seemed in rare form getting out of his black and yellow Mustang. It looked like he had been spending some of the money that Liam had earned for him on a new image for himself. He wore a brand new leather jacket with a pair of cowboy boots that looked custom made, and he was smoking what seemed to be a very expensive Cuban Cohiba cigar, the stogie resting comfortably on his lower lip while the brown spit dribbled from his chin.

"What are you doing here?" Liam was unimpressed with his new attire or his new nicotine appendage.

"I'm here on behalf of Aaron. I must say I'm a pretty happy fellow knowing that you're going to race again. I'm sure Aaron's influence and his pocketbook had something to do with Johnny changing his mind. Made me realize I couldn't refuse either."

"It's not your thing, Toby, there are no motorcycles involved this time."

"I know, I know, but that's okay. Don't ever say that Toby wasn't one to change for the good of the people. Besides, haven't you heard? Aaron asked me to oversee all his races in these parts, whether they involve motorcycles, cars, trucks or even goddamn horses," he blurted out with a malevolent and disgusting chuckle.

"Huh, sounds like you're not thinking about the people but yourself." Liam knew Toby never did anything unless there was a dollar sign attached to it.

"I'm here because I want to support you, Liam. I care about you, and since your last race, I want to make sure you don't get hurt again." Toby's sincerity was as fake as Gina's crimson nails.

"I don't need your care, Toby and I don't need you. This race has nothing to do with you, and I would appreciate it if you would mind your own business. Understood?"

"Whoa, what's this? When did Liam Larson grow a pair of balls? You better be careful, you wouldn't be where you are now if it wasn't for me or have you forgotten so quickly? Maybe that accident damaged more than your leg." Toby's mouth was full of stogie spit. "Furthermore, I told you I'm working for Aaron now, so this is my business."

"You don't scare me, Toby. You do what you want, bet on Johnny or me I don't really give a damn. If it's money you want to make, then I'm sure that's what you'll get, but I'm not going to help you make it. Once this race is over then I'm finished, I've got more important things to do than trying to win races so scumbags like you can profit off of me."

"Hmmmm… funny how you've changed your tune so suddenly. Would a certain red-haired girl have anything to do with this?"

"That's none of your damn business," Liam said coming nose-to-nose with Toby's.

"Interesting… well, I'm sure you've worked all this out with Aaron since he is still your boss. Whatever you mean by being 'finished' I'm sure you mean just for a while. You are under contract with Dent Enterprises well after this race is over or have you forgotten about that too? You break the contract with Aaron, and you'll dread the day you ever met him. I don't think he'll be too happy about your new plans, but then again, if you're so sure about them, I'm sure Aaron is aware of them also. You'd have to be a fool not to share that with him, and you're not that… are you, Liam?"

Liam rubbed his fists together. He wanted to punch that stogie Toby was smoking down his throat until it came out his ass, but before he could react on his diabolical thought, Parker interceded. "Don't do it, man, he's not worth it."

Liam backed down. "You're one damn lucky bastard, Toby. If Parker hadn't been here you'd be sucking your next pint of beer through a straw, you asshole! Now get the hell out of here! I've got work to do! You have no business here with me!"

Toby raised his arms in an act of defeat. "It's all good, friend, no need to get all riled up, remember I like that in you. You always win when there's fire in your piss. Just remember what I told you." Toby gave a nod in Parker's direction. "Nice seeing you again, Parker. I'll be seeing you around, Liam. I'll be seeing you real soon." Toby let out another maniacal chuckle.

"Man, that asshole burns me up!" Liam decided to go ahead and throw his punch anyway, right into the wall next to him. "You should have let me take care of him, Parker. Now he thinks he can run all over me."

"You have more important things to worry about than Toby," Parker said. He gave Liam a grave look.

"What's up, man? Do you know something I don't?"

"Toby was right."

"Right about what, Parker?"

"Aaron. He called earlier looking for you. He said you're not answering your cell.

"I don't have to answer to him every time he calls me. He doesn't own me; I just race for the man."

"Well, you better let Aaron know that. He acts like you're his property, Liam, and he pretty much gave Joe and me the impression that if you didn't get back with him, one of his boys would find you."

"That bastard doesn't scare me."

"I'm just telling you what he told me. He's banking on you to win this race, and he wants to see you tomorrow at Ripley Road for a test run."

"Huh? The truck isn't even ready, Parker. I'm not doing it. I'm not bending to Aaron's will just because he thinks he can do whatever he wants whenever he wants. He may own half of Ohio and West Virginia, but he doesn't own me. Never has and never will."

"I don't want any trouble either, Liam, but I think we should just go along with him until the race, and once it's over, then you can kiss both Aaron's ass and Toby's goodbye. We don't want to ruffle any more feathers than we already have. I think Aaron already thinks you don't plan on racing after the eleventh, I'm sure that's why he sent Toby here. If that's what you're planning, you better make sure that Aaron hears it from you first. That guy doesn't play fair, how do you think he got where he is today?"

Liam looked at Parker, he knew he was right and by all accounts he knew he should listen to him, but he just didn't want to. He had been Aaron's puppet long enough.

"Hey, I know you're done with those scumbags but don't start going backward because of your anger with them. You've got your eye on the prize, and that's all that matters. Just do as they say, they don't have to know the truth, Liam. Those assholes can't handle it anyway; just let them believe that you're still their man and then when it's over….well it will just be over. You don't want to lose Jenny again because of Aaron or Toby. Do you hear me, friend?"

"Yeah, I hear ya', friend. I'll show up tomorrow but Parker, you and I know the truth, and that's how we're going to keep it. I know Toby will tell Aaron what I told him, I just don't care anymore, but we can't let anyone else know that I plan on quitting. I'll make Aaron believe that I'm still working for him and in the process, make Toby look like an ass for spreading the rumor."

"What about Johnny?"

"I haven't decided yet," Liam said looking at both Parker and Joe now. "We seem to be on the same page, but I still don't know how much I can trust him. He still loves Jenny, and he may let that get in the way."

"He seemed pretty genuine to me. It seems as though he had thrown in the towel."

"Yeah, but Parker, he's been playing this game with me for two years now. I have to be careful with him. I want to be able to trust him, I think I can, but I don't know for sure. I guess only time will tell."

"But aren't you playing the same game too?" Parker added.

"Maybe, but my intentions are different than his. We made a pact and I'm holding him to it, and that's all the either one of you need to know. Clear?"

"Sure, Liam, whatever you say." Joe grabbed his keys. "I gotta go, but I'll be back tomorrow. Don't forget to lock the doors when you close shop, all right?"

Liam and Parker gave Joe a nod.

"Come on," Liam said to Parker, "we've got some work to do if I'm going to have this truck ready to show Aaron tomorrow."

****

They arrived at Ripley Road bright and early the next morning, Parker following Liam in his lime green truck. Their hope was to scope out the road before Aaron and his boys arrived, but they were too late. Aaron and his crew were already there waiting for them.

"Nice to see you, Liam, I'm glad you decided to show up. You've been a hard man to track down since our last talk."

"Yeah, well, I've been busy."

"I can see that. So... what do you think? Are you going to be ready for the race? It's only a few days away."

"Yeah, I'll be ready."

"Have you seen Johnny?" Aaron asked.

"No, should I?"

"I guess not. I didn't know if maybe the two of you were scheming together on how you were going to run the race. You country kids sometimes have your own ideas; I hope that's not the case this time; I have a lot riding on you winning this race. I hope that's your intention as well. I would hate for you to let my investors or me down."

"I haven't let you down yet, have I, Aaron?"

"Well, your track record has been excellent up until your hiccup last November. You're not going to let that happen again are you?"

"Aaron, it seems you've lost your faith in me. I can guarantee you that you and your investors will be more than happy with my performance in this race. All I ask is that you let me prepare for it my way and not yours. I've been doing this for years; I don't need any help from you or Toby. I have Parker and Joe, and that's all I need. You want this race to mimic the first one, then you'll let me prepare for it the way I did the first time, with my crew and not yours."

Aaron let out a wicked laugh. "Boy, I do believe you are learning the game. Sure, I'll back off and so will my boys but just remember, you are under contract with me to win, and that's exactly what I expect from you. Don't let me down." Liam smiled at Aaron as he clapped his hands together and rubbed them vigorously. "Well, I don't have all day, enough of this small talk; let's see what your black beast can do. I've heard it's got quite a little engine in it; let's see if it lives up to the rumors I've heard."

"Sure, I'd be glad to show you." Liam stepped into his truck. He started his F-150 and let the engine come to life. Aaron was pleased with the sound and gave Liam a toothy grin. He then stood back to give his prized driver ample room to show him what this truck could really do. Liam revved the engine a few more times to let it warm up and then gunned the gas as he charged his truck down the road. He drove the truck all the way to the end and into Devil's Bulge. Parker held his breath waiting for Liam to make the sharp turn. He lost sight of him after he went into the bend; he looked nervously over at Aaron, who stood with his arms crossed, showing no emotion as he waited for the truck to reappear. It seemed like forever before Liam turned the corner and headed back towards them, it was only then when Parker exhaled. Liam crossed the imaginary finish line and whipped his truck into park, jumping out of the cab.

"So, were you happy with that?" He was exuding with a cocky and confident attitude.

"Not bad, Liam, not bad at all, I guess your little black beast does live up to its name. Just be sure that you don't let that cocky attitude of yours ruin the race. I would hate to have what happen the last couple of times on this road happen to you again. This road seems to have it in for you and like I said, if you lose this race for me, I'll have it in for you too; remember I only sign winners, Liam. Don't... let... me... down, understand?" Aaron emphasized each word pushing his forefinger into Liam's chest. "I'll see you on race day, buddy." He flicked a goodbye gesture with his hand and got on his Silver Harley Roadster and drove away, his posse following close behind him.

"How did it feel?" Parker asked.

"It felt good."

"Really?"

"Yeah, really, Parker."

"Are you ready?"

"Yeah, I don't think I'm the one you should worry about, Parker, let's just hope Johnny is up for this."

"He will be, Liam."

"Yeah, I guess we'll see." Liam seemed to zone out for a minute. "Hey, now that I've taken care of business, do you mind if I head out?"

"Sure, everything okay?" Parker could hint some elusiveness in Liam's behavior.

"Yeah, there's just something I have to do while I'm thinking about it, and now is as good as time as any. I'd like to take care of it before the race."

"Is this something I should be worried about?"

"No, not at all my friend, just checking something off of my bucket list," Liam said with a slight grin.

"Does this have anything to do with Jenny?"

"Everything I do has to do with her, Parker," Liam answered with a tender note to his voice.

"Alright, I'll be here if you need me."

"Thanks, man; but I've got this. Oh… just so you know, this thing I have to take care of is going to take me away for a couple of days, but I'll be back for the race."

"What? Now you've got me worried, what's going on? Don't you think we need to be concentrating on the race, we've only got a few days, if you're going to be gone two of those days that doesn't leave us anytime to make sure you're ready to race Johnny."

"You saw me today; I'm as ready as I'm going to be. I can do the race blindfolded. You know as well as I do there's nothing more we can do, right now we're just buying time until game day. Trust me, I'm ready, but I've got to do this first. Okay?"

Parker was at a loss for words. "Okay. But you better be in touch. I don't want the eleventh to roll around, and you come up MIA. Aaron will be all over this place looking for you, and I won't be able to help him."

Liam put his hand on Parker's shoulder. "Listen, you've been my anchor for as long as I can remember, you've been there for me when no one else was. I trust you, and I need you to do the same for me right now. I won't bail on the race or you. Just give me these days and then I promise, you'll see me on race day."

"Okay, man," Parker said with some reservation.

"Hey, if I called you sometime in the middle of the night, could I count on you to help me, without asking any questions?" Liam asked surreptitiously.

"Yeah, of course, I'll always have your back, but man, you've got me dumbfounded."

"It wouldn't be the first time," Liam said. See ya, friend." Liam offered Parker no more information as he hopped into his truck and drove off.

****

It was well after midnight when Liam walked into his bedroom. He tried to walk lightly over the wooden floor, but his uneasy stagger was a dead giveaway. Jenny stirred under the covers as he made his way to her. She never woke. Instead, she just lay there as the moonlight filtered in through the window and cast a glow over her skin. Liam stared at her, still in awe that she was actually here with him. Finally, after over a year of mistrust, doubt and ill-conceived fears, he had her back again where she belonged and where he needed her to be. Her beautiful auburn hair flanked her face as she continued to stir in her sleep. He touched her cheek, causing her to groan softly while she slept. His heart was racing. Her absence in his life had been the biggest mistake he had ever made. He didn't care about the race, he didn't want to do it, it wasn't important to him anymore, all that mattered was Jenny, and no matter what Aaron or Toby or even Parker had to say, he didn't have anything to prove anymore. His demons were all gone; all that was left was an angel who had come into his life one Friday night at a football game.

He climbed into bed with her and wrapped his body around hers, snuggling her tightly, inhaling her scent. This was all he needed. He moved her hair away from her eyes to see her angelic face. She awoke and turned to him. Even half asleep, she was still the most beautiful sight he had ever seen.

She moaned again in satisfaction, pulling herself closer to his bare chest. "You're home," she said sweetly. "I missed you."

Yeah, I'm home."

"Did you have a good day?" she asked, taking his forefinger and kissing it intermittently. How did the test run go?"

"Great and my day... well it just got a whole helluva lot better."

"It has?"

"Yes."

Jenny snuggled closer to him. They're bare bodies entwined in the sheets and each other. "I love you, Jenny."

"I love you too." He groaned in pleasure as she lifted herself up and started kissing him on his lips and continuing her way down his neck to his chest and finally ending at his stomach. She then sat up and straddled herself over him. He locked his hands into hers and held her tightly.

"What?" she whispered, her lips touching his in a very erotic and teasing manner.

"I want us to get married."

She smiled. "I want that too, babe. And we will, as soon as you are done with this race." She bit his nose in a seductive but still very playful manner.

"You don't understand, Jenny, I don't want to wait until after the race is over. I can't wait any longer. I love you, and I've been waiting to marry you since I first laid eyes on you. I knew that very first moment when I saw you that I was looking at my soul mate, my best friend, and my wife. I feel like I've been waiting for this my whole life, please, baby, will you marry me... now?" he asked sitting up making sure to keep her close in his grasp. He held on to her left hand as he kissed her ring finger. "I gave you this ring because I was ready to marry you two years ago, please, Jenny, let's do it now; all I have to do is make a phone call."

Jenny looked shocked as he pleaded with her. "But..."

"No buts, babe. I know you had this idea of having our whole family there but don't you just want to do this?"

Jenny didn't answer Liam right away. In the time that there was silence between them, he began to doubt her feelings for him and maybe they had somewhat subsided since their time apart. "Jenny?" he asked nervously.

But her silence was only because she was waiting for the shock to wear off. "Liam... of course I will marry you, baby. Yes, yes, yes, yes!" she repeated, swinging her arms around his neck.

"Oh my God, Jenny, I didn't think you were going to say yes. Thank you so much for not giving up on me." He brought her face to his and kissed her with all the raw emotion he had built up inside of him. He then hopped out of bed, confusing his bride-to-be.

"What are you doing?" she asked. "Do you mean right now, Liam? It's two o'clock in the morning!"

"I told you, I didn't want to wait." Liam threw Jenny her clothes. "Here, put these on, and I'll meet you downstairs in five minutes."

"Five minutes, are you crazy, Liam? Can I at least take a shower or brush my teeth? I would like to look presentable to you on our wedding day or wedding night," she said as she looked at the clock.

"No, how can you improve on perfection? You look gorgeous just the way you are. Now hurry up, I don't want to waste any more time, we've got a wedding to go to!" he said grinning from ear-to-ear.

She knew he meant it. She quickly got dressed stumbling over her clothes while trying to put them on. She still found time to run a brush through her hair and brush her teeth. She looked in the bathroom mirror as she rushed in applying a quick coat of mascara, lip gloss and a few spritzes of Liam's favorite perfume. She stood there momentarily when she suddenly realized what was happening to her. "My wedding, I'm getting married, I'm actually marrying Liam." Her epiphany made her giggle uncontrollably. She twirled around the bathroom almost falling over from her self-inflicted giddiness. She grabbed the sink to balance herself only to giggle even more. She knew Grandpa Mack was sound asleep in the room next to her. She opened the bathroom door slowly to keep the squeak it made to a minimum. She tiptoed over the floorboards until she had made it downstairs to find Liam waiting for her.

"Sorry, I think I stole six minutes instead of the five you said I could have."

"No apologies, my love, so you stole a minute, you stole my heart the minute your eyes touched my soul," he said eloquently. "Are you ready?"

"Yes, but how... where what?" Jenny was fumbling with her words, trying to understand how Liam was pulling this off. "Don't we need a minister and witnesses?"

"Can you try to trust me, and realize that all the necessary arrangements have been made for this very important occasion? I promise that I won't let you down."

"Liam, I don't want any fanfare or frills, that's not who I am or who you are, promise me that it won't be like that. I don't need any of that stuff, just you and me that's all I want."

"Jenny, all I've ever wanted to do was give you the world, and I intend on doing that tonight. Now come on, we're going to be late to our own wedding if we don't leave right now." He picked her up and carried her to the truck. It had somehow been mysteriously decorated with their names and the words congratulations and forever written on it.

There were no blindfolds or secret destinations this time as Liam drove, Jenny knew this route too well, especially over the past year, he was taking her to Serenity Hill. She couldn't believe how nervous she had become, especially when he turned down the narrow, country road that led to the pasture. The night was alive as the stars above them danced in the moonlight. They came to a stop, and Liam brought Jenny out of his truck and into his arms. She skimmed the Hill's surroundings; her eyes lead her to the gazebo.

"Liam!" He didn't say a word but gave her his famous wink. She stood in awe at the sight before her. The entire gazebo was covered in white lights that were intertwined with pale blue lavender roses. Blue rose petals blanketed the floor while white and light blue tulle hung from the ceiling and cascaded around them. Jenny couldn't help but cry at the sight of it. "You did all this? When? How?" she asked as he gently put her down.

"I had a little bit of help." Liam looked over her shoulder. She turned to see Parker and Kendra walking from behind the oak tree. "Oh my God, Liam. I can't believe you."

"I told you I would give you the world," he said showing her the majestic scenery surrounding them. He held both of her hands in his. "I love you, Jenny; I can't wait for this moment to happen."

"Shall we begin?" The minister appeared from behind the gazebo.

Jenny spoke one word, all the while keeping her eyes glued to Liam. "Yes."

They took their places in front of the minister as Kendra handed Jenny a lavender bouquet of roses and then took her place next to Parker. The ceremony was beautiful and simple in nature, just the way Jenny and Liam wanted it. The formality that most ceremonies provided was replaced with an effervescent ease as they stood in front of the minister. Jenny in a simple white blouse, with jeans and no shoes and Liam in his signature jeans and cowboys boots. As Liam had promised, there was no fanfare or frills only the presence of the stars that continued their dance against the backdrop of the midnight sky. The minister spoke eloquently as he recalled two young kids who met at a football game but by no means by chance. How the boy fell in love one August afternoon when he found his soul mate. And how a shy girl who was reluctant to let the boy into her life, who had been scorned by others, found she was still drawn to him. And realized, in the end, her heart and love lie with him. They   were connected, when one breathed in the other exhaled. The minister continued his story as he told how life pulled the young lovers apart, but how destiny brought them together again. The couple exchanged simple bands etched in silver with both of their initials engraved on the inside.

As the minister pronounced them husband and wife, he continued by calling them soul mates, Kindred Spirits brought together by fate, never to be separated again in this life or beyond. They kissed while Parker and Kendra clapped and laughed joyously, there were no bands or orchestras to serenade them yet music still could be heard in the wind that ambled gently through the trees and once again, Liam and Jenny danced.

Chapter Twenty-One
One Helluva Ride

"Hello, Mrs. Larson." Liam kissed her softly on the lips as she succumbed to his will. She was barely awake but still, her soul longed for him.

"Mmmmmmm... hello, Mr. Larson," Jenny said, her eyes finally meeting her groom's.

"I can't believe we finally did it." Jenny stroked the stubble on Liam's face.

"Are you happy?" Liam asked.

"More than happy, I'm ecstatic and numb all over. I'm feeling a thousand things all at the same time, and they're all wonderful. I knew this feeling would be great, but I never expected it to be this amazing. We're married, can you believe it? It's finally real, no more thinking about it or talking about it, wondering if or even when it would happen. It's finally official. Are you happy?"

"Jenny, are you kidding? I couldn't be any happier; this is all I've ever wanted. If I die today, I'll die a happy man knowing we're connected forever. I feel blessed. Thank you for saying yes to me." Liam held her ring finger in his hand, playing with the silver band that bonded them forever.

"Liam, I don't ever want to leave here. Can't we just stay here forever?"

"I promise, Jenny, after the race we never have to leave this place again. I don't care where we are as long as we are together. Remember, you are my home."

"I love you, Liam." she paused.

"What is it?" he asked. He could sense something in her voice.

"I need to tell you something. Even though I've never agreed with the racing, I understand why you did it and the importance behind it. The gravity of the situation is much larger than my reasons for you not doing it, and I just want you to know that I'm really okay with it. I get it now. I know by racing Johnny, you'll finally be able to rid yourself of your demons and finally close that chapter. I'm behind you, and I want you to go out there and know that you have my full support. I know where it's coming from and that it's not about proving who the better racer is."

"You didn't have to tell me this, I already know it, but you're right, I don't have to prove anything anymore, but Johnny and I do have an obligation, and we have our own reasons to see it through."

"Even though I understand your reasons for the race I'm still confused about Johnny's. I don't understand what changed his mind. His heart is failing him, this race; if it goes badly could be the end for him."

"Yeah, but he's adamant about doing it, he doesn't want people to treat him differently just because of his heart. He kept that a secret for a long time and he did it while leading a normal life, he doesn't want that to change now. He'll be fine, Jenny, and so will I. This race is just going to be a show for Aaron and his company."

Jenny smiled at Liam. "Have I told you lately how much I love being Mrs. Larson?"

"Yes, but you can tell me again, I love hearing it."

Liam leaned over her and began to caress her. She allowed his hands to explore her body as she surrendered herself to his primal needs one more time. They made love over the next two days, their desires reaching new heights as their unbridled and insatiable appetite satisfied their lust for each other.

Monday finally arrived. Jenny's blissful honeymoon with her groom was rudely interrupted by the cruel fate of reality. She watched Liam walk along the path that led to his mother's grave. He seemed deep in thought as he knelt down and touched the cold granite, his head bowed as he began to pray. He prayed for a long time before finally kissing the cold stone and returning to Jenny's side.

"Are you okay, Liam?"

"I'm fine. I just needed to talk her. Jenny... it's time, I've gotta go."

"I know." Jenny's voice tried to sound upbeat for Liam.

"I won't be long, if you want, I can take you back to the house, and you can wait for me there. I'm sure Grandpa has called your parents by now, and I know they'll want to talk to you."

"I know, but I'll wait for you here, I'd rather that we talk to them together, if you don't mind. Besides, this is where I told you I would be."

"Whatever your heart desires, my love. I won't be long."

"I love you, Mr. Larson."

"I love you more, Mrs. Larson."

"Keep safe, and please come back to me."

"I'll be back in a heartbeat, Jenny that is my word to you." Her eyes were heavy with tears, she was trying to remain strong and show the strength and support that she promised she would, but it was harder than she thought. Liam pulled her to him and kissed his worried bride emphatically before leaving, hoping to diminish the fear she was carrying.

Jenny couldn't walk Liam to his truck; instead, she stayed in the gazebo and watched him drive off. The oddest feeling came over her as she lost sight of him, she felt weak, and her knees began to tremble, almost buckling beneath her. She grabbed the blanket that still carried his scent and wrapped it around her frightened body. "In a heartbeat," she whispered and thus begun her wait.

A few hours later she heard what she thought was the sound of a truck making its way up the country path. It was different from the F-150's sound, and as she rose from her seated position, she noticed the outline of a white Bronco. Johnny drove slowly and finally came to rest only a few feet from her. He stared at her, both of them locked into each other's trance. She hadn't spoken to him since that day with Kendra.

"Hello, Jenny."   Johnny's greeting was warm and welcoming as he stepped out of his Bronco.

"Hi, Johnny. I didn't expect to see you."

"I know. I just wanted to see you one more time before the race. Besides, the news is all over town about you and Liam getting married here the other night."

"Oh… so you know?"

"Yeah, I do. I wanted to be one of the first to tell you congratulations."

"Thank you. I'm sorry, Johnny, that I didn't tell you. It happened so fast that nobody knew. I didn't even know until that night. Liam just didn't want to wait any longer."

"You don't owe me an explanation, Jenny, I'm happy for you... for the both of you. It's what's right."

"Really, Johnny?"

He came closer to her and embraced her. "I didn't come here to make you feel bad or to confess my feelings for you or to tell you that you made a mistake because you haven't. You and Liam are meant for one another, and it's time I finally realized that and bowed out of the race." He was trying to remain strong in front of her.

"Do you mean that literally, Johnny?"

He began laughing thinking about what he had just said. "Oh, I guess that did sound like I wasn't going to do the race, didn't it? It's still on; as a matter of fact, once I leave here I'm going straight to Ripley Road, from what I hear, there is a huge crowd gathering for this historic race," he said with a note of sarcasm. "Who knew I would gain so much notoriety for just falling in love with you."

"So, it's kind of crazy there, huh?"

"I guess. I've heard that Aaron Dent has turned this quiet little race into a three ring circus. He's got people selling t-shirts and vendors selling food and drinks, you would think it was the Black Walnut Festival."

"What about the police? If they're acting like this is some sort of party, the police are sure to know about it."

"Apparently, Aaron has made friends with them. If rumor holds true, they're getting a cut from the winnings tonight."

"I can't believe it; leave it to Aaron to get the local police to help him with his show. Does Liam know about this? Have you spoken to him?"

"No, I haven't, and I'm sure he knows; plus, there's no need for us to talk, Jenny. We both know why we're there and what we have to do."

"What is that supposed to mean?"

"Nothing more than we're just racing against each other."

"You sound like Liam, he said the same thing. It sounds like there is a new variable to your agenda. Would it be your mom's uncle?"

"Liam told you?"

"Yeah, he did. Wow, I must say, that little bit of info threw me for a loop, what a small world."

"Yeah, pretty crazy isn't it? I couldn't believe it when I found out but no worries, Jenny, this isn't a death match between Liam and me, all it's going to be is a race to satisfy all the crazy, frenzied fanatics out there. He's doing it to fulfill his promise to Aaron, and I guess you could say it I'm doing it to honor my great uncle. Maybe I have something to prove for his sake, but I'm not going to do it to hurt Liam. I'm just there to race and to finish…people seem to only remember that it was Liam who didn't cross the finish line, they forget that I didn't cross it either. Remember?"

"Yeah, I guess that's right," Jenny said as she thought of him being pulled from the wreckage. "Johnny?"

"Yeah, Jenny?"

"Not to change the subject, but how are you feeling?"

"Really Jenny, you don't have to worry about me, you sound just like mom. But to ease your mind, I'm fine, I'm good as gold," Johnny said, laughing at his own expense.

"You're always the jokester when I'm trying to be serious with you, aren't you?"

"I know, but there's no need for the concern, this race isn't going to kill me, a bum heart already has claims on that." Jenny didn't find Johnny's statement amusing, and the look on her face let him know it. He became quiet, turning his attention away from her. "Well, I just had to see you before the race; I wanted to make sure you were all right. It's been one helluva ride between us and I've loved every minute of it."

"What's this? This sounds like a final goodbye? Won't I see you after all this crap is over?"

"Probably not. I think after tonight you and Liam need some time together and I don't need to interfere with that time. I've got my own time to worry about," Johnny said clutching his silver pocket watch.

"Does your mom know you carry that with you?"

"Yes, it makes her feel good to know that I have it with me. She misses seeing you, Jenny but she understands why you never came back to say goodbye to her."

"I miss her too. I'm sorry about that, everything just came to a head with me, and I felt like I was suffocating. I never meant to leave without telling her goodbye, but at the time, I didn't see any other way and then as time went on, I just never made the time to go back. She's always been so good to me, I feel bad, Johnny.

Please tell her I'm sorry. She truly inspired me."

"Don't worry, Jenny, she already knows, you're forgetting who you're talking about. She knew the minute you left she wouldn't see you again, it's all good." Johnny inhaled deeply. "Well, girl, I better go before they think I bailed on the race."

"Johnny, I don't know if it matters anymore, but I will always love you. Thanks for being there for me."

"Anytime, Jenny, like I've always said, you will always hold a special place in my heart. I love you too. And for what it's worth, I have no regrets for being honest with you or the actions I took to display that honesty." They embraced once more, holding on to each other for one final moment. He pulled back from her, "you know, you should really wish me luck tonight; I've yet to win a race against your guy," he said laughing.

"Good luck." Jenny kissed him softly on his lips.

He touched his lips after they parted from hers. It was as if he was still holding on to that special feeling, validating once more where his heart lived. With one last smile, Johnny hopped in his truck and waved goodbye. She waved back as he disappeared behind the bend that Liam had taken only hours earlier.

*****

The shop was unusually quiet while Liam played with his wedding band, he seemed to be preoccupied sitting in his truck while Parker and Joe did a final check on the F-150. Only hours earlier, half the town seemed to be there wishing Liam well and good luck, but all of them left, leaving the three men to themselves to do their final preparations.

"Looks like you're ready, Liam." Parker hopped into the truck next to him.

"I'll follow behind you guys," Joe said to both of them.

Liam didn't respond to either of his friends.

"You alright, man?" Parker asked. Liam still didn't indulge Parker with an answer. It finally took Parker shaking Liam's arm for him to get his friend's attention. "Hey, man is anything wrong?"

"Huh? Sorry," he said rubbing his eyes. "I guess I was out of it for a minute."

"Yeah... everything okay? You seem to be elsewhere, are you thinking about Jenny?"

"I'm always thinking about her, Parker and yeah, I'm okay. I'm just ready to get this over with; it's been a long time coming. Is the truck ready?"

"Yeah, it looks great; I see no problems for tonight."

"Are you sure? Did you check the tie-rod?"

"No, was there a problem with it?"

"Not really, just making sure and thinking out loud."

"Are you sure? We really can't risk taking any chances, Liam."

"It's fine, it was more of me just going over the list in my head, that's all. I trust my truck, it's never let me down, and I know it won't tonight." Liam continued to carry a blank stare. "Parker?"

"Yeah?"

"After this race, I'm finished with racing; it's really over for me, I know I told you this already, but I want you to understand that I'm not blowing smoke up your ass. I want to be with Jenny, and I'm not going to have anything or anyone interfere with that."

"I know that... sounds as if you're leaving or something. Are you talking about taking some time off for a honeymoon? Because if you are, you know that Joe and I can cover for you, the shop will still be here when you get back, just like it's always been."

"Yeah, I think Jenny and I need some time to be together away from Spencer. We've both earned this. You probably won't see us for a while, so can I ask a huge favor from you... as a friend?"

"Sure, anything, Liam, what is it?"

"I think if Grandpa knew that we weren't coming back for a while he might worry."

"I don't think so, Liam. He knows the shit you guys have been through, he'll want this for you guys as much as anybody."

"I know, but still, I don't know when we'll be back, can you give him this letter and check in on him once in a while for me. He still thinks he can run that farm by himself with one arm tied behind his back. I'd appreciate it if you could let him know that you were there for him."

"It sounds like this honeymoon could be a permanent vacation, Liam. Are you trying to tell me something?"

"No worries, man, and no questions, all right? Can you just do this for me?"

"Sure, like I said, I have your back."

"I knew I could count on you. There's one more thing I need to ask of you. After the race, I'm going to split as fast as I can. I'm not sticking around to talk to anybody. I plan on telling Aaron my intentions, but besides that, I'm going back to Jenny. I need you to give this to Johnny. I don't plan on talking to him either, and I need him to have this letter, he'll understand what it means once he reads it." Parker didn't ask Liam any more questions; he just took the second letter from Liam.

"So, are we going to do this or not?" Parker was trying to change the tone of their atmosphere.

"Yeah, let's do this." Both of them gave out a loud holler leaving the shop. Liam's truck flew out of the parking lot leaving a trail of dust in its path.

****

Liam and Parker arrived at Ripley Road with Joe following behind them. Just as Johnny had told Jenny, Aaron Dent had turned this quiet little race into a racing enthusiasts dream. Liam recognized at least a dozen different reps from various racing magazines that were there to see if they could become potential sponsors. Most of them had become friends of his, meeting them at many of Aaron's events and parties. It was crazy the amount of people that were lined up to see a race that would be over in a matter of minutes. And in the middle of the frenzy was none other than Aaron himself, along with his sidekicks Toby and Gina. Liam grunted in disgust.

"Finally, my prized driver has graced us with his presence." Aaron held out his arms to hug Liam.

"You're an hour late, Liam, where the hell have you been?" Toby sneered at the both of them.

"I'm here, just like I said I would be." Liam was undaunted by Toby's threatening demeanor.

"I wanted you to test run the truck one last time before the race, but we can't do that now. You better have this machine of yours in tip-top condition. I don't want any surprises tonight, you… will… win, right? There is no other choice. I heard through the grapevine that you had a talk with Johnny a few weeks ago. You two don't have your own ideas planned for tonight do you?" Aaron asked suspiciously.

"None that I can think of." Liam gave Aaron his best cynical smile.

"As you can see, there are a lot of people here to see you, Liam; I don't want your head somewhere else. I need you to focus; this could be a huge payout for all of us and could lead to more important races in the future."

"You have my focus, where else would it be, Aaron?"

"I heard about you and Jenny getting hitched, not good timing on your part, Liam. You should have discussed that with me first. I have plans for you that do not include a wife tagging along."

Liam's face started turning a beautiful flame of red as Aaron talked about Jenny.

"Liam, remember why we're here," Parker said. "There's no need to start a fight before the race." Liam knew Parker was right. He had to be smart, and these tactics of Aaron's were only to get Liam fired up anyway.

"First, I don't need to discuss my personal life with you or get your approval or permission, it's none of your damn business, and second, my wife supports me and just for the record, I'm ending this tonight, Aaron. I was going to tell you after the race, but I see it's best to let you know now. There will be no future races for me."

"You can't quit on me now, you're still under contract with me for two more months."

"Contracts can be broken, Aaron."

"Not mine."

Liam didn't give Aaron the satisfaction of a comeback; instead, he saw Johnny drive up and pull across from them, he left Aaron, Toby and Gina still wondering what the hell was going on.

"Hey, you ready for this?" said Liam.

"As ready as I'll ever be. Are you?" Johnny replied.

"Yeah. Are we still good about what we talked about earlier?"

"Yeah, Liam, I'm still on board. This is it, isn't it? I'm not going to see you after the race?"

"No, man, I'm leaving as soon as it's over; Jenny's waiting for me."

"I see, well congrats on the marriage. It's about time. If you weren't going to do it, I was thinking about asking her myself."

"I bet you were." Liam looked around as he saw the large crowd begin to take their places. "Do you need any help?" Liam was watching Johnny do a check under his hood.

"You'd be willing to help the enemy?"

"I'd be willing to help you, Johnny," Liam said with sincerity.

"Sure." The two of them, along with Parker helped tighten some loose bolts and pour in some more oil before giving Johnny the thumbs up. Liam walked around and checked the Bronco's tires and then turned to Johnny extending him his hand.

"What's this, more civility?"

"Good luck, Johnny, may the best man win."

Johnny gave Liam his hand, and they both gave each other a firm and long handshake. They stood before one another and realized that the two-year feud between them was finally over. After tonight, there would be no more fights, no more accusations, and no more lies; both of them would go their separate ways knowing that if their paths were to ever cross again, they would meet as friends. With one more nod, the two former enemies stepped into their respective vehicles and drove to the starting line. The crowd roared with excitement as they watched the Black Ford and White Bronco take their positions. Aaron Dent took his spot. The potential sponsors corralled around him and waited to see if Liam's driving ability really did live up to its reputation. Aaron sat in his chair like he was the king of the world. His toothy smile grew with each rev of Liam's engine.

Julia Shipman walked between the two trucks to her designated spot; she wore a deep cut shirt paired with biker mini shorts and thigh-high boots, all in white, of course. She came dressed for the occasion. Parker and Joe stood anxiously on the side and away from the Dent following. Parker put his hands in his pockets as he felt the two letters between his fingers. He let out a heavy sigh. Liam nodded in Parker's direction, giving him an ominous but grateful stare. This was it, there was no turning back.

Julia turned to the crowd, she waved the white flag high in the air, the crowd once again roared with a euphoric fever as the sound of Liam and Johnny's names echoed against the hills. She turned back to face the two opponents who were both grasping their steering wheels until their knuckles had turned a bone white. All eyes were on her, and she knew it. She slowly raised the flag high; the thunderous noise that occupied the air only moments earlier had come to a deafening halt as a dead calmness replaced it. The wind was the only sound to be heard as it whipped around the flag. She moved her head to Liam, he nodded yes, and then she turned to Johnny as he did the same. They were both ready. She inhaled deeply along with everyone else; the start of the race was upon them. She squeezed the flag tightly, looking up at it, her body exhaled, the solid white cloth left her grasp, the wind whistling it around as it fell poetically downward, hitting the pavement with a crashing thud.

Liam and Johnny gunned their gas at the exact same moment, their tires screeching into the asphalt as their trucks barreled down the road. The noise returned to its feverish pitch. The crowd's frenzied energy shaking violently as they watched the two trucks pass them in a chaotic haze. Both drivers were neck and neck. Aaron stood from his seated position remaining calm, watching closely for Liam to take the lead. Johnny seemed to be a half a length ahead of Liam as he tried to maneuver his Bronco past the F-150 before taking the onslaught into Devil's Bulge. But Liam had turned into a master driver since his high school days. He knew exactly what to do, and he allowed Johnny to take the lead, knowing he would have to slow down before entering the wicked turn... and when he did, Liam would take that opportunity to pass Johnny and then take the race for himself. A few hundred feet before Devil's Bulge, Johnny's Bronco was still a half a length ahead of Liam, it gradually slowed down allowing Liam's F-150 to catch up. The two drivers glanced at each other, knowing what was before them. The plan was set into motion. Johnny slammed on his brakes; his steering wheel began to shake uncontrollably. The crowd watched in horror, Johnny tried desperately to keep his truck from careening out of control; all the while no one had realized that Liam had taken the lead and disappeared into Devil's Bulge.

"What the hell is going on?" Parker asked Joe.

"Your guess is as good as mine. Something's not right, something's wrong with Johnny's Bronco."

But Johnny's White Bronco wasn't ready, as a matter a fact, it had been leaking oil since the beginning of the race, and the left rear tire had a hole in it that was causing air to slowly escape from it. These two factors were detrimental and had now prevented Johnny not just from finishing but winning the race. Johnny fought with his Bronco to keep it from overturning on him. The truck fought back frantically, but Johnny navigated his way off the side of the road. Spectators ran wildly to get out of his way. It finally came to a stop landing on its side. It gave out a loud hiss while Johnny sat sideways staring at Devil's Bulge.

"Are you okay?" Parker ran to Johnny's aid.

"Yeah, I'm fine, only my ego is bruised… again," Johnny said climbing out and dusting himself off while he kept his eyes on the bend before him. He saw nothing but the remnants of debris and dust that Liam's truck produced when it passed him.

"Are you sure, is it your heart?"

"No, Parker, I feel fine, it's my truck. My wheel started vibrating and then I heard this loud pop. Dammit!" Johnny kicked his truck, throwing his hands in the air in frustration. A crowd gathered around him, but most eyes were still glued to Devil's Bulge waiting to see the return of the black F-150.

Seconds turned into minutes and still there was no sign of Liam. It had been almost five minutes since he disappeared behind Devil's Bulge, not long in most cases but an eternity in the racing realm. He should have made the turn effortlessly minutes ago and been well on his way to crossing the finishing line, but there was no sign of Liam or his truck. He seemed to have disappeared like a ghost in the night.

Chapter Twenty-Two
Redemption

Aaron was leery as he voiced his concern to Parker. "What the hell is going on? Where's Liam?!"

"I don't know. Your guess is as good as mine." Parker thought about his conversation with Liam before the race and wondered if this little disappearing act had anything to do with what he meant.

Aaron, for the first time since the race, began to show signs of emotion. He got on his walkie-talkie looking for some answers to what happened to his prized driver. "What do you mean you don't know? Don't you see him?" Aaron threw down the walkie-talkie in disgust as he stormed past Johnny and Parker. "Dammit!"

"Something's not right, Johnny; Liam should've been back by now," Parker said. Johnny didn't say a word; he just stared along with everyone else at the bend. The crowd was cheering Liam's name, waiting impatiently to see the black F-150 appear from Devil's Bulge. The noise was thunderous, but Parker heard something that seemed to escalate over the uproar of the crowd. He walked past everyone, almost in slow motion; he sensed something. No one noticed Parker's mannerisms except for Johnny.

"What is it, Parker? Do you see something?"

"No, but I think I heard something. Come on!" Parker insisted.

Parker began running faster while Johnny tried desperately to keep up with him. Aaron and Joe both noticed the boys' frantic behavior and began running after them too. By the time they caught up with them, the entire crowd was behind them. They couldn't believe what they saw once they made it past Devil's Bulge. In a culvert about a hundred yards past the bend, flipped over and smoke rising from the carnage, lie the F-150, the wheels still turning somehow, unaware that it was no longer in the race.

"Oh my God, not again! Liam!" Parker and Johnny both yelled out in horror. Liam was pinned inside. The smell of gasoline was filling the air. "We have to get you out of here; it's going to blow up!" But there was no response from Liam's bloodied and limp body.

"Liam, get up man!" Aaron yelled pushing his way in. "Let me handle this." He slapped Liam's face. "Come on, wake up, buddy, you're okay… you're okay." But still, Liam didn't answer. He just lay there as blood poured from his head and down his rugged face, his eyes half open, the sparkle that once resided in them was now absent, leaving them dull and listless.

"We need an ambulance!" Johnny yelled running through the crowd. "Someone call 911, Liam is hurt! Hurry!" The screams of Johnny's voice reverberated throughout the air. The crowd's euphoric chants had been replaced with screams of fear and panic. Ripley Road had turned into a place of mayhem and confusion. "I gotta call his grandpa," Johnny said to Parker.

"What about Jenny? Someone needs to let her know what happened!" Parker exclaimed.

But Johnny already knew that answer. "I think she already knows." his voice was grim.

"Grandpa's on his way!" Joe yelled from the crowd.

"It doesn't look good, man. I... I don't know..." Parker began to fumble with his words, becoming choked with emotion.

Johnny placed a hand on his trembling shoulders. "Come on, I hear the ambulance, let's go help them."

The two men turned around only for Johnny to turn back again; something had caught his eye, his face turned as pale as a ghost as he looked in front of him. The abrupt and strange behavior caused Parker to turn around too; both of them became frozen as they stared at the enormous buck with the missing antler that ambled before them, his presence larger than life. He gave a huff towards them before disappearing into the woods.

"Oh my God, it can't be... it can't..." Johnny stuttered.

"It is. You don't think that's what happened again?"

Johnny leaned down to the F-150, the wheels still turning, embedded in the silver fender on the right side of the truck was a tuft of brown fur, spotted in blood. Johnny pulled it away from the truck and examined it carefully and then looked at Parker in disbelief. "Yeah, I think that's exactly what happened. Look." Johnny gave Parker the fur.

"I can't believe this, it just can't be, the same damn deer exactly two years later?! It's just too weird," Parker said as he scratched his head. But it was, and both of them knew it.

Johnny and Parker both stared at the mesmerizing pelt knowing that this seemingly harmless animal had been the cause of Liam's misfortune. The larger than life animal had stood before them, undaunted by their presence or the catastrophe he had caused. The look he gave them was a look of redemption, payback for what had happened to him the first time. Neither one of them spoke another word, both of them still standing, still frozen in time while the mayhem around them continued to move at a furious pace.

All the excitement of the day had been replaced with a ghostly silence as Liam's friends, colleagues and admirers hovered around him. The medics were pulling him carefully from his truck while the engine hissed with what little life it still had in it. Parker and Johnny stood by their friend, talking to him with words of encouragement. Liam hadn't responded to any of it, he remained limp as the medics tried frantically to get a response from him.

"Let me through, let me through!" Everyone could tell by the huskiness of the voice who it belonged to. The crowd parted for Grandpa Mack. "My boy, my boy! Oh dear Lord, not my boy, not again!" Grandpa wailed. He looked to Parker and Johnny for answers. "What happened?" And then he saw Aaron Dent. "This is all your fault, you did this you damn bastard!" Grandpa charged towards him, grabbing the man's leather jacket and throwing him to the ground. Toby Raines and about five other of Aaron's men jumped on Grandpa only to have Parker, Joe and Johnny come to their elder's side.

"Stop this!" Johnny made himself a barricade between all of them. This isn't going to do Liam any good to have you guys battle it out. It wasn't anybody's fault that this happened, and it doesn't matter anyway, what does matter is Liam, and right now, he's in a really bad way. He didn't have the heart to mention the deer he and Parker had just seen.

Aaron's men pulled back. Joe and Parker held on to Grandpa trying desperately to wrangle himself free from them. "What happened tonight? Why is my boy lying on the ground over there?"

"We don't know, Grandpa. We didn't see the accident. He was winning, he actually passed Johnny but Johnny lost control and Liam drove on. We had no idea something was wrong with Liam, he was doing great, we were all waiting for him to come out of Devil's Bulge. But he didn't. That's when we realized something was wrong. Parker said trying to give some answers to Grandpa.

But Grandpa was beyond being consoled at this point, he knew where the answers lie, and it was with his son, the boy he had raised since the tender age of six. He knew that even though his mind was in the race, his heart wasn't. He hadn't been the same boy since the night of the first accident. It didn't help that he had lost his way with drinking and the likes of Toby, Gina, and Aaron. These cruel animals who called themselves humans were nothing more than leeches that lived off of his grandson and now, as Liam lay still on the hard pavement that made up the infamous Ripley Road, they gathered their belongings, unwilling to admit their part in this horrific night.

"We're out of here, Johnny, let me know how your friend is," Aaron said callously.

"You're not going to the hospital?"

"No, I think it's best that I don't. Besides, he has who he needs around him right now, and I have the distinct impression that I'm not one of them. Even though the two of you didn't finish the race, you'll still get a cut from tonight's profits; I'll send you your share in the mail to you."

"So, that's it? You're leaving just like that? Is this how you operate? Look around you, there's been an accident, your prized driver is hurt, don't you even care about him or is it just about the money with you?!"

"What are you trying to say, Johnny?"

"I'm trying to say that you're nothing but an asshole! Liam is lying on the ground not even twenty feet from you and you don't even give a damn! Why do you have to leave so soon? I'm sure if the race had been finished you would be making some sort of plans to celebrate, you don't have the time to see him off to the hospital to make sure he's going to make it?"

Aaron remained calm while Johnny continued his rant. Toby waited for Aaron to give him his cue to pounce on Johnny but instead, Aaron told his fellow colleagues to pack up and head on out. "This is so interesting coming from you, Johnny. I must say, I'm surprised by your emotional pull to your former friend. I thought you two were sworn enemies or was I mistaken?" Johnny didn't pleasure the asshole with an answer. "Well, it doesn't matter anyway; I got what I came for. I was hoping for a better finish to the race, but I must say you and Liam still out did yourselves. I guess this race between you two is just not meant to be finished but still, what a helluva show you guys put on for this town and for me. I can see why so many people flocked to see this momentous event. If you can't cross the finish line what better way than to have both of you, burn out. I like this ending better, it keeps the audience wanting more and that's exactly how I make my money. I think I see another race in our future, Mr. Bryant. I'll be in touch." Aaron began to walk away only to be interrupted by Johnny's fist.

"That was for Liam and his grandpa. There will be no more races, Aaron, by Liam or me. This was it, you know that."

"Yeah, I guess I do, but like I said, it doesn't matter. I still got what I came for, not only did I make a shit load of money off of him, after tonight, everyone will know who I am, and that's all I care about it. You're pretty good, Johnny, I was impressed. If you ever get your heart taken care of, you should look me up, I can take you places, just ask your friend." Aaron paused before getting into his car, "And as far as Liam is concerned, give him my best. Damn, what a shame. I hope he makes it. He's a good kid." He looked over at Liam; the paramedics were working frantically on him. "Hmmmmm... I could have taken that boy places, he had quite the future in front of him, too bad it's over. Oh well, sometimes you win, sometimes you lose." The sheer coldness of Aaron's voice made everybody sick to their stomach. It took everything in their power not to go after him, but their concern was for Liam, unlike Aaron.

****

It was a somber scene at the hospital. Dr. Garrett met the three men in the hallway. "How is he Doc?" The words staggered out of Grandpa's mouth as he tried to hold back his tears. He had been in this position one too many times.

"We're prepping him for surgery, Mack. I'm not going to sugar-coat this, but he's in really bad shape. He flat-lined twice on his way here. He has a lot of internal bleeding, and his chances of survival aren't good. You need to be prepared, Mack. I'm sorry." Dr. Garrett placed his hand on Grandpa's broad shoulders as he witnessed this man who had lived through so much in his life succumb to the horrible news of his beloved grandson. Grandpa's body gave in and fell to the floor. Parker and Johnny both followed him trying to console the man they had only known as Grandpa. Liam, who was in a cold, stark room just a few feet from them flat-lined for the third time.

The wails from Liam's grandpa could be heard throughout the hospital as he surrendered to his misery.

Chapter Twenty-Three
Coming Home

    The night was long. Liam awoke to the sound of his name being called. He looked all around him but could not find where the voice was coming from. He felt strange when he stood up. He began to walk only to find that his gait had changed; the pronounced limp that he had carried for so long was now completely gone. "Jenny? Is that you? Where are you, babe? I can't find you." But the voice that called for Liam had grown silent; he was all alone walking along the path. He found himself at Serenity Hill. He looked for his bride, this is where she said she would be waiting for him, but he didn't see her anywhere. His heart grew faint as he wondered if she had left him, maybe her time waiting had grown long, and she had become impatient. "Jenny?" he yelled again. This time, he heard the voice but was startled when he turned to find out who was calling for him.

    She walked wistfully towards Liam, her long hair framing her porcelain face as ringlets of it floated around her as it caught the wind. She looked as she always had to him: beautiful. "Mom?" A feeling of love swept over him at the sight of her. His voice was subdued and almost frightened as he spoke her name. He didn't know if she was real; if this time was real. He became frozen while she made her way to him. Her moves were effortless, stopping only inches from him, her enigmatic stare infiltrated right through him with his eyes.

"Liam," she said softly. He was mesmerized and in awe of her presence and still, he wondered if he was dreaming. "It's okay, Liam, you don't have to be afraid of me."

"I don't think I'm afraid, I'm just trying to grasp what's going on, are you real, Mom?"

"I am as real to you as the heavens are to the angels, my dear." She reached out her hand to his. Her touch was warm and reminded him of his childhood.

"Why are you here Mom? I don't understand."

"I'm here to let you know that it's alright to let go."

"All I want to do is to be with her, Mom."

"I know, dear. The two of you have a love that transcends through time; it's a rare and uncommon bond that cannot be broken."

"But it hasn't been an easy love, Mom, it's been so hard. I didn't know if we would make it. I've fallen, and I've failed her. I thought I was strong enough to handle the pressures that I faced, but I haven't been, and in the process, Jenny has seen a side of me that makes me ashamed."

"Ashamed? Liam, don't you realize that the shame you think she feels for you is instead a feeling of pride and a greater love for you. The struggles you have endured have only deepened her feelings for you."

"She left me, Mom."

"She's never left you, just as I have never left you, my son. That is why I'm here, you need to know that the decision you made was the right one. I know your heart, Liam and I can hear it beat for Jenny. You need to let go, and finally, go to her, she's never left you, she's been waiting for you just as she promised.

"I just want to do what's right for her. I don't want to hurt her anymore, she doesn't deserve that."

"The only thing that could hurt her is if you don't keep your promise."

"I love you, Mom. I've missed you so much."

"I've always been right here, Liam," Jessica said as she pointed to Liam's heart. She looked away to the horizon that overlooked the ridge. "I have to go son, and so do you. It's time."

"But I want to talk to you; please, can't we spend some more time together."

Jessica didn't answer; she leaned in and gave her son a heartfelt kiss on his forehead. "I love you too, Liam, I always will; now go to Jenny, her wait has been long enough." She turned from her son and walked away. Liam kept his eyes on her as she faded from his view.

He was alone again. He felt torn, he wanted to see if his mom would return but he felt destined to continue his walk. His body was being pulled, but he didn't understand why or to where; he only knew that he had to keep moving and that this would lead him to Jenny."

"I'm coming home, baby, I'm finally coming home."

Chapter Twenty-Four
The Walk

      I felt strange staring at the house; my head dizzy from the feeling. It was quiet, but the two oak trees that resided on either side of the intimidating structure seemed to chant my name as the wind stirred among its leaves. I approached the house taking the broken steps that Liam had promised me a hundred times that he would fix. I chuckled softly as my right foot went into the fragmented wood. I could still hear him saying, *"Watch your step, babe,"* he would then proceed to take my arm to keep me from falling, always the gentleman. I walked onto the porch and stood in front of the enormous wooden door with the ornately beveled window panes framing it. My heart was beating at an uncomfortable pace as I grabbed the tarnished doorknob; it turned effortlessly welcoming me into its internal realm. The butterflies had returned. They were still there giving me feelings of enchantment once I was inside. I proceeded cautiously and then stopped. A formidable sensation kept me from moving on, for some odd reason I was immobile, unable to go on, even though I yearned to be here. Maybe I was afraid of what lie ahead, knowing that my visit would not produce the desire I coveted.

      And yet, as I perused my surroundings I couldn't help but feel a sense of calm and tranquility as the images of times past flashed before me. I took it all in, inhaling sharply, digesting everything. The house still looked the same, which was a very satisfying and welcome site as my memories flashed in front of me. I began to smell the scent of freshly brewed coffee and homemade cinnamon buns coming from the kitchen, their aroma wafting through the air. I could have sworn I heard Grandpa and Liam's voices while they talked about the day ahead of them. To my left was the living room. The same floral sofa that Liam and I sat on so many times still graced the middle of the room. I envisioned the countless times we occupied it while we engaged in so many of our heartfelt conversations. His adoring blue eyes always absorbed in mine as if he were to look away from me I would somehow disappear from his sight.

My eyes slowly pulled away from that vision and gravitated towards the one corner in the room. I felt overwhelmed at the sight; before me stood my Christmas tree. I could see the branches heavily laden with the blue and silver ornaments that Liam so lovingly adorned on it. But more importantly, I could hear the excitement in his voice as he presented it to me, his words still quivering when he spoke, afraid that for some reason, I might not like it. He was so wrong, always so worried that he wasn't making me happy when his very existence made me happy. Just being with him made me the happiest person on Earth, not the material things that he constantly bestowed upon me. I smiled. My gaze left the room, the image leaving an everlasting impression on me. I continued my walk down the long and unobtrusive hallway, still looking around each corner for him to appear. Even the sight of Blue would be nice, but there was nobody here, only my own footsteps to break the silent monotony. I approached the staircase; my eyes again were diverted to the right where I saw the kitchen. The clinking of glasses and the shutting of cabinet doors could be heard. It was Liam and me laughing while we made ourselves something to eat. I shook my head realizing that what I thought I was seeing and hearing was only a memory, but still, I stood watching the scene play out before me as if it was truly happening, each frame reliving a time in our lives together. A tear fell from my face. One of so many that I had shed since Liam had entered my life.

I turned to the stairs once more. I pondered on whether I should continue this tour or leave. There really was no reason for me to be here; I knew where I needed to be, but in order to get there I had to make this house part of my journey. I had been everywhere else; this was my last stop before my final destination. I grabbed the railing and held on to it tightly, causing the knuckles in my hand to turn a bone white. For some reason, seeing the sallow color of my skin was very amusing to me. Another smile crept onto my face as I stared at the paleness. I began my walk slowly up the staircase. I wanted to relive each step as if I was experiencing them for the very first time. And in a strange way, I was. I could only remember a handful of times when I actually climbed these stairs on my own accord. Normally, I was in the comfort and embrace of Liam's arms; he never wanted me to walk on my own when he could hold me in his embrace. I made it to the top; I stood fixated by the long hallway in front of me. Behind me was the room that held so many secrets that begged to be revealed: but in the end, the surreptitious room was better left unattended and undisturbed. So, as a manner of respect for its hidden contents, I felt inclined to leave that door closed. Down the hall was Liam's bedroom, or our bedroom, as he wanted me to think of it. A sudden rush bewitched me. *I told myself I could do this, that it would be easy.* But it wasn't and now, more than ever, I wanted to leave. *To just turn around and never look back, but that would be the coward's way out, and I had waited far too long to let this moment pass without incident. I closed my eyes, repeating to myself that I could do this that I was strong enough to handle what was ahead of me, that this too, would be okay.*

But as my eyes remained shut and the darkness I prayed for consumed me, I heard him speak to me. *"It's okay Jenny, I'm here. You can do this, don't be afraid, babe."* Liam's sweet voice trying to comfort me as only he knew how.

"I can't Liam; I just can't, not without you." My tearful voice barely audible even to my own ears.

"Yes, you can, Jenny. Don't be afraid. Go on." His voice was so calm and reassuring, as though he knew what I could do better than I knew myself.

The trepidation of continuing overwhelmed me. I felt more like I was standing at the edge of a cliff than the back of the hallway.

"Keep going, Jenny," Liam continued to whisper. I looked down as I told my right foot to move in front of my left. *"Keep going, Jenny."*

The usual few seconds it took to arrive at the bedroom seemed to be taking forever now. Each door I encountered seemed to be a blur as I passed it. I knew what I was going to find when I entered the room, and the mere thought of that was scaring me to death. My gait was slow and cautious. My heart beating a thousand beats faster as my pallid hands approached and enclosed the intricate doorknob that would lead me inside.

"Jenny, open the door." Liam's voice was ever so sweet, so very adamant.

With a deep breath I did, the other side of the door revealed Liam's bedroom. I became instantly comforted, the calmness and tranquility I yearned for encompassing me with its gentle embrace. The anxiety was gone, swept away with the rush of air that the door stirred on its opening. Besides Serenity Hill, and even more so than Brush Creek Road, this was the one place that had become a sanctuary for Liam and me. The one place we could go to when we wanted to escape from the world. That's why I had come back here, that's why it was so important for me to be here before I moved on. I needed to be in our room, surrounded by our belongings and the memories we made here. I could feel Liam's presence, and even his touch on me as a shiver ran up my arm. In this room, I was with him again.

I entered the room and made my way to the bed, sitting down gingerly; the black comforter giving in to my weight. Finally, I could breathe. I gazed affectionately at the room. Not much had changed. As a matter of fact, everything looked exactly the same. I reflected on the pictures of Liam and me that sat on the nightstand. There was the goofy one of him and me as he held me upside down and made the funny face. Then there was the one my mom had taken the night of homecoming. It seemed like a lifetime ago since those pictures were taken. A feeling of melancholy overcame me as I remembered back to those times, a time when if I had only known then what I knew now, I would have embraced them even more. I laid my head on the pillow and sharply inhaled the scent that belonged only to Liam. It inebriated my senses. I squeezed the pillow tightly praying that somehow, I could make Liam appear before me, but the only thing that appeared were more of my tears. I wanted him, I needed him, my body ached for him. I was tired of waiting for him; my impatience waning with each passing moment that he was away from me.

"Please stop crying, baby. I love you."

"I love you too, Liam. I love you so much. Please come back to me, please. I miss you so much."

"I'm on my way, love; I'm only a heartbeat away." If only I could honestly believe that.

I could have sworn Liam's arms wrapped around me, squeezing me as our bodies conformed to one another, letting me know that he was here. But as I turned to face him, to look into his crystal-blue eyes, I only found myself facing an empty room. I knew I only imagined it, but it felt so real that I thought for sure, he was too. I arose from the bed and made my way to the door. I had seen enough and I knew it was time for me to leave.

I turned one more time to gaze upon the room. I wanted to take everything in for one last time, memorizing each detail so I would never forget, knowing my body would never grace this room again. I was given a gift, but I couldn't be selfish with it. It was time for me to let it go, one chapter ended, and another one was waiting to begin. I was ready to leave when out of the corner of my eye I saw it, peeking itself from behind the huge oak bed. It was just one corner of it, but enough for me to recognize it, Liam's football jersey, the number eleven staring at me as bold and as brilliant as it had from the very beginning. I picked up the frame that protected this ominous and portentous number that had followed us from the beginning and continued to remain in our lives even now. I stared at the lines that made this number and recalled a time when I was afraid of it, considering the digit a warning, or better yet a threat, but in reality, it had been a guide, a tool to pilot Liam and me on our passage, a blessing in disguise.

The number didn't bring us together, destiny had done that. The number just happened to be there to steer us along our way, to remind us who we are and where we belonged. We were brought together because we were meant to be, not by chance but by fate, plain and simple. Whether the number was there or not, our destiny had already been sealed for us to be with one another a long time before our bodies had even touched. Liam and I knew that. Everybody did, including Johnny Bryant. I do believe he needed to enter my life for me to realize that I didn't need him in my life, as weird as that may sound. At least not in the way he wanted it to be. He had always been there for me. And just like Liam, he had loved me too. Even though my heart and unconditional love lie with Liam, a small part of my love belonged to Johnny, too.

I took one final look at the room. It was finally time to move on, I had seen enough. The room seemed to be suspended in time, just as I felt.

I left closing the door behind me. My walk was again slow but eager this time as the hallway faded behind me. I traveled forward; I could see Grandpa Mack in his room sitting in his rocking chair, Blue at his feet, fast asleep and content. The stairs creaked beneath my feet; they too were saying goodbye to me with each step I took. I reached the bottom of the staircase and glanced once more into the living room. I was positive I could see a light dimly flicker on and off, the room was also bidding me farewell. I gave a slight smile and nod towards the inanimate space before leaving.

Outside, Sugar Dumplin' was grazing on the grass; the sun was setting on the horizon. The sunset was vivid in its color, the end of another day and the promise of a new tomorrow. I blew a kiss into my hand and threw it to the wind. An act of appreciation for the abundant memories it had given me. As I walked away from the house, I could see clearly now that the narrow path in front of me had widened. I knew what it meant because I had seen it only one other time on a dark and rainy road, the number eleven was still there to guide and reassure me. I fervently walked as my anticipation grew. I knew it wouldn't be much longer. This was not the end but the beginning, and everything before this very moment was only the prelude.

The walk in front of me was not meant for me to go alone. It had been so long, the fact that it was finally here made me giddy. Through all the trials and tribulations our relationship had given us, we never forgot what we meant to one another. Yes, there were moments of doubt and we did lose sight of each other, but it was only momentary. Our love had been born long before we had; it was just waiting for our earthly bodies to find each other.

Now as I began my walk, I look back and realize that Liam's and my journey had been a learning experience to help us through this process, to get us to this point. Our journey had made us stronger, not only physically, but mentally through our mind and spirit. And allowing certain people to enter our lives that would not only befriend us but help mold us and guide us in the direction through the choices that we made, whether they be right or wrong. The answers were always there. Instead of realizing that, I decided to make it harder on myself and in the process, made it more difficult for everyone I loved. But now I felt at peace, everything was in place, the puzzle almost completed, only one piece missing, but not for long. The walk was beautiful and serene and even though I had never been here before, in my dreams I had been here many times. The crooks and crevices in the broken stone path, the green moss that grew along the side, even the buttercups and violets that popped up sporadically before me were all familiar to me. Welcoming me and reminding me of what lie ahead.

I could feel the warmth of him; with each new hint of the wind that touched my face I could feel him. He was near. It seemed I had been waiting for this moment an eternity...and maybe I had. I lost track of time, time always stood still when it came to Liam and me. I could sense him now; his presence was growing stronger with each step I took. We could feel each other without the other being present; he knew he was close to me as well.

"I'm coming, Jenny."

"I know, Liam."

I wasn't afraid, but anxious as the approaching moment grew closer. I continued my walk and focused on the path's shape as it curved ahead of me. For the longest time, I took it as the one. My one. Liam had his own path...his one. And together, side-by-side our paths, our ones, made the number eleven. How funny it seemed now as I reminisced about it, looking back at our beginning.

In the distance, I could see a shadowy figure approaching me. It was Liam. He closed in on me embracing me with his strong and comforting arms that I had missed for so long. I finally felt alive for the first time in a very long time.

"Hello, my love. Have you been waiting for me?" He tenderly leaned in and kissed me.

"Only for a lifetime," I said.

I didn't want to let him go. It had been so long since we touched, since I felt him against me, or smelled his scent. He smiled, and his crystal-blue eyes ignited with the love he had for me and reassured me that this time; we would never be separated again. We kissed, and a fire erupted inside of me instantly. I had longed for this feeling for so long.

"No more sorrow, babe, only happiness," Liam said with reassurance.

I turned to look behind me for only a moment. The path behind us was etched with memories from the past that brought us to this point in our lives. I saw our family and friends as they stood quietly next to one another. Consoling each other as Liam's casket was slowly lowered into the ground next to mine.

Two Hearts turn into one from Above
Finally, Forever Together, Their Love
Liam and Jenny

You see, Liam had died in the accident, his body mangled and broken beyond the repair from any doctor. Nothing could save him that night. But to be honest, he didn't want to be saved; he wanted to be with me. This was his plan as well as his destiny. He made great strides after my death to try and move on without me, but it turned out to be too hard for him. He came undone at the seams and although he knew I was with him in spirit that wasn't enough. He knew our time together was soon but he had no idea of when or where or even how, his intuition led him to believe, to be prepared, and so he made peace with his life, knowing he couldn't leave without making things right with the ones he would leave behind.

His death had come long before the accident. Yes, physically he had finally died, but his soul died the night I perished, two months after the accident on April 11th. I lived long enough for Liam to give me his last name and for our future to be secured as husband and wife forever. I never woke up; I never got to see the relief in Liam's eyes as mine met his knowing that I had finally awakened from my two-month slumber. Instead, I felt only the cold and loneliness that death brought to me. I remained in a coma until June 11th and finally succumbed to my injuries with Liam always by my side. He lost all hope after my death. His life was nothing more than a broken record that kept replaying the past to him over and over again in his mind. He couldn't endure it. The thought of leaving this world on his own accord crossed his mind many times, but he knew I would disapprove. I believe there was a special hell for souls who took their own lives, a place so desperate and sad, that no spiritual being would forgive. A place that did not know love or cared to, a place where souls were destined to walk alone and a place where they were to live their eternity in hopelessness, gloom, and desolation.

I wanted Liam to be with me, I waited for him patiently, but he knew he had to come to me when it was his time; when the heavens above had ordained it, just as they had ordained mine. I wanted to help him, and I tried through his dreams, but even those sometimes turned against him.

No one could reach him. He was an empty shell. He spent his days drinking and his nights racing. He carried the weight of the world on his back. There were no more happy times for Liam, his demons following him as he blamed himself for the accident and ultimately, my death. He was a dead man walking with a heartbeat, surrounded by family and friends, yet still all alone in the world.

But I was still with him if only in spirit; and he knew that. At night, when his tired body would finally give in to a restless but still much-needed slumber, I would come to him in his dreams. Talking to him, consoling him, telling him how I much I loved him and that he was never alone, telling him that it was only a matter of time, to hang on until we could be together once again. He felt at times as though those dreams were his nightmares, reminding him of the fateful night that was the perpetrator to my demise, frightening occurrences to remind and torture him even further. But I knew he heard me.

Although I had no idea of the hour or even the time of day, I knew our long-awaited reunion would be soon. I knew his time on Earth was very limited and that our time together in eternity was closely approaching. My new body ached with the excitement and anticipation of his arrival. And as I finally held his hand in mine, I relished with the realization that my patience had strengthened me.

****

"I love you, Jenny."

"I love you too. I've missed you so much."

Liam picked me up and held me tight in his embrace. "Oh, babe, it's me that has missed you. I will never leave your side again, Mrs. Larson."

"You promise, Mr. Larson?"

"Do you remember our wedding ceremony, Jenny?"

A huge smile sprung from my face. I recalled the event as if it had happened yesterday. It didn't happen on Serenity Hill, our wedding happened moments before I passed away.

"Yes, how could I forget? You stood next to my bedside as you held tightly to my hand. I was wearing the white dress you had given me. Even though my eyes were closed, I could still see you. I was leaving but not until I was your wife. You were so handsome in your white shirt and black pants. You had a lavender boutonniere in your lapel, just for me. You laid a dozen lavender roses next to me; they were so beautiful. I was unable to speak to you, but you heard my heart. I remember the sensation that ran through me while you held onto my hand tenderly as the minister performed the ceremony. You placed a silver band on my finger and then placed an identical one on yours. The minister pronounced us husband and wife, and you gently kissed me as our families looked on. You whispered in my ear how much you loved me. There were so many emotions running through you, happiness that we were finally united as one, but such sadness as my imminent death was so near. I also remember you never left my side, and you were with me when I finally did take my last breath, never allowing me to be afraid or alone."

"I told you I would never leave you and I meant it. I felt your love that night, Jenny. I felt your love every day after your death. Your love is what kept me going until I couldn't go on any longer. It was meant to be this way, you and me together, forever."

Liam pulled me to him, holding me in his tight but ever gentle embrace as he kissed me the only way Liam knew how... with all his heart and soul. Our lives were now, finally, and forever, one. He gently released me as we smiled at each other lovingly.

"I have something for you, Liam."

He knew what I was about to give him. I've only seen this look on him when he talks about his love for me. A pure love that I could only give him; and now, as I placed our son, Guardian, in Liam's arms, I saw the same look of love come across Liam's face again.

"He's been waiting for you."

Liam didn't speak, but the smile that broadened as he held Guardian spoke volumes. Liam had once told me that he had only been in love once and that's when he saw me. Now as he gazed upon at our son, I could see he had fallen in love all over again.

"Forever, Jenny?"

"Forever, Liam, the three of us forever."

We slowly walked on our path, Liam cradling Guardian and I cradling Liam's arm. The light was brighter now as we approached it, a calming of peace, love, and tranquility engulfed us. I wasn't afraid anymore of what lie ahead of me because I knew I had the loves of my life by my side to experience it.

****

In death as in life you may not always understand what's in store for you, but would you really want to know anyway? Isn't the element of the unknown, the surprise factor so much better than the actual knowing? Most of us fear death, but I see death as something to embrace and look forward too. It's the beginning, not the end. I didn't know if I would ever be with Liam again after April 11th; that daunting number that seemed to scare me more than bring me the reassurance that I begged from it. It was always just there to guide me. I understood that now and so did Liam. But as I looked ahead at the path that we were about to embark upon, the two courses that formed an everlasting eleven that disappeared into the horizon, I realized it was a conduit to our forever journey, and forever was looking incredible to us. The saying that all roads lead home rings very true for Liam and me. We were finally on our way home, and we had traveled many roads to get there.

Chapter Twenty-Five
The Storyteller

"Tell me more, Grandpa, tell me more, pleeeese!" The little girl begged as she climbed onto her grandpa's lap.

"Well, come on up and I will," The elderly man said helping his eager granddaughter to his lap. He chuckled at the sight of her enthusiasm as she begged for him to begin. He'd told this story to her at least a hundred times before but she never grew tired of it, and in reality, neither did he. It was a part of him that he would never forget as he held his permanently tanned and weathered hand to his heart. It beat in rhythm to his granddaughter's sweet and harmless pleas.

"I love your stories, they're the best," she said as she shimmied herself into his lap. Her grandpa looked to the sky where he witnessed the soft and tranquil rain descending from the clouds that were coming to a close once hitting the ground.

"Are you sure you want me to tell you again? You've heard this story a hundred times, Jennifer."

"Mmm-hmmm," she murmured taking a sip of her juice, she was so excited in anticipation of the story that most of the purple, sugary contents spilled onto her chin instead of going into her mouth.

"Well then, I better get started, sweetheart."

"Yes, yes, yes!" The little girl said giggling with genuine excitement.

And so the elderly man began his tale...once again.

He began as he always did by telling his beloved granddaughter of a time long ago when a young boy and young girl fell helplessly and hopelessly in love. He told of how this young boy who, on one hot summer August afternoon on his way to football practice had his heart forever taken by a beautiful girl he had yet to meet with auburn hair and hazel eyes. He was the all-American football player, the adoration of the community and she was the shy and reclusive majorette. Grandpa continued his tale by speaking of the determination the boy had in meeting her and the apprehension the girl carried. His love for the girl grew with each new day and how happy he was when she finally felt the same for him. Their love was rare and beautiful in the most pure and simplistic of forms, and their lives were filled with all that young love brought with it. But even in their ideal and perfect world, the young girl carried a fear that brought her unease and dread most every day. She was scared of this foreboding element that she thought would mean the demise of their happiness. It was only when she allowed herself to open up and share her fear with him that she felt her trepidation would leave her, but still, that was not to be.

He continued telling his granddaughter of how a mere number, a simple digit held so much anxiety in this girl's life and even though she carried the support of her mate, it still hovered over her at all times. But still, she remained hopeful as she fell deeper in love with her football player. Their lives were forged together by their feelings for one another, their love was destined to be; as if it was Kismet and nothing in this world could ever change that, or so they thought. But that was until the New Year when an old friend of his came to town and fell in love with his girl as well. *He* didn't mean to fall for the girl with the auburn hair, *he* knew she loved another, but his heart had been damaged and only when *he* saw her did it begin to beat again. *He* pursued her with a vengeance, uncaring that *he* was wrong in doing so. The pursuit continued to no avail and still, *he* fought for her love. She not only loved someone else but she loved one of his oldest friends, which made his plight even more foolish. Even his mom, who held the gift and grown fond of the girl, tried to tell her son that it was wrong. She saw the disastrous outcome but still *he* pursued what he already knew was the impossible until there was no other choice left.

The two young men chose to end their feud by racing against each other on none other than the eleventh, that number that had haunted the girl from the very beginning. If she ever was afraid of the number before, she was petrified of it now. The race was supposed to be simple, once down and once back, the winner claiming victory; not of her but of their posterity. But still, it did not matter to her who won the race; her heart belonged to only one. It was with the one who made her heart skip a beat, the one whose crystal-blue eyes entranced her every time he looked her way, and the one who loved her as much as she loved him. And although her feelings for the newcomer at times made her question her loyalty, it was always brief, for nothing could compare with what she felt for her football player. *He* tried in vain to convince her of his affection, but in the end, it still did not matter to her; she rode the race with the boy who her destiny belonged to, leaving the boy with the damaged heart to ride alone.

"The race was held on a bleak and rainy Saturday night, and the entire school seemed to be there to cheer on the Black Ford F-150 and the White Bronco. There would only be one winner at the end and both boys prematurely claimed that title, if not for the race but for the girl's heart. And so, as the race began and the trucks sped away, and destiny began to step in.

The elderly man paused as he took a sip of his water.

"Don't stop now, Grandpa, please continue," the little girl implored him.

"Well, sweetheart you know what happened next. The deer came out of nowhere causing Liam to lose control and crash. It was the worst accident those parts had ever seen. Everybody ran to help the two injured lovers, but it was *him* who made it to them first. *He* immediately helped the girl that belonged to the other out of the twisted wreckage only to have the one she loved look on helplessly, in disbelief. That was the beginning of the demise for both the football player and his majorette.

For two months, he kept vigil by her side while *he* kept his from afar. But even with all the heartfelt prayers and care that she received, she was still doomed to leave her earthly body. She had lost their baby the night they brought her in but she knew that her soul mate would be devastated if she would leave him too, so soon. She knew the guilt he carried even though it wasn't his fault. She didn't blame him, she loved him, but her injuries prevented her from telling him, so instead she lay in wait while he had time to be with her. But her time was slipping away, and so her beloved arranged to have the ceremony that would bind them together forever.

"On a beautiful, sun-filled day, two months to the day of the accident, the beautiful girl with the auburn hair who lay peacefully in a charming but simple white wedding dress became his bride while their loved ones looked on. Moments later, after the minister pronounced them husband and wife, he kissed her softly as she took her final breath. He felt the breath leave her body as his lips touched hers, and at that very moment, he had begun to die with her. He knew he would not be able to carry on without her, no matter how much support he received from those who cared about him. No one could break through the wall he had built around him. It was only a matter of time before his end."

"Grandpa?"

"Yes?"

"I thought you told me that she used to talk to him? How could she do that if she had died?"

"She came to him in his dreams."

"But you said that she talked to everyone, did she come to them in their dreams too?"

"Yes, dear, that's exactly what happened. Everybody was so distraught and beside themselves after her untimely death, and she could see it, she felt their pain. While Jenny waited for Liam to come to her, she stayed close to those she had left behind by visiting them in their dreams. Everything that happened after the accident, her going to college, the two of them marrying at Serenity Hill, conversations they carried on with her; even her time with Johnny was all just a dream, their own individual dream but still just a dream. None of them had the opportunity to say good-bye to her. They played out scenes as if she really was alive. It was their way of grieving and finally being able to say good-bye and move on."

"Grandpa, does your heart still hurt?"

The elderly man clutched his granddaughter's precious, little hand in his, giving her a most loving and gentle smile. "Not anymore, dear. It used to hurt but I was given a gift by a very dear friend, and now my heart is better."

"It was from him, wasn't it; the football player gave you his heart?"

"Yes, Jennifer."

"So, you guys weren't enemies after all?"

"No, not really, we were just in love with the same girl, and we had a misunderstanding that seemed to last longer than it should have; but in the end, I realized that my love for her could never compare to what he felt for her. They were meant to be together, they were Kindred Spirits, and something that rare and special can never be torn apart."

"Are they together now?"

The grandfather looked towards the sky once more, the rain had ended giving way to a sapphire-blue sky that showcased a beautiful double rainbow crossing over them in a perfect arch. "Yes, I would definitely say they are together, hand-in-hand and heart-to-heart."

"What about her family?"

"Well, her death was very hard on them as you can imagine, and they found themselves in a lot of pain and misery. Everywhere they looked they saw her, and it reminded them that she would never return, so her parents closed the business and moved away, leaving Billy the apartments. It was too much for them to stay here."

"Grandpa, what about the number eleven?"

"In the end, I think they realized that they were the number, two bodies that formed two parallel lines, side-by-side, that went on forever just like their love. The number was only there to let them know that their destiny was with each other."

"What about your destiny, Grandpa?"

"I still carry my love and always will. I was given the opportunity to share in both of their lives, and I was given the gift of life by both of them. One by her unique beauty and insight that I needed to carry on here, on Earth, and his by the gift of life with his heart, so he could be with her. In the end, we all got what we wanted. He is where he belongs... with her, and I am where I belong... with you," he said kissing his beloved granddaughter's forehead.

"He left you a letter didn't he, that's how you knew that you would get his heart, right?"

"Yes, he left two letters, one to his grandpa and the other one to me."

"What did his grandpa's letter say?"

"I don't know, he died keeping the contents of the letter a secret. But that's okay, it was for him and him alone."

"But you have your letter; can you read it to me?"

"Of course." He put her down where she stayed, juice box in her hand. He returned moments later with a worn and yellowed envelope that contained the contents that would change his life forever. His hands were swollen and shook when he moved them, giving way to his age and the hard work he had done all his life, but still, he unfolded the fragile parchment carefully and began to read it to her.

The Letter...

Dear Johnny,

If you are reading this, well then, I am gone. Hell, I guess our race was never meant to be finished, but don't feel sorry for me or even sad because I bit the big one, you know as well as I do I'm where I belong, and I'm finally happy. It's ironic but while I sit here writing this, I think about me being gone, and I'm not afraid. I think I will finally feel alive because I don't feel that way now, especially with Jenny gone, I'm just not the same, even though I've tried, my life meant nothing after her death. I had a feeling something bad was going to happen to me, ever since those damn nightmares began. And as time went on, and so did my unraveling, the feeling got worse. I just couldn't shrug it off. So, I knew that I had to prepare myself...just in case, and that's why you're reading this letter from me.

Don't ask me why but I figured that my feeling was going to come true by race time, but it just seemed fitting. Maybe it was intuition, I don't know, but I just knew that if something was gonna happen, it was going to happen on the 11th. Hell, Jenny and that damn number. She was always trying to convince me to take heed of it, but I didn't want to put any stock into it, my only concerns were for her, my love for her was and is constant and eternal. I know you loved her too, Johnny and how can I blame you for that? I don't want you to think that I left this Earth hating you, you were always my friend, but it was just hard knowing how you felt for her.

So, as I finish this... call it my last will and testament to a friend, I want to give you my heart. I know you need it much more than I do. By coincidence or by fate, I found out that we shared the same rare blood type while I was in the hospital. Can you believe it? It is only right that it goes to you.

I don't need it where I am going. Jenny didn't so much take my heart as she took my soul, so please take my heart, Johnny and live the life I couldn't and love the way you should. Remember us as the friends we once were and if you must, the enemies we became but most importantly, remember us as the brothers we will forever be. Don't be sad for Jenny or for me, our lives aren't ending, they are just beginning. We are finally together and whole again, Kindred Spirits if you will, loving, laughing and dancing with each other as we begin our eternal journey. Take care my friend and may your life bless you with the love, life, and laughter you so deserve.

Your friend,

Liam

While the elderly man carefully and neatly folded the worn letter back into its original form, his granddaughter watched in fascination to his methodical movements.

"Grandpa?"

"Yes, my dear."

"I'm glad Liam and Jenny are finally together."

"Me too, my dear."

"Grandpa?"

"Yes, my dear."

"I like Jenny's name."

"I do too."

"Grandpa?"

"Yes, my dear?"

"Have you?"

"Have I what, my dear?"

"Have you been able to live, love and dance?"

A gentle and captivating smile arose on the grandfather's face as he pondered his granddaughter's intriguing last question. He picked her up and swung her around, both of them laughing incessantly. He held her close to his heart, her tiny little arms placed securely around his neck. "Yes, Jennifer, I would have to say with all my heart."

Even this late it happens:
The coming of love, the coming of light
You wake, and the candles are lit as if by themselves,
Stars gather, dreams pour into your pillows, sending up
warm bouquets of air
Even this late the bones of the body shine
And tomorrow's dust flares into breath

~Mark Strand

Jamie Kincaid

      Jamie Kincaid grew up in Spencer, West Virginia. She has been a lover of words and a storyteller since she was a little girl. And although she carries two degrees, one in Marketing from Glenville State College in Glenville, West Virginia and the other in Education from Buffalo State College, in Buffalo, New York, her affair with writing always remained. She has traveled and lived in many areas but if you were to ask her where her home is, she would tell you in a heartbeat that it is and always will be Spencer. In her spare time when she is not writing and taking care of her family, you can find her running miles and miles. She lives in Ohio with her husband and their three beautiful children and her golden retriever who remains faithfully by her side while she continues to write her next tale.

She would like to thank her family and friends for their love, support, and belief in her. And for those wonderful friends who always came to her rescue to help her out of computer situations, (you know who you are!) And for Him, who lifted me up and made me realize this is who I am and that it was only a matter of time before the world would know that too, seeing her stories in print can only be described as epic for her, a dream come true.

Liam and Jenny... they are in each and every one of us, believe in fate, true love, kismet... pickles, wild horses, silly jokes, sweet tea, endless talks, endless nights, drives to nowhere, heart and soul, you 'n me, always here, always and forever, destiny 831.

The Kismet Series:
Kismet: Book One

Jenny King detested the mere thought of Liam Larson. She didn't understand why every girl at Spencer High was intoxicated with him. But that was all before October 11th. It was a simple gesture; Liam, the all-star football player for the Spencer High Yellow Jackets, handed Jenny her baton. That encounter would change their lives forever. From then on, they became inseparable.

Jenny begins to notice a strange coincidence that seems to follow them; the number 11. It has become their shadow. When Liam begins indulging in street racing, Jenny becomes unraveled. He is always in heat number 11, or his time ends up with 11 in it. Jenny is convinced that the number is plaguing her for a reason.

Soon, Johnny Bryant, a friend of Liam's, moves to Spencer. He played football for the Walton Tigers, their number 11, and moves to Spencer when his mom, Gertie Bryant, a numerologist and psychic opens a spiritual shop. Johnny falls for Jenny and tells Liam that until there is a ring on her finger; she is his for the taking. Fights between Liam and Johnny over Jenny take center stage, and the boys decide that they need to end their feud by racing each other on April 11th. The day arrives with a vengeance, bringing with it a horrible rainstorm. Jenny persuades Liam to let her ride with him. Johnny pulls up next to them in his white Bronco. Liam's black Ford F-150 growls as they await the start. The race begins, and both trucks barrel down the wet and dark road. Jenny glares as she sees the road turn into the ominous number 11.

Her ghosts become real. It's Kismet.

The Kismet Series:
Karma: Book Two

After the crash last summer, and her recovery, Jenny and Liam move in together. They are ready to leave their past behind and start planning their future. Liam makes peace with Johnny, and they become partners in an auto body shop.

Liam loves Jenny more than his own life, but can't seem to let go of his nightmares and demons. He starts racing again, hoping that it will help. It doesn't. In fact, it makes things worse when he hooks up with Toby and Gina, two shady characters who are using Liam to win motorcycle races and money for them. Liam begins drinking and Jenny feels helpless. With Liam growing more distant, Johnny tries to convince Jenny that they should be together. She begins to question her love for Liam but finally realizes that it is he alone, who holds her heart.

On the day she is telling Johnny goodbye, Liam finds Jenny with Johnny and becomes enraged. He walks away, screaming the awful words, "You're Dead To Me!" Her world ended. Their love seemed to be over even before it had the chance to fully bloom. Jenny comes to understand that there is nothing left for her to do but leave town after Johnny's mother, a "seer" tells her all is lost.

As she drives away, she wonders about the number 11 and if her past with Liam is a result of their life now... a life that they are living apart from each other. Was this a result of bad Karma? Jenny believed her love with Liam was undying; that it was conceived before they were born.

They were Kindred Spirits... but only time would tell if this would be true.

The Kismet Series:

"Keep: The Prequel"
Coming Soon!

Visit the author's Website at:
www.JamieKincaid.com

Visit the author's Facebook page at:
The Kismet Series

Made in the USA
Charleston, SC
09 February 2017